THE HIPPOPOTAMUS POOL

Books by Elizabeth Peters

NIGHT TRAIN TO MEMPHIS
THE SNAKE, THE CROCODILE AND THE DOG*
THE LAST CAMEL DIED AT NOON*
NAKED ONCE MORE
THE DEEDS OF THE DISTURBER*
TROJAN GOLD
LION IN THE VALLEY*
THE MUMMY CASE*
DIE FOR LOVE
SILHOUETTE IN SCARLET
THE COPENHAGEN CONNECTION
THE CURSE OF THE PHARAOHS*
THE LOVE TALKER
SUMMER OF THE DRAGON
STREET OF THE FIVE MOONS
DEVIL-MAY-CARE
LEGEND IN GREEN VELVET
CROCODILE ON THE SANDBANK*
THE MURDERS OF RICHARD III
BORROWER OF THE NIGHT
THE SEVENTH SINNER
THE NIGHT OF FOUR HUNDRED RABBITS
THE DEAD SEA CIPHER
THE CAMELOT CAPER
THE JACKAL'S HEAD

*Amelia Peabody mysteries

ELIZABETH PETERS

THE HIPPOPOTAMUS POOL

A Time Warner Company

Warner Books, Inc., 1271 Avenue of the Americas, New York, NY 10020

Printed in the United States of America
First Printing: April 1996
10 9 8 7 6 5 4 3 2 1

Library of Congress Cataloging-in-Publication Data

Peters, Elizabeth.
The hippopotamus pool / Elizabeth Peters.
p. cm.
ISBN 0-446-51833-6 (hard)
I. Title.
PS3563.E747H54 1996
813'.54—dc20

95-31886
CIP

Book design by Giorgetta Bell McRee

To George and Dennis

ACKNOWLEDGMENTS

I have badgered and bored almost all my Egyptological friends about this book. I am particularly indebted to the following for supplying offprints, photographs, suggestions and encouragement:

Dennis Forbes, editor of KMT (who also suggested the title); George B. Johnson, his skilled colleague and photographer extraordinaire; The Wilbour Library of Egyptology of the Brooklyn Museum; Dr. Donald Ryan, who passed on Tetisheri's good wishes; the entire staff of the Epigraphic Survey at Chicago House, Luxor, especially the Mudir, Peter Dorman, who dragged me, kicking and screaming, up to the top of Drah Abu'l Naga; Dr. Daniel Polz, who has politely refrained from finding Tetisheri's tomb before I could do so; The Oriental Institute, its library and its director, Dr. William Sumner; Dr. Peter Der Manuelian, who designed the map and the tomb plan. He followed my (often confusing) instructions, so any errors and/or anomalies are my responsibility.

And Dr. Edna Russman, who was the first to mention to me the possibility that the statuette of Tetisheri might be a copy of an ancient original rather than an out-and-out forgery. She graciously admits that Emerson may have hit on the idea earlier.

CHARACTERS APPEARING OR REFERRED TO IN *THE HIPPOPOTAMUS POOL*

Abd el Hamed—antiquities dealer and forger, living in Gurneh

Abdullah ibn Hassan al Wahhab—reis (foreman) of Emerson's Egyptian workmen

Ali—a suffragi (room steward) at Shepheard's Hotel

Ali, Mohammed, Selim, et cetera et cetera—Abdullah's sons, who also work for the Emersons

Ali Murad—antiquities dealer and American consular agent in Luxor

Amherst, William—Cyrus Vandergelt's assistant, a young Egyptologist, who has very little to do with the story

Berthe—a woman of mystery, one of the Emersons' former enemies

Brugsch, Emile—assistant to Maspero, first archaeologist to enter the cache of royal mummies at Deir el Bahri

Budge, Wallis—Keeper of Egyptian and Assyrian Antiquities at the British Museum; notorious for his questionable methods of acquiring objects for the museum

Carter, Howard—newly appointed Inspector of Antiquities for Upper Egypt

Daoud—Abdullah's nephew

Emerson, Amelia Peabody—Victorian gentlewoman, archaeologist, and expert in crime

Emerson, Evelyn—Walter's wife, granddaughter of the late Earl of Chalfont

Emerson, Radcliffe—Amelia's husband, "the most eminent Egyptologist of this or any other era," known to Egyptians as the Father of Curses and to his wife as Emerson

Emerson, Walter—Radcliffe's brother, a specialist in the languages of ancient Egypt

Emerson, Walter Peabody—son of Amelia and Emerson, called Ramses by his friends and an afreet (demon) by almost everybody else

Forth, Nefret—ward of Amelia and Emerson, granddaughter of the late Lord Blacktower

Layla—Abd el Hamed's third and most interesting wife

Mahmud—steward of the Emersons' dahabeeyah

Marmaduke, Gertrude—hired by the Emersons to tutor their children

Maspero, Gaston—reappointed in 1899 to his former position as Director of Antiquities

Murch, Chauncey—American missionary and dealer in antiquities in Luxor

Newberry, Percy—English Egyptologist

O'Connell, Kevin—star reporter of *The Daily Yell*

Petrie, William Flinders—Emerson's chief rival as the founder of scientific archaeology

Quibell, J. F.—newly appointed Inspector of Antiquities for Lower Egypt

Riccetti, Giovanni—formerly in control of the illegal antiquities trade in Luxor, he intends to regain that position by any means necessary

Sethos, aka the Master Criminal—formerly in control of the illegal antiquities network in Egypt, the chief adversary of Amelia and Emerson (and Ramses)

Shelmadine, Leopold Abdullah, aka Mr. Saleh—is he the reincarnation of the High Priest Heriamon or a member of a gang of tomb robbers? Or both?

Todros, David—Abdullah's grandson

Vandergelt, Cyrus—American millionaire excavator and enthusiastic amateur of Egyptology

Washington, Sir Edward—a younger son with a talent for archaeological photography and a questionable reputation with the ladies

Willoughby, Dr.—English physician residing in Luxor

INTRODUCTION

For the convenience of readers who may be encountering Mrs. Emerson's journals for the first time, we have obtained permission to reprint this excerpt from *The National Autobiographical Dictionary*, 45th edition.

The date of my birth is irrelevant. I did not truly *exist* until 1884, when I was in my late twenties.[1] It was in that year that I set out for Egypt with a young lady companion, Evelyn Forbes, and found the three things that were to give meaning and purpose to my life: crime, Egyptology and Radcliffe Emerson!

Emerson (who was beginning that remarkable career in archaeology which is described elsewhere in this dictionary) and his brother Walter were digging at the remote site of Amarna in Middle Egypt. Shortly after Evelyn and I joined them, the work was interrupted by a series of extraordinary events featuring what appeared to be an animated mummy. The unmasking of the villain who had inspired this apparition did not interfere unduly with a successful season of excavation.[2]

My marriage to Emerson took place soon thereafter, as did the union of Evelyn to Emerson's brother. The birth of our only child, Walter Peabody Emerson, familiarly known as Ramses, necessitated a brief hiatus in our annual expeditions to Egypt. It was not until the autumn of 1889 that an appeal from the widow of Sir Henry Baskerville, whose death under mysterious circumstances had interrupted his excavation of a royal tomb at Thebes, took us back (with what delight the Reader may imagine) to Egypt. We were of course able to finish Sir Henry's work and solve the mystery of his death.[3]

We had left our son with his aunt and uncle in England that season, since his extreme youth (and certain of his habits) would have imperiled him (and everyone around him). However, he had from an early age demonstrated a keen aptitude for Egyptology, so (at the insistence of his doting father) he accompanied us to Egypt the following year. We had hoped to work at the great pyramid field of Dahshûr that season, but the spite and jealousy[4] of the then Director of Antiquities relegated to us the nearby site of Mazghunah—probably the dullest and least important archaeological site in Egypt. Fortunately our work was enlivened by our first encounter with the enigmatic genius of crime known as Sethos, or, as I preferred to call him, the Master Criminal.

The details of this amazing man's career are shrouded in mystery, but it must have begun in the late 1880s, in the Luxor area. A few years later he had disposed of all rivals and ruled supreme over the illegal antiquities trade. All the objects looted from tombs and temples by unauthorized diggers, Egyptian and European, passed through his hands. Superior intelligence, a poetic imagination, utter ruthlessness, and an incomparable talent for disguise contributed to his success; only his most trusted lieutenants were aware of his true identity.

We were able that year to foil Sethos's attempt to rob the princesses' tombs at Dahshûr and to escape his attempts on our lives.[5] He got away from us, though, and we found him on our trail again the following season. However, certain developments of a private nature (which are not within the scope of this article) gave us reason to believe we had seen the last of him.[6]

In the autumn of 1897 we set out for the Sudan, which was being reconquered by British-led Egyptian troops after a long period of occupation by the Dervishes. We had planned to excavate in the ruins of the ancient Cushite capital of Napata, but a message from Willy Forth, an old friend of Emerson's who had been missing for over ten years, sent us out into the wastes of the Western Desert in search of him and his family. The details of that astonishing adventure (perhaps the most remarkable of our lives) have been recorded elsewhere[7]; it resulted in the rescue of Forth's daughter Nefret from the remote oasis where she had dwelt since her birth.

The winter of 1898–99 saw Emerson and me again at the site of Amarna. We had left Ramses and Nefret (now our ward) in England, and I looked forward to reliving the fond memories of my first meeting with my admirable spouse. The startling events that interrupted our excavations that year involve private personal matters that are inappropriate in an official biography;[8] suffice it to say that we encountered for the third time our great and terrible adversary, the Master Criminal, and several of his henchmen, as well as a mysterious female known to us only as Berthe. The thrilling denouement of this adventure saw Sethos felled by an assassin's bullet, the dispatch of the assassin by Emerson and the disappearance of Berthe and the henchmen. . . .

I have often been asked to account for the frequency of our encounters with criminals of various varieties, but in my considered opinion it resulted inevitably from two causes: first, the uncontrolled state of excavation during the period in question, and second, the character of my husband. From the first, and at first almost single-handedly, Emerson fought tomb robbers, inept inspectors of antiquities and unprincipled collectors in his crusade to preserve the historic treasures of Egypt. Needless to say, I was ever at his side in the pursuit of knowledge and of villains.

1. Sic? This is not consistent with other sources. However, the editors were of the opinion that it would be discourteous to

question a lady's word.

2. *Crocodile on the Sandbank*

3. *Curse of the Pharaohs*

4. Mrs. Emerson refused to alter this statement, despite the editors' objections to its prejudicial nature.

5. *The Mummy Case*

6. Mrs. Emerson's reticence on this subject is difficult to understand, since she has described these events in the fifth volume of her Memoirs, *Lion in the Valley.*

7. *The Last Camel Died at Noon*

8. For the details of these private personal matters, cf. *The Snake, the Crocodile and the Dog*

CHAPTER ONE

The Trouble with Unknown Enemies Is That They Are So Difficult to Identify

Through the open windows of the ballroom the soft night breeze of Egypt cooled the flushed faces of the dancers. Silk and satin glowed; jewels sparkled; gold braid glittered; the strains of sweet music filled the air. The New Year's Eve Ball at Shepheard's Hotel was always an outstanding event in Cairo's social season, but the dying of this December day marked an ending of greater than usual import. In little more than an hour the chimes would herald the start of a new century: January the first, nineteen hundred.

Having just completed a vigorous schottische in the company of Captain Carter, I sought a quiet corner behind a potted palm and gave myself up to speculation of the sort in which any serious-minded individual would engage on such an occasion. What would the next one hundred years bring to a world that yet suffered all the ancient ills of mankind—poverty, ignorance, war, the oppression of the female sex? Optimist though I am, and blessed with an excellent imagination (excessively blessed, according to my husband), I could not suppose a single century would see those problems solved. I was confident, however, that my gender would finally achieve the justice so long denied it, and that I myself would live to see that glorious day. Careers for women! Votes for women! Women solicitors and women surgeons! Women judges, legislators, leaders of enlightened nations in which females stood shoulder-to-shoulder and back-to-back with men!

I felt I could claim some small credit for the advances I confidently expected to see. I myself had broken one barrier: as the first of my sex to work as a field archaeologist in Egypt, I had proved that a "mere" woman could endure the same dangers and discomforts, and meet the same professional standards, as a man. Candor as well as affection compels me to admit that I could never have done it without the wholehearted support of a remarkable individual—Radcliffe Emerson, the most preeminent Egyptologist of this or any century, and my devoted spouse.

Though the room was filled with people, my eyes were drawn to him as by a magnet. Emerson would stand out in any group. His splendid height and athletic form, his chiseled features and bright blue eyes, the dark hair that frames his intellectual brow—but I could go on for several pages describing Emerson's exceptional physical and mental characteristics. Humbly I acknowledged the blessings of heaven. What had I done to deserve the affection of such a man?

Quite a lot, in fact. I would be the first to admit that my physical characteristics are not particularly prepossessing (though Emerson has, in private, remarked favorably on certain of them). Coarse black hair and steely gray eyes, a bearing more noted for dignity than grace, a stature of indeterminate size—these are not the characteristics that win a man's heart. Yet I had won the heart of Radcliffe Emerson, not once but twice; I had stood at his side, yes, and fought at his side, during the remarkable adventures that had so often interrupted our professional activities. I had rescued him from danger, nursed him through illness and injury, given him a son . . .

And raised that son to his present age of twelve and a half years. (With Ramses one counted by months, if not days.) Though I have encountered mad dogs, Master Criminals, and murderers of both sexes, I consider the raising of Ramses my most remarkable achievement. When I recall the things Ramses has done, and the things other people have (often justifiably) tried to do to Ramses, I feel a trifle faint.

It was with Ramses and his adopted sister Nefret that Emerson stood chatting now. The girl's golden-red hair and fair face were in striking contrast to my son's Arabic coloring and saturnine features, but I was startled to note that he was now as tall as she. I had not realized how much he had grown over the past summer.

Ramses was talking. He usually is. I wondered what he could be saying to bring such a formidable scowl to Emerson's face, and hoped he was not lecturing his father on Egyptology. Though tediously average in other ways, Ramses was something of a linguistic genius, and he had pursued the study of the Egyptian language since infancy. Emerson feels a natural paternal pride in his son's abilities, but he does not like to have them shoved down his throat.

I was about to rise and go to them when the music began again and Emerson, scowling even more horribly, waved the two young people away. As soon as she turned, Nefret was approached by several young gentlemen, but Ramses took her arm and led—or, to be more accurate, dragged—her onto the floor. The frustrated suitors dispersed, looking sheepish, except for one—a tall, slightly built individual with fair hair, who remained motionless, following the girl's movements with a cool appraising stare and a raised eyebrow.

Though Ramses's manners left something to be desired, I could not but approve his action. The girl's lovely face and form attracted men as a rose attracts bees, but she was too young for admirers—and far too young for the admiration of the fair-haired gentleman. I had not met him but I had heard of him. The good ladies of Cairo's European society had had a great deal to say about Sir Edward Washington. He came of a respectable family from Northamptonshire, but he was a younger son, without prospects, and with a devastating effect on susceptible young women. (Not to mention susceptible older women.)

The seductive strains of a Strauss waltz filled the room and I looked up with a smile at Count Stradivarius, who was approaching me with the obvious intention of asking me to dance. He was a bald, portly little man, not much taller than I, but I love to waltz, and I was about to take the hand he had extended when the count was obliterated—removed, replaced—by another.

"Will you do me the honor, Peabody?" said Emerson.

It had to be Emerson—no one else employs my maiden name as a term of intimate affection—but for an instant I thought I must be asleep and dreaming. Emerson did not dance. Emerson had often expressed himself, with the emphasis that marks his conversation, on the absurdity of dancing.

How strange he looked! Under his tan lurked a corpselike pallor. The sapphire-blue eyes were dull, the well-cut lips tightly closed, the thick black hair wildly disheveled, the broad shoulders braced as if against a blow. He looked . . . he looked terrified. Emerson, who fears nothing on earth, afraid?

I stared, mesmerized, into his eyes, and saw a spark illumine their depths. I knew that spark. It was inspired by temper—Emerson's famous temper, which has won him the name of Father of Curses from his admiring Egyptian workmen. The color rushed back into his face; the cleft in his prominent chin quivered ominously.

"Speak up, Peabody," he snarled. "Don't sit there gaping. Will you honor me, curse it?"

I believe I am not lacking in courage, but it required all the courage I possessed to accede. I did not suppose Emerson had the vaguest idea how to waltz. It would be quite like him to assume that if he took a notion to do a thing he could do it, without the need of instruction or practice. But the pallor of his manly countenance assured me that the idea terrified him even more than it did me, and affection rose triumphant over concern for my toes and my fragile evening slippers. I placed my hand in the broad, calloused palm that had been offered (he had forgot his gloves, but this was certainly not the time to remind him of that little error).

"Thank you, my dear Emerson."

"Oh," said Emerson. "You will?"

"Yes, my dear."

Emerson took a deep breath, squared his shoulders, and seized me.

The first few moments were exceedingly painful, particularly to my feet and my ribs. I am proud to say that no cry escaped my lips and that no sign of anguish marred the serenity of my smile. After a while Emerson's desperate grip relaxed. "Hmmm," he said. "Not so bad, eh, Peabody?"

I took the first deep breath I had enjoyed since he took hold of me and realized that my martyrdom had been rewarded. For so large a man, Emerson can move with catlike grace when he chooses; encouraged by my apparent enjoyment, he had begun to enjoy himself too, and he had fallen into the rhythm of the music.

"Not bad at all," Emerson repeated, grinning. "They told me I would like it once I got the hang of it."

"They?"

"Ramses and Nefret. They were taking lessons this past summer, you know; they taught me. I made them promise not to tell you. It was to be a surprise for you, my dear. I know how much you like this sort of thing. I must say it is a good deal more enjoyable than I had expected. I suppose it is you who . . . Peabody? Are you crying? Curse it, did I tread on your toes?"

"No, my dear." In shocking defiance of custom I clung closer to him, blotting my tears on his shoulder. "I weep because I am so moved. To think that you would make such a sacrifice for me—"

"A small enough return, my darling Peabody, for the sacrifices you have made and the dangers you have faced for me." The words were muffled, for his cheek rested on the top of my head and his lips were pressed to my temple.

A belated sense of decorum returned. I strove to remove myself a short distance. "People are staring, Emerson. You are holding me too close."

"No, I am not," said Emerson.

"No," I said, yielding shamelessly to his embrace. "You aren't."

Emerson, having "got the hang of it," would allow no one else to waltz with me. I declined all other partners, not only because I knew it would please him but because I required the intervals between waltzes to catch my breath. Emerson waltzed as he did everything else, with enormous energy, and between the tightness of his grasp and the vigor of his movements, which had, on more than one occasion, literally lifted me off my feet, it took me some time to recover.

The intervals gave me the opportunity to observe the other guests. The study of human nature in all its manifestations is one no person of intelligence should ignore—and what better place to observe it than in a setting such as this?

The styles of that year were very pretty, I thought, without the exaggerated outlines that had in the past distorted (and would, alas, soon again distort) the female form. Skirts fell gracefully from the waist, sans hoops or bustles; bodices were modestly draped. Black was a popular shade with older ladies, but how rich was the shimmer of black satin, how cobweb-fine the sable lace at throat and elbow! The sparkle of gems and of jet, the pale glimmer of pearls adorned the fabric and the white throats of the wearers. What a pity, I thought, that men allowed themselves to be limited by the meaningless vagaries of fashion! In most cultures, from the ancient Egyptian until comparatively modern times, the male swanked as brilliantly as the female, and presumably took as much pleasure as she in the acquisition of jewels and embroidered and lace-trimmed garments.

The only exceptions to masculine drabness of attire were the brilliant uniforms of the Egyptian Army officers. In fact, none of these gentlemen were Egyptians. Like all other aspects of the government, the army was under British control and officered by Englishmen or Europeans. The uniforms denoting members of our own military forces were plainer. There were a good many of them present that night, and in my imagination I seemed to see a faint shadow darkening those fresh young faces, so bravely mustachioed and flushed with laughter. They would soon be on their way to South Africa; where battle raged. Some would never return.

With a sigh and a murmured prayer (all a mere woman can offer in a world where men determine the fate of the young and helpless) I returned to my study of human nature. Those who were not dancing sat or stood around the room watching the intricacies of the cotillion, or chatting with one another. A good many were acquaintances of mine; I was interested to observe that Mrs. Arbuthnot had gained another several stone and that Mr. Arbuthnot had got a young lady whom I did not recognize backed into a corner. I could not see what he was doing, but the young lady's expression suggested he was up to his old tricks. Miss Marmaduke (of whom more hereafter) had no partner. Perched on the edge of her chair, her face set in an anxious smile, she looked like a bedraggled black crow. Next to her, ignoring her with cool discourtesy, was Mrs. Everly, wife of the Interior Minister. From the animation that wreathed her face as she carried on a conversation across Miss Marmaduke with the latter's neighbor, I deduced that the lady, swathed in black veiling, was a Person of Importance. Was she a recent widow? No lesser loss could dictate such heavy mourning; but if that were the case, what was she doing at a social function such as this? Perhaps, I mused, her loss was not recent. Perhaps, like a certain regal widow, she had determined never to leave off the visible signs of bereavement.

(I reproduce the preceding paragraphs in order to demonstrate to the Reader how much can be offered to the serious student of human nature even in so frivolous a social setting as that one.)

It would be my last social event for some time. In a few more days we would leave the comforts of Cairo's finest hotel for . . .

Well, only Heaven and Emerson knew where. It was one of

his engaging little habits, to delay until the last possible moment before telling me where we would excavate that year. Irritating as this could be, it had a certain titillation, and I amused myself by considering the possibilities. Dahshûr? We had never finished exploring the interior of the Bent Pyramid, and pyramids, I must confess, are a passion of mine. Amarna would be equally to my taste, however, since it was there that my first romantic experiences with Emerson took place. The Theban area, too, had its attractions: royal tombs in the Valley of the Kings, the majestic temple of Queen Hatshepsut . . .

My meditations were interrupted by Nefret and Ramses. Her rose-petal cheeks aglow, the girl dropped into the chair at my side and glowered at her foster brother, who stood with arms folded and face expressionless. Ramses had graduated to long trousers that year—the sudden elongation of his lower limbs having made that decision advisable on aesthetic if no other grounds—and with his curly hair brushed into a rampant crest, he resembled a critical stork.

"Ramses says I may not dance with Sir Edward," Nefret exclaimed. "Aunt Amelia, tell him—"

"Sir Edward," said Ramses, prominent nose quivering, "is not a suitable person for Nefret to know. Mother, tell her—"

"Be quiet, both of you," I said sharply. "I will be the judge of who constitutes a proper associate for Nefret."

"Hmph," said Ramses.

Nefret said something I did not understand. I supposed it to be one of the Nubian swearwords to which she resorted when in a temper. Temper, and the heat of the room, would have reduced any other female countenance to an ugly state of red-faced perspiration, but she could never appear other than beautiful; her cornflower-blue eyes sparkled wickedly and the sheen of perspiration that bedewed her skin made it glow as if lit from within.

"Ramses," I said, "please go and ask Miss Marmaduke to dance. You owe her that courtesy, since she is to be your tutor."

"But Mama—" Ramses's voice cracked. Ordinarily he was able

to control the inevitable fluctuations, from soprano to baritone, that mark a lad's adolescence; on this occasion emotion had made him lose control, and his use of the childish form of address which he had recently abjured was further indication of perturbation.

"I believe your hearing is not deficient, Ramses," I remarked.

Ramses's countenance resumed its normal impassivity. "No, Mother, it is not, as I am sure you are aware. I will of course obey your command, for such I take it to be despite the manner in which it was couched, though I cannot but regard the use of the word 'please' in this context as a meaningless—"

"Ramses," I said loudly, for I knew perfectly well what he was up to; he was quite capable of continuing the sentence until it would be too late to lead the unfortunate Miss Marmaduke onto the floor.

"Yes, Mother." Ramses turned on his heel.

Her good humor restored, Nefret laughed and gave my hand a conspiratorial squeeze. "It serves him right for being so impertinent, Aunt Amelia. Miss Marmaduke is a perfect old maid!"

I had to admit the accuracy of the description. Miss Marmaduke was, by her own admission, still under the age of thirty, but she looked years older. Being taller than the average, she had acquired a habitual stoop; her mousy-brown hair stuck out in wisps from the pins and combs that attempted to confine it. However, the comment was rude and unkind, and I felt bound to point this out.

"The comment was rude and unkind, Nefret. She cannot help being plain, poor thing. We were fortunate to find her, since you and Ramses must not neglect your education this winter, and we were unable to hire a suitable tutor before we left England."

Nefret made a face. I went on, "I would not have said so in Ramses's presence, since he is already too inclined to think himself omniscient, but in this case I am forced to agree with him. Sir Edward has an unsavory reputation with regard to women—especially very young women. You are only fifteen and peculiarly vulnerable to such attentions."

"I beg your pardon, Aunt Amelia." She was out of temper with *me* now; her eyes snapped. "I believe I know more about the matters to which you refer than an English girl of fifteen."

"You *are* an English girl of fifteen," I replied. "And yet, in some ways, you are barely two years of age." I paused, considering this striking analysis. "How interesting! I had never thought of your situation in quite those terms, but they are correct. The customs of the strange society in which you spent the first thirteen years of your life were so unlike those of the modern world that you have had to begin all over again—and forget a good deal of what you had learned, especially about—er—certain dealings with persons of the opposite gender. I am only trying to protect you, child."

Her lovely face softened and again she took my hand. "I know that, Aunt Amelia. I am sorry if I was rude. I was angry with Ramses, not with you; he treats me as if I were a child and he a stern guardian. I will not be bullied by a little boy!"

"He is younger than you, to be sure," I said. "But he has only your best interests at heart. And you can no longer look down at him, can you?"

I was unable to repress a smile as I watched Ramses doggedly guiding Miss Marmaduke through the mazes of the dance. She was trying to minimize her height by drooping and bowing her head, so that her high pompadour kept brushing his face. The contortions of that face, as Ramses heroically controlled his need to sneeze, made me feel more kindly toward my son. He would not have behaved like a gentleman if I had not made him, but now that he had taken the bit between his teeth, he was performing gamely against considerable odds. Miss Marmaduke had no more sense of rhythm than a camel, and her long-sleeved, high-necked black gown was inappropriate for a ball.

My ball gowns are usually crimson, since that is Emerson's favorite color. The one I wore that evening was of quite a different shade. Nefret saw my expression alter; quietly she said, "You are thinking of the baby."

It had been Nefret I sought on that terrible June morning, after the call came from Walter. We had had the telephone installed only the month before; little did I imagine that it would be a source of such shocking news.

I left Rose, my invaluable and tenderhearted parlormaid, sobbing into her apron, while our butler Gargery, his own eyes moist, tried to comfort her. Nefret was not in the house. After I had searched the stables and the gardens, I knew where she must have gone.

Some might think it a strange sort of monument to find on the grounds of a quiet English country house. In point of fact, fake ruins and pyramids had been quite the mode, and many a wealthy traveler to Egypt had brought back stelae and sarcophagi with which to adorn his property. The small brick pyramid, located in a quiet woodland glade, was not a modish ornament, however. It stood over the remains of a prince of Cush. He had lost his life in a vain but heroic attempt to restore Nefret to her family, and at the request of his brother, who had carried the quest to its triumphant culmination, we had given the gallant youth honorable burial in the manner of his own people. A little chapel, its lintel carved with the sun disk and the name and titles of the dead boy, stood at the base of the monument. Nefret went there from time to time; she had known Tabirka well, for he had been her playfellow in her youth. I myself occasionally spent a quiet hour near the pyramid; it was a pleasant place, surrounded by trees and wildflowers.

I found Nefret seated on the stone bench near the chapel, weaving flowers into a garland. She looked up when she heard me approach; I suppose my face must have betrayed the shock I felt, for she at once rose and led me to the seat.

"I am going to Chalfont Castle," I said distractedly. "I have tried to reach Emerson and Ramses; they were not at the house in London or at the Museum, so I was forced to leave a message for them. I dare not delay, I must go to Evelyn at once. Will you come with me?"

"Of course, if you want me."

"It may comfort Evelyn," I said. "How is she to bear it? It was with Walter that I spoke . . ."

I would have gone on sitting there, in a stupor of disbelief and grief, if Nefret had not raised me to my feet and led me toward the house.

"I will help you pack, Aunt Amelia. And accompany you, of course. How did it happen?"

"Suddenly and—thank God—peacefully," I said. "She was perfectly well last night when Evelyn tucked her into her cot. This morning the nurserymaid found her . . ."

I began weeping, I believe. Nefret's slender arm went round my waist. "Don't grieve, Aunt Amelia. I have asked Tabirka to look after her. His courage is as high as his heart is gentle; he will protect her from the perils of the darkness and carry her safely to the arms of the god."

I had paid scant attention to Nefret's little speech at the time, hearing only the comfort it was meant to convey. When it came back to me some time later, it gave me a queer feeling. Had I told her of the baby's death? I could not remember having done so, and yet she had known—known before ever I spoke. Even more alarming was her reference to the ancient (and of course erroneous) religion she had supposedly abjured. Was that why she crept away to her foster brother's chapel—to whisper prayers and make offerings to the old gods she secretly worshiped?

(The little offerings I occasionally left on the altar were simply tokens of respect, as I am sure I need not explain. And I am sure the bottles of Bickle's Best Brown Stout I once found arranged in a neat row had been intended in the same way. They could not have come from Nefret, since the purchase of spirituous liquors was impossible for her. It was legally impossible for Ramses too, but Ramses had his methods—most probably Gargery, his devoted admirer.)

Evelyn and her husband Walter, Emerson's younger brother and a distinguished Egyptologist in his own right, were our dearest friends as well as our closest kin. They were devoted to their children, and I expected I would find Evelyn prostrate. But when Wilkins the butler, his own eyes red-rimmed, announced our arrival, she came quickly to meet us, and outwardly at least she appeared less distraught than he.

"We have been more fortunate than most families, dear sister," she said, with a set, rigid smile. "God has left us five healthy children. We must bow to His will."

It would have been difficult to criticize this admirable demonstration of Christian fortitude, but as the summer went on I thought she was overdoing it. Tears and hysteria would have been preferable to that terrible smile. She would not wear mourning and became almost angry when I did so. And when, after anxious consultation with my husband and hers, I told her we had decided to remain in England that winter instead of going out to Egypt as we always did, she turned on me with the first bitter words I had ever heard from her. I should and must go. Did I have such a poor opinion of her that I believed she could not get on without my support? She did not need me. She did not need anyone.

Including her own husband. She and Walter now occupied separate sleeping chambers. Walter would not speak of it to me, he was too modest and too loyal to complain, but he was less reticent with Emerson—and Emerson is not reticent at all.

"Confound it, Peabody, what the devil is she up to? She will kill Walter; he loves her devotedly and would never think of—er—going with another woman. Men have their needs—"

"Oh, bah," I exclaimed. "Don't talk such pernicious nonsense to me! Insofar as that is concerned, women have needs too, as you of all people ought to be well aware . . . Emerson, let go of me at once. I will not be distracted, not at this time."

"Curse it," said Emerson. "She is doing it to punish him. Like Lysistrata. Peabody, if you ever dared pull a trick like that on me—"

"But my dear, it is not a trick on Evelyn's part. I doubt she knows herself why she is acting as she is. *I* know, of course. She is angry—angry with heaven. She can't get back at God, so she is punishing the rest of us, and herself most of all. She blames herself for the child's death."

"Don't spout your psychological mumbo-jumbo at me," Emerson shouted. "The notion is absurd. How could she blame herself? The physician said—"

"The human spirit is not rational, Emerson," I said poetically. "I know whereof I speak; I myself have occasionally felt a pang of illogical guilt when Ramses got himself into some horrible scrape, even when it was entirely his own fault. Evelyn feels guilt and fear as well. She wants no more hostages to fate."

"Ah," said Emerson. He considered the idea. "But, Peabody, there are ways—"

"Yes, my dear, I know. Leaving aside the efficacy of those methods, and the impossibility of raising them with Evelyn at this time . . . It's all beside the point, Emerson; we don't need practical solutions just now, we need a way of rousing her and I—I don't know how to do it." I turned away. This time, when Emerson took me in his arms, I did not protest.

"You'll think of something, Peabody," he said gently. "You always do."

But I had not, and four months had passed since that conversation. We had delayed our departure longer than usual, in the hope of seeing an improvement that did not, alas, occur, and because there were a number of new arrangements to be made this year. For the first time Ramses and Nefret were to accompany us and I was determined their education should not be interrupted. It proved to be much more difficult than I had anticipated to find a tutor of either sex. Most of the applicants I interviewed had declined the post after hearing that they would be expected to spend the winter in a tent or an Egyptian tomb. (A few hung on until after *they* had been interviewed by Ramses.)

So when, shortly after our arrival at Shepheard's, I was approached by Miss Marmaduke, I could only regard it as an unexpected stroke of good fortune. Her credentials were excellent, her recommendations had come from the highest social circles, and her reason for seeking employment could only increase her value in my eyes; for, as she explained, she had come out on a Cook's Tour and fallen in love with Egypt. Hearing from mutual acquaintances of our imminent arrival and our need of someone to educate the children, she had delayed her departure in the hope of obtaining a position with us—and, as she shyly explained, learning something about the antiquities of the country. This pleased Emerson, who had not been much taken with her when he first met her. He had hoped to begin training a lady Egyptologist but had been unable to find a suitable candidate. There were few women students at that time, since most professors would rather have had a homicidal maniac in their classes than a female. Miss Marmaduke had also some secretarial experience, and was quite willing to assist in the clerical duties all properly conducted archaeological excavations require.

(And the fact that Emerson had not been much taken with her was an additional point in her favor. Emerson is a very modest man. He has no idea of the effect he has on females.)

When the next waltz began and Emerson approached me I rose to meet him, determined to forget care in the pleasures of the dance. However, instead of leading me onto the floor he tucked my arm in his.

"Will you come with me, Peabody? I am sorry to rob you of your terpsichorean pleasures, but I feel sure that if given a choice, you would prefer the alternative I propose."

"My dear Emerson!" I exclaimed, blushing. "The activity to which I assume you refer would always be my first choice, but can't it wait? It would not be proper to leave the children unchaperoned."

Emerson gave me a surprised look and then burst out laughing. "That activity will certainly have to be postponed—though, my dear Peabody, I hope not for long. We have an appointment. It may be a complete waste of time, but there is an outside chance that the fellow has useful information. Now don't ask questions, we are already late. And don't fuss about the children. They are old enough to behave themselves, and Miss Marmaduke's presence should satisfy the proprieties. That's why she is here, hang it, to watch over the children."

"Who is the individual we are about to meet?"

"I don't know. But," Emerson said, forestalling the objection I was about to make, "the message I received from him this morning contained some intriguing information. Knowing where I plan to excavate this season, he offered—"

"He knows more than I, then," I said sharply. "When did you decide that, Emerson, and why is a total stranger more familiar with your thoughts than your own wife and professional partner?"

Pulling me along, Emerson crossed the landing and started up the last flight of stairs. "Cursed if I know, Peabody. That was one of the things that provoked my curiosity. It was a deuced odd communication; the writer was clearly a man of intelligence and education, but he was equally clearly in a state of some agitation, demanding secrecy and hinting at unspecified but horrible dangers that threatened him. His claim that he knows the location of an unrobbed tomb is undoubtedly balderdash—"

"What?" The word came out in a high-pitched squeak, for the rapidity of his movements had left me short of breath. "Where?" I demanded. Emerson stopped and looked at me reproachfully.

"You needn't scream, Peabody. At Thebes, of course. Specifically . . . but that is what we are about to discover. Come along, my dear, come along, or this mysterious individual may have second thoughts."

A man stood before the door of our sitting room. He was not Emerson's mysterious visitor; he wore the uniform that distinguishes the employees of Shepheard's, and I recognized him as the suffragi who was on duty during the night hours. Seeing us, he sprang to attention. "Emerson Effendi! See, I have done as you asked. I have guarded your door. This person—"

"What person?" Emerson demanded, looking up and down the deserted hall.

Before Ali could reply, a form emerged from behind a turn in the corridor. It moved as silently as the specter it resembled; enveloped from shoulders to heels in folds of dark fabric, a broad-brimmed hat pulled low over its brow, it came to a halt some

feet away. The nearest light was behind it and I felt sure it had chosen that position with deliberate intent, for the brim of the hat shadowed its features.

"Ah," said Emerson, his good humor restored. "You are the gentleman who requested an appointment? I apologize for being late; it was all Mrs. Emerson's fault. You don't object to her joining us, I hope?"

"Not at all." The comment was brief, the voice low and husky—obviously disguised.

Emerson opened the door. "After you, my dear Peabody. And you, sir, come in."

I had left one lamp burning, for a number of unpleasant experiences had taught me it is unwise to enter a totally darkened room, but it gave only enough light to assure me that there were no assassins or burglars lying in wait. I was about to press the switch that would turn on the overhead lights when a hand closed over mine. I let out a little cry of surprise and Emerson exclaimed, "What the devil—"

"My heartfelt apologies, Mrs. Emerson," said the stranger, releasing my hand—and just in time too, for Emerson had already seized him by the collar. "I did not mean to startle you. Please don't turn on the lights. I am taking a terrible risk by coming here; allow me to preserve my anonymity until we have reached an agreement—if that can be done."

"Confound it," Emerson exclaimed. "I warn you, Mr. Saleh . . . Ah, but am I to take it that the name you gave me is not your own?"

"It will suffice for the present." The stranger had moved away, into a pool of shadow. He raised his hands to his face. Was he praying? I thought not. An anticipatory shiver of excitement rippled through my limbs.

Emerson emitted a loud groan. "Oh, good Gad! Are we to have another of these melodramatic distractions? I suppose one season of simple archaeological excavation, uninterrupted by criminals, was too much to expect. Had I but known . . . Well, curse it, the damage is done. Even if I were to follow my instincts, which tell me to throw you out the door before you can utter a word,

Mrs. Emerson would insist on hearing you out. She dotes on melodrama. If you have adjusted that mask to your satisfaction, Mr. Whoever-You-Are, sit down and start talking. I am a patient man, but my time is valuable and I strongly suspect that this will be—"

"He can't start talking until you stop, Emerson," I said. "Take that chair, Mr.—er—Saleh. May I offer you something to drink? Tea, coffee, brandy, whiskey?"

"Whiskey. Thank you."

Mumbling to himself, Emerson waved me toward the sofa and went to the sideboard. Ignoring his complaints, I seated myself and studied the stranger curiously. The black cloak had fallen back; under it he wore ordinary European clothing. The name he had given was Egyptian, but the fact that he had accepted an alcoholic beverage meant he was not a Muslim—or at least not a very good one. I was unable to make out his features, since the mask of black silk covered his entire face and was fastened, in some manner I could not ascertain, under his chin. An orifice roughly oval in shape exposed his lips, and I assumed there were other openings to permit vision, though not even a gleam of eyeballs was visible under the brim of his hat.

Emerson handed me a glass and offered another to our visitor. He put out a hand to take it.

He must have been watching me as closely as I had examined him; seeing me stiffen, he let out a little coughing sound that might have been a laugh. "You are quick, Mrs. Emerson. Was that why you offered me refreshment?"

"It was an outside chance," I said calmly. "But it is more difficult to disguise one's hands than one's face. The spots of old age can be covered, but not the protruding veins that are equally distinctive. Scars, calluses, birthmarks, the very shape of palm and fingers—or, as in this case, a distinctive article of jewelry. . . . Since you did not take the precaution of removing your ring before you came here, may I take it that you would not object if I asked to examine it more closely?"

"I had intended to let you do so, in confirmation of the story

I am about to tell you." He removed it from his finger and placed it on the palm I had extended.

Even an uneducated tourist would have recognized the basic design. In pharaonic times, scarabs were popular amulets, which carried a hieroglyphic inscription or a name on the flat undersurface. Replicas, some honestly proclaimed as such, some purporting to be ancient, were sold to tourists by the hundreds. In this case the scarab was not of the common faience or stone; it was, or appeared to be, solid gold. It had been fastened to the shank of the ring in a manner familiar to me from ancient examples: twisted gold wires on either side of the scarab-shaped bezel allowed it to pivot. When I turned it over I was not surprised to see the hieroglyphic signs that spelled a name. I recognized the name, but it was not one of the ones commonly found on such trinkets.

I handed the ring to Emerson, who studied it with a scowl as Mr. Saleh began to speak.

"This jewel has been handed down from generation to generation for over three thousand years. It is the symbol of the office of High Priest of the ka of Queen Tetisheri, whose name you see on the scarab. Only the body perishes; the immortal spirit, the ka of the Egyptians, passes on from one fleshly tenement to another. It has been my sacred duty over the long centuries to ensure the survival and the rebirth of that great queen. In my first incarnation, as Heriamon of Thebes, I was her faithful—"

Emerson's roar made the window glass rattle. "Hell and damnation!"

"Emerson!" I exclaimed. "Do calm yourself. And be careful of the ring, it is twenty-two-carat gold and quite fragile."

"Peabody, I will be damned if I will put up with this sort of thing." The blood that had rushed to his tanned face turned it a pretty shade of mahogany, but he put the ring carefully into my hand before clenching his own hand into a fist and shaking it under my nose. "Reincarnation! Either he is a lunatic or he is inventing this lunatic tale in order to cover up a more sinister plan." He jumped to his feet and lunged at the stranger.

Warned by Emerson's initial scream of rage, the stranger had also risen. The pistol he now held in his hand brought even my impetuous husband to an abrupt halt. "Hell and damnation," Emerson repeated, in a softer but even more ominous voice. "What is it you want, then? If you dare lay hands on my wife—"

"I have no intention of harming either of you," was the quick response. "I go armed for other reasons, but I was not unprepared for your reaction. Only hear me out. What harm can it do?"

"Go on," Emerson said curtly.

"What I told you is true. This body is only the latest of many my ka has inhabited. You may believe it or not; that is immaterial to me. I mentioned it only to explain the source of the knowledge I am about to offer you. I know the location of her tomb. I can lead you to it—a queen's tomb, with its treasures intact."

Emerson's breath caught. He did not believe it—but oh, how he wanted to! He would not have sold his soul for wealth or the face that launched a thousand ships, but a royal tomb! Mephistopheles himself could have made no offer more seductive to the heart of an Egyptologist, even that of a scholar who prizes knowledge above vulgar fame. Emerson's contributions to the field of Egyptology had won him the acclaim of his peers (and, I am sorry to say, a certain degree of vulgar fame as well), but he had never made that one outstanding discovery all archaeologists dream of. Could this be such a discovery?

"Where?" he demanded.

"Drah Abu'l Naga." The stranger stepped back and lowered the pistol. Like me, he had observed the signs, not of belief but of the desire to believe.

In the days when he possessed a beard, Emerson had been wont to tug at it in moments of deep thought. Now sans beard, at my insistence, he had to content himself with rubbing the cleft in his chin. "Logical," he muttered. "But if you know anything about Egyptology, which you obviously do, you could have reasoned that out. Devil take it, Saleh, or whoever you are, what are you really after? If you know where such a tomb is located, why would you offer it to me?"

"If I told you the truth, you would not believe me. No"—for I had attempted to return the ring to him—"it is mine no longer. The trust has passed on."

"See here," said Emerson, controlling his temper more successfully than I had imagined possible. "If you are implying that Mrs. Emerson is your successor—future incarnation—oh, the devil!"

"You, not she," was the calm reply.

I held my breath, anticipating the threatened explosion. To my surprise, Emerson relaxed and a glint of humor warmed his stern face.

"That is a more seemly alternative than the other. Just how is the transfer of personality and/or sacred duty effected, Mr. Saleh? I trust you don't expect me to undergo the standard purification rituals. Mrs. Emerson disapproves of beards, but I doubt she would allow me to shave my head, and not even for the honor of being high priest of Tetisheri would I give up my roast beef and—er—certain other activities."

"Mockery is your defense against the truth, Professor. You will learn soon enough that our fates are foreordained; your destiny will come upon you and you will accept it. Until that time, believe, if you prefer to do so, that I have come to ask your help for purely practical reasons.

"The secret cannot be kept much longer. For a thousand generations we have protected her from the tomb robbers of Gurneh, from Greek and Roman and Byzantine thieves, from the predators of Europe and America. There are ways of leading searchers astray. When all else failed . . ."

"Murder?" I breathed the word.

"When all else failed. But now there are too many searchers for treasure, and the number continues to increase. Foreign archaeologists swarm over the cliffs of western Thebes, and the Theban thieves are busier than before. If she must be found, better it should be by a scholar than by the local robbers; they will destroy what they cannot carry away, sell the treasures to any purchaser, scatter them to the far ends of the earth. You will give me your promise—your solemn oath." The hand that held the weapon had fallen to his side; he took a step closer to Emerson. "You will not allow her mummy to be violated. You will keep her funerary equipment intact and undamaged, treat her remains with reverence. Do you swear?"

The deep, solemn tones echoed like a prayer, or a curse. Emerson shifted uneasily, but he met the other man's gaze straight on.

"I cannot swear," he said. "If it were within my power, I would do precisely as you ask, though in all honesty I must tell you my motives would not be the same as yours. Such a find would be unique; scholarly principle would demand it be kept intact, guarded and carefully preserved. Your assessment is correct: if tomb robbers find it first, they will tear the mummy to pieces and destroy what they cannot carry off. It would be a tragedy in scientific terms. . . . Oh, good Gad, why am I wasting time in futile speculation? There is no such tomb, and even if there were, I could not give you my word, for mine would not be the ultimate decision."

"You have said enough. You have spoken the truth. Few men would do that. And no man would fight to preserve her tomb as you would."

"That is true," I said, for Emerson remained silent. "And you know, Emerson, there is a good chance we could succeed. As the excavators we would have certain claims to the contents of the tomb; if we gave up those rights to the Museum, in exchange for M. Maspero's promise that he would keep the objects all together—"

"Oh, do be quiet, Peabody!" Emerson turned on me, glaring. My dear Emerson is never more handsome than when he is in a rage. His large white teeth were bared, his eyes glowed like the eastern sky when the approach of night deepens the azure depths, his lean cheeks were becomingly flushed. Speechless with admiration (and with the impossibility of making myself heard over his bellowing), I gazed on him.

"It is just like you to plan an entire campaign of action on the basis of a fantasy," Emerson went on bitterly. "My patience is running out, Saleh. I will give you"—he took out his watch—"precisely sixty seconds longer. If at the end of that time you have not produced something tangible to prove your claim, I will throw you out."

Saleh had returned the pistol to his pocket. Coolly he resumed the chair he had abandoned and picked up his glass. "The ring is not proof enough?"

Emerson snorted, and Saleh went on, irony coloring his voice, "Not to a mind as rigidly logical as yours, I suppose. What would satisfy your requirements?"

"Precise directions," Emerson replied promptly. "The entrance must be well hidden or it would have been found before this. There are many acres of rough, broken ground in the region you mentioned."

"I thought you would say that." Saleh had finished his whiskey. Placing the glass on the table, he reached into his pocket and took out a folded piece of paper. "I was told . . . I . . ."

His voice broke in a horrible, rattling gurgle. One hand went to his throat; the other clenched, crumpling the paper it held. Emerson jumped forward, but he was too late; a violent, convulsive movement threw the stranger out of the chair and onto the floor.

"Get back, Peabody," Emerson said, reinforcing the suggestion with a sharp shove. I got back in time to avoid a kick from the recumbent man; his limbs thrashed in uncontrolled, tetanic spasms that jerked his body back and forth, as if he were performing some prone and primitive dance. Emerson threw himself onto the writhing body and interrupted his eloquent curses long enough to gasp instructions. "Fetch a doctor, Peabody—go yourself, don't—damnation!—Captain Cartright or—oh, good Gad!"

Even his formidable strength was taxed by the effort of holding the sufferer, in order to prevent injury not only from the furniture but from the violent spasms of his own tortured muscles. I needed no further admonitions; picking up my skirts, I ran.

By the time I reached the ballroom I was in a considerable state of breathless agitation and physical disarray. People fell back before my wild rush. At first the room was only a blur of color and movement; there were too many cursed uniforms, I could not locate the one I wanted. Forcing myself to calmness, I saw Captain Cartright guiding a stately dowager in purple plush through the mazes of the cotillion. I rushed to him and caught him by the arm.

"You must come at once, Captain Cartright! An emergency—strychnine poisoning . . . convulsions . . ."

"Good heavens," exclaimed the person in purple, whom I now recognized as the wife of Cartright's commanding general. "What is the meaning of this? The woman is mad or intoxicated!"

We stood in the center of a circle of gaping faces, for my voice, I daresay, had been shrill enough to attract attention.

"Instantly," I insisted, shaking the captain. "He is dying! My sitting room—"

"Yes, of course, Mrs. Emerson," Cartright said quickly. "Where are your rooms?"

"This way," said a voice behind me. It said no more; as Cartright followed after the speaker, I saw that it was Ramses. He was moving rapidly even for him, squirming through the crowd like an eel.

Now that help had been dispatched, I felt it would be advisable to catch my breath before hurrying back. Breathing slowly and deeply, I pondered the precipitation of Ramses. It was his insatiable curiosity, of course, but he might have had the courtesy to offer an arm to his mother.

Another gentleman did so. It was Mr. Jenkins, the assistant manager, and it may have been a desire to end the disturbance, rather than concern for me, that prompted his action. The dancing had stopped altogether and people were staring rudely. "What is wrong, Mrs. Emerson?" he inquired, leading me off the floor.

Realizing he had not heard my announcement to Captain Cartright, I decided not to enlighten him. He would only make a fuss. Hotel managers do not like to hear of dead or dying guests.

"It is all taken care of, Mr. Jenkins," I replied, hoping that was the case. "Thank you."

Anxious as I was to return to the scene of the action, I could not in conscience do so until I had made sure Nefret, now abandoned by Ramses, was safe in the charge of Miss Marmaduke. But that lady's chair was now occupied by someone else, and as I continued to scan the room I caught sight of Nefret, alone and unescorted, entering from the direction of the Moorish Hall.

The sight of her would have aroused the direst suspicions in any maternal breast—the faint smile, the flushed cheeks, the slight disarrangement of her hair. The Moorish Hall, with its soft divans and pearl-inlaid furniture, is the most romantic setting imaginable; mashrabiya screens and painted arches enclose shaded recesses that might have been designed for lovers.

With a muttered "Good Gad," I hastened to her. When she saw me, an even more betraying flush brightened her face. She began, "Oh, Aunt Amelia—"

"Come with me at once."

"I was only—"

"Not now, Nefret. Hurry."

By a fortunate chance, the lift was waiting. I directed the attendant to close the door and take us directly to the third floor. The presence of others prevented speech between me and my errant ward; she stood staring straight ahead, biting her lip and—I did not doubt—inventing alibis. However, as I hurried her along the corridor it began to dawn on her that my agitation might have a more serious cause than her misbehavior.

"What is wrong?" she exclaimed. "Has something happened? Oh, heavens—not to the Professor!" For such was her name for Emerson, who would have responded unfavorably to being called "Uncle Radcliffe." He dislikes his given name, which is one of the reasons why I never employ it.

Not until I heard Nefret's question and the alarm that deepened her voice did it dawn on me that Ramses might have jumped to a similar if erroneous conclusion. No wonder he had been in such a hurry. "Confound the boy," I muttered, "I would have reassured him if he had waited a moment. It is his own fault."

He and the captain had not arrived long before us. Ramses, arms folded and shoulders stiff, was looking particularly enigmatic. Cartright knelt by the fallen body. He glanced up as I entered and said, "I must have misunderstood, Mrs. Emerson. You will be relieved to know that there is no indication of poisoning; it is only—"

A long, quavering cry stopped him. The cry came from my throat, for I had seen that the form sprawled supine and senseless upon the floor was not that of the stranger.

Pushing the doctor aside, I fell on my knees and gathered his bleeding head into my arms.

"Emerson! Oh, my dear Emerson!"

"It is only a bump on the head, Mrs. Emerson," Cartright said, picking himself up. "No cause for concern, I assure you."

"No cause for concern!" I cried wildly. "You know not whereof you speak, sir. The last time he suffered such a blow . . . Emerson!" For his eyes had opened, and his gaze had focused on my face. "My dearest Emerson, speak to me. Who am I?"

CHAPTER TWO

A Lady Cannot Be Blamed If a Master Criminal Takes a Fancy to Her

"Now be fair, Peabody," Emerson said. "It is no wonder the poor chap believed you to be hysterical. That was a damned—er—deuced idiotic question."

I rubbed my cheek. It still stung.

"The phraseology was certainly open to misinterpretation," I admitted. "But is it any wonder I was overwrought? Are you certain . . ."

"You are my wife," Emerson said. Removing the pipe from his mouth, he employed the stem as a pointer. "That is our son Ramses. That is our daughter Nefret. The animal presently occupying her lap is the cat Bastet. The larger four-footed creature is another cat, Anubis by name. This bit of material on my head, placed there over my strenuous objections, is called sticking-plaster. It covers, quite unnecessarily, a slight bump and a small cut."

"I do wish you wouldn't be sarcastic, Emerson. It is particularly trying to my nerves."

"I am endeavoring to change the subject, my dear."

The reminder was justified. Neither of the children knew the whole truth about the terrible events of the previous winter, when another blow on the head had destroyed Emerson's memory even of ME.

My efforts to keep Ramses in the dark about his father's bout of amnesia had failed, but he did not know about our most recent encounter with our great and terrible adversary, the Master Criminal. It would have been impossible to explain all that had transpired without admitting that an illicit passion for my humble self had prompted certain of Sethos's activities.

Not that I had anything to be ashamed of. A lady cannot be blamed if a Master Criminal takes a fancy to her. Nevertheless, it was not a subject I particularly wanted to discuss with my son.

At least I devoutly hoped Ramses was unaware of those facts. I did not count on it, because Ramses had ways of finding things out. Our workmen, and other individuals who ought to have known better, believed he was a djinni, whereas, in fact, he was only one of the world's most efficient snoops. In his younger days he had been only too prone to discussing the information he had acquired by such morally questionable means, but of late he had become more taciturn. I don't know which was worse. The discussions were often very embarrassing, but wondering what might be going on in Ramses's mind was a nerve-racking exercise.

The ball was still in progress; the distant strains of music and laughter floated in through the open window. The temperature had dropped rapidly, as it does in Egypt after sunset. A cool breeze lifted the curtains and stirred the filmy chiffon ruffles trimming the loose collar and elbow sleeves of my wrapper.

After slapping me (with the kindest of intentions, as Emerson had indicated), and assuring himself that Emerson did not require his services, the young surgeon had taken his departure. Obviously he regarded my earlier reference to poison as no more than an example of female hysteria, and although under normal circumstances I would have felt obliged to set him straight (in justice to myself and my sex), under these circumstances I allowed the delusion to remain.

The four of us—six, including the cats—had gathered in the sitting room, where we sat sipping restorative cups of tea. I had changed into a loose-fitting, but, I believe I may say, becoming negligee of white silk cut en princesse. Emerson had also changed clothing, not because of damage to his evening attire (most of the blood had come off on me when I clasped him to my bosom), but because he prefers to wear as little as possible. In addition to his evening pumps he had also removed his coat, waistcoat, tie, and shirt. The last-named garment had a stiffly starched front and attached collar, and buttoned up the back, so I could not dispute his claim that it was "the most confoundedly uncomfortable piece of clothing in existence, except, oh, yes, Peabody, I grant you, except for corsets, but you never wear them anyhow." He had replaced the garment with one of his work shirts, open at the neck and rolled up to the elbows. He was smoking his pipe, and stroking the cat that lay across his knees.

Like his female counterpart Bastet, Anubis is a brindled Egyptian cat, larger and wilder than European varieties of felines. He was Emerson's—or, to be more accurate, since cats cannot be said to belong to anyone, he had condescended to concentrate his attentions on my husband. Bastet, who had been with us longer, favored Ramses, to such an extent that some superstitious persons considered Bastet to be Ramses's feline familiar, with magical powers of her own. She certainly was devoted to the boy (though of late she had begun to share her favors with Nefret), and Ramses would go nowhere without her. We had brought Anubis as well, since our servants in Kent refused to be left alone with him. I confess that Anubis made me a trifle uncomfortable too. Larger and darker than Bastet, he had not her benevolent nature. It could not be said that the two were friends. On the occasion of their first meeting Anubis had attempted to force his attentions on Bastet and she had knocked him head over heels. Their relationship at present could best be described as a negotiated truce.

Curled on Nefret's lap, the cat Bastet purred hoarsely as the girl's hand moved across her head. Nefret had not changed her dress; bright-eyed and alert, she demanded an account of what had happened.

"Unless," she added, with a prettily curled lip and a flash of blue eyes, directed at Emerson, "you, sir, are of the school that believes females should be kept ignorant and out of harm's way."

"Don't play your little games with me, young lady," Emerson replied good-humoredly. "Even if I were of that opinion, experience has taught me the futility of insisting upon it." Sobering, he went on, "I had intended to tell you and Ramses the whole story, for I have a strange foreboding—er—that is to say, I have a feeling this evening's adventure may presage danger to come."

Whereupon he launched into his account. It was somewhat verbose but quite well-organized, so I did not interrupt.

Ramses did. "Hmmm," he said, stroking his chin. "Very interesting. May I ask, first, whether Mr. Saleh's fit was feigned? Was it he, or another person, who struck you? Where did—"

"I don't know," said Emerson loudly. "If you will allow me to finish, Ramses . . ."

"I beg your pardon, Father. I was under the impression that you had finished; otherwise I would not have—"

"Hmph," said Emerson. "The fact is, the fellow's struggles, or fit, or feigned fit, ended shortly after you left, Peabody. He was limp and unresponsive, so I went to the sideboard to get him a glass of brandy. That is all I remember. It must have been Saleh who banged me on the head, though, since I only turned my back for a few seconds and I am sure I would have heard the door open."

"Not if another person was already in the room," I said, before Ramses could point this out. "In concealment, behind the draperies or on the balcony."

"Ridiculous," said Emerson, for he could see where this line of argument was heading. "How could another person have got in? The suffragi—"

"Is susceptible to bribery. I suggest we interrogate him immediately."

"Out of the question, Peabody. Your theory is pure fantasy."

"Let us assume," said Ramses, "since there is no indication of another person being present, and since there are a number of logistical difficulties, such as how he could have got in without being observed by the suffragi, and how he could have departed, dragging an unconscious body—"

"Oh, for pity's sake, Ramses," I snapped. "Let someone else speak occasionally. Nefret has been trying to get a word in for the past five minutes. The points you have made are valid, though my initial suggestion, that the suffragi might have been bribed or temporarily absent from his post, would account for the seeming anomalies. Furthermore, I cannot conceive why Mr. Saleh should come here for the admitted purpose of giving us information and then suddenly change his mind and resort to physical violence in order to get away, for if he had changed his mind, he had only to say so; there was no need, surely . . ."

My breath gave out. Nefret was first out of the starting gate this time.

"Quite right, Aunt Amelia, that is just what I was going to say. It is much more likely that some unknown second party wanted to silence Mr. Saleh before he could betray the secret. And that means . . . But you see what it means, Aunt Amelia!"

"Oh, good Gad," Emerson groaned, taking his pipe from his mouth. "Nefret, don't encourage her. You may consider that an order."

"He is just making one of his little jokes," I told Nefret.

Emerson said, "Damn," and banged his pipe against the ash receptacle.

I said, "Language, Emerson, please."

Emerson said, "You drive me to it, Peabody."

"But Nefret is correct, Emerson. The fellow's symptoms were consistent with those of strychnine poisoning, and I detected a distinct odor of bitter almonds."

"I beg your pardon, Mother," said Ramses—for his father had gone red in the face and was incapable of articulation. "But I fear you are confusing your poisons. Prussic acid is the one that smells like almond extract. Furthermore, both prussic acid and strychnine act very quickly. Are you suggesting that the postulated poison was in the whiskey you served him? That was the only substance he imbibed within the requisite time period, but had whiskey been the medium, you and Father would also have been affected."

"That is precisely the point I intended to make," said Emerson.

"Did you get a look at the map, Father?" Ramses asked.

"What map? Oh—you mean the paper Saleh was about to show me? I don't know that it was a map. I had requested—demanded, in fact—specific directions. His reply was, 'I thought you might ask that.' He then took the paper from his pocket."

"Precisely," Ramses said. "So it must have been a map, or a verbal substitute therefor."

"Or a blank sheet of paper," Emerson grumbled. "Confound it, Ramses, you are as bad as they are. The most logical explanation is that the fellow is a lunatic. He believes in his own fantasy, that he is the reincarnation or the descendant of an ancient Egyptian priest, but when he was forced to produce evidence he went into a fit rather than admit the truth to me or to himself. By this time he is safe at home, wherever that may be, and no doubt he is firmly convinced that he and I were attacked by demons or by an imaginary enemy. That is the way these people think."

"Why, Emerson," I exclaimed. "You have been reading up on psychology."

"Bah," said Emerson. "I have not the time to waste on such nonsense. Unfortunately, I have been acquainted with enough lunatics to understand how their minds work. Now, see here, all of you. The fellow's story was pure fabrication, but if he believes it he may approach us again, and he may be dangerous. Keep on the alert, at least until we have left Cairo."

"And when will that be?" I inquired.

"Soon." Emerson smiled at me. "I have a little surprise for you, Peabody, one I am sure you will like."

"When?" I strove to speak firmly, for his behavior really was maddening; but it is difficult for me to be firm with Emerson when his keen blue eyes soften and his well-cut lips part in a smile.

"Tomorrow. I want to get an early start, so we had better go to bed. It has been a tiring day."

"Especially for you, my dear Emerson," I said, directing a hard stare at Ramses.

"Father certainly should rest," said that young hypocrite, who obviously had no intention of allowing his father to do so. "One question, if I may. The ring you mentioned—"

"Is missing," I said. "Ramses—"

"You neglected to put it in a safe place?"

"I dropped it onto the table when Mr. Saleh collapsed, being more concerned with his condition than with a bit of lifeless metal," I said, with heavy sarcasm. "It was not there when I returned. I trust, Ramses, that your question was not meant to imply criticism of my behavior?"

"Certainly not, Mother. I know you bitterly regret your failure to retain that interesting bit of evidence, and I would not for all the world add to—"

"Go to bed, Ramses."

Nefret had risen obediently. Eyes lowered, hands clasped, she went to Emerson. "Good night, sir."

He took her golden head in his hands and kissed her on the brow. "Good night, my dear. Sleep well."

"Good night, Aunt Amelia." She came to me and I kissed her as Emerson had done.

Ramses had recently decided that he was now too old for kissing—of his parents, at any rate. Further than that I was not in a position to say. Gravely he shook hands with his father—a process that amused Emerson very much. "Good night, Father. Good night, Mother."

"Good night, Ramses. Don't leave your coat on the chair; take it with you and be sure to hang it up."

Nefret had already slipped away, carrying Bastet with her. Her room opened off the sitting room, as did ours. Ramses occupied a chamber next to ours but not connected with it.

"How fortunate we are to have such intelligent, obedient children," Emerson said fatuously. "I told you, Peabody, that Nefret would be no trouble."

"Your naïveté constantly astonishes me, Emerson. I don't know what prompted Ramses to obey an order without arguing, for once in his life, but Nefret was trying to escape a lecture. I must have a word with that young woman. She behaved very improperly this evening. I caught her coming out of the Moorish Hall—you know what that place is like, Emerson!—and I strongly suspect that she was there alone with a man!"

"You contradict yourself, Peabody. If she was with a man, she was not alone."

"You are not taking this seriously, Emerson."

"And you are taking it too seriously, Peabody. You have no proof that anything untoward occurred. Admonish the child if you must, but can't it wait until morning?" Emerson yawned and stretched.

I now make certain that the buttons on Emerson's shirts are sewn with double thicknesses of thread, since they were always popping off when he disrobed in haste or when he expanded the impressive breadth of his chest. This was an old shirt; the buttons slipped handily out of the holes, and as he extended his arms to their full length, quite a large expanse of his person, smoothly tanned and artistically modeled, became visible.

"Really, Emerson, you ought to be ashamed of yourself," I said. "If you think you can distract me from my maternal obligations in that crude, unsubtle fashion—"

"Unsubtle? My dear Peabody, you don't know what you are saying. Now if I had done this . . . or this . . ."

Leaving the cat Anubis in the sitting room, we retired to our own.

The air was still cool and fresh when we left the hotel the following morning. I am always an early riser, and my curiosity about the surprise Emerson had promised made me all the more anxious to be up and about. But never believe, Reader, that curiosity, or

Emerson's interesting attentions, had made me neglect my duty as a parent.

I had gone to Nefret's room immediately upon arising. She was the picture of girlish innocence as she slept, tendrils of red-gold hair framing her face, lips sweetly curved. The name her father had given her well became her, for in ancient Egyptian it meant "beautiful."

I stood watching her for a while with mingled appreciation and foreboding. I would be the first to admit that my maternal instincts are not well developed—though in my own defense I must add that the raising of Ramses would have discouraged any woman. Having got him, as I hoped, through the most perilous period of life, I had found motherhood thrust upon me once again, and I believe I will not be accused of exaggeration when I claim that no mother ever faced such a unique challenge as Nefret. Only her quick intelligence and her desire to please had enabled her to adjust to a way of life so different from the one to which she had been accustomed.

She had not done it without argument. As her confidence grew and her trust in us increased, her criticism of civilized conventions intensified. Why should she swathe herself in layers of heavy, uncomfortable garments? Why should she not talk openly and freely to young men, without the presence of a chaperone? Why must she lower her eyes and blush and remain silent in company, when her opinions were as interesting as those of anyone else?

These rules *were* absurd. I admitted as much, but I had to insist she follow them. Young and inexperienced, at a time of life when certain physiological developments render a female susceptible to masculine blandishments, she was fair game for men like Sir Edward Washington, and the fortune she would inherit when she came of age would bring suitors swarming around her. We were her only protectors—effective protectors, to be sure, for few men, however infatuated, would risk the wrath of Emerson by taking advantage of his ward. I pondered, as I had done before, about the advisability of adopting her legally. Could we do it? Would she want us to? She was fond of us, I felt certain, but perhaps that degree of intimacy would not please her.

With a sigh, I abandoned these musings and turned my attention to the issue at hand. Gently I shook her awake.

She answered my questions without dissembling and accepted my lecture in silence, but she was still pouting when Emerson helped her into the carriage.

Emerson did not observe the pout. He would not have observed it (men being what they are) even if something had not distracted him. A series of sounds like the honking of a giant goose heralded the appearance of a monstrous object before whose advance the crowd of beggars, vendors, tourists and donkeys scattered. Motorcars were still a rarity in Cairo, and this one was being driven at quite an excessive speed—a good fifteen miles per hour, if I was any judge. It was bright red in color, and an equally brilliant crimson jacket adorned the chauffeur, whose face glowed with pride and pleasure.

"A Stanley Steamer," Emerson breathed. "Peabody, what would you think of—"

Leaning forward, I jabbed the coachman with my parasol. "Drive on, if you please."

However, he was unable to do so since the motorcar was blocking the way. Instead of objecting to the delay, as would have been his normal custom, Emerson leaned forward, studying the vehicle with greedy eyes. Thus far I had managed to resist his suggestion that we purchase one of the horrid things, but I feared I was losing ground.

Other guests were less tolerant than Emerson. The occupants of the carriage behind us raised their voices in loud complaint, and several ladies waiting for their carriages put handkerchiefs to their faces and backed away as the vehicle emitted an explosive popping sound and a burst of evil-smelling smoke.

The owner of the motorcar, identified as such by his long coat and visored cap, had emerged from the hotel. All eyes turned toward him, some in angry reproach, some (female) in interested appraisal. Smiling, he offered his arm (and, one may assume, his apologies) to a lady who had stumbled over her long black skirts as she retreated. After handing her over to her attendant, he sauntered slowly down the steps and took his place behind the wheel.

"Who is that young jackanapes?" Emerson demanded, jealousy (of the machine) making him neglect to finish the sentence my instruction to the driver had interrupted. "He looks familiar."

Nefret had slumped down in the seat and turned her face away. It was Ramses who replied, with a suspicious glance at his sister. "That is Sir Edward Washington, Father, and he is not so very young. Thirty years of age if he is a day."

"Quite elderly, upon my word," said Emerson. "As I was saying, Peabody, what would you think—"

"Where are we going, Emerson?" I asked.

"Confound it, Peabody, I wish you would leave off—"

"The coachman is awaiting instructions, my dear."

The motorcar having driven off, Emerson consented to give those instructions, standing upright on the seat and mumbling into the fellow's ear in order to prevent me from hearing. I said with a smile, "So this is part of the secret, is it? Would I guess the truth if I knew our destination?"

"Not likely," Emerson declared. "But you are devilish keen in such matters, my dear, and you always claim afterward that you knew all along. Perhaps if I blindfolded you—"

"Not likely," I assured him, taking a firm grip on my parasol.

Emerson laughed. He was in high good humor, the motorcar forgotten, and I realized that the children must be in on the secret too. Ramses's narrow countenance looked almost affable, and Nefret's silvery laughter blended with Emerson's deep chuckle. I will say for the girl that she had not a sulky disposition. She had got over her annoyance with me; though, if truth were told, I was not altogether over my annoyance with *her*.

She had been with Sir Edward—and in the Moorish Hall!

"But he was a perfect gentleman, Aunt Amelia. He did not even try to kiss me, though he wanted to."

"Good Gad! How do you know that? Did he have the audacity to—"

"No, certainly not. But I could tell. I did my best to encourage him—in a ladylike manner, of course—but perhaps I have not yet learned how—"

"Nefret!"

"You always tell me I must be receptive to broadening experiences. That would have been a broadening experience. And, from what I have observed, a very enjoyable one."

I did not doubt where, and under what circumstances, the little minx had had the opportunity to observe *that*. Emerson is an impulsive individual, and he is sometimes careless about closing doors. A certain degree of self-consciousness made my lecture on ladylike behavior milder than it might otherwise have been.

Nefret certainly looked like a little lady that morning, in a pale-green gingham frock and a charming bonnet of blue and green straw woven to resemble feathers. Broad-brimmed hats or boaters were in vogue for young ladies that year, but this hat had taken her fancy and I saw no reason to discourage a moderate degree of individuality in matters of dress.

Ramses was fairly presentable too, though I knew that condition would not endure. We had left Anubis at the hotel, but the cat Bastet, on the carriage seat between Ramses and Nefret, stared interestedly around her, like any tourist. I emulated the cat. Not that I would have spoiled Emerson's innocent pleasure by claiming I had anticipated his surprise, but I was curious to know whether I could do so.

I began to get a glimmer of an idea when we crossed the Kasr en-Nil Bridge and saw, on the farther bank, the pennants and flags and funnels of various vessels. That vista had changed since my early days in Egypt; tourist steamers and tugs had largely replaced the graceful sailing vessels called dahabeeyahs. From what I had heard, the Cook's steamers were comfortable enough, providing everything from a proper English breakfast of eggs and bacon, oatmeal and marmalade, to an army of servants in red tarbooshes. The steamers made the run from Cairo to Luxor in five and a half days.

Only imagine, I thought, when I heard someone boast of that speed. Five days and a half for the wonders of Egypt; five and a half days in the society of shallow-minded, frivolous individuals, who "did" Egypt at top speed and in determined isolation from the country and its "dirty natives." I was in full accord with Emerson; if we wanted to get somewhere in a hurry (which he usually did), better the railroad, which made no pretense at instilling culture.

Yet, as the carriage proceeded along the bank fond memories overcame me, and though I knew it to be folly my eyes sought a vanished shape—that of my dear dahabeeyah the *Philae*, on which I had traveled during my first, never-to-be forgotten visit to Egypt. A few of the graceful vessels were still to be seen. Some of our friends clung to the good old customs, and I was pleased to see the *Istar*, which belonged to the Reverend Mr. Sayce, and just beyond it, Cyrus Vandergelt's boat, *The Valley of the Kings*.

"Is Cyrus arrived, then?" I asked, for I fancied I had solved Emerson's little mystery and wondered why he had made such a fuss about lunching with an old friend. "Is that the reason . . . Oh! Oh, Emerson!"

For a vision had appeared to me; a dream had taken on reality. I knew her with the knowledge of the heart, as some poet has said (probably in quite another context), though she was singularly changed, shining with fresh paint and bright new awnings, and though the name on the bow was not the one that had been hers. The name . . . The name was . . . My own.

I burst into tears.

"Good Gad, Peabody, don't do that!" Emerson gathered me into his arms. "You never used to do that. This makes twice in two days! What has come over you?"

"I am so happy," I said between sobs.

"Hmph," said Emerson. "I don't recall that you reacted in that manner to my proposal of marriage, or to—er—certain other incidents that I remember with an intensity of emotion corresponding to the one you claim to feel."

"It is not the same thing at all, Emerson."

"Indeed? Well, we can discuss that at another time. Sit up and straighten your hat and blow your nose and tell me that you are pleased."

Ramses offered me a handkerchief. It was very nasty, like all

Ramses's handkerchiefs, so I declined with thanks and found my own.

"Speechless with delight would be nearer the mark, Emerson. Is it really the dear old *Philae?*"

"Not any longer. She is now the *Amelia Peabody Emerson*—yours in name and in fact."

With an effort I conquered my emotion. "It was a noble gesture, my dear. That you should sacrifice yourself—for I know how you dislike traveling in this manner—"

"It was the most sensible course of action," Emerson declared. "You know we are still arguing about where we plan to excavate for the next several years; until we settle on a particular site, we cannot construct permanent quarters. The boat will serve in that regard until we do. It is an infernal nuisance having to pack up our books and papers every year, and now we won't have to stay at that bloo—blooming hotel."

"Yes, Emerson, of course," I murmured, conscious of a faint qualm. "But you know, my dear, it will require some time to get our staterooms in proper order."

"All done," said Emerson, beaming with obtuse satisfaction. "I have been working on this for months, Peabody; I began searching for a boat last spring, before we left Egypt, and when I saw the *Philae*, I knew it was just the thing. She was in sad condition, to be sure, but I ordered the proper repairs to be made, and as you can see they are complete."

"Bedding," I began. "Linens, dishes—"

"All supplied. I had a quantity of articles shipped out this past summer. But why are we sitting here talking? Come and inspect your new domain, Peabody." He jumped lithely from the carriage and helped me out. "No doubt you will want to make a few small changes, women always do—hurry along, Ramses, give Nefret your arm, the bank is cursed slippery—but I am sure you will find everything to your satisfaction."

The bank *was* cursed slippery, littered with a variety of unpleasant objects from rotting fruit to dead rats. I clung to Emerson's arm and nerved myself to ask the question whose answer I dreaded.

"Who was in charge of the arrangements, Emerson? Was it . . . Surely it was not . . ."

"Why, Abdullah, of course," Emerson answered, steadying me as I staggered. "Watch where you step, Peabody."

"Abdullah," I repeated faintly. "Of course."

He was waiting at the top of the gangplank, and when I saw the familiar form, its snowy robes and turban matching the white of his beard, affection overcame my dread of what he had done—or, to be more accurate, probably not done. Abdullah had been our reis, or foreman, for many years. He and the members of his extensive family had been trained by Emerson in the methods of scientific excavation; they were not only indispensable and valued assistants, they were trusted friends. To complain of the fact that, like all men, Abdullah had not the faintest notion of what constituted decent housekeeping would have been unreasonable.

So I addressed him as "my father," and knew it pleased him, though dignity and the watching audience—the aforesaid members of his family, all jumping up and down and calling out in welcome—prevented him from displaying emotion. Formal Arabic greetings can take quite a lot of time. To my surprise Abdullah cut them short and said, with an odd look at Emerson, "There is someone here to see you, Father of Curses."

"What?" Emerson freed himself from the fond embrace of Daoud, Abdullah's nephew, and directed a formidable scowl at his foreman. "Here? What the devil do you mean, letting a stranger on board, when this was supposed to be a private family occasion? Get rid of him."

Abdullah began, "He insisted—"

That was an error, and he ought to have known better. Emerson's roar hurt my ears. "Insisted? Oh, he insisted, did he? Where is he? Devil take it, I will throw him overboard myself!"

Abdullah's bearded lips twitched. "That feat would tax even your powers, Emerson. He is on the upper deck."

Emerson charged toward the stairs. I followed close on his heels, for I dared not allow Emerson to encounter a visitor when he was in one of his rages. It had occurred to me, as it must have occurred to the reader, that "Mr. Saleh" had called again, but I immediately dismissed the idea; only a man of extraordinary importance could have persuaded Abdullah to violate his orders. The Khedive? The British Consul-General? Lord Kitchener? In his present state of mind Emerson was quite capable of throwing any or all of these distinguished personages overboard.

The upper deck, which formed the roof of the cabins, had been fitted out with chairs and lounges, awnings and little tables, to form a pleasant open-air parlor. My housewifely eye could not help noticing that the awnings sagged and that the rugs clashed horribly with the upholstery of the chairs; but my full attention was captured by the individual who sprawled upon the largest of the sofas—yet scarcely large enough, I feared, to stand up under the strain.

He occupied its full length, his head and shoulders raised by a pile of cushions, his enormous girth swelling up from his chin and down to feet as small as a woman's. On them he wore dainty slippers so heavily embroidered with gold and sequins that the underlying fabric could not be seen. An emerald the size of a pullet's egg adorned his cloth-of-gold turban. By contrast, his robe was puritanically plain, without so much as a row of braid: light gray in color and voluminous as a tent, it caught the light with the rich glow of velvet. Squatting behind him, motionless as statues, were two men wearing a kind of livery consisting of loose trousers and matching vests and turbans of the same unadorned gray.

Emerson had come to a dead stop. "So," he said. "You are still alive. I hoped one of your innumerable enemies had finished you off."

Though the vast shape of his body resembled that of a beached whale, the fellow's face was heavy rather than fat, especially around the clean-shaven jaws and chin. They protruded like the muzzle of an animal, and when the wide lips parted, they displayed teeth yellow as old ivory.

"Courteous as ever, O Father of Curses," he said, in English almost as pure as Emerson's. "Will you not present me to the honored Sitt your wife and to your beautiful and talented children?"

The beautiful and talented children had, as I might have expected, followed us. The visitor appeared quite struck by them, especially by Nefret. He stared, openly and rudely, until Emerson stepped in front of the girl as if to shield her from that intent gaze.

"No, I will not," he said. "Nefret, we will join you in the saloon shortly. Go with her, Ramses."

When Emerson speaks in that particular tone, not even Ramses disobeys him. The visitor laughed. "Then I will present myself. You need no introduction, Sitt Hakim; your fame is in the streets and the sûks and the palaces. I am Giovanni Riccetti."

"Good heavens. I know your name, of course." And indeed I did. Emerson had mentioned it on several occasions. In his time Riccetti had been the most notorious antiquities dealer in Egypt.

"You do me too much honor, Sitt. I have long looked forward to this moment."

"Never mind that," said Emerson. "What are you doing here? They said you had retired."

"I have. I live in scholarly seclusion, enjoying the modest fruits of my labors—my flowers and fountains, my books, my studies, other harmless—"

"Ha," said Emerson. "Your habits were not always so harmless, Riccetti. Come to the point. What do you want?"

"To be of service to you. Only the regard I feel for one so distinguished could have drawn me from my quiet courtyard, where the tinkle of fountains and the scent of roses . . ." He broke off and raised a long pale hand, sparkling with gems. "Now, my friend, don't lose that notorious temper of yours, it is bad for your health. There are rumors in the sûks that may affect your health as well. Did you have a visitor last evening?"

The flush of anger faded from Emerson's face, leaving it hard as granite. "You must know I did, or you would not ask."

"Would you care to tell me what transpired at that meeting?"

"No. Would you care to tell me why you have the impertinence to inquire? Do you know the fellow?"

"He was well known in certain circles."

"Those same circles in which you were once so prominent?"

"Whatever connections I once had were severed long ago. But I still . . . hear . . . of certain matters."

Neither of them paid the least attention to me; eyes locked, they exchanged questions and answers in rapid succession, like fencers striking and parrying blows. I suspected this was not the first time they had faced one another thus, and that Emerson had learned that he must play the game by his opponent's rules if he hoped to gain any information.

He is not a patient man, however. His next question: "What matters?" was too blunt; it produced only a faint smile and a shrug.

Emerson tried again. "He called himself Saleh. What is his real name?"

"Leopold Abdullah Shelmadine. His father was English. He was employed as a clerk in the Interior Ministry."

Emerson was silent. He had not expected such a direct response. Before he could comment, Riccetti continued, "You can obtain his address at that office, but it would be a waste of your time to go looking for him. He did not return to his house last night, nor has he been seen since he entered the hotel."

"Good heavens, Emerson," I exclaimed. "Is not this confirmation of . . ."

Emerson turned on me, his eyes blazing. "Amelia, I beg that you will keep out of this. Can't you see that he is trying to trick you into an unguarded statement?"

"I?" I cried indignantly. "If he knows of me he should know such a device would never succeed."

"Quite," said Emerson, baring his teeth in such a way that I decided it would be wiser to refrain from further comment at that time.

"Quite," Riccetti repeated. "Your husband does both of us an injustice, Mrs. Emerson. I have given him more information than he has given me, and I will add one more word of friendly warning before I take my leave." He lifted his arms; the men crouching behind him leaped up and raised him to his feet. "Be on your guard, my friends. There are those who would prevent you from carrying out your plans and others who would help you if they could. Be sure, before you act, that you know one from the other. Good day, Mrs. Emerson; it has been an honor to meet you. Farewell, Emerson—until we meet again."

Leaning on his servants, he waddled toward the stairs.

We watched in silence until the top of the gold turban had sunk out of sight. Then Emerson led me to the rail. The litter must have been on board the boat, though I had not observed it; now it moved slowly down the gangplank, the gray silk curtains tightly closed, the muscular arms of the men who carried it straining to hold it level. Not until it had reached the bank and moved away did Emerson speak.

"He must have wanted something very badly to go to all that effort. I wonder if he obtained it."

"He wanted to know what had happened to Mr. Saleh—Mr. Shelmadine, rather." Emerson nodded, and I went on, "It was not necessary for you to silence me so peremptorily, my dear. I was well aware of what Riccetti was doing, and would never have betrayed anything of importance."

"Ha," said Emerson. Feet thudded up the stairs and he turned to address his son and heir. "Devil take it, Ramses, I told you to stay in the saloon."

"With all respect, sir, you did not. You told me, if memory serves, and I believe it does, to accompany Nefret to that chamber, which I did, and since I had the distinct impression that you meant her to remain there, though that command was not specifically expressed either, I remained as well, since she gave every indication of leaving—which," Ramses concluded, with a gasp and a start, "she has done."

Nefret, whose golden head was visible below him on the stairs, must have given him a sharp shove, producing the gasp and the start. He maintained his position, however, arms extended to prevent her from advancing any farther.

"Go back down," Emerson said.

"But Father, that gentleman—" he started again, and Nefret made a loud comment in Nubian. I recognized only Ramses's name, but entertained no illusions as to the import of the speech.

"Hell and damnation," shouted Emerson. "Curse it, I came here to show your dear mama the surprise I designed for her, and show her I will—every confounded cupboard, every cursed corner and every bloody nail in every wall! Get yourselves back down those stairs, both of you, or I will—I will—"

"Yes, Father, of course. Nefret will have to go first." Ramses glanced over his shoulder, smirking in a way that would have induced any right-thinking female to slap him. Nefret tried. She then descended, her heels clicking like castanets, and Ramses followed at a discreet distance.

"Such dear, obedient children," I remarked.

Emerson grinned. "Normal children, at any rate. Now come along and squeal with rapture at frequent intervals or I will—I will—"

He did—briefly, however, since sounds of verbal combat could be heard from below.

I took copious notes as we proceeded. There were—how well I remembered!—four staterooms, two on either side of a narrow passage, and a bathroom with water laid on. The saloon looked much as I remembered it, with high windows along the curved side; the ivory paneling had been freshly painted and the gilt trim renewed; with an indescribable thrill of emotion I realized that the crimon curtains might well be the same ones Evelyn and I had selected all those years ago. They were certainly faded and tattered enough. Emotion notwithstanding, they would have to be replaced. I made a note.

Emerson began to look a little surly as my list lengthened, and I had to increase the frequency and intensity of my squeals of rapture. They had an equally soothing effect on Abdullah. His look of apprehension (for he and I had had a number of little disagreements on the subject of proper accommodations) was soon replaced by a smile; and indeed I had not the heart to complain. I realized I would have to find some subterfuge in order to do the necessary shopping, since both Abdullah and Emerson were sublimely unconscious of any deficiencies.

"Tomorrow, then," Emerson declared. "We will come on board early, Abdullah. Have everything in readiness."

"Er—perhaps we ought to speak with the captain, Emerson," I suggested.

He and the other members of the crew had awaited us when we arrived; the exuberance of Abdullah's relations and the violent reaction of Emerson to the news of a visitor had prevented us from greeting them as we ought to have done. I made haste to compensate for this rudeness with an extravagant display of affability. The reis, a tall, upstanding chap with a neat black beard, looked so like Hassan, my former captain, that I was not surprised to learn he was the latter's son.

"I have heard many stories about you, Sitt Hakim," he said, his steady black eyes holding the same glint of humor with which his father had often regarded me.

"I'll wager you have," said Emerson. "Your esteemed father is well, I hope?" Without waiting for an answer, he continued, "So, Hassan, we will leave tomorrow."

Egyptians had become accustomed to Emerson's manners, which by Arab standards were uncouth in the extreme; Hassan smiled, but he informed us with the greatest possible courtesy that we could not possibly sail next day. The cook had been unable to obtain vegetables of the proper quality, the steersman had hurt his back, and so on. I had expected this, which was why I had not argued with Emerson about the time of departure. After some discussion and (on Emerson's part) cursing, a compromise was reached. We would depart on the Thursday, two days hence.

We retrieved the cat and Ramses from the saloon, where he had remained looking over the library, and returned to our carriage. Ramses had possessed a hat when we started out. When I asked him what had become of it he looked even blanker than usual.

"I regret to say that I do not know, Mother." Without drawing breath, he went on, "Who was that corpulent gentleman and what did he want?"

"I hope he is not a friend of yours," Nefret said. "What a horrible man! He looked like a statue of Taueret."

I had myself been struck by the resemblance. The goddess Taueret was often shown as a hippopotamus standing erect. In appearance she was certainly one of the most grotesque of all Egyptian deities, but her aspect was benevolent, for she was the patroness of childbirth. I said automatically, "One should not judge individuals by their appearance, Nefret."

"Nefret has it right, though," Emerson declared. "He *is* a horrible man. His name is Riccetti. Some years ago he was the Austrian consular agent in Luxor and one of the most successful antiquities dealers in the country."

"Ah," said Ramses. "By successful, I presume you mean to imply dishonest."

"That depends on one's definition of dishonest," Emerson admitted. "In most cases the consular agents did not actually break the law, since the laws about selling antiquities were too vague to restrict their activities unduly. They operated like any other merchants, in more or less amiable competition. Riccetti was different. It was rumored that he had been a member of the Red Hand or another such secret terrorist society, and certainly his methods supported that assumption."

"Good Gad," said Ramses. "What precisely did he do?"

"Never mind," Emerson said curtly.

"Oh," said Ramses.

Emerson smiled at Nefret, whose wide eyes were fixed on his face. "Don't be concerned about Riccetti, my dear, he only stopped by to—er—to say hello. He retired years ago, with enough money to keep him in comfort all his life. The trade pays well, especially in the Theban area. I told you about the village of Gurneh, which is built in the midst of an ancient cemetery. The residents of that pleasant little community are skilled tomb robbers and manufacturers of forgeries, some of them good enough to fool even the experts. Budge of the British Museum—"

"I beg your pardon, Father," said Ramses, "but Nefret knows all this. I told her."

In this case I did not blame Ramses for interrupting. When Emerson gets on the subject of Mr. Budge of the British Museum he is inclined to use bad language and lose track of what he is saying.

Emerson glowered at his son. "Oh, indeed? Well, it won't hurt either of you to hear it again. If you will spare me your criticism, Ramses, I will proceed to matters with which even you are not familiar—to wit, the career of Giovanni Riccetti."

Ramses subsided, twitching with impatience, while Emerson took his time about filling and lighting his pipe. I knew why he was rambling on at such length; he did not want to discuss Riccetti's reasons for coming to see us.

"It is said," Emerson continued, "that the loot from the cache of royal mummies at Deir el Bahri was marketed by Riccetti. Some of the funerary papyri and ushebtis turned up in European collections, leading eventually to the arrest of the thieves and the discovery of the tomb by the authorities, but I suspect that the most valuable objects were sold to wealthy collectors who prefer not to display their prizes. The collecting mania . . ." He went droning on, recapitulating a story we all knew by heart, until he broke off with a cheerful, "Ah, but we have arrived; there is the hotel."

"One further question, Father, if I may," said Ramses.

Emerson, who had thought he was safe, braced himself. "Yes, my son?"

"Are all antiquities dealers so very fat? You remember Abd el-Atti."

Relieved, Emerson burst out laughing. "Only those who practice Turkish habits, Ramses. It might be considered an occupational hazard, I suppose, for men with too much wealth and no self-control."

"Turkish habits, Father? Do you mean that Signor Riccetti is a lover of—"

"Food," said Emerson loudly, giving me an agonized look. "Food, drink, sweetmeats, wine, spirituous liquors of all kinds . . ."

"Overindulgence and insufficient exercise," I said, responding to his unspoken plea. "Mens sana in corpore sano, Ramses, as I have often said."

"Yes, Mother. But—"

"Time for luncheon," Emerson declared, pulling out his watch.

"Suppose we go straight in, my dears? I am famished. Here, Peabody, let me help you down. Nefret, my dear—"

He bustled us into the dining room. Ramses appeared to have taken the hint, for I did not suppose he had forgotten the subject. I promised myself to have a little talk with him, on the propriety of discussing certain topics in the presence of his sister. However, I had an uncomfortable feeling that Nefret probably knew a great deal more about such topics than did Ramses. Perhaps I had better have a little talk with Nefret too.

After luncheon Emerson excused himself. "A few errands, my dears. I won't be long. Er—Peabody, why don't you make arrangements for one of those delightful little dinner parties of yours? It has become a pleasant custom, meeting with our friends on our arrival in Egypt."

"Pleasant little custom?" I repeated incredulously. "Delightful? Emerson, you despise formal dinner parties and you always complain bitterly about them."

"I cannot imagine where you got that idea," Emerson declared with the utmost sincerity. "Vandergelt has not yet arrived, but some of our archaeological acquaintances must be in town; Newberry and Sayce and—er—Newberry."

"I will be glad to, Emerson," I replied, conquering my astonishment and wondering what the devil he was up to now. In fact, the request suited certain of my own purposes very well.

"Excellent, excellent. I look forward to meeting Newberry and—er—again. Until teatime, my dears."

And off he went, without giving any of us a chance to ask where he was going. I thought I knew, though. I would have insisted on accompanying him if his absence had not provided me with an opportunity to begin my shopping. Besides, I told myself, I would get it out of him later—and without the children knowing.

But why the devil was he so anxious to see Mr. Newberry?

I scribbled a few hasty notes and dispatched them, and then we set out for the Khân el-Khalîli. Nefret had been in Cairo only once, and then for scarcely three days. Everything was new and fascinating to her; eyes wide, lips parted, she was constantly distracted by the wares of goldsmiths and silk merchants. Naturally I bore this with my customary good humor. Ramses kept wandering off, as was his habit; like his father, he had acquaintances everywhere, and I had become resigned to seeing him greeted familiarly by pickpockets, beggars and sellers of forged antiquities.

Our last stop was at Paschal and Company in the Ezbekîyeh, where I was able to obtain a number of the household articles Emerson had overlooked. Glancing first at my list, which was still far from complete, and then at the sun, I concluded we had done enough for one day, and led my entourage back to the hotel.

A great splashing and a burst of unmelodious song from the bath chamber informed me that Emerson had already returned. I was tidying myself when he joined me in our room, and I was pleased to see that he was in an excellent humor. His first act was to demand that I thank him properly for his kindness, which I did, but the sound of voices in the adjoining sitting room forced me to put an end to that.

"The children must be ready," I said. "How astonishing. I told them to meet us for tea in fifteen minutes, but I never expected Ramses would be so prompt. Hurry, Emerson; here, let me tie your cravat. Where is your hat?"

"I won't wear a cursed hat," Emerson said calmly. "What news from our friends, Peabody? Have you arranged your dinner party?"

"I did not look to see if any messages had been delivered, Emerson, but I will do so now."

There were no letters or notes on the table, and when I looked for the suffragi I did not find him at his post. Concluding that he must be attending to the needs of some other guest, I led the party downstairs. Several messages awaited us at the desk; after collecting them we went to the terrace and selected a table.

I must say we made a handsome group. Emerson's imposing form always attracts attention, especially from the ladies. Nefret's white frock was in the latest mode, with a high net collar and long close-fitting sleeves. Her hair flowed down her back in waves of red gold, and the hat tipped over one eye was of fine white straw trimmed with silk bows and flowers. Ramses was looking remarkably smart. I had observed signs of dandyism of late; he was, however, in that uncomfortable intermediate stage between child and man, when a boy may be transformed all at once from a proper young gentleman to a grubby urchin. All the more reason, I thought, to appreciate the young gentleman. I gave him an approving smile.

He was not looking at me. He was watching Nefret, who demanded our attention by holding out her arm and exclaiming, "Look, Aunt Amelia. Isn't it beautiful?"

It was. The bracelet circling her slim wrist was of fine gold mesh and exquisite workmanship. She had admired it earlier that day at the shop of Suleiman Basha.

"Where did you get that?" I demanded.

She knew what I was thinking. Her lips curved demurely. "Why, from Ramses, Aunt Amelia. It is not improper, is it, to accept a gift from one's brother? I have already thanked him."

The bewitching smile she gave him would have been thanks enough for most men. I had never seen Ramses blush, but on this occasion his high cheekbones darkened just a trifle. "For you, Mother," he said, offering me a parcel wrapped in tissue.

It was a small figure of a seated cat formed of blue-green faience. It wore a tiny golden earring, and a loop of gold wire around its neck enabled it to be hung on a chain.

"Why, Ramses," I exclaimed. "How thoughtful of you. Er—it must have been extremely expensive."

Courtesy—a quality even children deserve—prevented me from putting the question more bluntly. "Where did you get the money?" was what I meant.

"I borrowed it from Father," said Ramses. "However, I intend to pay him back at the earliest possible opportunity, in part from my savings and in part from my allowance as it falls due."

"Thank you, Ramses," I said, and with Nefret's assistance unfastened the chain from my neck and added Ramses's cat to the scarab that had been Emerson's bridal gift. "I will hang it on its own chain later."

My appreciation was sincere, but my doubts as to Ramses's true motives were considerable. I had found the opportunity of having a little talk with him earlier, pointing out, among other things, that while I could only approve his brotherly concern for Nefret's reputation, he stood a poor chance of influencing her by scolding her and ordering her about.

"Bullying her will only make her more determined," I explained. "Any woman of character would react in that way."

"Ah," said Ramses. "Most interesting. I confess I had not considered that aspect. Why I should have been so obtuse I cannot imagine, since I have had ample opportunity to observe the truth of your analysis in your own . . . Hmmm. Thank you, Mother. You need say no more. I am able, I hope, to learn from example, and I will proceed in a way you and Father will approve."

I was not at all certain I approved. A lady always appreciates a little gift, but at his present rate of income Ramses would be in debt for a good many months. He was an expert haggler, but the gifts must have cost a pretty penny, especially the bracelet. Did Ramses think he could bribe Nefret into submission?

She was turning her arm, admiring the sparkle of sunlight on the gold, and smiling happily.

Perhaps he could at that.

After reading the messages I was able to inform Emerson that our dinner party was arranged for Friday evening.

"But we are sailing on the Thursday, Peabody."

"We will have to postpone our departure until Saturday, that is all. You were the one who asked me to arrange the party,

Emerson; such things can't be done on the spur of the moment, people have other engagements."

"Oh, bah," said Emerson.

He did not, as I had expected, inquire whether Mr. Newberry was joining us. In fact I had not heard from him at that time, but later that evening I received a note of acceptance, and duly reported this to Emerson.

He appeared to have lost interest in the matter. Without looking up from the papers that had occupied him since we returned from dinner, he only mumbled under his breath. Not until I began to prepare for bed did he abandon his labors.

I had felt it best to wait until he was in his most vulnerable mood before questioning him about his errands. "What did you learn about Mr. Shelmadine?" I inquired.

"Who?" Emerson tossed his shirt in the general direction of a chair.

"Saleh, as he introduced himself. You went to his office today, didn't you?"

"No. Why the devil should I do that?"

"Where did you go, then?"

"The Museum, the French Institute, the Department of Antiquities. This," said Emerson, seating himself and removing his shoes, "is an archaeological expedition, Amelia. I am not surprised to discover that this fact has slipped your mind, but it is foremost in my own. I was engaging in necessary research."

"Then you will not be interested in what I learned today."

Emerson rose to his feet. "Almost certainly not."

His blue eyes took on a familiar gleam as he watched me. I reached for my wrapper.

"What are you doing?" Emerson demanded.

"That should be obvious. Oh dear, I seem to have got my arm in the wrong sleeve. You might give me a hand here, Emerson."

Emerson did so. Flinging the offending garment onto the bed, he wrapped his arms around me and said resignedly, "All right, Peabody, you are determined to tell me, so we may as well get it over with. What is it, assault, theft, murder?"

"It may be murder. The body has disappeared."

"Whose body?"

"Ali's body."

"Which Ali? There are dozens of them among our acquaintances."

"Ali the suffragi. There is another man on duty this evening. When I asked after Ali, the fellow said he had left his position—gone off, without a word. You see what that means, Emerson."

"Of course," said Emerson. "He was murdered. What else could have happened? There is no other conceivable reason why an individual would fail to turn up for work. The little matter of a missing corpse—"

"The Nile is near at hand, Emerson."

"So are the opium dens, Peabody. And the houses of prostitution."

In that he was unfortunately correct. The area immediately behind the hotel was one into which no lady would venture, even when escorted.

"Emerson, you rambled on quite unnecessarily this afternoon about tomb robbers and other subjects. Was it to prevent Ramses from pursuing his inquiries about Signor Riccetti's habits?"

"It certainly was not a subject I cared to discuss. Particularly in the presence of Nefret."

"You can tell me, though."

Emerson hesitated for a time. Then he shrugged and said with some irritation, "I don't know why I bother trying to keep such things from you, Peabody. Your own lurid imagination has probably supplied the answer. Nothing was too vile for Riccetti. Assassination, murder, torture—and intimidation. His rivals knew that if they defied him, not only they but their friends and families would be at risk. Even their children."

He had said enough. Intelligence and imagination (both of which I possess to an unusual degree) combined to present a series of ghastly pictures. It is impossible to guard all those one loves every instant of every day, and children are particularly vulnerable.

Even mine. "Emerson," I cried, "Ramses and Nefret must be

warned. She is not so timid and helpless as you believe, and she will be better able to guard herself if she knows the truth."

"Now, Peabody." Emerson's grasp tightened protectively. "Do you suppose that bastard would dare attack *my* wife or *my* children? He knows better. Come to bed, my dear, and forget your fancies."

Yet a strange foreboding (of the sort that frequently comes upon me) told me he was no more persuaded than I.

CHAPTER THREE

Abstinence, As I Have Often Observed, Has a Deleterious Effect on the Disposition

In a social sense our little dinner party was a great success. How could it be otherwise, with so many old acquaintances gathered together, discussing Egyptology and engaging in harmless (I engage in no other variety) gossip about absent friends? Among the latter were Professor Petrie and the lady he had recently espoused. They were absent, at any rate, though Emerson would probably describe Petrie as a friendly rival rather than a friend. (And he might omit the adjective.) As for myself, I had only the kindest of feelings toward Mrs. Petrie, even if she had consistently refused my invitations and (I had been informed) made several critical remarks about me.

The Reverend Mr. Sayce gave me an entertaining description of Mrs. Petrie. His initial introduction to her had occurred when she was descending a ladder, and the clerical eyes had been shocked by seeing, under her loose tunic, bare calves and breeches reaching only to the knee.

Realizing somewhat belatedly that a derogatory comment about ladies in trousers might imply criticism of present company, he had hastily added, "Now in your case, Mrs. Emerson, it is quite different. Your Turkish—er—trousers are quite . . . They are not so . . ."

"Form-fitting?"

The Reverend blushed. I could not resist teasing him just a little, so I went on gaily, "But you have not yet seen my new working costume, Mr. Sayce. My Turkish—er—trousers were too voluminous for convenience; I have replaced them with trousers less generously cut, but of course I wear a long jacket reaching below—if you will excuse me for mentioning them—the hips. I will just give Mrs. Petrie some friendly hints next time I meet her. Where are they working this year?"

The Reverend gratefully availed himself of this change of subject.

A number of our friends had been unable to attend the party. M. Maspero, who had (amid general rejoicing) returned to his post as head of the Antiquities Department, was in Luxor with Howard Carter, the new Inspector of Antiquities for Upper Egypt. It was a splendid advancement for Howard, and at my suggestion we all raised a glass to congratulate him and Mr. Quibell, who held the corresponding post in Lower Egypt.

I had placed Mr. Newberry between myself and Emerson. Since Nefret and I were the only ladies present, the proper balance of male and female was impossible, and I might well have ignored this rule anyhow since I was extremely curious to discover why Emerson had been so keen on the sort of social meeting he usually protested with teeth bared. I might as well have spared myself the trouble. Emerson spoke not a word that gave me the slightest clue, nor would he discuss the subject later when we were alone. I was so vexed with him I thought seriously of refusing to participate in the activities he initiated in order to distract me. However, since I knew distraction was not Emerson's sole reason for initiating those activities, it would have been childish and petty-minded of me to object.

We went on board the dahabeeyah next morning. It had been

a singularly uneventful three days, with no word from the Hippopotamus Man, as Nefret called him, or the mysterious Mr. Shelmadine. There had not even been a body pulled from the Nile. So I was informed, at least, by the gentleman at police headquarters, which I visited one afternoon when Emerson thought I was paying calls. (In fact I was paying calls—on the police. I deplore prevarication and only resort to it when circumstances demand it.)

My aversion to prevarication compels me to add that Ali the suffragi had not been pulled from the Nile either, for the simple reason that Ali had never been in it. He had returned to his duties the day after I had observed his absence, claiming he had been ill. He appeared to be quite touched by my interest in his health (though that did not prevent him from requesting additional baksheesh). The information he provided was not worth additional baksheesh (though that did not prevent me from giving it, on general principles). He had not seen our visitor leave, nor had he observed anything unusual that night. He had been busy running errands and attending to the needs of the other guests in his charge.

It was all very discouraging. I could only hope that something interesting would develop soon.

However, the pleasure of being once more on board ship, and the innumerable duties that awaited me—hanging curtains, arranging stores, discussing menus with the cook, instructing the steward in the proper method of brewing tea—kept me busy and occupied. So did the little fits of temper and general grumpiness that prevailed among the crewmen and servants. The month-long fast of Ramadan had begun; eating and drinking are forbidden between sunrise and sunset, and abstinence, as I have often observed, has a deleterious effect on the disposition. The intemperate noctural gorging that succeeded the setting of the sun had equally unfortunate effects. It was all part of life in Egypt and I had become accustomed to coping with it.

I fully expected that after a few days Emerson would regret his decision and begin complaining about the slowness of our progress. However, he had arranged for a tug to accompany us.

Romantic it was not, but the ugly little boat was preferable to the old custom of ordering the crewmen to the tow ropes whenever the wind failed—especially since Emerson had been in the habit of stripping to the waist and going out to "give the poor fellows a hand."

He did not complain. He was fully absorbed in some mysterious research that occupied him all day and half the night. To my extreme annoyance he refused to discuss it with me, saying only, "It will be made clear at the proper time, Peabody. I want to get my arguments in order before I present them to you." And with that I had to be content.

When my duties permitted, I sat on the upper deck. There is not a great deal to see in the way of pyramids after one leaves the Cairo area, but as the banks glide slowly by and green fields are succeeded by picturesque cliffs, a mood of lazy contentment seizes the watcher. Nefret spent a good deal of her time there, reading and studying and, I felt certain, daydreaming about the subjects that occupy a girl of her age. I could only hope the hero of those daydreams was not the dastardly Sir Edward.

The stewards fought for the privilege of waiting upon her. She had won their hearts by treating them with the same smiling courtesy with which she behaved to everyone (except Ramses—he had fallen back into his old habits, which was only to be expected, and Nefret responded as was only to be expected of *her*). She had lived among dark-skinned people all her life. Some had been her inferiors in rank, some her superiors; some had been villains of the deepest dye, others the noblest of men. She knew what some people never learn: that each individual is to be judged on his own merits and that superficial physical characteristics have nothing to do with character.

Busy as I was, I did not neglect my Egyptological studies. I had become known for my little translations of Egyptian fairy tales and legends. I had a new one to work on this year, and I spent several hours each day in the saloon in Emerson's company (though all I ever got from him in the way of conversation were the usual muttered expletives when he hit a snag). Emboldened by my growing skill in translating the hieroglyphs, I had decided to try my hand at hieratic, the cursive script used on papyrus in place of the ornamental but cumbersome picture writing which was employed on monuments. The hieratic of the particular papyrus I had selected was particularly elegant, and fairly close in form to hieroglyphs, but I was brooding over a particular squiggle one afternoon three days after our departure, when Emerson threw down his pen, rose, and spoke.

"How is it going, Peabody?"

"Quite well," I said, casually sliding a sheet of paper over one of the books as Emerson came to me and looked over my shoulder.

"Hieratic? How adventurous of you, my dear. I thought you always asked Walter to transliterate your documents into hieroglyphs."

"He was so preoccupied this year, I didn't like to ask. It is excellent hieratic, as you see."

"As hieratic goes," said Emerson, whose interests incline toward excavation rather than linguistics. "What is the text?"

"Apophis and Sekenenre. I intend to give it a new title, of course. 'The Hippopotamus Pool.'"

Emerson did not reply, so I went on to explain. "You remember the historical context? The invading Hyksos had conquered most of Egypt, but the valiant princes of Thebes held out against them. Then to the ruler of Thebes, Sekenenre, came an insolent message from the heathen king, hundreds of miles to the north in Avaris: 'The roaring of the hippopotami in your pools prevents me from sleeping! Hunt them and kill them, that I may rest.'"

"A somewhat free rendering," said Emerson dryly. Before I could prevent him, he twitched the paper away. "Ah. You are borrowing from Maspero's translation."

"I am not borrowing from it," I said in a dignified manner. "I am *referring* to it and to various other versions—just to check one against the other."

"Quite proper," said Emerson. "Would you be willing to interrupt your work? And send for the children, if that is agreeable to you. It is time we had a little conference."

"Ah, indeed? You are condescending to inform us of our future plans?"

"I told you I wanted to get my thoughts in order. I have now done so, to such good effect that I am even willing to risk the disruption of those thoughts by our son. Go and fetch him and Nefret, will you, my dear?"

I sent one of the stewards after Nefret, who was, as usual, on deck, but deemed it advisable to collect Ramses myself. The servants had refused to enter Ramses's room ever since the time one of them had gone there to change the bed linens and been confronted by a strange man with a wen on his forehead and a hideous scar drawing his upper lip into a snarl. (Ramses's notions of disguise, at which art he had become only too proficient, ran at that time to the melodramatic.) I had made him remove and reassume the wen, the scar and the snarl in the presence of the assembled staff, but they preferred to believe in his magical powers.

That day I was confronted, not by a character out of sensational fiction, but by a stench so appalling I stepped back, pinching my nostrils together.

"Ramses, are you mummifying things again?"

Ramses turned from his workbench. "I told you, Mother, that I have given up the study of mummification for the present, having ascertained to my satisfaction that my basic theory is correct. In order to refine that theory it would be necessary for me to mummify a human cadaver, which, given current laws and social attitudes, seems a difficult if not impossible—"

"Thank heaven for that. What are you—No, never mind, don't tell me. Come along; your father wants to see us."

"He is ready, then, to take us into his confidence?"

"So I believe. Hurry and wash your hands. And your face. And change your shirt. What are those peculiar—No, don't tell me. Just change it."

Ramses obeyed, retiring modestly behind a screen in order to replace the offending garment—a somewhat absurd procedure, since, like his father, he was accustomed when on the dig to go about bare to the waist. When he was ready we started for the saloon.

"Please do refrain from interrupting your father every few minutes, Ramses," I said. "He is the most affectionate of parents, but the habit would irritate anyone, and I don't want him to be distracted."

"Yes, Mother," said Ramses.

Emerson had arranged the chairs in a semicircle facing the table he used as a desk, and was sitting behind it trying to look professorial but not succeeding because Nefret was perched on the arm of his chair. When we had all taken our seats, Emerson cleared his throat and began.

"We will be working in western Thebes this season, in the Seventeenth Dynasty cemetery. I have every expectation of discovering a royal tomb—that of Queen Tetisheri."

"But Emerson," I exclaimed. "You said—"

Emerson fixed me with a hard stare. "If you will allow me, Peabody."

"I beg your pardon, my dear. But you said—"

"The ring Saleh—Shelmadine . . . Why do so many of the people we encounter have more than one name? That ring and Shelmadine's fantastic story did not affect my decision. It had been made before we arrived in Cairo.

"As you all know, the third volume of my *History of Egypt*, on which I am presently at work, begins with the rulers of the Seventeenth Dynasty. It is a very confused period about which little is known, and I realized some time ago that it would be necessary for me to conduct further excavations in the area before I could hope to present a coherent account.

"This resolution was strengthened last spring, when we spent several weeks at Abydos before returning to England. Despite the fact that our work was once again interrupted by events I need not recount, since they are known to you all—for though Nefret was not with us, I feel certain she has been apprised of the details by Gargery and both of you . . ."*

He stopped, having lost track of where the sentence had got

*The volume of Mrs. Emerson's diaries describing these events is among those which appear to have been lost or destroyed.

to, and began again. "Despite those interruptions, we discovered a shrine containing a stela that mentions Queen Tetisheri."

"A remarkable discovery," said Ramses. Turning to Nefret, he explained, "Abydos was the holiest city in Egypt, the burial place of the god Osiris. Memorials to the dead were often erected at Abydos even when the persons so honored were buried elsewhere. Such was the case with Tetisheri. The inscription on the stela we found describes how her grandson, King Ahmose, raised a memorial shrine to her at Abydos. According to my translation of the text of the stela—"

"I have here," said Emerson loudly, "a translation of the text made by your uncle Walter. You will admit his authority, I hope? Thank you. He will appreciate your condescension. Now as you all know, the stela made something of a stir in archaeological circles. A good many people knew of it, and some may have anticipated my decision—"

"To return to Abydos this season?" I inquired. I trust my voice and expression did not show the disappointment I felt. Much work remains to be done at Abydos, but it is not one of my favorite sites. There are not even any pyramids worth mentioning.

"No, my dear," said Emerson, the tone of his voice suggesting that he had some other epithet in mind. "The inscription makes it clear that Tetisheri's original tomb was at Thebes. And by a strange coincidence, the Drah Abu'l Naga mentioned by our multi-nomened visitor is the exact area in which a tomb of that period would most likely be located."

"Very true," said Ramses eagerly. "We have the testimony of the Abbott Papyrus and the discovery of the coffins by Mariette in—"

Half an hour later we were all gathered round the table examining papers, maps and photographs, and engaging in animated discussion.

All of us except Emerson. Hands clasped behind him, he was looking out the window and humming softly under his breath.

Or was he humming?

"Emerson," I said tentatively.

He turned, his features wreathed in a benevolent smile. "Yes, my dear? You wanted me for something?"

The last sentence definitely had a bite to it. I hastened to remark, "I only wanted to say, my dear Emerson, that, familiar though I am with the brilliance of your intellect, this surpasses anything else you have ever done. We will search for the tomb of Tetisheri at Thebes! I must admit I am not entirely clear in my own mind as to precisely where in that largish stretch of cliff on the West Bank you mean to begin, but I feel certain you have it all worked out, and will enlighten us at the proper time."

"Hmph," said Emerson. "I might already have enlightened you, Peabody, if you and Ramses had not kept on interrupting me. However, it will make better sense to you when you see the actual terrain. We will postpone the remainder of the explanation until then. I am deeply honored that you approve my decision."

"Quite," said Ramses. "However, Father, if I may raise a minor objection—"

"Ramses, you are always making objections," Nefret exclaimed. She slipped her arm through Emerson's and smiled up at him. "I am sure the Professor knows exactly what he is doing. A queen's tomb! It is thrilling."

"Hmph," said Emerson, in a much more affable tone than the one he had previously employed. "Thank you, my dear."

"You are absolutely correct, Nefret," I added. "The Professor always knows what he is doing. In my opinion historians have never given enough attention to the ladies, and what a remarkable woman this Tetisheri must have been—the first of that line of great queens who wielded so much power during the Eighteenth Dynasty."

"I believe," said Ramses, "that in your opinion, Father—which is, I hasten to add, mine as well—she was the mother of that king Sekenenre whose horribly mutilated mummy was found in the royal cache. His wounds suggest that he died in battle."

"You were once of the opinion that he had been murdered by the ladies of the harîm," Emerson interrupted, amusement warming his blue eyes.

"I was at that time only three years of age," said Ramses in his most dignified manner. "The manuscript about the hippopotamus pool that Mother is presently translating suggests that war between the Hyksos and the Theban princes was about to be resumed. The wounds that killed Sekenenre and the hasty form of mummification employed support the idea of death on the battlefield."

Nefret had been sorting through a pile of photographs on Emerson's desk. "This is his mummy?"

It was a hideous face, even as mummified faces go—and few of them would look well framed and set on a mantelpiece. The shriveled lips were drawn back in a distorted snarl. Heavy blows had smashed the bones of the face; one long symmetrical slit in the skull must have been caused by a sharp-edged weapon, an ax or sword.

Most girls would have shrieked and covered their eyes if confronted with such an image. Nefret's voice was calm and her countenance unmoved except by remote pity. But then, I reflected, she had known many a mummy in her time. A distinct asset for a would-be archaeologist.

"Yes, that is his," Emerson answered. "Hard to imagine from that shriveled residue, but he was a handsome, well-set-up chap in his day, and barely thirty years of age when he met his death."

I joined Nefret, who went on looking at the photographs. "An unsightly portrait gallery indeed," I remarked. "It is sobering to reflect that those grisly remains, now so withered and naked and broken, were once divine monarchs and their beautiful queens. Of course we must never forget what our faith teaches us: that the body must return to the dust whence it came, whereas the soul of man . . ."

"Is immortal?" In a particularly sardonic tone Emerson finished the sentence I had left incomplete—for I had belatedly realized where it was heading. Concerned as I was about Nefret's questionable religious beliefs, I had thought to administer a little lesson on Christian dogma. What I had forgotten was that the immortality of the soul was also Egyptian dogma, and that Emerson might not want to be reminded of our strange visitor and his talk of reincarnation.

"Er—yes," I said.

Nefret was too absorbed with her mummies to heed the exchange. "All of them look as if they had been in a war," she murmured, contemplating an emaciated cadaver whose nose was decidedly askew.

"He may well have been in a war," Emerson said. "That is Ahmose, Tetisheri's grandson, who defeated the Hyksos and reunited Egypt. His injuries are postmortem, however—inflicted by thieves who unwrapped the mummies looking for jewels. The poor corpses had rather a hard time of it, unwrapped and mutilated by thieves, rewrapped by pious priests—some of whom were not pious enough to refrain from removing objects the thieves had overlooked—violated again, moved from one hiding place to another in the futile hope of preserving what little remained of them. Not all of them were lovely and beautiful in their lives, though. This little old lady was practically bald by the time she arrived at the embalmers', and those protruding front teeth did not add to her charm."

"Who is she?" Nefret asked.

Emerson shrugged. "The mummies got jumbled up a bit, which is not surprising when you consider that they were moved several times. Some are unidentified, and many, I believe, were mislabeled. It will probably take years to sort them out, if it can be done at all."

"The techniques of mummification changed over the course of time," Ramses said. "One might determine thereby the approximate period in which the individual lived."

"Enough of mummies," I said in disgust.

"This is more to your taste, I suppose," Emerson said, as Nefret held up a photograph of a massive gold bracelet.

"I remember seeing these jewels in the Cairo Museum," Nefret said admiringly. "Is it certain that they belonged to Queen Ahhotep? The cartouche is that of King Ahmose—her son, I believe?"

"They were found in her coffin," Emerson replied. "So they must have been given to her by Ahmose, who was indeed her son. If the gifts he bestowed on his grandmother Tetisheri were as rich as these . . ."

"It is surely too much to expect that her tomb was not robbed in antiquity," Ramses said.

"We must not get our hopes up," Emerson agreed. "A number of objects belonging to royal personages of the Seventeenth Dynasty have been discovered in modern times, including the jewelry of Ahhotep. The only one bearing the name of Tetisheri is this statuette."

There were four photographs in all, showing the statue from the front, the back, and both sides. It portrayed a young woman seated in the stiff formal pose common to such sculptures. Her garment was the simple, close-fitting shift worn by women of all ranks, supported by straps that framed her little breasts, but on her head was the vulture crown of a queen. The feathered wings framed a delicate young face.

Ramses began, "If it came from her tomb—"

"It certainly came from the Theban area. I first saw it in 1889, in the shop of an antiquities dealer in Luxor," Emerson said. "It was one of a pair."

"I did not know that," Ramses admitted with chagrin.

"Few people do. In fact, only the base of the second exists, and it is badly damaged, but it is an exact replica of the base of this statue. Before we left Cairo I went round to the French Institute, where the broken base has been rotting away ever since that moron Bouriant acquired it—God knows where or when, since he never bothered keeping records. It makes my blood boil," said Emerson, grinding his teeth, "to think how much knowledge has been lost by the carelessness of archaeologists. One can't expect any better from illiterate tomb robbers, but scholars are almost as bad, especially that bastard—"

"Emerson."

"Er—hmph," said Emerson, scowling at me as if it had been my fault that he had employed language no young lady should hear. He really did try, poor man, but he had not been named

Father of Curses for nothing, and old habits are hard to break. I had more or less given up nagging him about it. It did not appear to bother Nefret, whose Nubian vocabulary included a number of words I had never asked to have translated.

"It is a lovely thing," I said, studying the photograph and wondering what there was about it that struck me so oddly. I had seen the statue several times, for it was in the British Museum. Never before had it affected me as it did now. Frowning, I went on, "Mr. Budge did not purchase it for the Museum until 1891, I believe. If you knew of it earlier you might have abandoned your principles just for once. A gift like that would have quite won my heart."

"If your protestations can be believed, your heart had already been won," said my husband coldly. "You know how I feel about buying from dealers, Amelia. Your principles are more elastic, which is why I never mentioned the statue to you. And besides—"

He broke off.

"Besides what, Emerson?"

"He was asking too much."

Emerson's forthright, candid character makes it very difficult for him to lie to me. His expression at that moment was a dead giveaway—a blend of sheepishness and attempted insouciance. He was holding something back.

Ramses had (confound the child) been absolutely correct. Emerson's analysis had cast new light on the confused history of the Seventeenth Dynasty, and was to win acclaim when it was published several years later, but it was of no help in pinpointing the location of the tomb we were after. Emerson would not sound so confident unless he had other information he had not shared with us.

There was one source from which he could have got such information. I should have been ashamed of myself for suspecting Emerson of deceiving me, but it would not have been the first time he had done so. Supposing, I thought, Mr. Shelmadine had recovered from his fit and was able to communicate with Emerson before the latter was struck unconscious? If that were the case,

Emerson's only reason for concealing the truth *must* be that the knowledge of it would imperil me. (At least that was what Emerson always claimed.) And the corollary—mark my reasoning, Reader—was that it would imperil Emerson to an equal degree.

I shook off the dark foreboding this realization inspired. I had no proof that it was so. And if it was, I would get it out of Emerson one way or another.

Ramses was examining the photographs of the Tetisheri statue with unusual concentration. Then he looked directly at Nefret. She had turned away, and as Ramses's eyes moved from her delicate profile back to the photograph, and back again to Nefret, I saw it too.

Nonsense, I told myself. The resemblance was coincidental. All young women of a certain type look much alike. Maturity has not yet stamped their features with a distinctive cast of character. Thousands of girls have delicate pointed chins and rounded cheeks.

The remainder of the voyage was without incident, except for one occasion on which Emerson got away from me and I discovered him on the lower deck with Hassan and the men telling vulgar stories and smoking hashish. At least the men were smoking hashish. Emerson was smoking his pipe. I had no reason to doubt his assertion that he had smoked nothing else.

If I have not mentioned Miss Marmaduke (which in fact I have not) it is because she kept to her cabin for the first several days, suffering, as she claimed, from a mild case of catarrh. Such afflictions are common to newcomers, so, aside from visiting her daily to supply medication and inquire after her condition, I respected her request to be left alone. I hoped I had not made a mistake in employing such a feeble individual and one, moreover, who appeared to lack the neatness of mind and person I had expected. I was willing to make allowances for the faintly unpleasant odors that pervaded her room—they were not those of illness but of a herb or variety of incense, which I supposed were intended to be medicinal—but her references to prayer and meditation as a means of restoring her health forced me to warn her not to repeat those references to Emerson. He believes that God helps those who help themselves—or would, I daresay, if he believed in a god of any variety.

Whether it was prayer or the herbal incense or my medication or simply the passage of time, Miss Marmaduke reemerged into the world much improved in appearance and in manner. At dinner that evening I was surprised to see her wearing a forest-green frock that flattered her sallow complexion and displayed a figure more shapely that I had expected. For the first time since I had met her she looked as young as she claimed to be—in her early twenties, to be precise.

When I complimented her on her frock she lowered her eyes. "I hope you do not think me frivolous, Mrs. Emerson. My illness, brief and inconsequential though it was, made me realize that I had wandered from the way. The physical body and its trappings, of grief or vanity, are meaningless; I have rededicated myself to the higher path."

Good Gad, I thought. She is almost as pompous as Ramses.

Ramses it was who responded, with a long-winded lecture in the course of which he referred to the system of Hegel, *The Kabbalah* and Hindu mysticism. I have no idea how he picked up such stuff. After a while Emerson, who is quickly bored by philosophy, turned the conversation to Egyptian religion. Miss Marmaduke responded with wide-eyed interest and breathless questions. It was constantly Professor this and Professor that, and what is your opinion, Professor?

Being a man, Emerson did not at all object to these attentions. Not until the end of the evening was I able to raise the rather more important subject of lessons.

"Whenever you like, Mrs. Emerson" was the immediate response. "I have been ready all this time—"

"There is no need to apologize," I said rather brusquely. "You could not help being taken ill, and before that we were busy making the arrangements for departure. Tomorrow, then? Excellent. French, English history—you may start with the Wars of the Roses, they have already got to that point—and literature."

"Yes, Mrs. Emerson. Under the last heading, I had thought poetry—"

"Not poetry." I am not certain what prompted that response. It may have been the memory of an uncomfortable discussion with Ramses on the subject of certain verses of Mr. Keats. "Poetry," I continued, "is too sensational for young minds. I want you to concentrate on neglected masterpieces of literature composed by women, Miss Marmaduke—Jane Austen, the Brontë sisters, George Eliot and others. I have brought the books with me."

"Whatever you say, Mrs. Emerson. Er—you don't think that *Wuthering Heights*, for example, is too sensational for a young girl?"

Nefret gave me an expressive look. She had hardly spoken all evening—a sure sign, with her, that she had not taken a fancy to her new tutor.

"I would not suggest it if I did," I replied. "Tomorrow at eight then."

Emerson had begun to fidget. He felt I was making an unnecessary fuss about the children's education, since in his view the only subjects worthy of study were Egyptology and the languages necessary to pursue this profession. Now he stopped tapping his foot and looked approvingly at me.

"Eight o'clock, eh? Yes, quite right. You should retire early, Miss Marmaduke, this is your first day out of bed. Ramses, Nefret, it is late."

So encouraged, the others retired, leaving us, as Emerson had intended, alone.

"Miss Marmaduke is certainly a changed woman, Emerson."

"She looks much the same to me," said Emerson vaguely. "Have you spoken to her about trousers, Peabody?"

"I was not referring to her attire, Emerson, but to her demeanor."

"Oh. It seems much the same to me. Come along, Peabody, early to bed, eh?"

Later, when Emerson's deep breathing assured me he was deep in the arms of Morpheus and the moonlight lay in a silver path across our couch, and the soft sighing of the night breeze and the ripple of water should have induced repose in me—later, I lay sleepless, pondering the transformation of Miss Marmaduke, or Gertrude, as she had asked me to call her.

There was one obvious explanation for the improvement in her appearance and manners. Emerson's magnificent physical attributes and gentle manners (toward females) frequently prompted women to fall in love with him (hopelessly in love, I hardly need say). This would not have been the first time it had happened.

In fact, now that I came to think about it, it happened almost every year! The young lady journalist, the tragic Egyptian beauty who had given her life for his, the mad High Priestess, the German baroness—and, most recently, the mysterious woman called Berthe, whom Emerson had described as being as deadly and sly as a snake. He denied she had been in love with him, but then he always denied it (either through inherent modesty or fear of recriminations).

Really, it was getting monotonous. I hoped Miss Marmaduke was not going to be another of Emerson's victims. It was possible that she was something more sinister. Had it been an example of my well-known prescience that made me see her as a great black bird? Not a crow or a rook, however—a larger, more ominous bird of prey.

The vultures were gathering.

When a conqueror passes on, lesser men divide the broken fragments of his conquests. Witness, for example, the events following the death of Alexander the Great, when his generals carved the leaderless empire into kingdoms for themselves. It might seem extravagant to compare Alexander with Sethos, our great and evil opponent, yet they had had much in common: ruthlessness, intelligence, and, above all, the indefinable but potent quality called charisma. Like Alexander's empire, Sethos's monopoly over the illegal antiquities trade in Egypt had rested on his abilities alone. Like Alexander's, his empire was now leaderless—and the carrion birds were hovering.

Riccetti must be one of them. His retirement a decade or more ago might not have been voluntary. No, not voluntary, I thought;

he had been forced out of the business by Sethos, who was now removed from the scene. Was "Miss Marmaduke" a hireling of Riccetti's, or a competitor? How many others were after our tomb? And which of them "would help us if they could"? That statement of Riccetti's was meant to imply that he was one of the second group, but of course it could not be taken at face value. Honesty is not a conspicuous characteristic of criminals.

The death of Sethos had not freed us from peril. On the contrary, it had multiplied the number of our enemies. Emerson's (and my) unending war against the illegal antiquities trade had focused on us the enmity of the dealers in that trade, and if the tomb for which we searched was indeed unknown and unlooted, every thief in Egypt would try, by any means possible, to get to it before we did.

Naturally I had no intention of discussing this interesting development with Emerson. He had certainly arrived at the same conclusion; but, being Emerson, he had chosen to ignore the dangers and would continue to do so until someone dropped a rock on him. As usual it was up to me to take the precautions Emerson refused to take—to guard him and the children, to be constantly on the alert for peril, to suspect everyone. No matter. I was up to the job. I rested my head against the shoulder of my oblivious husband and succumbed to sweet, dreamless slumber.

On the afternoon of the tenth day the boat rounded the curve in the river and we saw spread out before us the great panorama of Thebes. On the East Bank the columns and pylons of the temples of Luxor and Karnak glowed in the rays of the setting sun. On the west a rampart of cliffs enclosed the bright green fields and the desert that bordered them.

The West Bank was our destination, and as the dahabeeyah maneuvered in toward the shore, we were all at the rail. Miss Marmaduke had been unable to fit into my trousers, though I

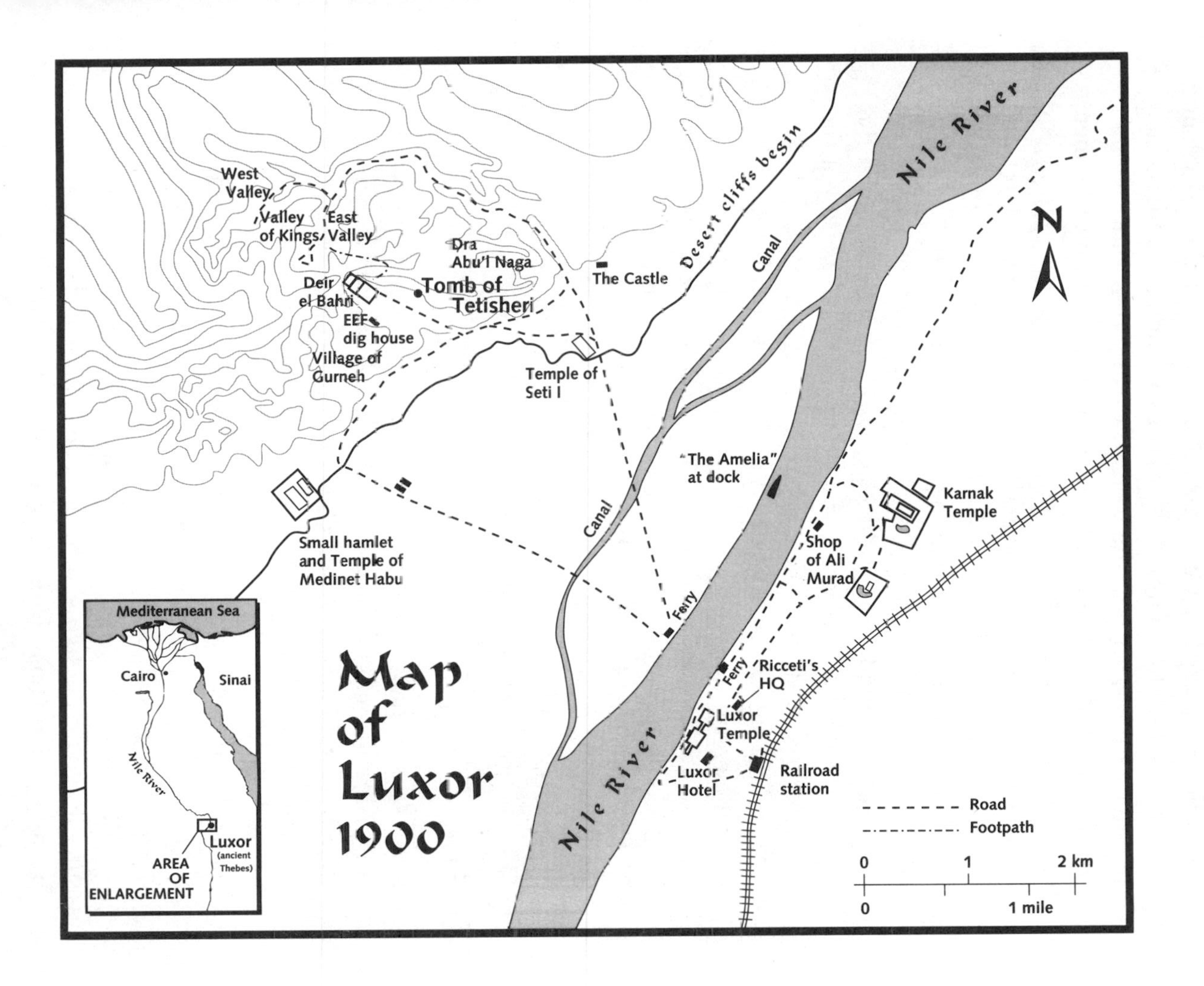
Map
of
Luxor
1900
N
Nile River
Desert cliffs begin
Canal
West
Valley
Valley
of Kings
East
Valley
Dra
Abu'l Naga
Tomb of
Tetisheri
The Castle
Deir
el Bahri
EEF
dig house
Village of
Gurneh
Temple of
Seti I
"The Amelia"
at dock
Karnak
Temple
Small hamlet
and Temple of
Medinet Habu
Shop
of Ali
Murad
Ferry
Ricceti's
HQ
Luxor
Temple
Luxor
Hotel
Railroad
station
Road
Footpath
0
1
2 km
0
1 mile
Mediterranean Sea
Cairo
Sinai
Nile River
Luxor
(ancient
Thebes)
AREA
OF
ENLARGEMENT

had offered a pair. (She was a good deal larger in that region than she had appeared.) Complying—as she explained at unnecessary length—with my wishes, she wore a walking skirt short enough to display neatly booted feet, and a shirtwaist and pith helmet. A wide leather belt defined her waist. She looked quite presentable, but no masculine eye would linger on her when Nefret was present. I had caused to be made for the girl costumes similar to my own: trousers and matching coats of flannelette or serge, covered all over with useful pockets. Stout little boots, a shirt and neatly knotted tie, and the usual pith helmet completed the ensemble. Her hair was clubbed at the nape of her neck, but she did not look at all like a pretty boy.

The first person we saw was Abdullah. He and his crew had come down by train the previous week, and I did not doubt he had set men to watch for us so that he could be on hand when we docked. He and the others were staying in Gurneh. Abdullah had innumerable friends and relations in the village, and it was conveniently close to the area in which we would be working.

After he and his entourage had come on board we went to the saloon for conversation and refreshments—whiskey and soda for us, gossip for the others, since the laws of Ramadan were still in effect. Abdullah, stately as a biblical patriarch, seated himself in a carved armchair. The others—Daoud, Abdullah's nephew, his sons Ali and Hassan and Selim—settled down comfortably on the floor, and Ramses settled down next to Selim, who had been his close companion (i.e., partner in crime) one memorable season. Though only a few years older than Ramses, Selim was now a married man and the father of a growing family. He had kept his boyish joie de vivre, however, and he and Ramses were soon deep in conversation.

"All is well, Emerson," said Abdullah. "We have procured the supplies you requested and have made it known that you will be hiring workers. Shall I tell them to come tomorrow?"

"I think not," Emerson replied. He took out his pipe. By the time he had finished fussing with the cursed thing and got it lit, Abdullah, who knew Emerson well, was watching him intently.

Such deliberation on the part of a man who was notorious for his impatience presaged an important announcement.

"We are all friends here," Emerson began. "I trust you as my brothers and I know that my words will remain shut in your hearts until I give you leave to share them."

He spoke English for the sake of Nefret and Gertrude, but the formal, sonorous speech patterns were those of classical Arabic. They had the effect he intended; solemn nods and exclamations of "Mâhshallâh," and "Yâ salâm!" followed.

"There is a lost tomb in the hills of Drah Abu'l Naga," Emerson went on. "The tomb of a great queen. I have had a quest laid upon me by those whose names must not be named; I have taken a mighty oath to find that tomb and save it. My brothers, you know there are those who would prevent me if they knew my intent; there are those who would . . . oh, curse it."

His pipe had gone out. Just in time, too; he had become carried away by his own eloquence and was in danger of overdoing the melodrama. I caught the eye of Abdullah, whose face was preternaturally grave but whose twinkling orbs gave him away, and I said, "The Father of Curses speaks well, my friends, don't you agree? I am sure that you, who are his brothers, will swear an equally mighty oath to aid and protect him."

The others were not as critical as Abdullah; emphatic assurances, in Arabic and English, followed, and tears of emotion sparkled in Selim's long lashes. Emerson looked at me reproachfully, for he does enjoy making speeches, but since I had summed up the general situation so neatly, there was nothing more for him to add.

"So," said Abdullah. "When will you begin hiring?"

"Not for another day or two. I will let you know."

Shortly thereafter our men took their departure. Ramses and Nefret accompanied them as far as the gangplank, and I sorted through the mail Abdullah had delivered.

"I am afraid there is nothing for you, Miss Marmaduke," I remarked.

She took the hint. Rising, she said, "The messages I await will not come by post. You will excuse me?"

"She has been reading too much poetry," I said, after she had gone. "I had hoped to find something from Evelyn, but there is only this letter from Walter. It is directed to you, Emerson."

The envelope contained a single sheet of paper, which Emerson handed over to me as soon as he had scanned it. "Not very informative," he said. "He is well, she is well, the children are well."

"She is not well or he would have elaborated on her improvement," I murmured. "Is there anything else of . . . What is that?"

"As you see, it is a clipping from a newspaper." Emerson's heavy brows drew together as he read. I held out my hand and Emerson passed over the clipping with a muttered "Oh, curse it."

It was a short paragraph from the English-language newspaper in Cairo, dated a few days after our departure, and it described the discovery of a body that had been drawn from the Nile. It was that of a man of middle age, five feet ten inches in height, but precise identification had not yet been made, since no personal possessions had been found on the body and the face was unrecognizable. The police requested the assistance of the public in reporting anyone of that general description who might be missing from his accustomed haunts.

"Mr. Shelmadine!" I cried. "We must communicate with Cairo at once, Emerson!"

"If you go near the telegraph office I will have you locked up," said Emerson with a snap of his teeth. "Control your outrageous imagination, Peabody. The description might match half the male population of Egypt."

"He did not return to his house, Emerson; Riccetti told us so. It would take approximately three days for gases to form in the body and bring it to the surface."

A furious gesture from Emerson warned me of Nefret's return. "Gases?" she repeated. "What are you talking about, Aunt Amelia?"

"Nothing," said Emerson, grimacing at me.

"One of the principles of criminal investigation," I explained, knowing that if I did not tell her she would go and ask Ramses, and that he would be more than happy to show off.

Nefret seated herself and crossed her slim ankles. "What sort of gases, Aunt Amelia? I have observed the phenomenon but never understood its reasons."

Emerson threw up his hands and stamped out, leaving me to explain the processes of decomposition. Nefret listened with interest and asked a number of intelligent questions.

We went ashore early the next morning. Emerson had meant to go alone, I believe, but that hope was doomed from the start. Short of ordering me to stay behind—an order I would have flatly refused to obey, as he well knew—he could not prevent me from accompanying him, and I was determined to go because I suspected he was about to pursue that one essential clue he had not chosen to share with me. Ramses was equally determined, and once Emerson had given in to Ramses he could not refuse Nefret's request. The only person he succeeded in heading off was Miss Marmaduke, because she was the only one who had to obey his orders. Handing her a sheaf of notes, he asked her to transcribe them.

I had not heard Emerson tell Abdullah of his plans, but he must have found a way of doing so, since Abdullah was waiting for him. I also deduced that Abdullah had not expected *me*, since he had not washed the donkeys.

Emerson swore a great deal when I insisted on doing so. It was only his engaging habit; Emerson is always kind to animals, and the poor little donkeys were never properly cared for. I had got the process down to a fine art by now. It took less than an hour to wash the little creatures, apply ointment to the sores under the filthy saddlecloths, and replace those saddlecloths with clean ones supplied by me. Ramses assisted with the medication. Nefret held the donkeys' heads and murmured sympathetically in their ears, and I confess they behaved a good deal better than they usually did when being washed.

Emerson was still complaining when we mounted our steeds. "If we had a motorcar . . . ," he began.

"Now, Emerson, be sensible," I interrupted. "How would you get one to Luxor? There are no roads."

Emerson's reply was inaudible because his donkey, still skittish from its unaccustomed ablutions, had broken into a trot.

Our destination, as I had of course suspected, was the village of Gurneh.

We had enjoyed encounters with the citizens of this insalubrious spot before. Located on a hill near Deir el Bahri, its dwellings mingle with the tombs of the ancient dead. In early times, its dwellings *were* the tombs, and the occupants resisted, sometimes by force, any effort of the authorities to relocate them. Their attitude was understandable. Why go to the trouble of building a house when there is a nice cool tomb handy? Besides, as Emerson once remarked, a fellow likes to be close to his work. The Gurnawis were the most accomplished tomb robbers in Egypt.

The other flourishing industry of Gurneh was the manufacture of forgeries, which were offered to tourists and, in some notorious cases, gullible archaeologists, as the genuine article. Emerson's and my dealings with the Gurnawis were complicated by the fact that a number of them were related to Abdullah. It made things a bit awkward for Abdullah too. His loyalty to Emerson (and, I hope I may say, to me) was paramount, but we tried to avoid little embarrassments such as arresting his nephews and cousins.

Leaving our donkeys at the bottom of the slope, we followed Emerson along the upward path, which led past tomb entrances and mud-brick houses and sometimes through their courtyards. Emerson's destination appeared to be a more pretentious dwelling, larger and in better condition than most of the others. I noticed that Abdullah had fallen behind, and spared breath enough to direct a question at Emerson.

"Is it one of Abdullah's family you mean to visit, Emerson?"

Emerson stopped and offered me his hand. "A trifle out of condition, are you, Peabody? How are the children?"

"Climbing like goats, both of them. They stopped to talk

with . . . good Gad, what villainous-looking men! Acquaintances of Ramses, I suppose. Answer my question."

"What question? Oh. No."

He went on, pulling me with him.

A walled courtyard fronted the house itself. Our approach had been observed; as soon as we got there, the door of the house opened and a man appeared. A heavy stick in one hand and a boy, on whose shoulder he leaned, supported his stooped body. Lifting his head he blinked at us and croaked, "Marhaba—welcome. Is it you, O Father of Curses? Even to old, failing eyes like mine that majestic form is unmistakable; and so it must be the honored Sitt your wife who is with you, though she is only a dim vision of loveliness to—"

"Yes, yes," Emerson interrupted. "Essalâmu 'aleikum, and so forth, Abd el Hamed. Will you invite us in?"

"You honor my house," said Abd el Hamed morosely.

Turning, he transferred his entire weight to the bony brown shoulder of his attendant. The boy stiffened and bit his lip; Hamed's fingers were like claws, and he had dug his nails hard into the boy's flesh. Not that there was much of it. I could have counted his ribs, since he wore only a pair of ragged knee-length drawers. He appeared to be a year or two younger than Ramses, though with such unfortunates, undernourished and mistreated, it was difficult to estimate. Bruises stained his bare shins and the big toe on his right foot was a festering sore.

Emerson had seen too. With a ripe Arabic swearword he pushed the boy aside, tucked the old man under his arm, and proceeded into the house.

The room was like the others I had seen in such houses—the floor of beaten earth, the walls of mud-brick, the windows high and narrow. Aside from the divan running along one wall, the only article of furniture was a low table. Emerson deposited the old man on the divan, removed the chickens that had been roosting there, and invited me to sit down.

"Yes, rest yourself, honored Sitt," said Hamed. "I will call my women to prepare—"

"No need to disturb them," Emerson said genially. "I am in the market for antiquities, Hamed; let us just see what you have, eh?" In one long stride he reached the curtained doorway at the back and passed through into the next room.

Squeals of surprise and alarm greeted him, and Hamed, miraculously recovered from his infirmity, leaped up and scuttled after Emerson. I followed, with Ramses and Nefret hot on my heels.

The room was a workshop, and the cries had been uttered by a child whom Emerson was holding by the collar of his filthy galabeeyah. Shelves around the room held a collection of ushebtis, scarabs and other small antiquities. The simple tools of the trade lay scattered about—a small furnace for melting the glassy faience, molds of various kinds, chisels and gravers and files.

Emerson released the child, who fled through another door. Selecting an object from the shelf, he held it out to me. "Not so bad, eh, Peabody? Hamed's workshop turns out the best fakes in Luxor. Not that these are his best; they are saved for serious collectors like Wallis Budge."

Ramses had picked up a large scarab fashioned of green faience. "This is really quite good, Father. However, the hieroglyphs are faulty. He has copied a text of Amenhotep III, but the owl sign—"

Surprisingly, it was the boy, not Hamed, who interrupted him. Snatching the scarab from Ramses he confronted him, eyes blazing. "It is right, son of a blind camel! I know the signs!"

Emerson had not appeared to be watching Hamed, but his booted foot intercepted the stick before it could strike the boy's shin. "So you made this, my son? What is your name?"

The lad turned. Anger had given his thin face animation; he would have been a nice-looking boy if his features had not been distorted by dirt, bruises and a fierce scowl.

"What is your name?" Emerson repeated inflexibly.

"David." The reply came from Abdullah, who was standing in the doorway. "His name is David Todros. He is my grandson."

CHAPTER FOUR

Candor Is Not a Conspicuous Characteristic of Criminals

"What is a grandson of yours doing in a place like this, Abdullah?" I demanded.

Abdullah's eyes fell before my indignant gaze. "It is not my doing, Sitt Hakim. I would have taken him into my house. He would not come. He would rather be starved and beaten by this criminal than—"

"Be a servant to the Inglîzi," the boy interrupted. His eyes, feral as those of a trapped animal, darted around the room. I stood in one doorway and Emerson in the other, so flight was impossible. He might be cornered, but he was still defiant; he pursed his lips and spat—not at me or Emerson, for he was not so rash as that, but between the feet of Ramses. My son's expression did not change perceptibly. However, I could have told David that he had made a serious error in judgment.

"You prefer to be a slave to this man?" Emerson inquired evenly. "The Inglîzi do not beat their servants."

The boy's lip curled. "They hire them to fetch and carry and then dismiss them. I learn a trade here. I learn—" He brandished the scarab at Emerson. "The signs are right. I know what they mean!"

"Oh, indeed," said Emerson. "Read the inscription, then."

It had been copied from one of the commemorative scarabs of Amenhotep III; I recognized the names and titles, which David rattled off, indicating the signs with a filthy forefinger, but he stuck after a while. Ramses, who undoubtedly knew the text by heart, opened his mouth. Catching his father's eye, he closed it again.

"It is well done," Emerson said. "And so is the workmanship. What else have you made for Hamed?"

The boy gave his master a wary look and shrugged. Hamed, who had settled himself on a stool, decided it was time to assert himself.

"Father of Curses, you are the greatest of men, but by what right do you break into my house and question my apprentice? I will show you my poor collection if you like. Let the boy go. He knows nothing."

"The boy may go when he chooses," Emerson said, in the same mild voice. Hamed, who knew that voice, swallowed audibly. "And where he chooses. David, we are hiring workers. If you come to us, now or at any time, you will be well treated."

He moved away from the door.

David looked from him to Hamed, and, for the first time, directly at his grandfather. Abdullah's stern face did not change. I was the only one, I believe, to see the look in his eyes.

Ducking his head, the boy ran out the back door.

"Oh, go after him," Nefret cried. "We cannot leave him with this terrible old man."

"The choice must be his," Emerson said.

"Yes, yes." Hamed shot Nefret a malignant look. "The young Sitt has a tender heart, she knows nothing of evil. You did wrong to offer him a place with you, Emerson Effendi. The boy is dangerous, he will attack like a wild dog. I keep him only out of charity."

"A quality for which you are well known," Emerson said. He tossed the scarab negligently into the air and waited till the last second before catching it. Hamed squawked in alarm. "Well, my dears—"

An outburst of cries, thuds and thumps interrupted him. They came from beyond the door through which the boy had vanished. Emerson vanished in his turn, for he, like myself, had recognized an all-too-familiar voice. How Ramses had slipped out without being observed I did not know, but he obviously had, for he was not in the room.

A short passage, more like a rough tunnel than a corridor, led into a room cut out of the rock of the hillside. The only light came from a few small crude pottery lamps, but it was sufficient for me to see, not only the traces of paint on the walls, but the tableau vivant before me.

Emerson had separated the two boys and held them apart, one hand on Ramses's shirt collar and the other gripping David's bony shoulder. I could not tell what damage Ramses had inflicted on the other boy, but it was evident that at least one blow had struck Ramses, for his prominent nose was streaming blood.

Both were too breathless to speak at first. Then Ramses dragged his torn sleeve across his face and gasped, "He was eavesdropping, Father. He ran when I confronted him and I went in pursuit and when I cornered him, for, as you see, this is a dead end, he—"

David called Ramses something extremely rude in Arabic. Ramses called him something so much ruder that even Emerson blinked, and David's eyes widened—with, I thought, a certain degree of admiration. Emerson shook them both.

"There are ladies here," he said, in the same language. "The Inglîzi do not use such words in the presence of women. Perhaps you did not know that, David. But you, Ramses—"

"I apologize, Mother," Ramses muttered.

"You had better apologize to Nefret too," I said, moving farther into the room so that Nefret could enter.

"Oh, good Gad. I did not see her there. However, I cannot suppose that she understood."

"Wrong again," said Nefret. "You called him—"

Ramses raised his voice. "Mother, Father, he was—"

"Eavesdropping?" Emerson released his grip on the boys. They exchanged threatening glares but deemed it wiser to leave it at that. "He lives here, Ramses, and you are a visitor. What he does is none of your affair."

"I will not apologize to him," Ramses said sullenly. "He hit me first."

"What a cowardly excuse!" Nefret exclaimed. "He is younger and smaller than you. For shame, Ramses! Poor boy, did he hurt you?"

She placed a gentle hand on David's arm. Ramses appeared to be struck dumb—with indignation, probably. David was even more surprised. He looked from the slim fingers, pale against his skin, to the face that smiled so bewitchingly at him, and for a moment . . . But I decided I must have imagined that fleeting response, for he darted out, brushing past Nefret and bumping into Hamed, who sent a flurry of curses after him.

"Have a look, Peabody," Emerson said, picking up one of the clay lamps and approaching the nearest wall. "The old rascal has built his house smack up against an Eighteenth Dynasty tomb. The corridor leading to this chamber was an ancient thief's tunnel. One of Hamed's ancestors, no doubt."

"How do you know it is Eighteenth Dynasty?" I asked curiously. "There is almost nothing left of the decoration."

"The majority of the private tombs in this area are of that period. And one can make out a few outlines here"—he moved the lamp—"and here. It appears to have been a banqueting scene, similar to those in the tombs of Ramose and Nebamon. This tomb was never finished. Observe that the back wall is still rough; the surface was not smoothed or plastered in order to provide an even surface for the draftsmen who laid out the outlines of the scene, and the painters who followed them. Hamed has enlarged the original tunnel, which was inconveniently narrow. And this opening was probably—"

We had all listened interestedly, for it is a privilege to hear an expert like Emerson expound on methodology; but when he approached the rough opening in the back wall, Hamed squawked in protest.

"Father of Curses, you go too far. That is a private place. The—the women—"

"You keep your women in this dark hole?" Emerson inquired. "As I was saying, Peabody, this opening was meant to lead into another rock-cut chamber, but it was never completed; and now it forms a handy storage cupboard for Hamed here."

The space was approximately ten feet square and five feet high. It was filled with sculptured forms. Stony faces stared out at us, some human in outline, some grotesque similacra of beast or bird—falcon and feline heads, ibis and crocodile. The shadowed eye sockets of a ram-headed sphinx sent out a glint of reflected light from a speck of mica in the stone.

"The sculptors' storeroom," Emerson remarked, as Hamed stamped and swore.

"They are copies, yes," muttered Hamed. "What is the crime in that?"

"None—unless you sell them as genuine." He hesitated for a moment and then shook his head. "Come, Peabody."

I waited until we were outside the house before I spoke. "Upon my word, Emerson, that was a somewhat abrupt departure. Why did you not remain until you had achieved your purpose? For I cannot believe—"

"I had not achieved my purpose, no. But it would have been useless to pursue the matter. I will have to return another time. Without," Emerson added, distributing an impartial glower among us all, "the rest of you. I might as well have shouted my business aloud to the whole of Gurneh!"

"Which you are doing now," I pointed out. A group of curious idlers had assembled while we were within, and Nefret was besieged by ragged urchins demanding baksheesh.

"Oh, damnation," said Emerson. Thrusting his hand into his pocket he pulled out a handful of coins and flung them.

This would have been a fatal error coming from anyone else—the only way to avoid repeated demands is to give nothing—but Emerson was well known to the Gurnawis, even the children.

After scrabbling for and squabbling over the coins, the onlookers reluctantly dispersed, and we started back down the hill.

"Now then, Abdullah," said Emerson, in a more moderate growl, "what the devil do you mean by failing to warn me that one of your descendants was in the employ of that old villain? Had I but known I would have proceeded differently."

"I did not know that is where you were going," Abdullah muttered. "I thought you intended to visit our house."

"I do. We will go there now. Well, Abdullah? Who is the boy?"

"The son of my daughter."

"Where is his mother?" I asked.

"Dead."

"And his father?"

"Dead."

"Really, Abdullah," I said in exasperation. "Do we have to wring every word out of you? Never mind, I believe I am beginning to understand. You called him David, not Daoud. Was his father a Christian—a Copt?"

"He was nothing," Abdullah burst out. "Even Christians are People of the Book, but he gave himself up to drunkenness and cursing God."

"Hmph," said Emerson. "He sounds a very sensible—ouch!"

I had just given him a little pinch. Emerson's opinions on the subject of religion are somewhat unorthodox. (Heretical might be a better word.) Freedom of conscience is the right of every human being, and I would never dream of questioning Emerson's, but there are occasions on which a frank expression of opinion may be counterproductive as well as rude.

Plodding along ahead of us, Abdullah threw the phrases over his shoulder. "My daughter was here, living with her uncle. He was arranging a marriage for her—a fine marriage, a marriage any girl would want. Michael Todros stole her away, and by the time my brother found them out, she was to bear his child. What other man would have her then? And she . . ." The words came hard to him, even now. "She would not leave him. When she died bearing the child I tried to take it, but Todros would not consent, and now—now he too is dead, dead of the drink and drugs given him by Abd el Hamed in payment for David's work, and still the boy will not give up his evil ways. Todros taught him to hate his mother's family, and he stays here, in the village of his kin, shaming them before their faces."

Nefret, close behind us, said, "Don't be sad, Abdullah. We will get him back."

"Quite right," I said firmly.

"Hmph," said Ramses.

Abudullah had exaggerated only a trifle when he said (though not in those precise words) that his renegade grandson lived too close for comfort. The house he and our men had hired was on the outskirts of the village; the residence of Hamed was visible from its door. We paid a brief call on them so that I could inspect the premises, for I felt obliged (by friendship as well as duty) to make certain they were comfortably housed. Since men seem to measure comfort by the degree of dirt and confusion that prevails, I deduced that they were very comfortable.

After the obligatory consumption of tea and bread, we mounted our donkeys. "So long as we are here, we may as well have a look round, eh?" said Emerson. "And show Nefret something of the area. She has not been here before."

"The nobles' tombs," Ramses suggested.

"No, no, it is too fine a day to spend underground," Emerson said, in a voice that brooked no argument. There are many sights of interest in Western Thebes, but I knew what was in his mind; his eyes were fixed on the hills to the north of where we stood—the brown, barren slopes of Drah Abu'l Naga.

We passed the temple of Deir el Bahri, where Emerson dismounted in order to walk with Abdullah and Daoud, who had accompanied us. His intention, I am sure, was to spare the poor donkey, but the truth is Emerson looks ridiculous mounted on a small donkey and superb when he is striding boldly forward, shoulders squared and head bared to the elements.

Admiring the symmetry of his form and wondering where the devil he had lost his hat, I paid little heed to the monotonous cadences of Ramses's voice. He was riding beside Nefret. They appeared to be back on friendly terms, probably because Nefret was so anxious to learn that she was willing to put up with Ramses's condescending lecture. I did not doubt, however, that he would pay for that condescension in due course. Women have their little methods.

The sun was high overhead by the time we stopped, and I began to wonder whether I would get any luncheon that day. I feared not. Emerson's narrowed eyes had the intent sapphirine glitter that indicated he was hot on some archaeological trail from which it would take more than food to distract him. I persuaded him to let the others rest for a while—he would have disdained such a suggestion on his own account—and passed round the canteen of cold tea that hung from my belt.

There was little shade. The hills of Drah Abu'l Naga are not precipitous cliffs like certain other sections of the Theban mountains, but ascend more gently to a summit some five hundred feet above the plain. The rugged slopes are pockmarked with dark openings, the entrances to tombs now empty and long abandoned, many filled with rubble and drifted sand. Pale ribbons of paths wind back and forth and up and down, clearly visible against the darker buff of the rock. Emerson shaded his eyes with his hand.

"Those columns south of here belong to the temple of King Sethos I, Nefret. We'll have a look at it another day; there are some features of interest, but it is much later in date than the period with which we are presently concerned. And there"—he pointed toward the place where the hill sloped down to the desert plain—"beyond that spur is the road to the Valley of the Kings."

"Shall we go there?" Nefret asked eagerly. "I have never seen the royal tombs."

"Not today."

I managed to suppress a sigh of relief. I was beginning to be very hungry, and a few sips of tea had not gone far to assuage my thirst.

Emerson took a wad of paper from his pocket and unfolded it. It appeared to be a rough map or plan, and we crowded round him, awaiting explanations. Instead of offering them Emerson said, "Hmph," and walked away.

We trailed after him, Abdullah towing the donkeys. After a short time Emerson stopped. "Hmph," he said again.

"Emerson, do stop grunting and exposit," I exclaimed.

"Hmph?" Emerson stared blankly at me. He went on, as if talking to himself. "There is no proper map. Why the devil doesn't someone make one?"

"Emerson!"

"You needn't shout, Peabody, my hearing is excellent," Emerson said reproachfully. "I am trying to locate the spot in which Mariette found the coffin of Queen Ahhotep. Impossible, I fear, since that bloody idiot—"

"The lady who owned the beautiful jewelry?" Nefret asked. "Was it in her coffin?"

She knew it had been, she was only trying to get Emerson back on track, and I must admit she succeeded better than I might have done.

"Quite right, my dear. You know the story, of course?" Without waiting for her to answer he proceeded to tell it. "It really is one of the most curious incidents in archaeological history. Mariette, that bloody—oh, very well, Peabody, I admit the fellow deserves the credit of founding the Antiquities Department, but the fact is he was more concerned with impressing noble visitors than conducting a proper dig. He was swanking around in Cairo when his unsupervised workmen came across the coffin, with the mummy and the jewelry. Even when he was notified of the discovery he didn't start for Luxor; he wrote a letter, the damned fool, and by the time it arrived, the local governor had got his hands on the coffin and opened it. The mummy was probably in poor condition, like others of the period, so the governor simply pitched the bones and bandages and sent the jewelry off to the Khedive in Cairo. By that time it had finally dawned on Mariette that he might be missing something; he managed to intercept the boat and rescue the jewelry."

"It is a miracle it wasn't stolen," Nefret exclaimed. "How could Mariette have been so stupid? Yet his is one of the great names of Egyptology."

"That sort of thing was only too common fifty years ago," Emerson answered. "Peabody would probably say one is obliged to give one's predecessors credit for what they did accomplish, but how anyone, at any time, could have been so feeble-witted as to suppose that a group of indigent, illiterate workers could resist the temptation . . . Ah, well. The most interesting point about the queen's coffin, and that of King Kamose, which was discovered under similar circumstances a few years earlier, is that both were found, not in proper tombs or tomb chambers, but buried under the rubble and loose scree at the base of these hills. Somewhere in this neighborhood." He gestured. There was certainly no sign of any excavation; the same tumbled rock, the same bare brown slopes stretched out to right and left.

"Thanks to Mariette's ineptitude, we can only guess as to the exact location," Emerson went on. "The mummies and funerary equipment were still in the coffins. Why they were left here instead of being removed to a cache of royal mummies like the one at Deir el Bahri we will never know; but here they remained, safe and forgotten, for three thousand years. Until that moron Mariette—"

"You have made your feelings about the gentleman quite clear, Emerson," I interrupted. "So you believe the original tombs must be close by?"

"Not necessarily."

"Then why . . . No, don't tell me. Should we not return to the boat and continue the discussion there?"

"Nonsense, Peabody. It is only half past twelve."

Further debate was halted by the approach of an individual on horseback. I was pleased, though not surprised, to recognize Howard Carter.

"I thought it must be you passing by Deir el Bahri just now," he exclaimed, dismounting and shaking hands all round. "For I heard this morning that you had arrived. Since you did not stop, I set out to track you down."

"I am delighted that you did," I replied. "We were about to return to the dahabeeyah. Won't you join us for luncheon?"

He was easily persuaded, and Nefret was even more easily persuaded to mount his horse. She had learned to ride the previous year and a pretty picture she made, her slim brown hands light on the reins and tendrils of red-gold hair curling over her temples. Howard insisted on walking alongside her, though I assured him it was unnecessary. Nefret had an uncanny rapport with animals of all species, including the human. Howard, who had only met her once before, was instantly at ease with her.

"I took up my duties on January first," he explained, after I had congratulated him on his appointment. "But my new house is not yet ready, so M. Naville has most generously allowed me to stay at the expedition house of the Egypt Exploration Fund."

"Hmph," said Emerson, whose relations with M. Naville (like his relations with most archaeologists) were not of the most cordial. Before he could enlarge on his opinions of the gentleman I said, "It will be a great responsibility, Howard, and you will have a great deal to do."

"More than one man reasonably can, I fear," Howard admitted. "But M. Maspero was good enough to assure me that I have his full confidence and support. He has just been here, you know. What a pity you missed him by only a few days."

"Isn't it," said Emerson.

"The territory is enormous," I said. "And your duties include, I believe, not only conservation and protection of the monuments but excavation and supervision of other excavations."

"Not your excavations," Howard said with a smile. "You certainly do not require supervision from anyone, much less me. But please let me know if I can be of assistance in any way. Is it to be the Seventeenth Dynasty cemetery this season?"

The subject occupied us until we reached the *Amelia*, where Abdullah and Daoud left us. Emerson interrupted his lecture long enough to present Miss Marmaduke, who was waiting in the saloon. She had finished sorting Emerson's papers and asked what she should do next.

"If you have no duties for me this afternoon, I thought I might take a little walk," she said hesitantly. "I am so anxious to see the wonderful temples and the Colossi."

"You have been here before, though, haven't you?" I asked. "On the Cook's Tour?"

"Yes—yes, of course. I meant, see them again. The tours do not give one much time."

"Good heavens, Emerson, what a slave-driver you are," Howard said with a laugh. "An ardent student of Egypt who has not been allowed to explore? Insist on your rights, Miss Marmaduke. You will find Mrs. Emerson a strong supporter."

"Leave off inspiring my staff to mutiny, Carter," growled Emerson.

Howard, who knew him well, only grinned, but Gertrude cried out, "Oh, sir, I did not mean—"

"Then you should learn to say what you mean. You won't get anywhere in this group by beating around the bush." But his irresistible smile and the softening of his keen blue eyes brought an answering smile and an even softer look to Gertrude's face. Curse it, I thought, if Emerson goes on in this way he may find himself in an extremely embarrassing situation.

Do not suppose for a moment, Reader, that I was jealous. Jealously is an emotion I despise, and anyhow, it was obvious that Emerson had not the slightest interest in poor Gertrude.

It was agreed that we would escort Howard back to Deir el Bahri after luncheon and then show Gertrude some of the sights of Thebes. It would not have been sensible to let her go off on her own, for she had not the strength of character to resist beggars, importunate donkey drivers and antika sellers, and Howard's jesting remark had made me realize we had rather neglected her. I still had no proof that Gertrude was a spy and an enemy; if my suspicions were in error we owed her the same courteous treatment any employee should receive.

That settled, Emerson turned the conversation to the subject that was his real concern. He thought he was being subtle, but it is impossible for Emerson to deceive me.

"I trust that among your other projects you mean to stamp out the trade in illegal antiquities," was how he began.

Howard glanced at me. I gave him an encouraging nod, which emboldened him, I believe, to venture an opinion that, though correct, was bound to irritate Emerson. "Professor, you know as well as I do that it is impossible under present conditions. I will attempt as best I can to thwart or arrest tomb robbers and illicit diggers, but once the stolen antiquities reach the dealers, there is little I can do. They always claim they didn't know the objects were acquired illegally, and I can hardly demand the arrest of the ones who are consular agents for foreign governments."

"True," I said sympathetically. "Nor can you arrest the foreign collectors who buy from the dealers."

"Arrest?" Howard looked horrified. "Good heavens, no; what a scandal that would cause! It isn't only private citizens, but officials of certain museums. I name no names, you understand."

"Why the devil not?" Emerson demanded. "We all know you are referring to Budge. He is not the only offender, but he is certainly the worst. Confront the swine. Tell him—"

"Emerson," I exclaimed. "You must not say such things. Howard, pay no attention. You will only get yourself in trouble if you follow my husband's example. Tact, my dear Howard. You must be tactful."

"Well, of course," Emerson said virtuously. "That is my method. Tact, subtle persuasion."

"Such as calling Mr. Budge a rascal and threatening to knock him flat?"

Howard's long chin quivered as he strove to repress his amusement, but when he spoke it was with utter sincerity. "Professor, your forthright manners and absolute integrity have been an inspiration to us all. A man might do worse than to emulate you. I want you to know—that is, I am well aware that I owe this appointment in large part to you and Mrs. Emerson. Your influence with M. Maspero—"

"Nonsense," said Emerson gruffly.

"But, sir—"

"Let us hear no more about it." Emerson reached for his pipe. "Has anything unusual turned up on the market lately?"

"There is always something," Howard said wryly. "As a rule I don't hear of it until it has been purchased by a collector."

Emerson gestured impatiently. "Be specific."

"Well . . . I suppose there is no reason why I shouldn't tell you. Recently a wealthy American tourist showed me a number of objects he had purchased in Luxor. They made me wonder whether some rich and important tomb had not been discovered. Please," he added hastily, seeing Emerson's expression, "don't ask me for the gentleman's name. I am hoping to interest him in supporting our work here and I would not like him to be—er—discouraged."

"You mean threatened," I said, while Emerson sputtered indignantly. "We will not press you for the gentleman's name, Howard, but there can be no objection to your telling us where he acquired the artifacts, can there?"

"I can deny you nothing, Mrs. Emerson. He bought them from Ali Murad. As the American consular agent, Murad feels himself secure. You won't get anything out of him."

"You think not?" Emerson bared his teeth. The expression was certainly not a smile.

After luncheon we rode back with Howard to Deir el Bahri, and lingered for a while admiring the temple and discussing the astonishing career of its builder, Queen Hatshepsut, who had proclaimed herself pharaoh. When I first beheld the site, only a few unimpressive fragments of the structure were visible amid huge heaps of piled-up sand and rock and the tower of the Coptic monastery which had given the place its name. (Deir el Bahri means "Monastery of the North.") Several seasons of work by the Egypt Exploration Fund had stripped away the covering, including the monastery, and exposed one of the most beautiful and unusual temples in Egypt—colonnades rising in successive steps toward the frowning cliffs that framed them, ramps leading toward the rock-cut sanctuary.

"In my opinion," I said, as we stood before a series of reliefs depicting the queen's birth, "Hatshepsut ought to be adopted by the women's suffrage movement as its patron saint or symbol. Coolly and efficiently, without civil war, she supplanted her nephew Thutmose III and proclaimed herself a man and a pharaoh! She was the first—"

Ramses cleared his throat. "Pardon me, Mother—"

I raised my voice. ". . . the greatest of those remarkable Eighteenth Dynasty queens who were directly descended from Tetisheri herself. At that time, as all reputable scholars agree, the right to rule passed through the female line, from mother to daughter. Unless he married the heiress princess, the king could not legitimately claim the throne."

"Hence the prevalence of brother-sister marriages in the royal family," Nefret said. "It makes perfectly good sense when you think of it in those terms."

"Hmph," said Ramses critically.

Nefret laughed. "Why, Ramses, I had no idea you were such a romantic. Love doesn't enter into royal marriages, my boy, not even in your civilized European societies."

I don't know whether it was the laugh, the patronizing "my boy" or the horrid accusation of being a romantic that incensed Ramses most. His face darkened. "Confound it, I am not—"

"That will be enough of that," I said sharply. "Nefret is correct; and according to Egyptian religious dogma the princess had special sanctity because her father was not the king, but the god Amon himself, as these reliefs we are inspecting indicate. Here you see Hatshepsut's mother—um—er—greeting Amon, who has come to her to—er . . ."

Pipe between his teeth, Emerson grunted, "Amon bears a striking resemblance to the queen's husband, Thutmose II, don't you think?"

"No doubt the god embodied himself in the king," I admitted.

"It would have been damned difficult for him to do the job without a body," said Emerson.

I decided we had gone as far as we ought with that subject. Nefret was trying not to laugh, and Gertrude looked shocked.

"Here," I said, moving the party on with a few little nudges, "we see the delivery of the great obelisks for the queen's temple at Karnak. They were made for her by Senmut, one of the most talented of her officials, who was Steward of Amon—"

"And her lover," said Nefret.

"Good Gad," I exclaimed. "Who told you that?"

"Ramses," was the demure reply.

"I don't know where he got that idea." I hurried on before Ramses could tell me where he got that idea. "The queen would never have taken a low-born lover. Her dignity and pride would have prevented it, and the nobility of her kingdom would have resented it bitterly."

"The same objections have been made to the rumors about Her Gracious Majesty Victoria and a certain groom," Emerson agreed.

When Emerson is in one of *those* moods it is impossible to keep him quiet. Abandoning the career of the great queen Hatshepsut, I turned to Howard. "You were responsible for copying these paintings, I believe? Have you any recent sketches to show us?"

Fortunately he had. After we had admired them we left him to his work.

I rather expected Emerson would drag us back to Drah Abu'l Naga, but evidently he had abandoned the idea of serious work for that day; we went in the other direction, in order to visit the Ramesseum and the temple of Medinet Habu. There were not many tourists, since most of them prefer to "do" the West Bank in the morning, but there were enough to annoy Emerson, and both places teemed with ragged children demanding baksheesh, self-appointed "guides," and sellers of dubious antiquities. Needless to say, none of them approached *us*.

Miss Marmaduke made a good show of enjoying herself. She stuck close to Emerson, for which I could not entirely blame her; not only was he a mine of information but his presence kept her from being harassed by the hovering beggars. Since she was incapable of doing it efficiently I had to keep an eye on Ramses, who kept wandering off.

By the time we started back, the sun was sinking westward and I decided it was too late for tea. We had an early dinner instead. Gertrude drooped over her plate, and confessed, when I courteously inquired, that she was very tired. "My fatigue is mental as well as physical, Mrs. Emerson. There has been so much to absorb! The Professor's wonderful explanations of Egyptian religion have given me a great deal to think about. If you will excuse me, I will go straight to bed."

"You will soon become accustomed to our pace," Emerson said, but the corners of his mouth quirked in a way I knew well. Had he deliberately set out to tire Gertrude? The ruse had not succeeded with Ramses and Nefret; both were bright-eyed and full of conversation, and when Emerson suggested they retire, Ramses protested.

"It is only nine o'clock, Father. I want—"

Emerson drew him aside. He thought he was speaking softly, but Emerson's best attempt at a whisper is audible ten feet away. "Your mother and I have an appointment in Luxor, Ramses. No, you cannot accompany us; I need you to stand guard. I know I can depend on you."

Ramses began, "What—"

"For once, my son, do not argue. I will explain later."

After Ramses had departed I said, "Another mysterious appointment, Emerson? I warn you, you *will* have a revolution on your hands if you persist in your high-handed methods. Have I not earned your confidence? Do I not deserve your trust? Will you—"

"Yes, yes, my dear. Only make haste, it is getting late."

I had only time to snatch up a parasol as Emerson led me from the room.

Our small boat was waiting, and so too were Abdullah and Daoud. Once we were on board, Daoud pushed off and then took his place at the tiller.

Moonlight cast a silvery path along the dark expanse of water, and the lights of the town seemed reflected a thousandfold in the starry vault of heaven. Emerson's arm stole round my waist.

The setting was romantic in the extreme. I was not. Emerson had taken Abdullah and Daoud into his confidence while keeping me in the dark, and what is more, they were only a few feet away. I sat stiff as a statue until Emerson's arm tightened to such a degree that the breath left my lungs in an explosive gasp.

"Peabody, will you please stop grunting and squirming?" Emerson hissed. "Abdullah will think I am—er—forcing my attentions on you. I don't want him to overhear."

My well-known sense of humor conquered my annoyance, for really, it was an amusing idea—that Emerson would force his attentions on me (or that Abdullah would disapprove if he did). Physical resistance would have been undignified, so I yielded to his embrace.

"Where are we going?" I demanded.

"To the antiquities shop of Ali Murad."

"You have made an appointment?"

"Certainly not. We will drop down on him like a pair of thunderbolts."

"An apt image," I agreed. "What are you hoping to find, Emerson?"

"Well, now." Emerson released me and took out his pipe. He had given up any pretense of whispering—it is not something he is very good at anyhow—and I noticed that Abdullah was leaning in our direction, listening as hard as he could. So he too was in the dark as to Emerson's real purpose.

"One of the local thieves has found that tomb, Peabody," Emerson said. "It is the only possible explanation for recent events. The ring our midnight visitor showed us must have come from Tetisheri's burial, unless you are credulous enough to believe it has been handed down from generation to generation since the second millennium before Christ. If thieves are at work in the tomb, other objects must have been taken too. They would end up in the antiquities markets in Luxor."

"That is why you went to see Abd el Hamed in Gurneh!"

"Precisely. He is related to every tomb robber in the village.

They bring their stolen goods to him and he passes them on to the antiquities dealers. I meant to drop in on him without warning and have a look round, but by the time we finished dealing with the boy, the element of surprise had been lost."

He paused to swear. He was having trouble getting his pipe lit in the stiff breeze.

"It is a logical theory," I admitted. "But I see one difficulty, Emerson. No—two. If the tomb has been located, it will soon be too late, if it is not already too late, to save it. The Gurnawis are master thieves. And—my second point—if Mr. Shelmadine was involved with the people who found the tomb, why would he offer to show it to us?"

Emerson gave up trying to light his pipe. Stuffing it into his pocket he replied, "Your viewpoint is unduly pessimistic, Peabody. At the very worst we can locate the tomb itself, and it is unlikely that the contents have been completely removed. The local thieves of Gurneh do not—cannot—work with the efficiency and openness of a legitimate archaeological team; not only must they operate in secret, but they dare not flood the market with objects whose source would eventually be questioned. Remember the Abd er Rasul brothers. They had been taking papyri and ushebtis from the royal mummy cache for almost ten years before they were caught, and there was still a good deal left."

"Yes," I breathed, my imagination fired. "But my second point—"

"I knew you were going to bring that up," Emerson said. "Leave it for the moment, Peabody; we have arrived."

Declining the offer of a carriage, we set out on foot. There were a good many people still abroad, for visitors preferred to rest during the heat of the afternoon and resume activities after the temperature had dropped, and during Ramadan the shops remained open long into the night. Ali Murad's house, which was also his place of business, was near the temple of Karnak. One of his employees stood outside the open door, inviting passersby to enter by catching hold of their sleeves and tugging at them. When he recognized Emerson his eyes opened very wide and he darted toward the door.

"No need to announce us," Emerson said genially, intercepting the fellow and ushering me in. "Ah, there you are, Ali Murad. I trust business is good?"

It appeared to be excellent. There were half a dozen customers in the small room and Murad himself was in obsequious attendance upon the most prosperous-looking pair—Americans, I deduced, from their peculiar accents.

Ali Murad was a Turk, with great curling mustaches; a red fez perched on his head and rings covered his hands. His control was better than that of his hireling; only a fleeting grimace betrayed his surprise and alarm.

"Emerson Effendi," he said smoothly. "And his lady. You honor my poor house. If you will be seated and take coffee with me—"

"I am sure Abdullah would be delighted to accept the invitation," Emerson said, taking me by the arm. "This way, Peabody."

He moved with catlike quickness, reaching the curtained doorway at the back of the shop before Ali Murad could intercept him. Abdullah was close on our heels.

I had visited the shop before, but had never gone beyond the front room. Obviously Emerson had. The doorway led into a small odorous vestibule. Before the curtain fell back into place, cutting off most of the light, I saw a floor of cracked tiles and a pile of rags and papers under a flight of narrow stairs. Without pausing, Emerson headed up the stairs, towing me after him. Abdullah had not followed us. I deduced that he had been instructed to prevent anyone else from following us. Indignant cries from the shop supported this assumption.

At the top of the stairs Emerson paused long enough to light the candle he took from his pocket. The house was larger than it had appeared from the street; a regular rabbit's warren of corridors and rooms filled the upper floor. Emerson kept hold of my hand and I kept tight hold of my parasol. People may jeer all they like about my parasols—Emerson often does—but there is no more useful article to be had, and mine were specially made, with heavy steel shafts and tips rather more pointed than is customary.

The upper floor was not unoccupied. I heard soft, unpleasantly suggestive sounds from behind some of the closed doors. I could also hear the sounds of footsteps in rapid pursuit of us. Either Ali Murad had got past Abdullah or the latter had been instructed only to delay him.

Finally Emerson stopped and held up his candle. I spun round, ready to defend him, for Murad had caught us up. When he saw my parasol he stopped and cried out, raising his ringed hands.

"Don't be such a bloody coward, Murad," Emerson said. "You don't suppose a lady like Mrs. Emerson would attack a man in his own house, do you? This is the right room, I believe. I hope you have the key; I would regret having to kick the door down."

Watching Emerson like a man in the presence of a savage dog, Murad made one final attempt at dignity. "You break the law, Emerson Effendi. You defy the Star Spangled Banner. I will summon the police."

Emerson laughed so hard he had to lean against the wall.

Cursing under his breath, Ali Murad unlocked the door. The windows of the room were covered with heavy wooden shutters; from the quantity of dust that shrouded them I concluded they had not been opened for a long time. There was no need for light. Potential customers were never brought here, the merchandise from this special storeroom was carried down to them.

A few tables and a few shelves, cluttered with small objects, constituted the furnishings. Ali Murad's housekeeping left a great deal to be desired. The artifacts had not been arranged in any particular order; ushebtis lay next to vessels of stone and pottery, and on top of ostraca. The floor had not been swept for heaven knows how long; the litter covering it would probably repay an excavation in itself.

As Emerson moved slowly round the room, one object after another appeared in the limited candle glow and then vanished again into shadows. He stopped before a slab of stone, square-sided except for its rounded top. It was a stela from some tomb, probably Nineteenth Dynasty, to judge by the quality of the sculptured scene at the top. Hieroglyphic inscriptions covered the rest of the surface.

I heard a grinding sound. It emitted from Emerson—from his

teeth, to be precise—but he moved on without comment. His behavior made Ali Murad very nervous. Like me, he knew that when Emerson controlled his temper to that unusual degree it was because he was up to something.

The objects in the room were genuine and every one of them had come from an illegal source—stolen by workers from a legitimate excavation or pillaged from a site that was supposed to be protected. Inspectors like Howard Carter had an impossible job; they could not guard every tomb and every temple in Egypt, and so long as collectors were willing to pay high prices for carved blocks and painted scenes, so long would the monuments be vandalized.

Leaning haphazardly against the back wall, or laid carelessly on the floor, were appalling examples of that vandalism—sections of paintings and bas-reliefs which had been hacked from the walls of tombs. I recognized one fragment, depicting the serene profile and elegantly coiffured head of a high nobleman, as part of a scene I had observed only five years earlier in a tomb at Gurneh.

I was standing quite close to Ali Murad, so I was conscious of a gradual stiffening in his posture when Emerson began examining the fragments, holding the candle close to each one in turn. At one point he let out a barely audible sigh of relief—and then caught his breath as Emerson turned back to a particular piece.

It was painted, not carved. The colors were bright and clear, except where dust had blurred them.

Before I could make out the details Emerson whirled round, holding the candle high. Whether he intended it or not, this had the effect of exaggerating the shadows that outlined his strongly marked features, which had not worn a pleasant expression to begin with. He looked positively demonic.

"Where did you get it?"

Ali Murad's voice broke like that of Ramses. "Effendi—"

"I'll have it out of you by one means or another," Emerson said.

Ali Murad's face, equally distorted by shadow, was a mask of pure terror. I suspected that Emerson was not the only one he feared. Caught between a rock and a hard place, as the quaint saying has it, he grasped at a frail strand of hope. "It is known that the Father of Curses does not employ the kurbash."

"Certainly not," Emerson agreed. "A whip is the weapon of a weakling. A strong man does not need it, nor does he resort to empty threats. You will tell me what I want to know because I am the Father of Curses, and my threats are not empty. Who was it? Mohammed Abd er Rasul? Abd el Hamed? Ah. I thought so. You see, Murad, how easy it was?"

He stripped off his coat and wrapped it carefully around the painted fragment before lifting it in his arms. Ali Murad's face shone greasily with perspiration, but at this act of flagrant brigandage he mustered enough courage to protest.

"You cannot do that. I will complain—"

"To the police? Come now. In violation of all my principles I am leaving you with the rest of your stolen goods. I won't even tell those American tourists the limestone head is a forgery. One of Abd el Hamed's, I would guess; it is not at all bad. Take the candle and light us down."

Abdullah, still on guard at the door, stood aside to let us pass. "All is well?" he inquired, in the tone of one who had expected nothing less.

"Yes, certainly," said Emerson, in the same tone. Turning to Ali Murad, who stood holding the lighted candle like a torchbearer, he bade him a pleasant good evening.

There was no response from the antiquities dealer. He appeared to be unaware of the fact that hot wax was dripping onto his hand.

As soon as we were out of the shop, Emerson handed Abdullah the fragment of painting. He walked close beside me, but did not offer me his arm, and his eyes kept moving, inspecting each passerby and examining every dark doorway. I did not really believe Ali Murad would attack us in order to retrieve his property—if one could call it "his." He had appeared to be thoroughly cowed, not to say petrified. However, I thought it wiser not to distract Emerson with conversation, and so I waited until we had reached the boat and were under way before I spoke.

"You did not look to see whether any other artifacts from the tomb might be there."

"It would have taken too long. You saw what a jumble the place was. I wanted to be in and out before the fellow could muster enough courage to call for help. This is enough. It proves what I suspected."

"Well done, my dear. How do you know this fragment comes from the tomb we are after?"

"I am familiar," said Emerson modestly, "with every tomb in Egypt and its decorative reliefs. That fragment is unknown to me."

The claim was dogmatic enough to verge on arrogance. Coming from Emerson it carried conviction, but not necessarily proof of his conclusion.

"But Tetisheri's tomb?" I persisted. "I was under the impression that queens' tombs of this period were not decorated."

"No queens' tombs of this period have been found," Emerson retorted somewhat acrimoniously. "We don't know *whether* or *how* they were decorated. If you will accept my conclusion for the moment, I will explain my reasoning when we have an opportunity to examine the fragment more closely."

"Certainly, my dear. I would never dream of questioning your expertise."

"Hmph," said Emerson. "We are on the right track, Peabody, I have no doubt of it. The next step is to—er—persuade Abd el Hamed to tell me which of the local looters brought the piece to him."

"And then we will—er—persuade the looter to lead us to the tomb. Oh, Emerson!"

"It may not be so simple, Peabody."

"No," I agreed. "For there are at least two groups of criminals after our tomb. One wishes to assist us, the other—"

"Amelia." The little boat had come gently to rest against the bank, but Emerson did not rise. Turning, he took my hands in his and bent over me. I had the distinct impression, even before he spoke, that he was not about to make a romantic gesture.

"I know what you are thinking, Peabody. Don't say it. Don't even think it."

"I had no intention of saying anything of the sort, Emerson. I know how the mere mention of that man's name maddens you—"

"What name?" Emerson's shout echoed across the quiet night. "We never knew his name, only a collection of aliases—several of them invented by you. Master Criminal indeed!"

"His men called him the Master, Emerson, you cannot deny that."

"I am not denying anything," Emerson declared untruthfully. "Devil take it, Peabody, I knew you were thinking of Sethos when you started to quote that absurd statement of Riccetti's. Assist us, indeed! No one is going to assist us! Riccetti was lying, and Sethos is dead. Why do you persist in romanticizing that rascal? He came to *your* rescue only because he wanted you for himself, the contemptible swine! He did his damnedest to exterminate *me*. Amelia, will you please stop thrashing around like that? You are not paying attention."

"You are shouting, Emerson. And squeezing my hands quite painfully."

His grip relaxed. Raising my hands to his lips, he kissed each finger in turn. "Forgive me, my dear. I admit I have felt an occasional trifling, fleeting touch of jealousy of that . . ." He glanced over his shoulder at Abdullah. "What are you grinning about, Abdullah?"

"I am not grinning, Father of Curses. It is the light."

"Oh. And," Emerson resumed, "I wondered for a time whether he really was dead."

"We saw him die, Emerson."

"I wouldn't put it past him to survive solely in order to annoy ME," Emerson declared. "However, Riccetti's reappearance proves that Sethos's organization is leaderless. The vultures are gathering."

"How extraordinary, Emerson! The exact same metaphor occurred to me only the other evening."

"That does not surprise me in the least."

"Then you admit that Riccetti may not be the only villain who is trying to take over the illegal antiquities trade? That Mr. Shelmadine was a rival of Riccetti's and was foully murdered in order to prevent him from disclosing information?"

"Confound it, Peabody, will you stop that? I admit nothing of the sort. I haven't the ghost of an idea why Shelmadine called on us, and neither have you, and I have not the strength to hear the sort of theories you are likely to propose."

There was a brief silence.

"Are you feeling well, Peabody?" Emerson inquired. "You failed to interrupt me."

"Our discussion had reached an impasse," I said. "We have not enough information to reach a conclusion—except that there are obviously two different groups of criminals involved. One wishes to assist us, the other—"

"Don't be a fool, Amelia," Emerson snarled. "That statement was Riccetti's, and I don't believe it for—"

He did not complete the sentence. The quiet of the night was rent by a piercing falsetto shriek. It was succeeded by the sounds of violent struggle, easily identifiable by me since I had become accustomed to them. It was not difficult to locate their source. We had landed as close to the dahabeeyah as Daoud could manage.

I observed that last detail as I leaped agilely out of the boat. The muddy bank was rather slippery; only the support of my trusty parasol prevented me from falling headlong. Emerson had not waited for me; he was already some distance ahead, covering the ground with great bounds. As he reached the foot of the gangplank a dark form rushed down it with such precipitation that Emerson, caught off balance, was sent sprawling.

I hesitated for a second, unable to decide whether to pursue the fugitive, assist my fallen spouse, or find out what had transpired on board. Another shrill cry from the deck decided me. Emerson regained his feet; dripping mud and cursing vehemently, he preceded me up the gangplank.

Someone had had the presence of mind to fetch a lamp. Nefret it was who held it; her hand was steady, though her face was as white as her nightdress. In its glow I beheld a scene like the conclusion of a stage melodrama. Blood spattered the deck and there were fallen bodies everywhere.

The cat Bastet sat beside one of the bodies, ears pricked and eyes glowing eerily. The body stirred and sat up.

Ramses's nose was bleeding again. The galabeeyah he wore in lieu of a nightgown had been torn half off him, baring his thin shoulders. In his right hand he held a long knife.

I looked from my son to the unconscious form of Gertrude Marmaduke, and then to the third recumbent body. Blood blurred the features, but I recognized the ribs and the festering toe and the bruised shins.

"Ramses!" I cried. "What have you done now?"

CHAPTER FIVE

The Fatal Fall of a Fellah

"I beg your pardon, Ramses," I said. "In the shock of the moment I spoke without thinking. I know, of course, that you would never be so uncivilized as to carry a knife or use it on a living creature."

"Your apology is noted and accepted, Mother. Though if truth were told—"

Emerson muffled him by pressing a cloth to his face. "Hold this in place, Ramses, it will stop the bleeding."

I glanced sharply at Ramses. Only a disheveled mop of curls and a pair of wide black eyes were visible over the cloth. The "truth" he had been about to tell might have been a comment on my own habit of carrying a knife (a different matter altogether), or an admission of something I preferred not to hear, so I did not pursue it. Having observed that nosebleed appeared to be the extent of his injuries, I turned my attention to the other boy, who was in far worse case.

Emerson had carried David to Ramses's room and put him on the bed. I had been less tender of my third patient, slapping her cheeks until she recovered from her faint and then shoving her into her room and ordering her to remain there until I returned. Ramses's cabin was uncomfortably crowded as it was, with five of us gathered round. Abdullah had arrived on the scene in time to see Emerson lift the limp, bleeding body of the boy. Though not a word had escaped his lips, he had followed us to the cabin and I had not had the heart to send him away. He had retreated to a corner where he stood like a stately statue, arms folded across his breast, face impassive.

"How is he?" Emerson inquired, bending over the bed.

"He is, to employ the word in its literal sense, a bloody mess," I replied. "Malnourished, flea-bitten, bruised and dirty. His assailant's knife inflicted two wounds. The one on his back is shallow, but this gash on his temple will require to be stitched up. I had better do it now while he is still in a swoon. Get a basin of clean water, Nefret, if you please."

Quickly and efficiently she obeyed, emptying the bloody water into the slop jar and rinsing the basin before refilling it. "What else can I do?" she asked.

Her voice was calm, her hands steady; the color had returned to her face. There was no danger of *her* falling into a faint at the sight of blood. "You might have a look at Ramses," I said.

Ramses sprang to his feet and backed away, clutching the torn remnants of his robe around him. "I do not require to be looked at," he said, the freezing dignity of the words somewhat marred by his blood-smeared face and torn garment. "I am perfectly capable of looking after myself should such be necessary, which it is not, since the only damage done was to my nasal appendage."

"Hmmm, yes," said Emerson, distracted by this candid admission. "I must show you how to defend yourself against that particular blow, Ramses. Your nose seems particularly—"

"Not now, Emerson, for pity's sake," I interrupted. "Leave him be, Nefret."

Nefret had backed Ramses into a corner. "I only want to help him, Aunt Amelia. He is behaving like a silly little boy. I am quite accustomed to the sight of—"

"Leave him be, I said. Bring the lamp over here, I cannot see to thread this needle. Ramses, wash your face and then tell me what happened."

"I was on guard, as Father instructed," Ramses explained. "I assumed he meant me to watch out for David. He had been following us all day."

"What?" I cried.

"He attempted to, as the saying is, lose himself in the crowd. The attempt was a failure, insofar as I was concerned. I believed it possible that he had been sent to spy on us by Abd el Hamed." Ramses completed his ablutions—more or less—modestly adjusted his robe, and squatted by the side of the bed, Arab fashion. "After I had extinguished my lamp, the cat Bastet and I took up a position by the window. The night was still, the air fresh and cool; my senses were at their keenest pitch, since I had been urged to retire long before the time to which I am accustomed. And may I remark, on that subject—"

"No, you may not," I said, without looking up.

"Yes, Mother. I sat, as I said, by my window, and although my mind was occupied with philosophical subjects, on which I would elaborate if I believed I would be allowed to do so, they did not interfere in the slightest with my concentration. It was the cat Bastet who warned me of the advent of an intruder, as I had anticipated she would, since her senses are keener than those of any human. A soft growl and a stiffening of the hairs along her spine alerted me. Before long I was rewarded by seeing a head appear over the gunwale. The head was followed by a body as the individual pulled himself up onto the deck, and it was then that I recognized David, for, though I had anticipated it would be he, I am not so rash as to leap to—"

"Ramses," I said.

"Yes, Mother. David—I knew him by his outline and by the way he moved—came creeping toward the cabins. I remained motionless, for I feared that precipitate action might enable him to elude me. As I waited for him to come within grasping range

I was somewhat startled to observe another head appear, and another, bulkier, form climb over the gunwale. Faced, as I believed, with two opponents, I was considering my options when the second individual leaped forward and I saw the moonlight glitter on an object in his raised hand. I saved David's life," said Ramses, without false modesty, "for my cry of warning enabled him to twist aside, so that the knife glanced across his back instead of entering his heart.

"I had expected the assailant would flee when he heard my voice, but he bent over David, who had fallen to the deck, and struck again. I therefore jumped out of the window and grappled with the fellow."

"Good heavens, Ramses," I exclaimed. "That was courageous but extremely foolish."

Ramses concluded it would be advisable to revise the statement. "Er—the word 'grapple' is not precisely accurate, Mother. The fellow managed to land one blow—on my nose, as you see—before I—uh—I kicked him."

"Where?" Nefret inquired innocently.

"Stop teasing him, Nefret," I ordered. "It was well done, Ramses. Ordinarily I would deplore any deviation from the rules of civilized combat, if there can be such a thing, but when one combatant is a large man with a knife, bent on homicide, and the other is a little—"

"I beg your pardon, Mother," said Ramses, reddening. "Do you wish me to continue my narrative?"

"Not at the present time," said Emerson. "The boy is awake, Amelia."

When I returned my attention to David I saw that his eyes were open. "I am going to have to clean and stitch this wound in your head," I said in my best Arabic. "It will be painful."

"No," said the boy through clenched teeth. "I do not need your help, Sitt. Let me go."

"Why did you come here, David?" Emerson asked.

"My dear, you should not question him now; he is in pain and requires—"

"I have no quarrel with your medical ethics or your altruistic intentions," Emerson replied, now talking English, as I had done. "You may dose him and bandage him and stitch him as much as you like, but first it is essential to ascertain the reason why he was attacked and take the necessary steps to prevent further harm to him—or one of us. Well, David? You heard my question."

The last sentence was again in David's native tongue, but I suspected, from the tightening of the boy's lips, that he had understood some, at least, of the preceding speech. Abdullah certainly had.

Emerson did not repeat the question; he stood waiting, inflexible as a judge. Then Ramses rose to his knees, and David's eyes turned to him. For a moment I had the uncanny impression that I was seeing my son reflected in a mirror that showed him, not as he was, but as he might have been had hard usage and poverty changed him. His eyes and David's were almost identical in color and setting, with the same fringe of thick dark lashes.

Neither spoke. After a moment Ramses resumed his squatting position and David looked at Emerson.

"After you went, Abd el Hamed tried to beat me," he muttered. "I struck the stick from his hands and ran away."

"He had beaten you before," Emerson said.

"Yes. I had run away before."

"But always before this you went back," Emerson said.

"He had nowhere else to go," Nefret exclaimed. "Must you continue, Professor? It is obvious that he—"

"No, my dear, it is not obvious," was the gentle but firm reply. "He could have gone to his mother's family. Is that not true, Abdullah?"

Abdullah nodded, but his face was so grim that only someone who knew him as well as I did would have sensed the softer emotion he was ashamed to display. I could understand why David, who knew his mother's family only from the bitter speeches of his father, would not want to seek refuge with them. And something had happened to the boy that day—Nefret's gentle concern, Emerson's interest and offer of help, even the vulgar, boyish tussle with Ramses—no single event, but a combination of all of them, had, perhaps without his conscious awareness, affected his decision.

"Hmph," said Emerson, who knew Abdullah as well as I did. "So you decided to accept my offer of help. Why did you wait until night?"

"I did not come to ask for help," David said haughtily. "I thought about the things you said—all day, as I lay hidden in the hills, I thought about them, and I thought, I will see the Inglîzi again and speak with them again, and then perhaps . . . But it would have been stupid to come openly, in daylight; I knew Abd el Hamed would be looking for me, trying to catch me and bring me back. I did not know he would go to such lengths . . ."

"You do not know why he would rather see you dead than out of his hands?"

"I do not know. Perhaps it was not Abd el Hamed. I do not know who it was, or why . . ."

His voice had become hoarse and faint. I said firmly, "Enough, Emerson. I am going to stitch this cut, and then he should rest. Hold on to him. Ramses, sit on his feet."

But before Emerson's big brown hands could close over the boy's bony shoulders, he was pushed aside and Abdullah took his place.

Having had considerable practice with Emerson, I made quite a neat job of my sewing. David did not groan or move a muscle; with his grandfather looking on, he would not have cried out if I had been amputating his leg. He was fairly done in by the time I finished, however, and Abdullah's brow was bedewed with perspiration.

I was itching to get to work on the boy with a bar of soap and a scrub brush, but I decided to spare him that exercise until he was rested. A few drops of laudanum, which he was too weak to resist, assured me that he would rest. I then ordered the others to their rooms.

"This *is* my room," said Ramses.

"True. You can sleep on the couch in the saloon."

"If you will consider a suggestion, Mother, it might be best for me to sleep here, on the floor. In that way—"

"You need not point out the advantages of the suggestion," I said somewhat curtly (for I thought I had detected a tinge of sarcasm in his introductory sentence). "It is a good one. There are extra blankets in the cupboard outside my room. Wake me if there is any change."

"Yes, Mother."

I waited until Nefret had left and Emerson had gone off with Abdullah before I said, "Were you hurt, Ramses? Be candid, I beg. Denial, if untrue, would be foolish, not courageous."

"I was not hurt. Thank you for inquiring."

"Ramses."

"Yes, Mother?"

He stiffened when I put my arms around him, but it was not from pain, and after a moment he gave me an awkward hug in return.

"Good night, Ramses."

"Good night, Mother."

I met Emerson in the corridor. "What did Abdullah have to say?" I inquired.

"Nothing. He is desperately cut up about the boy but is too proud to admit it. Confound the stubborn old fool; he behaves more like an Englishman than an Egyptian! Arabs are not usually so reticent about expressing their emotions. If he had been more affectionate with the boy earlier, David might have gone to him instead of coming here. I am prepared to accept David's explanations up to a point, but they fail to explain the ferocity of the attack on him. And I beg you, Peabody, don't start inventing theories! I am in no mood to listen to them, and I want to have a closer look at that fragment of wall painting. Daoud has taken it to our room."

"Daoud hasn't returned to Gurneh, I hope? I want him to—"

"What sort of idiot do you take me for? He is on the deck, outside Ramses's window. I say, Peabody, Ramses did well tonight, didn't he? I trust you told him so."

"There was no need for me to tell him so. Just let me look in on Gertrude for a moment, and then I will join you."

Gertrude was asleep, or pretending to be asleep. I went to our room.

"She is asleep."

"Or pretending to be asleep."

"Ah," I said, unbuttoning my jacket. "So that possibility occurred to you, did it?"

"Certainly. At this point in time I am prepared to suspect everyone of practically everything. What was she doing on deck in a dead faint?"

"I suppose she will claim that Ramses's cry of warning to David woke her, and that the sight of blood made her swoon. I believe we ought to dismiss her. Either she is a spy, in which case she is dangerous, or she is innocent, in which case she is a confounded nuisance."

Having removed my outer garments I put on my dressing gown over my combinations; I felt it wise to be prepared for action in case I was summoned in the night. For once Emerson paid no attention to this activity, which usually interested him a great deal. He was bending over the table, studying the painted fragment.

"Have a look, Peabody."

"Oh, dear," I exclaimed. "That is a king, Emerson, not our queen Tetisheri. The nemes headdress and the uraeus serpent on his brow—"

"Quite. Only traces of the cartouche remain, but it is probably that of Tetisheri's husband. He would be depicted in her tomb, and probably her grandson Ahmose would appear as well, if she lived on into his reign and was buried by him."

"Of course!" I bent over to examine the details more closely. "It is a handsome piece of work, isn't it? I had no idea artists of that period were so skilled."

Emerson frowned and fingered the cleft in his chin. "Neither had I. It makes me wonder if . . . Oh, the devil, Peabody, I can't be bothered delivering a lecture at this hour of the night. The mere fact that I don't recognize this piece is sufficient proof that it comes from an undiscovered tomb."

"Of course, my dear. Dare we hope that the rest of the tomb is decorated in the same way?"

"Unknown. However, this is certainly part of a larger scene. You were looking for something to rouse Evelyn, were you not? I think this might do the job."

"Why, Emerson," I cried. "What do you mean?"

"We must begin collecting a staff, Peabody. We will certainly want an artist. Carter is an excellent copyist, but he cannot be spared from his other duties. We need Evelyn, and it is high time she resumed the career she abandoned when she married Walter. We will need him too—there will be inscriptions, possibly papyri." Emerson had begun striding up and down the room, eyes glittering. "I will telegraph in the morning."

"So it is for your own selfish reasons that you propose this?"

Emerson stopped pacing and looked seriously at me. "Quite aside from the fact that I consider Evelyn to have a rare talent for capturing the spirit as well as the details of Egyptian painting, this is precisely what she needs at this time—distraction, hard work, commendation. She won't accept, however, unless we can convince her she is doing us a service. You must persuade her of that."

Tears of admiration dimmed my eyes as I gazed fondly upon Emerson. He is so large and so very loud that even I occasionally lose sight of his underlying sensitivity and perception. Few men would have understood a woman's needs so accurately. (To be sure, he had been often reminded of *my* needs, but he might have been forgiven for believing me to be unique.) He had hit the nail square on the head. Hard work, appreciation, the exercise of her God-given talent, and a soupçon of danger for spice—that was precisely what Evelyn required, and what she secretly yearned for. I found myself remembering a certain large black parasol. No one had known Evelyn possessed it until she had used it to thump a burglar into submission.

"You have hit the nail square on the head, Emerson," I said. "We will both telegraph in the morning. Even if we do not locate the tomb—"

"We will locate it, Peabody."

"How?"

"It is late, my dear. Come to bed."

I was up with the dawn, inspired even beyond my usual energy by the interesting activities that awaited me. Enemies closing in on every hand, a suffering patient awaiting my attentions, Evelyn to be persuaded—and a royal tomb to be found and rescued. We would probably have to fight off half the population of Gurneh if—when!—we located it. The prospects were delightful.

Leaving Emerson sleeping I hastened to Ramses's room, where I found both lads awake and engaged in low-voiced conversation—if conversation it could be called when Ramses was doing all the talking. After I had examined the patient I decided the first order of business was to feed him. I requested Ramses to fetch a tray. This seemed to surprise David a great deal. I presume he was not accustomed to be waited upon. He ate with good appetite, and when he had finished I explained what I intended to do next.

After some rather animated discussion, Ramses suggested I leave the job to him. I demurred at first, on the grounds that Ramses had yet to demonstrate his ability to wash himself, much less other people, but David's expression warned me that he would fight like a tiger if I persisted. Nothing less than complete submersion and prolonged soaking would have the desired effect, so I left him to the tender mercies of Ramses and went off to have my own breakfast.

The others had assembled, and after I had reported on my patient's condition, Gertrude said hesitantly, "I wish to offer my apologies, Mrs. Emerson, for my cowardly behavior last night. It was such a shock, coming on that terrible scene. But I ought to have had better control over myself. I promise it will not occur a second time. The Professor has told me about the poor boy. Would you like me to sit with him today while you are pursuing your archaeological activities?"

"Not necessary," Emerson replied. "I will require your assistance today, Miss Marmaduke. Get your gear together, we will be crossing over to Luxor after breakfast."

"Suspicious," I muttered, after she had taken her departure. "Very suspicious, Emerson."

"Everything strikes you as suspicious, Peabody."

"I don't trust that woman," Nefret declared. "She was on deck before me last night. What was she doing there?"

Elbows on the table, Emerson said, "I don't know. What was she doing?"

"She didn't have time to do anything, I was almost on her heels. As soon as she saw me she screamed and fell down. But if I had not come when I did, who knows what might have happened?" Nefret's eyes flashed. "Don't leave her alone with David, Professor. Her offer to sit with him was extremely suspicious."

Emerson looked from Nefret to me and back to Nefret. "It is like hearing an echo," he muttered. "I begin to wonder whether I am strong enough to manage two of them. Ah, well. 'Man tut was man kann.' I suppose Ramses shares your doubts about Miss Marmaduke? Yes; he would. Well, don't worry about David. One of our men will be on guard, and until I am certain about Miss Marmaduke's motives I will watch her closely. Why do you suppose I am taking the confounded woman with us today?"

When I returned to Ramses's room I found David back in bed, wearing one of Ramses's galabeeyahs. He had the look of a person who has just undergone torture of the most agonizing kind and he made no objection when I examined him—with, of course, due consideration for his dignity. The bruises, cuts and scrapes required only minimal attention, but the festering toe looked even nastier now that it had been washed. The nail was missing and the infection was deep. By the time I had cleaned and bandaged it Emerson was banging on the door demanding that I hurry up.

I bade him enter. "I am almost ready, Emerson. David, I want you to take this medicine."

"Laudanum?" Hands on his hips, Emerson eyed me askance. "Are you certain that is wise, Peabody?"

"He is in considerable pain, though he will not admit it," I replied. "He needs to rest."

"No! I must not—" David stopped, perforce, since I had pinched his nose with my fingers and tipped the liquid neatly down his throat.

"Don't worry," Emerson said. "One of your uncles, or cousins, or whatever the devil they are, will be on guard. You are safe here. Is there anything more you want to tell me?"

"No, Father of Curses. I do not know—"

"We will talk again later," Emerson said. "Come along, Peabody—Ramses."

"I trust," said Ramses, as soon as I had closed the door, "that you did not drug him because you suspect he would attempt to run away, Mother. He will not."

"He gave you his word, I suppose," I said sarcastically.

"Yes. And," said Ramses, "I have promised that if he remains with us, I will teach him how to read the hieroglyphs."

There was not time to continue the conversation. Gertrude and Nefret were waiting, and Emerson bustled us all into the dinghy.

Ramses began lecturing on the temples of Luxor and talked without a break during the voyage. This gave me a chance to collect my own thoughts, which were in need of organization. How busy we were become, and how many things required to be done! Identifying the would-be assassin of David was of prime importance, not only to prevent further assaults but to learn why someone was so intent on silencing him. That information might be got from the boy himself, if he was willing to talk—and if he knew.

First, though, were the telegrams to Evelyn and Walter. Reading over Emerson's shoulder as he wrote, I was moved to murmur, "Emerson, do you really believe it is wise to say we have found an unknown royal tomb? I don't doubt that the contents of that message will be all over Luxor by nightfall and in Cairo almost as soon. Every thief in Gurneh will be on our track, and M. Maspero will be very annoyed with us for not reporting to him immediately, and furthermore—"

"Write your own message, Peabody, and leave this to me," Emerson said, frowning masterfully.

So I did. An explanation for his behavior had occurred to me. I would have thought of it sooner if I had believed Emerson to be capable of such subtle dissimulation.

The telegraph office was located near the Luxor Hotel, and Emerson suggested we have coffee in the hotel garden. This leisurely attitude was so unlike him I knew he was up to something—several somethings, as it turned out.

"Not many people here at this hour," he remarked, surveying the scattering of tourists at the other tables.

"Most have already gone out to Karnak or across to the West Bank," I said, hooking my parasol over the back of my chair. "Only the lazy visitors, who are more interested in dissipation than improvement, would rise so late."

"It is a beautiful spot," Gertrude said dreamily. "What are those purple blossoms cascading over the wall behind us, Mrs. Emerson?"

"Bougainvillea," I replied (for botany is a favorite hobby of mine). "The climate is tropical; it permits the cultivation of such exotic blooms, as well as flowers familiar to us from our English gardens."

Emerson was watching people come and go. Becoming impatient, he interrupted my lecture. "Do you mind, Peabody? It is time we told Miss Marmaduke and the children of our plans."

"Proceed, my dear," I said, wondering what the deuce "our" plans might be.

Beating around the bush is not a habit of Emerson's. "I know the precise location of the tomb," he said.

Nefret and Gertrude responded with the exclamations of admiration a gentlemen expects from females when he has done something to impress them. Ramses responded with a question.

"And how did you ascertain that information, Father, if I may ask?"

"I have my methods," said Emerson, trying to look mysterious. "As to where . . . You will discover the answer to that tomorrow morning, when I lead you to the site. Thus far, Miss Marmaduke,

I am the only person who knows the precise location. Even Mrs. Emerson has not been taken into my confidence, for the simple reason that the knowledge might endanger her. Inexperienced as you are, you cannot comprehend how far the local thieves will go in order to learn such a secret."

Gertrude leaned forward, her hands clasped as if in prayer. "But surely, the more people who have the information—"

"I prefer to be the only one at risk," said Emerson heroically. "You cannot suppose I would endanger my wife or my innocent young children by sharing such deadly information."

No one who knew anything about me could possibly believe such an idiotic speech, and Ramses's attempt to look innocent was far from convincing. Gertrude might have persisted had not an exclamation from Nefret distracted her. It was only a stifled "Oh!" but it was pronounced in tones sufficiently intense to draw my eyes to the individual whose appearance had prompted it.

He had observed us; he was advancing, hat in hand, face wreathed in smiles. "What an unexpected pleasure!" he exclaimed. "Good morning, Professor and Mrs. Emerson—Miss Forth—Master Emerson. I dare not hope you will remember me—"

"Good morning, Sir Edward," I replied, stamping heavily on Ramses's foot. The impact jolted a gruff "Sir," out of him, which was as much as I could reasonably expect. Nefret's greeting had consisted of a smile and a dimple.

Emerson looked him up and down, from his fair head to his polished boots. "Good morning. We met last year, I believe. You were with the Northampton Expedition."

"I am flattered, sir, that you should recall such a fleeting encounter."

"You, an archaeologist?" I exclaimed in surprise.

The young man laughed good-naturedly. "I don't merit that honorable designation, Mrs. Emerson, though I *am* keen. Lord Northampton is a distant relation of my mother's—or, to put it another way, I am a very distant poor relation of his. He was good enough to employ me as a photographer last season."

How bitterly I regretted having spared her doting guardian the knowledge of Nefret's scandalous behavior with this person!

It was too late now; the look of calculation on Emerson's face made his intentions clear to me. In fact, I wondered if he had come to the garden in the hope of meeting with Sir Edward. He could have arranged to be informed of all new arrivals in Luxor. (And indeed I much regretted not having done so myself. The vultures would be gathering . . .)

Sir Edward had remained standing, hat in hand. Emerson waved him to a chair. "That motorcar of yours—" he began.

"Not mine, sir; it is the property of a friend who sometimes allows me to put it through its paces. We poor relations—"

"Yes, yes," Emerson broke in. "What would be the chances of getting such a vehicle to Luxor, do you think?"

"Good Gad, Emerson!" I exclaimed. "What a ridiculous idea! Even if you could get it here, what would you do with it?"

Sir Edward glanced at me. He appeared to be trying to compose an answer that would offend neither party. "One would need special tyres for desert travel, of course. But they are sturdy vehicles; last year a Stanley Steamer made it up to the top of Mount Washington."

"Named after a member of your family, perhaps?" I inquired with a pardonable degree of sarcasm.

"So I understand," was the smooth reply. "The first American President was descended from—"

"Returning to the subject of the motorcar," Emerson said.

"Emerson," I said rather sharply. "You are forgetting your manners. Miss Marmaduke has not yet been introduced to the gentleman, I believe."

Both acknowledged the introductions with a conspicuous lack of interest. Highly suspicious—or was it? She was not the sort of lady to attract the interest of an impecunious younger son. Sir Edward, however, was the sort of gentleman to engage the interest of any female. I decided that only Gertrude's reaction had been suspicious.

"So you were at Drah Abu'l Naga with Mr. Newberry," I said, hoping to distract Emerson from the motorcar.

I succeeded, for the moment. "Were you present when the fatal accident occurred?" Emerson asked.

"Accident?" Sir Edward looked as bewildered as I felt. It was the first time I had heard of such a thing. "There was no serious accident, Professor. We were singularly fortunate in that respect."

"One of your workmen fell off the cliff to his death," said Emerson. "I would call that a fatal accident."

"Oh, that." The young man's face cleared. "To be sure. Such things occur, however. No, I believe, though the exact date escapes me, that I was not present that day. Is it true, sir, that you are planning to work there this year?"

"How did you hear of that?" Emerson asked.

"From Mr. Newberry," was the prompt, easy reply. "He was most kind to me last year, and I called on him before I left Cairo. I am looking for employment, you see, and I had hoped he would recommend me."

Emerson opened his mouth. I said hastily, "How long will you remain in Luxor, Sir Edward?"

"All winter, if I am fortunate enough to find a position. We poor relations must work for a living."

This time I was not able to forestall Emerson, for his mouth had remained open. "I am planning to work at Drah Abu'l Naga, yes. If you will dine with us tomorrow evening on our dahabeeyah, we may have something to discuss."

Sir Edward expressed effusive delight and I glared at Emerson. "We must be going, Emerson," I said. "Unless you intend to waste the entire morning. You too, Sir Edward, should be up and doing."

"But my dear Mrs. Emerson, I rose at dawn." He did not bother to conceal his amusement. "I have already made the rounds of the antika shops; his lordship is a collector, as you know, and I had hoped to find something that would interest him. However, the best of the dealers was closed—indefinitely, I was told."

"What!" Emerson jumped to his feet, overturning his chair. "Is it Ali Murad of whom you speak?"

"Why, yes."

"Damnation!" Emerson shouted. The poor flowers trembled and cast a shower of purple petals over us. "Come, Peabody. Hurry!"

"You will excuse us, Sir Edward," I said.

"I hope it was nothing I said."

"Well, yes, it was, but you could not have anticipated his response," I admitted.

Sir Edward gallantly assisted Nefret to rise from her chair. She was careful not to look at him, not even when he plucked a fallen blossom from her hair with a smile and a murmured apology. As we hurried off I saw him tuck the little flower tenderly into his waistcoat pocket. He made sure Nefret saw too.

Fortunately I knew where Emerson must be going, since he was out of sight by the time we reached our destination. We found him kicking the closed door of Ali Murad's house.

"Do continue, Emerson, if it will soothe your nerves," I remarked. "Kicking the door can serve no other purpose. We might have anticipated this."

"Hmph," said Emerson. "At least *I* ought to have anticipated it. The old rascal is shrewder than I thought."

"And guiltier, Emerson."

"Possibly, Peabody, possibly."

"But would fear of us explain his flight? We already have the fragment and the information you wanted; why should he hide from us?"

Emerson let out a profane exclamation. "By Gad, Peabody, you are right again. The only confederate he named was Abd el Hamed. There was no danger to Ali Murad in that; we were already suspicious of Abd el Hamed and might have got his name from any one of several other sources. No. If Murad has gone into hiding it is because he fears someone else. We had better have another little chat with Abd el Hamed. If Ali Murad has warned him, he too may have run for cover."

"Or been permanently silenced," I said.

"Always looking on the bright side, Peabody. Quickly, back to the dinghy."

I would not have been unduly distressed to have found Abd el Hamed weltering in his gore. However, when we got to his house he was sitting on a bench in the courtyard enjoying the sunshine and smoking a water pipe. He appeared so ostentatiously at ease that I suspected he had been warned of our approach—and had, in fact, expected we would come.

Emerson cut short his unctuous greetings. "Still here, are you? Ali Murad is wiser than you; he has gone into hiding."

Hamed gaped in exaggerated surprise. "Hiding from what, O Father of Curses? No doubt Ali Murad enjoys a well-deserved holiday. Alas, I cannot afford such a luxury."

"In that case my hasty journey to warn you was wasted effort," Emerson said. "But perhaps you are unaware that the boy still lives."

The hit was a shrewd one. Hamed's hideous countenance was well schooled in deception, but the stem of the pipe slipped from his hand.

"Your servant was careless," Emerson went on. "Don't bother sending another. David has told me all he knows, and I would take it personally if he were attacked while under my protection."

Hamed had recovered himself. "I know nothing of this. I sent no one after the boy. He ran away from me. He is a liar, an ingrate, a thief—"

"Enough," I said. "Emerson, shall we not search the house?"

"Why bother?" Emerson smiled at Hamed, who was flapping around like a distracted hen. "We have a great deal to do before we begin work on the tomb tomorrow morning." Reaching into his pocket, he flipped a coin at the old man. "For your holiday, Hamed."

Followed by the usual curious crowd, including a goat and several chickens, we descended the hill and made our way to the house where our men were staying. Selim was the first to reach us; his first question was an eager "Is it true, Father of Curses, that you have found the tomb? Where is it? When shall we begin?"

Emerson frowned, but I could tell he was extremely pleased with himself. He shot me a meaningful glance before saying loudly, "That is a secret, Selim, known only to me. Come in the house, all of you. A wise man does not shout his business to the wind."

The conference did not take long, since Emerson (I had begun to suspect) had nothing particular to say. He pursed his lips and looked mysterious and threw out vague hints. The men were extremely impressed, however. After Emerson had told them to be ready in a day or two, we took our departure. Lingering outside the door in order to tie my bootlace, I heard one of them say in awed tones, "Only the Father of Curses could learn such a secret."

"No, it is the magic of the Sitt Hakim," Selim insisted.

"Or the magic of her son. It is known that he talks with afreets and demons . . ."

I did not repeat this exchange to Emerson. "What now?" I inquired, after I had caught him up.

"Luncheon," said Emerson. "Let me help you onto your donkey, Miss Marmaduke."

Emboldened by his affability, Miss Marmaduke said, "I am fascinated but bewildered by your activities this morning, Professor. Won't you explain to me why you went in such haste to that house in Luxor and what you said to that hideous old man?"

Emerson proceeded to explain. I have never heard such an unconvincing mélange of lies and half-truths, but then I knew Emerson better than she did. After rambling on at unnecessary length about tomb robbers and the royal cache at Deir el Bahri and other unrelated matters, he finished glibly, "I suspected it was Hamed who sent the killer after David. The boy knew too much—and now he has told me what he knew."

"So you will enter the tomb tomorrow morning? How thrilling! I can hardly wait." She raised shining eyes to Emerson.

Nefret, riding next to me, said something under her breath. I decided to take no notice.

It seemed to me that Emerson had overlooked one potential danger, but when I went to look at my patient I found that concern was, unhappily, unnecessary. When we all met at the luncheon table, I reported, truthfully, that David was too ill to be questioned.

"I feared it might happen. Infection is in the air here, and that foot of his has been festering for weeks. He is feverish and semiconscious. I intend to keep him under sedation, rousing him only to take liquids."

After lunch I went to sit with the boy, for I was genuinely

concerned about his condition. It was not long before Emerson joined me.

"Well done, Peabody. Marmaduke won't bother him if she thinks he . . . Oh, curse it! You were speaking the truth. He *is* ill."

Wringing out a cloth, I wiped the lad's face and bony chest. "I believe he will pull through, Emerson. I have dealt successfully with more desperate cases."

"I know it well, Peabody." Emerson placed a hand on my shoulder. "Though I have always been of the opinion that your success is due not so much to your medical skill as your dogged determination. No one would have the audacity to die when you are doctoring them."

I was about to respond with an equally tender speech when Ramses slipped into the room. "Now we can talk," he whispered. "Nefret is having a literature lesson with Miss Marmaduke."

"How clever of Nefret to think of it," I said.

"It was my suggestion," said Ramses. "Couched in such a manner that neither could refuse. Father—"

"Oh, dear," I exclaimed. "Now she will be planning how to get back at you. Ramses, I do wish you would try to get on better with Nefret. Sister and brother—"

"She is not," said Ramses, "my sister." Without giving me time to reply, he turned to Emerson. "Father, you have not yet deigned to take me into your confidence, but I believe I have anticipated your intentions. You have not in fact located the tomb. You hope to do so tonight, by following the thieves who do know its location."

"I had intended to tell you," Emerson said resignedly. "Since I took it for granted you would find out anyhow. The plan is this—"

A low moan from my patient drew our attention to him. He was stirring feebly, his eyes half open, but when I spoke to him there was no response, and the water I held to his lips dribbled down his chin.

"He must take water," I said. "Dehydration is the greatest danger. Emerson, do you hold—"

"Let me try, Mother." Ramses took the cup from me.

He spoke softly into David's ear. The response was astonishing. The dim eyes took on a spark of intelligence, and the swollen lips parted obediently. Supported by Emerson's strong arm, he drank.

"A little more laudanum now," I said, measuring the dose into the rest of the water. He took that too.

"Well!" I exclaimed, as Emerson lowered him onto the pillow. "How did you manage that, Ramses? And please don't tell me you mesmerized or threatened him."

"I saved his life," Ramses said. "We are blood brothers. Or will be, as soon as he can spare enough of that fluid to go through the proper ceremony. I did not feel it advisable at the present time."

"Quite right, too," Emerson remarked, watching me replace the bottle of laudanum on the table. "Er—Peabody—"

"Take the bottle, by all means, Emerson."

"I would rather you did it, Peabody. Just don't overdo it, eh? We want to ensure Miss Marmaduke will sleep well tonight, not be in a stupor for several days. And, Ramses . . ."

"Yes, Father?"

"Dismiss the idea at once. I strictly forbid it."

"But Father, if Nefret is awake when we leave, she will insist on accompanying us tonight! You surely do not mean to allow a female . . ." He stopped with a gulp and an apprehensive look at me. "A young female, a girl, in fact—"

"That decision is your mother's," said Emerson. "But I believe I know what she will say."

"Quite, Emerson. Young she may be, and female, but despite those frightful handicaps she has demonstrated her ability to take care of herself—and others." It was a low blow; Ramses did not like to be reminded of the time Nefret had rescued him from danger, but I felt he needed to be put in his place. Ignoring his reproachful look, I went on, "She is one of us."

"All for one and one for all," Emerson agreed cheerfully. "You may as well give it up, Ramses, I have been trying for years to keep your mother out of these affairs and I have never once succeeded. Nefret is of the same breed, I believe. So, Peabody, you will make sure Miss Marmaduke sleeps soundly tonight?"

"If you believe it to be necessary. She customarily retires early."

"I want to be certain she goes early to her bed and stays in it." Emerson fingered the cleft in his chin. "She may be as silly and harmless as she appears, but the fact remains that it was she who approached us instead of the other way round. Not that we had reason to suspect anything at the time."

"No; but the situation has changed and I agreed we should take no chances. When do you want to leave?"

"As soon after nightfall as is possible. They will do the same; they have a long night's work ahead of them."

I finished sponging David off and covered him with a light sheet. "You really think that the thieves will return to the tomb tonight?"

"If they do not, we have lost nothing," Emerson replied. "But there is a good chance they will believe my claim that I know the location and they will want to remove as much as they can before we get to work. We have been bustling busily back and forth, Peabody, threatening people and stirring things up; I might have learned the truth from any one of a number of sources."

"It was a most ingenious idea, Father," Ramses said in his most patronizing manner. "Mother, if you have other things to do I will sit with David for a while."

I thanked him. But I took the bottle of laudanum with me.

Since time was of the essence I did not wait to put the laudanum in Miss Marmaduke's coffee, as I had originally intended. I selected a rich burgundy to accompany the meal; the sticky black liquid dissolved quite well and the wine was dark enough to hide the color. Miss Marmaduke was not enough of a connoisseur to know that one should never serve Burgundy with chicken, but she certainly enjoyed it. I had to support her when she rose from the table, with incoherent apologies for her extraordinary fatigue.

Our preparations had been made. Daoud and Selim were to accompany us, while Abdullah remained at the dahabeeyah on guard. He did not like being left behind, but if we ran into trouble we wanted younger, more agile men to assist us. We gathered on deck waiting for Daoud to return from his scouting expedition. Our departure must be unobserved.

"Now is it clear?" Emerson said softly. "They will come by one of two paths—over the mountain path from the direction of Deir el Bahri, or along the base of the hill from the north. Ramses, you and Nefret and Daoud will cover the northern route. Remember, you are not to interfere in any way. Keep out of sight and well behind them. Once they have entered the tomb, mark the location and come to join us. We will be—"

"I am as familiar with the terrain as you, Father," said Ramses. "And you have already explained the plan three times. There is Daoud. He is beckoning us to proceed."

In single file we crept down the gangplank and sought concealment in the shadows of a group of palm trees. Here we assumed our disguises—galabeeyahs like those worn by the villagers, rags wound round our heads and scarves covering the lower parts of our faces. I must say Nefret made an unconvincing Arab, even with her bright hair hidden.

Though the hour was still early by European standards, the villagers of the West Bank kept country hours, rising with the sun and retiring when it set. Most of them. The ones we hoped to encounter worked only at night.

We met only curious goats and snapping dogs as we crossed the green fields of the cultivation, avoiding the clusters of rude huts. The moon was only half full, but it gave enough light to enable us to see the path. Starlight illumined the pale colonnades of the temple of Deir el Bahri, and from the Egypt Exploration Fund expedition house, now occupied by our friend Howard, shone a glow of lamplight. We gave it a wide berth; if Howard had known what we were up to he would certainly have disapproved, though primarily on the grounds of danger to us.

There was danger if Emerson's plan succeeded. The Gurnawis had attacked archaeologists before, and men like Riccetti were even less scrupulous of human life. After we had crossed the stretch of open desert and begun our ascent of the cliff, I ventured to speak.

"You think they will come by this path."

"Why else do you suppose I sent Ramses and Nefret in the other direction? That route is too roundabout for the men we are after; they will come from Gurneh, and the tomb must be high in the hills; the lower slopes have been picked over by archaeologists—if you can call Mariette an archaeologist—"

"Emerson."

"Hmph, yes. Give me your hand, Peabody; this stretch is a bit steep." He hauled me up onto a ledge, and then went on. "As you knew perfectly well, Peabody, I have been talking stuff and nonsense. I do believe the thieves will return to the tomb tonight, but this is a largish stretch of territory, and without more specific information than the abstruse scholarly clues I discussed with you some days ago we could wander these hills all night without finding men who will obviously be attempting to avoid scrutiny. Fortunately I have more specific information. You remember my asking Sir Edward about the death of a workman during last year's Northampton excavations? In fact I had already ascertained the truth of the matter from Newberry. Like Sir Edward—typical English snob that he is!—Newberry did not consider the fatal fall of a fellah important, but when I questioned him about it he was able to tell me approximately where the so-called accident occurred. He still doesn't know why I was interested," Emerson added, with an evil chuckle.

"But I do."

"Of course you do, Peabody."

"So that is why you were so anxious to see Mr. Newberry! Why the—why didn't you say so, and why didn't you mention the subject during our dinner party?"

"Because," said Emerson, giving me the sort of smile that drives wives to violence, "I had already called upon him. After considering the matter I decided it would be best to request a private interview. I had heard of the workman's death but paid it no attention at the time; not until after I realized that a number of people were after the tomb did it occur to me that the incident might be significant."

"The man had got too close to the tomb," I said. "Or actually came upon the thieves when they were at work. Well done, Emerson. You know the location, then?"

"Roughly. We had better stop talking now. Are you with us, Selim?"

When we reached the summit we paused to catch our breaths. Behind and below was the narrow strip of green bordering the Nile. Ahead, for hundreds of miles, lay a land as barren as a dead world. Clefts and wadis, canyons and deep valleys broke the surface of the plateau.

Paths, some of them ancient, crisscrossed its slopes. One of the oldest goes from the Valley of the Kings to Deir el Bahri and continues southward along the ridge toward the Ramesseum and Medinet Habu. We went north, following a less defined route that wound up and down the hillside. Despite his size, Emerson is as surefooted as a goat on such terrain and he seemed to be familiar with every inch of it, for always he chose the easiest way.

When he stopped, we were just below the top of the hill, with a steep slope below and a wilderness of broken ridges, canyons and clefts behind and ahead. We sat down in the shadow of a heap of stones and I passed round my canteen. Selim's eyes glittered. I knew his quick breathing was not due to exertion. It had been my suggestion that he accompany us and leave the older, more placid Daoud to watch over the children. Ramses could twist poor Selim around his little finger—and so could I. I smiled at him and raised a finger to my lips. He nodded vigorously.

Before long Emerson began to fidget. I had known he would. Waiting is not something he does well. I moved closer to him and kept him quiet for a while, but it was fortunate we had not much longer to wait. The moon had set and the hillside was in shadow. One of the approaching men must have stumbled or stubbed his toe. His involuntary cry of pain was loud enough to carry some distance.

Emerson started to rise. "Damna——!"

I clapped both hands over his mouth. After a moment he subsided and I felt it was safe to remove my grip.

"Sssh! Listen," I breathed.

The murmur of voices and the sounds of movement went on for some time, and eventually my straining eyes made out, not isolated forms, but a shifting section of darkness. How many of them were there? More than one or two, certainly. They seemed to be arguing. Gradually their voices rose, and one harsh whisper pierced the silence of the night.

"I tell you, he lied! What will the Master do to us if he learns—"

Another outburst of hissing argument drowned his voice. It died into silence; a temporary agreement must have been reached. The succeeding sounds were those of surreptitious movement. Pebbles rolled and rattled; something grated on rock.

Emerson could bear it no longer; he rose to one knee. I took firm hold of his turban and pressed my mouth against his ear.

"Emerson, wait until they have all entered the tomb. Then we can creep away—"

"And allow them to rob MY tomb?" His furious whisper echoed like the distant voice of an outraged deity. He twisted his head, leaving his turban in my hands, and surged to his feet. Pulling the robe over his head, he tossed it at me. "You and Selim go and fetch Carter."

"Emerson! At least take my—" But by the time I had freed myself from the tangled folds of his robe he was out of reach. Pistol in hand, I followed as fast as I dared. Selim, gasping with excitement, was hot on my heels.

I found Emerson; he was standing on a ledge some ten feet below the path. It was so small the toes of his boots protruded over an empty space as dark and narrow as the gullet of a crocodile.

"Ah, there you are, Peabody," he remarked. "Hang on a minute, I will be right back."

And without further ado he knelt, grasped the rock ledge with both hands, and swung himself down into the cleft.

Silence and caution were no longer necessary. Emerson would either fall into the tomb or past it, on his way to the bottom of the ravine, unequivocally informing those within of his presence.

Though every muscle and every nerve ached with the need for action, I forced myself to be calm. It was an exercise to which I had become accustomed after living with Emerson for so many years. Stripping off my own robe I tossed it aside. Then I lay down on the ground and lit a candle.

The slope was not precipitous; under ordinary circumstances I would not have hesitated to tackle it, using my trusty parasol as a stick. Under present circumstances, when a slip might precipitate me into a bottomless chasm, I decided not to take the chance. Regretfully laying parasol and candle aside, I instructed Selim to lie flat on the edge of the drop and give me his hand. Abdullah would have argued with me (though not for long). Selim never argued with me, but he would have if he had dared. Our faces were close together as I began the descent, clinging to his hand; his eyes were so wide his eyeballs gleamed like pigeon's eggs.

My feet had not quite touched the ledge when I had to let go of Selim's hand, for his head and shoulders as well as his arm were over the edge. There was a nasty moment when one boot slipped; the scrape of metal on stone was echoed by a muted cry from Selim.

"Do be quiet, Selim," I hissed. "I am on the ledge, it is all right."

"Oh, Allah! Sitt Hakim—"

"Sssh!"

It was not so much that I feared discovery—though if Emerson was in the clutches of a gang of desperate tomb robbers, surprise might be my best weapon when I burst in upon them—but the need to listen. I could see nothing below but blackness. I could hear sounds, though. The pit was not bottomless, but it must be very deep; the noises were faint and impossible to classify. The moans of a fatally injured man? The fall of a corpse—Emerson's corpse? My hands were so unsteady I had to strike three matches before I could light another candle.

A rope had been tied round a protruding rock spur; it vanished into the darkness, as Emerson had done. Kneeling, I felt of it. The strands were limp; no weight pulled them taut. Living or dead, fallen or triumphantly arrived at his goal, Emerson was not holding on to the rope. Grasping it, I lowered myself into the darkness.

I covered the first few feet more quickly than I had intended, but finally I got my knees wrapped round the cursed flimsy thing and was able to proceed more deliberately. It was a long descent—over ninety feet, as we discovered later. The sounds I had heard were no longer audible. Oh, heaven, I thought; will I be too late?

The darkness was intense. I might have missed the tomb entrance if the rope had not ended just below it. This came as a considerable surprise, and for an unpleasant moment or two I hung suspended only by my hands. Then the toe of my boot found a crack and my eyes made out a faint glow of light. Faint in fact, but bright as a beacon to eyes accustomed to utter blackness.

The tomb entrance had been cut in the side of the gully. It was approximately six feet square, but it was filled with rubble except for a narrow tunnel dug by the thieves. The light came from the far end of the tunnel. With the aid of the holes in the rock face—which, I began to believe, were not natural but man-made—I got into the tunnel. Crawling as fast as possible, I was only vaguely aware of the sharp stone scraps that scored my hands and knees.

I emerged somewhat suddenly into a small, dimly lit chamber. Before I could observe details I was grasped, pulled to my feet and caught in a tight hold that pinned my arms to my sides.

Though archaeological fever burned hot in my brain, at that moment I had eyes for no other object than Emerson. He lived! He was upright and unharmed! He was also extremely angry, and with reason. A robed and turbaned figure whose face was concealed by a scarf held a pistol pressed to his head.

"Confound it, Peabody," he began. "I told you—"

The man drew back his arm and struck. It was only a glancing blow, but I cried out in alarm. "Control yourself, Emerson! Don't risk another blow to the head."

Emerson was too furious to heed this excellent advice. "Take your hands off her, you—you—"

He stopped as the person who held me promptly obeyed—not Emerson's command, but a nod from the fellow who held the gun. I was no threat to them; my own pistol was in my pocket, nor would I have dared to use it when the other weapon was pressed against Emerson's temple.

The man who had held me was dressed like the first, and there was a third one too, equally anonymous in robe and turban and scarf. Where were the others? Had I been mistaken about their numbers?

Reassured as to Emerson's safety (for the moment at least), I had leisure to look about me. It was hard to make out details, for the only light came from a lantern of European design held by the third man, but I saw enough to raise my professional temperature. Stone chips and fragments of other materials covered part of the floor; in some places the debris had been removed or pushed aside. Toward the far end of the chamber it was piled high, halfway up the doorway on that wall. Framed by a heavy lintel and inscribed jambs, the opening had been blocked with neatly cut stones. A dark square broke the surface where one of the stones had been removed. This evidence of the robbers' penetration into the farther chambers—perhaps the burial chamber itself—was a trifle discouraging, but what I saw on the wall to the left of the door made me catch my breath. The tomb was decorated!

Piled-up chips and deep shadows concealed most of the painted surfaces. The feeble glow of the lantern illumined, and that dimly, only one portion of a single scene—the head and upper body of a woman, and the hands she had raised to shoulder height. Part of a hieroglyphic inscription named her; I could make out the curved shape of a cartouche, but not the individual signs. I knew her, though, as surely as if I had encountered an old friend. The wing of the same vulture crown depicted on her statue framed a familiar profile.

I started impulsively forward. Emerson's growl and the raised hand of one of the men reminded me that archaeological investigation might not be entirely appropriate at that time. After an exchange of glances and nods, the same individual whose gesture had stopped me spoke in a husky, obviously disguised whisper.

"You will not be harmed if you do not resist. Put your hands behind you."

He addressed Emerson, who glared at him.

"I believe, Emerson, that we ought to do as he asks," I said. "The alternative would be much worse and I do not see how even you can prevent them from doing whatever they choose."

The logic of this was irresistible, but I cannot remember when I have seen Emerson so aggravated. He kept up a rumbling undercurrent of curses while they tied our hands and feet. Emerson stubbornly insisted on remaining upright, but one of the men lowered me, gently enough, into a sitting position. Having completed the job they departed, crawling one by one into the tunnel. They left the lamp. I was grateful for that.

"I hope Selim had sense enough to run for help," I said anxiously.

Emerson's face turned purple as he strained at his bonds. Between grunts of effort he remarked, "I don't suppose . . . he could hear us . . . if we called out."

"Probably not. But he will find us eventually, he saw me descend. Do stop struggling, Emerson, you will only tire yourself."

"I want to get out of this damned place," Emerson said sulkily. "Didn't you bring your knife, Peabody?"

"Yes, my dear, I did, and I am endeavoring at this very moment to reach it. Calm yourself."

After a moment Emerson said, in quite a different voice, "They can't have removed the mummy or mummy case, Peabody. That doorway must lead to the burial chamber, but the opening is only eighteen inches square."

"I noticed that. And the paintings—oh, Emerson, it *is* Tetisheri's tomb! I would recognize her anywhere. How exciting this is! Ah—I have the knife. I will just hop over to you and . . . Goodness gracious, it is difficult to keep one's footing in all this disgusting debris. I believe it was a bone I just stepped on."

Emerson's head snapped round toward the entrance tunnel. Turning, he thrust his bound hands hard against mine, and after some fumbling got the blade of the knife between his wrists. "Hurry and get these cursed ropes off, Peabody. They are coming back."

CHAPTER SIX

Another Shirt Ruined!

The newcomer's approach was slow and deliberate. By the time his head appeared at the opening of the tunnel, Emerson was waiting.

My husband presented a horrifying picture, his face distorted in a snarl, his raised fists streaming blood—for, clumsy with haste, he had in the process of freeing himself inflicted several nasty cuts on his wrists—and I was not at all surprised when Selim yelped and retreated, like a turtle pulling back into its shell. Emerson reached in and dragged him out.

"What the devil do you mean, creeping up on us like that?" he shouted.

"Emerson, please lower your voice," I begged. "The noise is positively deafening in this confined space. I do wish you would not be so precipitate; just look at you, you are bleeding all over the antiquities. I could have told you it was Selim approaching."

"Then why didn't you?" Emerson picked up the knife and freed my hands and feet.

"You did not give me the opportunity, that is why. Fortunately I brought two handkerchiefs. Let me tie up your wrists, you cannot climb a rope when your hands are slippery with blood."

"Oh, bah," said Emerson. But he said no more because Selim was spouting questions and excuses. He had not known how to proceed. Had he delayed too long? Had he come too soon? What should he do now?

"Get out of here, I should think," I replied to the final question. "I hope you will not take this as criticism, Selim, for you acted quite properly, but if someone cuts that rope we will be in deep difficulty."

"Deep indeed," said Emerson. "Selim—I apologize for shouting at you, my boy, I was not myself—how did you elude the gentlemen who climbed that same rope a few minutes ago?"

"No one climbed it, Father of Curses. I saw no one. I heard terrible noises, the falling of rock, the voices of demons from the depths, but finally they died away. Sitt Hakim, I did not hesitate out of fear, I waited only because—"

"Impossible," I exclaimed.

"Hmmm," said Emerson, fingering his chin. "I suggest we postpone further discussion until after we have acted upon your sensible suggestion, Peabody. I will go first, then you, my dear. Put out the lantern before you follow her, Selim; some of these scraps are as dry as tinder."

Emerson was waiting for me on the lip of the opening, a lighted candle in his hand. "This explains one mystery," he said, indicating a second rope that hung down from the edge. "Our friends departed by means of the back door. Shall we follow their example?"

I took the candle from him and leaned out. "But it is a dead end, Emerson; I can see the bottom of the cleft, only a few feet below."

"Nonsense. The rope would not be here if it led nowhere. Curse it, Peabody, don't stand so close to the edge. I will go down and have a look."

Grasping the rope, he lowered himself. "Ah," he said, with satisfaction. "I thought as much. There is an opening. A bit narrow, but I believe I can . . . Stop where you are, Peabody, don't so much as stir until I give you permission."

Slowly he sank down out of sight; first his feet and lower limbs, then his body, and finally his head were swallowed up by shadows. Selim, still in the tunnel awaiting my word to proceed, began to wail.

"Oh, Sitt, what is happening? Oh, Father of Curses, do not leave me here!"

"Be quiet!" I said sharply, for my nerves were beginning to feel a certain strain. So thick were the shadows below, I felt as if I had seen Emerson swallowed up by black quicksand.

Then his head rose out of the depths. "All right, Peabody," he said cheerfully. "Wait until you feel three sharp tugs on the rope before you follow me; I would rather not risk a double weight. It is easy going once you squeeze through that narrow space, my dear; can you manage?"

The face that looked up at me wore an encouraging smile, but his furrowed brow was evidence of his concern.

"I got down this far, didn't I?" I replied. "Oh, Emerson, do be careful."

"And you, my love."

"Sitt Hakim," said a quavering voice from the tunnel. "Something is holding my foot. It is an afreet, I think."

Kneeling, my eyes fixed on the taut, quivering rope, I said over my shoulder, "Give me your hand, Selim. My power will pass through you down to your foot and the afreet will let you go."

Sure enough, he was able to free himself from the afreet (actually a bit of fallen stone), and I helped him out onto the ledge, suggesting that he remain motionless since the space was confined. Scarcely had he emerged than the rope went limp.

"Emerson!" I shrieked, unable to control my anxiety.

Three tugs followed, and then Emerson's voice, weirdly distorted. "Come ahead, Peabody."

Once I had got through the opening—quite ample in size for me, though it must have been a tight squeeze for my stalwart spouse—I was surprised to find a sloping surface instead of a perpendicular drop. Emerson had lit a candle and placed it on a ledge. His hands were waiting to grasp me by the waist and set me on my feet.

While we waited for Selim to join us I lit my own candle and looked around. The space was only a few feet in extent, and it looked as if it might collapse in on itself at any second: boulders of various sizes bulged from either side and from overhead. If I had not known there must be a way out I doubt I could have found it, for it was necessary to squeeze past one rock and around the jutting corner of another, until one final squeeze brought us out into the cool night air. We were on the slopes of Drah Abu'l Naga, only a few hundred yards from Deir el Bahri. Its colonnades glimmered pale in the starlight.

"No wonder the place has gone undiscovered so long," I gasped. "The tomb entrance cannot be seen from above or below. Who would suppose this pile of rocks concealed an opening?"

"I suspect there *was* no opening until recently," Emerson said thoughtfully. "But let us save speculation of that sort for a more leisured moment. We had better collect the children and get back to the dahabeeyah."

Leaving Selim to mark the spot, we went off arm in arm, Emerson matching his longer strides to mine.

"Cold, my dear?" he inquired, as a shiver ran through my frame.

"On such a beautiful night? Only look at the stars! It is excitement that moves me. What a discovery! What courage and what brilliance you displayed in locating it! I wonder you are not skipping with happiness."

"A pretty sight that would be. Never mind the flattery, Peabody; luck had as much to do with our success as my talents. And this evening's adventure has had several odd aspects. When I arrived in the tomb I fell into the middle of a small war."

"Please elaborate, Emerson."

"The men we saw descend into the tomb were members of an illustrious family of Gurnawi thieves. I recognized several of them. But they were not the men *you* saw, for by the time you arrived on the scene, the Gurnawis had been taken prisoner by another group of individuals who must have arrived sometime earlier via the lower entrance. When I emerged into the antechamber, one of the second group was waiting for me, pistol in hand, and I saw no reason to object when they bundled the Gurnawis out through the tunnel. Evidently the latter were persuaded to descend the lower rope while you were descending the upper."

"That seems a logical deduction. But how extraordinary, Emerson! You did not identify any of the second—first?—you know who I mean, the men who were waiting for me."

"How could I? They were wrapped to the eyebrows, and careful to say as little as possible. Which makes one wonder—"

"—if we might have recognized an acquaintance had they been less cautious. Yes, Emerson! Sir Edward—"

"What the devil are you talking about? I met him last year; he is a typical, annoying young aristocrat, but so far as I know, perfectly respectable. Nor," Emerson added with a chuckle, "was Miss Marmaduke one of them. (You were about to suggest her, were you not?) What I intended to say before you interrupted me was that I wonder if some or all of them were not Egyptians."

"That would explain their disguises and their reticence," I said. "At least we can be certain that none of them was Signor Riccetti."

"Impossible to disguise that bulk," Emerson agreed. "But he is in this up to his fat neck, I have no doubt of it."

"He may be as dishonest as he is obese, Emerson, but does not the encounter of this evening substantiate the statement he made—that there are those who would aid us if they could? No, my dear, please don't bellow"—for I knew the signs that preceded that exercise—"just listen. The second group of individuals meant us no harm. They did not even search me for weapons. In fact, if they had not been there when you entered the tomb, you might have been killed or seriously injured by the Gurnawis. They were, if I may be permitted to call them that, our Preservers."

"I cannot prevent you from calling them anything you like," Emerson replied furiously. "But the idea is even more fantastical than your usual theories. Abandon the subject, Amelia, if you please."

I did so, since I did not wish discord to cloud the pleasure of our starlit stroll. After a time Emerson began to whistle. It was the agreed-upon signal—the stirring strains of "Rule Britannia"—and in response a trio of ghostly forms materialized from the darkness.

Ramses was extremely annoyed at having missed "the fun," as he called it. Nefret was more interested in the strange men. In the intervals between Ramses's complaints she peppered us with questions until we reached the boat and Emerson ended the discussion with a reminder that there were a number of things that must be done without delay.

"Quite right," I said. "I must see how David is getting on, and make sure Gertrude is safely tucked in her bed; Howard Carter must be notified, and M. Maspero. And I am very worried about Selim, alone out there in the darkness."

"He won't be alone for long," said Emerson.

When I joined him in our room I was not surprised to learn that he meant to return to Selim at once. Attempting to dissuade him would have been a waste of breath. "At least take Abdullah and Daoud," I begged.

"My dear, I will be knee-deep in assiduous assistants by morning," Emerson said, stripping off his filthy, bloodstained shirt. Tossing it onto the floor, he grinned at me. "'Another shirt ruined,'" he quoted.

I could not joke. The premonition of danger was so strong it clung to my lips like the taste of bitter herbs. I caught hold of him. "Let me go with you."

Gently he loosened my clinging hands. "Now, Peabody, don't carry on. Abdullah has gone to collect the men; I will meet them at Deir el Bahri, and knock Carter up while I'm about it. I can hardly wait to see his face."

"You are taking Ramses. Why can't I—"

"Because you are needed here. Yours may be the post of greatest peril, Peabody. We still don't know why the boy was attacked. If it was to prevent him from telling us about the tomb, then he is out of danger, but I doubt that was the motive. It is most unlikely that he could have learned such a closely kept secret. He must be guarded, and you must watch Miss Marmaduke as well."

"Yes, I know. But—"

"I will take Anubis. How's that?"

"A great consolation," I said sourly. Upon hearing his name the cat, who was lying on the bed, sat up. Emerson snapped his fingers. Anubis jumped down and followed him to the door. In fact the knowledge that the cat would be with him did console me a little. Anubis's brindled coat and heavy muscular body, not to mention his surly disposition, were those of a feral animal, and he was utterly devoted to Emerson.

"Get some sleep, Peabody."

"Oh, certainly. The easiest thing in the world."

After he had gone I changed my own garments, which were in little better case than Emerson's. Descending cliffs on a rope and crawling through bat guano has a deleterious effect on one's wardrobe. Then I returned to David. He had been asleep when I first looked in on him, and I had left Nefret to watch him. He was awake now, his great black eyes fixed on Nefret, who was sitting cross-legged on the floor and staring owlishly back at him.

"He woke," she said.

"So I see." I sat down on the bed and felt the boy's forehead. It was cool. The fever had broken, but he was still very weak.

"Where he gone?" David asked.

I knew to whom he referred but before I could answer, Nefret said, "'Where *has* he gone.'"

David bobbed his head. "Where hasss he gone?"

"He is trying to learn proper English," Nefret explained, as I turned a critical eye upon her. "He asked me to correct him."

"I see. Well, David, Ramses has gone with his father. We have found the tomb. You know the one I mean."

David shook his head. "Many tombs. I do not know them."

"The tomb of which I speak is in El-Dira. It has been known

to certain men of Gurneh for several years. The Father of Curses and I found it tonight. He and Ramses have gone back to guard it, with our men. Now, David, it is late and you need to rest. Only answer one question. If you didn't know about the tomb, why did Hamed try to murder you?"

"I not . . ." He hesitated, glancing at Nefret, and went on slowly, "I do not know. I leave him. He try to make me stay. I said he was a . . ."

Again he hesitated, this time, I thought, because he had remembered Emerson's instruction on using improper language in the presence of females. The boy had a quick retentive mind and commendable ambition. We might make something of him—if we could keep him alive.

Leaving Yusuf, another of Abdullah's innumerable offspring, on guard, I sent Nefret off to get a few hours' sleep, though I doubted she would. As for me, how could I close my eyes when Emerson might be in danger?

I did because I knew I must, but I was awake with the dawn and ready for duty. Emerson had entrusted me with a number of vital errands and I performed them with my customary efficiency, though every particle of my being ached with the desire to abandon duties whose interest paled by comparison to the thrilling activities he was enjoying. It was mid-morning before I was able to mount my donkey and urge it (with words alone, since I have never struck an animal) toward the hills north of Deir el Bahri. Nefret and Gertrude accompanied me; I felt it advisable to keep the latter individual under my observant eyes from now on.

It was not difficult to locate the spot I sought. A good-sized crowd had gathered. I was amused to see among the onlookers members of several of the more notorious tomb-robbing families of Gurneh, trying without success to look pleased. Hussein Abd er Rasul greeted me with effusive congratulations and offered the assistance of himself and his brothers. I declined the offer.

Conspicuous by their European dress were Emerson and Howard Carter. His eyes shining with excitement, Howard congratulated me and then began to scold me. "Honestly, Mrs. E., you must not do this sort of thing! It is horribly dangerous. Why didn't you come to me?"

"You know Emerson," I replied.

"Yes, and I know you," Howard said forcibly.

"Not now, Howard." I turned to my husband, who was shouting orders at Abdullah. "Good morning, Emerson."

"Oh," said Emerson. "So there you are, Peabody. What kept you?" Without waiting for an answer, he cupped his hands round his mouth and called, "Ramses, come down from there this instant! I told you you would have to wait until Nefret and your mama arrived before you enter the tomb."

"So you have not been back inside?" I inquired. "Thank you, Emerson; it was good of you to wait for me."

Sleeves rolled to the elbow, bared black head shining in the sunlight, Emerson looked as fresh as if he had slept for eight solid hours, but affectionate concern prompted my next suggestion. "I brought tea and food, my dear; have something to eat and tell me of your plans."

Emerson put a casual arm around me and drew me out of the path of a boulder that went rumbling down the hillside. The spectators scattered and then reassembled, like a group of ants around spilled sugar.

"As you can see, Peabody, I am clearing the lower entrance. We can't continue climbing up and down that bloo—er—blooming rope. If the passage is widened we can use ladders or build stairs."

He accepted a cup of tea, and Ramses, who had joined us, remarked, "It may be possible to open the lower part of the passage entirely, Father. I believe it was an avalanche or earthquake that closed it in ancient times. Good morning, Mother. Good morning, Nefret. Good morning, Miss Marmaduke."

Emerson cut the civilities short. "At any rate, we won't be able to begin work in the tomb itself for several more days. Oh—here is your parasol, Peabody. You left it on top last night."

"Thank you, my dear, I am glad to have it back. You sent some of the men up to guard the upper entrance?"

"No need," Emerson replied, smacking a boiled egg against a

convenient rock. "Our fellows will be here below. If anyone tries to slide down that rope they will hear him, and . . . Well, I would not care to be in his position. Now then, Peabody, tell me the news. How is David? Did you telegraph Maspero and send messages to the others?"

It was like him to ask first after the sick boy. With an affectionate smile I reassured him as to David's condition, and went on, "The most amazing thing, Emerson. When I went to the telegraph office, I found a message from Walter. He must have sent it moments after our telegrams arrived."

"They are coming, then?"

"They intend to leave today. What on earth did you tell them? Walter's mention of 'deep concern' could hardly have referred to the tomb."

"I told them Ramses was ill," Emerson said calmly. "And that you were in a state of intense depression."

"Emerson, how could you?"

"I do not scruple to employ drastic measures when they are required, Peabody. In this case they were required." He popped another egg into his mouth and, speech being beyond him at that moment, gestured inquiringly.

"Oh, dear," I murmured. "Poor Evelyn; what a state she will be in. Well, there is nothing I can do about it now. As you requested, I left a message for Sir Edward repeating our invitation to dinner."

Emerson swallowed. "Curse it, Peabody, I told you to get him over here immediately. I want a complete photographic record of our work, from start to finish."

"Then why didn't you wait before moving those rocks? The original appearance—"

"The boulders are a natural phenomenon. I am speaking of—"

"How do you know they weren't deliberately placed there? Such information—"

"Because I examined the damned things!" Emerson shouted. "They could not have been—"

"Emerson, will you please stop—"

"Peabody, if you continue to—"

Realizing I was on the verge of behaving in an undignified

manner, I stopped speaking. Emerson stopped speaking because he had run out of breath. Ramses, who had been waiting for a lull in the conversation, said only, "Ouch!" because Nefret, rising, had stamped on his foot.

"I am so sorry, Ramses," she exclaimed. "How clumsy of me! I have got quite stiff sitting on this rock. Professor, I brought my new pocket camera. Its scope is limited, of course, but if you like, I will try a few photographs."

"Oh, have you one of those?" Howard exclaimed. "So do I. It does quite well out-of-doors, with a bright sun, but in shadow or darkness—"

"That is a problem we will have to work out," Emerson declared. "I believe reflectors will do the job. Go ahead, Nefret, and see what you can get."

Nursing his foot, Ramses remarked, "Sir, you said we could enter the tomb after Mother came."

"Mother and Nefret," said that young person, with a sweet smile at Emerson.

"It is a difficult climb," Ramses protested. "Even with a rope."

"And how do you know that?" Nefret demanded. "Have you tried it? You were told to wait."

"Never fear, Miss Nefret," said Howard, with an admiring glance at her flushed, indignant face. "We'll get you in by one means or another."

"There will be no difficulty." Emerson got to his feet and stretched. "I set Mohammed to work earlier constructing a rope ladder. I will take it with me when I ascend the rope, and anchor it firmly. The rest of you can follow—two at a time, the space is limited."

Abdullah, who had known better than to try to get a word in, cleared his throat. "I will go first, Emerson, and carry the rope ladder."

Emerson gave him a companionable grin. "Wait your turn, Abdullah. First Ramses and . . . er . . . no, ladies first. You and Nefret, Peabody, then Ramses and Carter, then . . . Excuse me, Miss Marmaduke, I did not mean to overlook you."

She had made it easy for him to do so. Seated a little distance away from the rest of us, head bowed and hands folded like a humble governess in polite company, she had not said a word. Now she looked up.

"It is kind of you to think of me, sir. I yearn to see that wonderful place, but I would rather not behold it until all is prepared."

"May as well wait till we have the steps up," Emerson said, visibly relieved. "Very well, then. Abdullah and Daoud after Ramses and Carter. Abdullah, tell the men to hold off working while we are on our way up there; the whole structure is extremely unstable and I don't want anyone mashed by a falling rock."

It had seemed to me that very little had been accomplished, but now I realized why Emerson was proceeding so slowly. Whether the entrance had been deliberately blocked (and I felt sure it had been, despite Emerson's dogmatic statement to the contrary) or closed by an accidental avalanche, the rocks were unstable; the removal of the wrong one could bring others tumbling down.

Emerson slung the rope ladder over his back, grasped the end of the rope and began to climb. Standing close to me, Nefret remarked, "Why do we need the ladder, Aunt Amelia? The slope cannot be steeper than forty-five degrees, and with the rope—"

"It is not so easy as Emerson makes it appear, my dear," I replied, watching uneasily as darkness engulfed my husband. "You are young and agile, but you have not his strength in the arms and shoulders. When he—" I broke off, shielding my face with my arm, as a shower of broken stone rained down.

"Look out below!" Emerson called—somewhat belatedly. "My apologies, my dears; this cursed stuff crumbles at a touch."

It was not crumbling rock I feared. Desperate men had awaited us the night before, and Emerson's position now was even more vulnerable. A missile falling from above could loosen his grasp; a sharp knife severing the rope would have the same effect, inducing a fall that would almost certainly be fatal. And the most dangerous moments would be the last, when he neared the entrance. I believe I did not draw a deep breath until I heard him repeat his warning, and the rope ladder came tumbling down the slope, accompanied by a rattle of stone. Needless to say, my foot was on the lowest rung as soon as it was within reach.

As soon as my head passed through the narrowest part I saw Emerson. He had lighted several candles and stuck them onto the rock face. Leaning over, he grasped my wrists and lifted me onto the ledge.

"Proceed, my dear, but watch out for bats. They were stirring uneasily."

"You have already entered the chamber?"

"Before ever I let down the ladder, Peabody. Do you suppose I would allow you and Nefret to venture here until I was certain there were no uninvited guests? You will have to feel your way, I did not want to leave an open flame unattended."

Many archaeologists would have considered Emerson's concern about fire unnecessary, and few men would have sent their wives into a pitch-black tomb chamber filled with bats and bits of mummy. I agreed with his precautions; and his unquestioning confidence in my abilities was the firm foundation on which our marriage rested. As I crawled along in the dark, with sharp edges of rock jabbing into my knees and hands, I acknowledged, as I had so often done, that I was the most fortunate of women.

My entrance into the chamber irritated several of the livelier bats and I had to speak sharply to them before they settled down again. I lit a candle. When Nefret and Emerson joined me I was still staring in disbelief at the object that had immediately engaged my attention.

I interrupted Emerson's introductory remarks.

"Look. I did not see it last night. Was it there when you entered the room just now?"

"Was what where?" Emerson demanded irritably. "I didn't carry out a detailed inspection, Peabody, I only made certain no one was . . . Oh, good Gad."

The statue was approximately two feet high and carved of black basalt. It had been placed next to the door leading to the burial chamber. Jaws parted to display its formidable teeth, swollen abdomen framed in bands of reflected light, it depicted the grotesque hippopotamus goddess, Taueret.

By the time everyone had had his or her turn in the tomb, it was mid-afternoon, and even Emerson conceded that we had better return to the dahabeeyah. However, as we jogged on side by side he kept up a grumbling monologue. "We haven't enough men, confound it. They will have to stand watch round the clock, and I dare not leave fewer than five of them on guard. Did you see the look on Mohammed Abd er Rasul's face this morning? I wouldn't put it past him and his brothers—"

"Emerson, you know you have done the best you could, so stop worrying about it."

I persuaded him to get a few hours' sleep. I hoped this would put him in a better mood, because I had arranged a little dinner party, of the sort Emerson particularly dislikes. Since it had been necessary to invite Sir Edward, I decided I might as well include several of our professional colleagues, who would be clamoring for news of the new tomb.

A bath and a change of clothing quite refreshed me, and I went to see what the others were doing. Gertrude was in the saloon transcribing the notes Emerson had made that morning. She looked tired, and would have liked to chat, but I excused myself. Her forlorn look made me feel a little guilty. Had I been wrong about her? If she was an enemy she was not a very efficient one. Thus far I could accuse her of nothing except making eyes at my husband, and there was nothing unusual in that.

I found Ramses and Nefret with David. All three of them were sitting on the floor around a tray of food—collected, clearly, by Ramses, since it consisted of a stomach-churning combination of Egyptian and English dishes. Upon seeing me Ramses got to his feet, as I had taught him. David promptly followed suit, and I exclaimed, "You should not be out of bed, much less standing. Let me see that foot."

A thick green paste covered the injured toe. When I asked,

where he had got the horrid stuff, David gestured at the window. Daoud, who had been watching with an avuncular smile, hastily withdrew his head. I called him back. Interrogation produced the information that the "salve" was an old family remedy consisting primarily of various herbs and mutton fat.

"Primarily?" I repeated suspiciously.

"It appears to have done no harm, Mother," said Ramses. "Though doubtless it was your treatment that has proved so efficacious. As you can see, the swelling has subsided and he can stand without pain." He went on without drawing breath. "Will you not join us? We are telling David about the tomb and having a council of war."

More flattered than I cared to demonstrate, I accepted the biscuit and glass of sugarcane syrup he offered me and took a chair.

"What makes you suppose a council of war is necessary?" I inquired.

"Surely that is obvious," said Ramses. "We have yet to account for the inexplicable behavior of the individual who visited your rooms in Cairo, for the equally strange visit of Signor Riccetti, and for the even more peculiar affair of the second set of tomb robbers."

"Only they weren't," Nefret said. "If they had gone there to rob the tomb, they would not have behaved so nicely to you and the Professor. *I* think they went there to protect you."

"Why the dev—— Why should they do that?" I demanded.

Ramses crossed his legs and looked at me seriously. Years of experience had given me some clues as to how to read that enigmatic countenance of his, and there was a glint in his eyes that made me extremely uneasy.

"Did not Signor Riccetti mention two different groups of individuals—those who would aid you and those who would interfere with you?"

Relief swamped me. Ramses was not supposed to know that, but the information was less uncomfortable than certain other facts he was not supposed to know. "I suppose you wormed it out of your father," I said resignedly.

"Father informed me of the matter," Ramses corrected. "In his opinion the information had become relevant in view of what occurred last night. Those events would seem to substantiate a statement that initially appeared—"

"Ramses, do you have to talk that way?" Nefret demanded. "David doesn't understand half the words you have used and your long-winded, pompous speech patterns are cursed aggravating."

I couldn't have put it better myself. Ramses blinked—an extravagant display of emotion for him—and Nefret went on, "Everything goes to prove what Aunt Amelia and I have known all along. The man who had the ring was sent by the leader of one group—probably Riccetti—and he was killed by someone from the other group."

"But how was it done?" I asked.

"You were the one who thought of it, Aunt Amelia," Nefret said. "The killer was on the balcony. He shot Mr. Shelmadine with a poison dart."

"Good Gad," I exclaimed. "Naturally I had thought of that, Nefret, but it really does seem . . . well . . . just a bit theatrical, doesn't it?"

"It is the only explanation," Nefret insisted. "The murderer may have bribed the suffragi to let him in, or, what is more likely, crossed to your balcony from another near at hand. It was dark, and our rooms were high above the street; no one would have seen him. Then, after he struck the Professor, he or a confederate sent the suffragi off on an errand and carried the body into a nearby room—the same one from which he had reached your balcony. They could get rid of the body later, in a trunk or box."

"Hmph," I said. "What do you say, Ramses?"

"It is a reasonable hypothesis—er—idea," said Ramses. "So we have been discussing who these mysterious individuals—er—people—might be. Who would have a motive—er—reason—to prevent us from excavating—er—clearing—er . . ."

He had taken Nefret's criticism to heart, but his attempts to simplify his vocabulary were not very successful. Nefret smiled patronizingly at him. "Allow me, Ramses. Obviously these people want to keep us away from the tomb so they can steal its contents.

That means they are or have been connected with the trade in illegal antiquities. Riccetti is certainly one of them. Then there is the man called Sethos . . . What is the matter, Aunt Amelia?"

"A crumb caught in my throat," I said. "How do you know of Sethos, Nefret?"

"From Ramses, of course. He warned me not to mention the fellow to you or the Professor, but I cannot understand why," Nefret said with seeming innocence. "He sounds a fascinating man. I am sorry I never encountered him."

"I am very glad you did not," I muttered. "It has been five years since we heard from Sethos, and as Ramses knows, his last message informed us he was leaving Egypt for good."

"And we have no reason to doubt that assurance," said Ramses. It was a statement, not a question, but his cool black eyes focused on my face as if awaiting a response.

"None," I said firmly. "Sethos cannot be involved in this business."

"Then," said Ramses, after a long, nerve-racking pause, "his empire is leaderless. We may be facing some of his former subordinates—er—lieutenants—curse it, the people who worked for him." He looked rather piteously at David, who nodded vigorously.

Ramses went on with more assurance. "Sethos had many assistants, of all nationalities and both sexes. Since most are known to us, it behooves us to ask . . ."

He broke off, looking self-conscious. Nefret said calmly, "Is Miss Marmaduke a spy for a group who want to rob the tomb?"

"She is not the only possibility," said Ramses, with a malevolent glance at his "sister." "Sir Edward is a highly suspicious character."

"I can think of at least two reasons why Sir Edward might wish to improve his acquaintance with us," Nefret murmured. "Neither involves a criminal motive."

David had been following the dialogue—for such it had become—with openmouthed interest, his head turning from one speaker to the other. How much *he* understood I could not say, but *I* was under no illusion as to where the discussion was heading.

Ramses said, "Hmph," as Emerson would have done when faced with incontrovertible female logic, and Nefret smiled at him.

"I agree, dear brother, that we should take nothing for granted. There are two of us and two suspects. I leave it to you to ingratiate yourself with Miss Marmaduke and worm her secrets out of her. Sir Edward will be my responsibility. I quite look forward to the challenge."

Emerson fussed and fumed when I told him of the dinner party. Not only did he refuse to wear evening dress (which I had expected), but he refused to dress at all, appearing in the saloon wearing his wrinkled work clothing and boots. He was the only one of the gentlemen (I do not include my son in that category) who had not made an effort. Howard and the other archaeologists wore their best suits and Sir Edward was in full evening kit, which set off his fair hair and well-knit form only too well.

He was unable to monopolize Nefret, however, because several of the other gentlemen (and Ramses) surrounded her. M. Legrain, who was in charge of the work at the Karnak temple, found her particularly fascinating. He was French, of course.

In such a group and on such an occasion, idle social chitchat soon gave way to professional conversation. We were besieged with questions about the tomb, but Emerson, usually decided to the point of dogmatism, was uncharacteristically cagey.

"At this stage I prefer not to commit myself. You know my views on excavation. The corridor is filled with debris; it will take some time to clear it and examine the material."

"But the burial chamber," Howard exclaimed. "Did the thieves enter it? Is the mummy intact? Surely you will investigate that before—"

"Surely not," said Emerson, giving him a frosty stare. "Mrs. Emerson and I are motivated by scientific principle, not idle curiosity."

"So Mrs. Emerson will be working with you?" The speaker was Sir Edward. Raising one eyebrow, he looked from me to Emerson and back to me. "Doing what, if I may ask?"

"Excavating," I said. "Examining the debris, noting any artifacts we may find and their precise location."

"In the tomb itself?"

"It would be difficult to carry out those activities anywhere else."

The eyebrow rose even higher. Then he laughed and raised his glass of wine. "My respectful salutations, Mrs. Emerson. I begin to see that a lady may be . . . in short, a lady, with all the grace, beauty and charm of her admirable sex, and still be as daring and capable as any man. My prejudices have been shaken; dare I venture to hope that continued association with you will shatter them entirely?"

"Speaking of that," said Emerson, and drew the young man aside.

This rather abrupt ending of the general discussion caused the others to break up into smaller groups. Ramses was deep in conversation with M. Legrain; as I approached I realized the latter was describing, with exuberant Gallic gestures, an event that had occurred at Karnak a few months earlier. Several of the monolithic columns of the Hypostyle Hall had collapsed, with a crash that shook the entire town of Luxor.

"It was an event formidable," Legrain exclaimed.

"It must have been," said Ramses politely. He added in a meditative voice, "Lucky for me I was not there at the time."

"Pardon?" said M. Legrain.

I came to a dead stop and stared at the back of my son's head. I was not tempted to ask him to repeat the statement—I had heard it quite clearly—but I could not believe what I had heard. I did have a tendency (an understandable tendency, considering his history) to blame Ramses for anything untoward that might occur in his immediate vicinity, but surely he did not suppose that I would suspect him of blowing up the temple of Karnak!

Could it be that Ramses was developing a sense of humor?

Ramses turned and saw me. There was certainly a gleam in his eye. In anyone but Ramses I would have called it a twinkle.

By the end of the evening even I had begun to flag a trifle, after a sleepless night and a day full of exertion, but as I sat before the mirror giving my hair its usual hundred strokes I mentally reviewed the activities of the day and felt satisfied that all was in order. Another cot had been moved into Ramses's room. M. Legrain had offered his assistance and that of his men. (Emerson, who had no intention of letting another archaeologist in on our discovery, had declined the offer.) Messages had begun to pour in—from M. Maspero, offering congratulations; from Cyrus Vandergelt, just arrived in Cairo, expressing his intention of proceeding as quickly as possible to "the shoot-out," as he put it; from other archaeological friends, asking what they could do to help. Emerson had offered Sir Edward a position as official photographer, adding that the offer might be withdrawn if Sir Edward continued to make eyes at his wife—

"For pity's sake, Emerson!" I exclaimed, dropping my brush. "He was only being polite. I hope you didn't express it so bluntly as that."

"What do you take me for, Peabody? I don't recall the precise words, but I was the soul of tact, as always."

His hands came to rest on my shoulders and his face was reflected in the mirror before me. I could not help laughing, he looked so pleased with himself.

"The young man doesn't give a curse about your wife, Emerson. It is Nefret he is interested in."

"He scarcely spoke to her all evening."

"Precisely. Emerson, what are you doing?"

"I am making certain," said Emerson, "that you will not be led astray by the attentions of a smooth-talking young aristocrat."

"But Emerson, you must be weary, and I have not finished my one hundred strokes, and it is late . . ."

"Then why are we wasting time in conversation?"

It was certainly a reasonable argument. Besides, I had intended to use all possible means to prevent Emerson from returning to the tomb that night. This means proved to be as effective as I had hoped.

However, we were not to enjoy a restful night's sleep. It was a little after two in the morning when the now familiar sounds of a violent struggle roused me. Long years of practice had trained me to respond alertly and instantaneously; I had retrieved my nightdress and slipped into it before Emerson came fully awake. I called out a little reminder—"Don't forget your trousers, my dear"—caught up my parasol, and ran to the door.

I found myself a trifle confused initially, for of course I had instinctively started for Ramses's room, which was across the corridor from ours. His door stood ajar, but so did another—that of Nefret's chamber. Light streamed through the opening and the continuing sounds of an altercation issued therefrom.

Parasol at the ready, I dashed in—and stopped short. Two individuals were struggling. I had anticipated as much. What I had not anticipated was that the individuals should be Nefret and Miss Marmaduke.

Advancing, I ordered them to desist at once. They broke apart, panting and trembling. Gertrude's loosened hair hung over her face and her nightgown had lost several buttons, but Nefret was in worse case. Her gown hung open to the waist and had been pulled off one shoulder. Catching my eye she hurriedly adjusted it and burst into speech.

"She struck him, Aunt Amelia! She was trying to—"

"Oh, heavens!" Gertrude sagged at the knees and leaned heavily against the wall. "I did not know! I thought—good God! He has come back! Don't let him go near her!"

"He" was David, accompanied by Ahmed, who had been on guard outside Ramses's window. Nefret had flung herself down on her knees at the foot of the bed. It struck me as an inappropriate moment for prayer, but before I could comment on this Nefret turned to me with a gesture of appeal and I saw to my horror that her raised hand was stained crimson.

"Help me, Aunt Amelia. And don't let that woman—"

"Certainly not," said Emerson, from the doorway. "Amelia, you had better do as she asks. No one else move."

I knew what I would see. Only one member of the party was not visible, and he was usually the first to turn up.

Ramses was curled up on the floor, half-hidden by the tumbled bedclothes and by the bed itself. Nefret was tugging at his bloody hands, which were clasped tightly over his side. His eyes were open.

Seeing me, he said, "Good evening, Mother. It was not David."

"Indeed?" I pushed Nefret out of the way, rather more forcibly than was necessary, and knelt by Ramses. He allowed me to lift his hands, remarking, "It would be advisable to stop the bleeding, I believe; I am beginning to feel a trifle giddy, and there are several things I want to say before—"

"I can well believe that, Ramses."

He had been holding a part of the sheet over the gash in his side. I folded another section into a heavier pad and pressed down on it.

"Ouch," said Ramses. "Mother—"

"Be quiet. Emerson, fetch my medical kit. Nefret, tear that sheet into strips."

Emerson was back almost at once. "How is he?"

"Luckier than he had any right to expect. The lung has not been punctured, probably because the knife struck a rib. Ramses, stop squirming. I know the alcohol stings, but I must disinfect the wound before bandaging it."

"I am not squirming," said Ramses, faintly but indignantly. "That was an involuntary physical reflex. And may I say, Mother, that I take exception to the word 'lucky.' Observing a glint of light along the blade of the knife I was able—"

"Be quiet, Ramses."

"He can still talk, at any rate," said Emerson, with a long breath of relief. "What the devil happened here?"

"The boy crept in and tried to—to—assault her," Gertrude cried. "I heard her scream and came at once, but he must have got out the window before I could—"

"That is a lie," Nefret said. "It was not David."

"It was dark." Gertrude's voice rose hysterically. "How could you see who it was? I saw his outline against the window."

"You saw Ramses," Nefret said. "He was the first to respond to my call for help. The man who . . . the man let me go and ran to the window. Ramses went after him." Her hands continued to move mechanically, tearing strips from the sheet, but she was as pale as her nightdress and her voice was unsteady.

"That will do, my dear," I said. "Emerson—"

He took her into a fatherly embrace. "We'll sort this out tomorrow," he said, clumsily patting the bright head that had come to rest on his breast. Emerson's hands, as I had cause to know, were never clumsy. It was rage that made them tremble now.

With seeming coolness he went on, "Miss Marmaduke, return to your room. I will speak with you later. Nefret, your aunt Amelia will take you to our room as soon as she has finished with Ramses. He had better remain here. I will stay with him. David—"

"It was not David." Ramses's eyes were half-closed, but he was alert enough to hear how his father's voice had hardened when he pronounced the boy's name. "He was just stirring when I left our room. The individual was larger and stronger than David, though dressed the same. Someone is trying . . ."

"You have made your point, Ramses," Emerson said. His arm around Nefret, he drew her toward the foot of the bed and stood looking down on his son. "Well, Peabody?"

"You can put him on the bed now," I said, tying a neat knot. "Carefully."

This operation having been performed, I covered Ramses and wiped the perspiration from his face. I believed him to be asleep or unconscious, but I might have known Ramses would insist on having the last word. His lips parted.

"Now you will be able to retain your reputation for honesty with Aunt Evelyn. When she arrives you can show her . . . a genuine . . ."

He would have gone on quite a bit longer, I suppose, if he had not lost consciousness. Leaving Emerson tight-lipped and silent by his bedside, and noting that David had settled down in the corner with a look that told me it would require force to remove him, I put my arm round Nefret and led her to our room.

There was no question about it, Ramses *was* developing a sense of humor. As I might have anticipated, it was a deuced peculiar sense of humor.

CHAPTER SEVEN

The Soft Voice of the Father of Curses Is Like the Growl of an Angry Lion

For once Emerson was up before me the following morning. He was trying to move quietly, but he is not good at that; a muffled swearword woke me and I opened my eyes to behold Emerson standing one-legged like a stork, holding his stockinged foot in his hands. I deduced he had stubbed his toe on the bedframe, since his mumbled maledictions were addressed to that article of furniture.

There was just enough light for me to make out his form. "And where do think you are going at this hour of the morning?" I inquired. I thought I knew, though.

"Curse it," said Emerson, in what he fondly believes is a whisper. "I didn't mean to wake you, Peabody."

"Then you should not stumble around in a dark room in your stocking feet." He had not answered my question, so I asked again. "Where are you going?"

"For a healthy morning stroll." Emerson sat down and began pulling on his boots.

"An excellent thought. I will join you."

Nefret still slept, her cheek pillowed on her hand. I slid out of bed and went behind the screen to dress. I did so with even greater celerity than is my habit because I feared he would try to leave without me, but when I emerged I found him standing by the bed.

"Will she be all right?" he asked anxiously.

"Oh, yes. The young have amazing powers of recuperation, and she was not hurt, only frightened."

"You are certain?"

"Yes, my dear. The fellow barely touched her. I believe she was more distressed about Ramses than about herself. How is he?"

"If there had been any cause for concern I would have told you at once," Emerson replied. "Selim is with him."

"Selim? But he was not here, he was . . ."

"Not so loudly, Peabody. You will wake her."

"I am awake." The blue eyes, their color now discernible in the strengthening light, popped open. "How is Ramses?"

"As I was telling your aunt Amelia, sound asleep, with no sign of fever."

"You are going somewhere, aren't you?" She scrambled out of bed, displaying in her haste a long stretch of slender limbs. "I will sit with Ramses."

The nightgown was my own; I had bundled up her torn garment and put it out of sight. Mine covered her, once she was on her feet, from shoulders to floor. Nevertheless, I felt it necessary to administer a little reminder. "Put on your clothes first."

"Such nonsense," Nefret muttered. "Oh, very well. Don't worry about Ramses, I will take care of him."

"I am sure you will," I said, hoping that Ramses would refrain from mentioning his heroic rescue every five minutes, and that Nefret's grateful affection would prevent quarreling for a few hours at least.

"Sir?"

Emerson, on his way out the door, turned. She looked him straight in the eye and said slowly, in her best Arabic, "Good fortune attend thy purpose, O Father of Curses."

Emerson gave me no time for more than a glance at my son, who was indeed sleeping quietly. When we left the dahabeeyah, Anubis materialized out of somewhere, as cats do, and followed us down the gangplank.

"Emerson," I said. "What did Nefret mean?"

"You understand Arabic, don't you?"

"Yes, but . . . It sounded to me as if she were encouraging—approving, at least—some action that . . ."

"I needed no encouragement, my dear," said Emerson mildly.

If I had not already known he was in no mood to trifle I would have deduced as much from the fact that the animals awaiting us were horses, not the little donkeys. Abdullah was waiting too, his face unusually forbidding. Emerson tossed me onto one of the horses and swung into his own saddle.

"Don't propose washing the cursed horses, Peabody, you will have time to fuss with them later. I have hired them for the remainder of the season and sent one of the men across to Luxor to buy saddles for us. These are, I confess, a trifle worn. Confound it, Abdullah, make haste or I will leave you behind. You, too," he added, glancing at the cat, who responded with an agile leap onto Emerson's knee.

"Emerson, did you sleep at all last night?"

"I entertained myself instead by planning what I mean to do to Hamed."

"But you cannot be certain it was—"

He was off before I could finish the sentence and I had to urge my steed to the best pace the poor creature could attain in order to keep up with him. I dared not let him get ahead; in his present state of mind he was capable of thrashing the old man within an inch of his life—an action he would probably regret, once he had cooled off—and Abdullah was not the man to prevent him. Family honor as well as the affection Abdullah hid from all eyes but mine would demand retaliation for the suspicion cast upon his grandson.

The necessity of restraining two infuriated male persons would be a challenge even to me, but I thought I could manage it—with a little luck. Luck, or more probably the fact that Hamed had learned of our approach, was with me. The old villain was nowhere to be found. The courtyard was empty of any but gallinaceous life, and the servants and apprentices had fled.

Emerson stormed through the house kicking over furniture and ripping down the curtains that served in lieu of doors. He even invaded the harîm—if one may use that word to distinguish a small room inhabited by two cowering females. A single glance showed him, and me, that neither could be Hamed; one was a wrinkled old crone and the other a black-eyed girl who could not have been more than thirteen.

They had neglected to veil themselves and they cowered only because it was expected of them. Both faces contemplated Emerson without alarm and with considerable interest. Saluting them respectfully, he looked under the divan and behind a curtain, and backed out.

"This is a waste of time, Emerson," I said. "He is not here. You have searched—"

"My dear Peabody, I have only just begun."

We returned to Abdullah, who was in the main room. Knife in hand, he was jabbing it randomly into the floor. "Nothing," he said, straightening.

"It will be in the master bedchamber, I expect," said Emerson, with a sardonic curl of his lip.

One room was certainly furnished more comfortably and garishly than the rest of the house. Rugs covered the floor. A divan was piled with cushions; beside it stood a water pipe and a tray with a bottle and glass. The glass was half full. Emerson picked it up and sniffed the contents.

"Brandy. He violates not only the commandment against spirits but the laws of Ramadan. Very well, Abdullah, let's get at it."

They did not bother to roll the rugs back. After a few stabs Abdullah grunted with satisfaction. "Wood. It is here, Emerson."

The trapdoor had been covered with a thin layer of dirt to make it look like the rest of the earthen floor. Emerson heaved it up.

Instead of the huddled figure of a fugitive I saw a pile of odd-shaped bundles wrapped in rags. The first one Emerson took out proved to be an exquisitely shaped alabaster (more properly, calcite) vase. The incised hieroglyphs on one side of it had been filled with blue paste.

"Ahmose Nefertari," Emerson muttered. "Royal wife, royal daughter, royal mother. Not our queen, Peabody. How many royal tombs have these bastards located?"

He put it carefully aside and reached again into the hole. The objects piled up: part of a finely carved wooden ushebti, royal by the headdress, but uninscribed; a heart scarab in green feldspar; several other ushebtis of glazed blue faience; a handful of turquoise and gold beads carefully wrapped in a cloth—and a small statue, ten inches high, that looked strangely familiar.

"Tetisheri!" I exclaimed. "There was a pair of statues, then. Or a trio."

"More likely an entire chorus. This is one of Hamed's copies, Peabody. I wonder how many others he made before he disposed of the original." Emerson rose to his feet and handed the statuette to Abdullah, who slipped it into the breast of his robe.

"Aren't you going to—er—confiscate the other antiquities?" I inquired.

"At the moment I don't want them, I want Hamed. Where the devil could the bastard have got to? I will search every confounded house in the cursed village if I must, but there should be an easier way of locating him. Perhaps if I inquired of the ladies . . ."

"They may fear him too much to betray him, Emerson. But that girl—she is so young, hardly more than a child. Can't we take her away?"

"I doubt she would come, Peabody. Oh, I share your abhorrence of the custom, but if you are in a reforming mood you might start closer to home. The laws of civilized England allow females to marry at the age of twelve."

For once my well-honed instincts and my understanding of

female psychology were in error. The ladies were only too eager to cooperate. They responded to Emerson's questions with rolling eyes and shrugs, but one of them—the elder of the two—mentioned, in a studiedly casual tone, that Hamed had recently embraced marriage for a third time.

"Ah," said Emerson. "She has her own house? She must be a pearl of beauty, to merit a separate setting—or a wealthy widow. Most likely the latter. Hamed loves money even more than he does . . . er, hmmm. Marhaba, Sitt; Allah isabbekhum bilkheir."

As we left the room I saw the girl creep closer to the old woman, who put a motherly arm around her. Polygamy is a vicious unnatural custom, which I would never understand or condone; but a tender blossom of affection may grow from a compost heap. I wondered if it had been jealousy on the girl's account—not of Hamed's unprepossessing person but of the attentions he bestowed on his new wife—that had prompted the older woman's betrayal.

Our presence and Emerson's noisy actions had drawn an audience. Most were the usual curious idlers of all ages and sexes (and species), but I saw several ugly faces in the crowd, and I said softly to Abdullah, "Should we go for reinforcements?"

His knife in his hand, the other hand in the breast of his robe, Abdullah looked down at me in surprise. "No, Sitt, why?"

He invited me, with a gesture, to precede him. I took a firmer grip on my parasol and followed Emerson.

One of the spectators cheerfully supplied the information he requested. The house was not far distant. It was quite an elegant establishment, larger and in better repair than many of its neighbors. The door was beautifully carved and very old. Emerson considerately refrained from kicking it open. He did not bother to knock, however.

The features of the woman seated cross-legged on the divan opposite showed the racial mixture one finds in Egypt, particularly in the south, and they had combined in an uncommon pattern of striking character—full lips and high cheekbones, wide-set eyes of a shade more green than hazel, a jutting nose like that of a Roman general. Her skin was dark brown, sleek as velvet.

After a disinterested glance at me she looked Emerson over, head to foot and foot to head, and her lips parted in a smile. She had obviously been expecting company, for she was dressed in her best. Silver hung from her ears and brow and jangled at her wrist as she raised a cigarette to her lips.

Emerson began, "Salaam aleikhum—er—"

She cut him short, gesturing with the cigarette. "My name is Layla, Father of Curses. He is there."

"There?" Emerson echoed rather stupidly. He had not expected such ready compliance.

"Hiding in a corner, like the weasel he is," was the contemptuous reply. "You would soon find him, so why should I not tell you before you wreck my poor house?"

"Very sensible," Emerson said approvingly. He plunged through the curtained doorway she had indicated. A shriek announced the discovery of Hamed. Emerson returned, dragging the fellow by the neck of his robe.

The woman uncoiled herself and followed him to the door. "If you would visit me, Father of Curses, for you I lower the price to—"

"Good gracious!" I exclaimed. "That will be enough from you, miss—madam—"

"Never mind, Peabody," Emerson said. "Curse it, do you suppose I am in the mood for . . . Even if I would, which I would never . . . Damn these women, they are always distracting a fellow!"

The spectators scattered when we emerged from the house, and then regrouped at a little distance, leaving three persons confronting us. They were the men I had noticed earlier, and their expressions were even uglier. Hamed, plucking at the fabric that constricted his throat, gasped, "Let me go. Let me go or they will . . ."

"Oh, I think not," said Emerson, tightening his grip so that the threat ended in a choked gurgle. "Peabody, your parasol, if you please."

I did not know precisely what he had in mind, but guided by his words and his gesture I brandished the implement in question.

Two of our opponents hastily backed away and one—the largest and most muscular—fell to his knees. "No!" he shrieked. "No, not that! Sitt Hakim, Emerson Effendi, please, I beg—not that!"

It was a dramatic scene: the cowering man, face shining with perspiration, hands raised as if in prayer; the awed ring of watchers; Emerson's impressive form towering over the suppliant; and the cringing, whimpering bundle of rags that was Hamed. I confess the parasol was a slightly discordant note, however. Torn between astonishment and amusement, I held my pose, and Emerson said, "Get up, Ali Mahmud, and go away. Peabody, you may lower your—er—weapon. Now then, Hamed, let us talk."

He sat the old man down on a rock. Abdullah, knife in hand, growled. "He is mine by right, Emerson. The honor of my family—"

"You can murder him after I have finished questioning him, Abdullah," Emerson said. "Or not, as I decide. Hamed, I told you I had tired of your attentions. I do not often repeat a warning. Who was the man you sent last night? I want a little chat with him too."

Hamed's eyes rolled wildly from Emerson to me to Abdullah. He was not deceived by Emerson's mild tone. It had become a proverb in the villages of Egypt: "The soft voice of the Father of Curses is like the growl of an angry lion."

"You will not let him kill me if I speak the truth? I am an old man, old and broken—"

"Who was it? One of your sons, I presume. Which?"

I was not surprised to find Hamed ready to play Abraham to Emerson's wrathful Jehovah. "Solimen," he blurted. "But he did no harm. He meant no harm."

Again Abdullah pushed forward. "No harm? To a young girl, a maiden who has never known a man, who is in the protection of Emerson Effendi and of Abdullah ibn Hassan al Wahhab? I would cut your scrawny throat for that, Hamed, even if you had not tried to put the blame on my grandson."

Hamed's squinting eyes widened to an extent I would not have believed possible for those deep-set orbs. The words burst out of him like bullets. "What do you say? It is madness, what you say! Emerson Effendi—Sitt Hakim—you do not believe . . . If I desired to die I would leap from the cliffs of El Dira, it would be easier than the death such a deed would bring on my head. Wahyât en-nebi, by the life of the Prophet, I swear—"

"Hmph," said Emerson. "Do you know, Hamed, I am almost inclined to believe you. What did he go there for, then?"

His grip loosened. Hamed let out his breath and readjusted the folds of cloth around his throat. I shared Emerson's opinion, that his terrified denials had been genuine, but the interval gave him time to gather his wits again.

Finally he muttered, "For the boy. He is mine, I paid well for him. It is my right to take him back."

"And Solimen went to the wrong room?" Emerson inquired helpfully, elbowing the snarling Abdullah back.

Hamed was shrewder than that. "He could not go through your son's window, there was a man on guard. The maiden woke before he could leave her room, and called out. Solimen is young and a fool, he lost his head, but he meant only to keep her from summoning help." He added, with a sly look at Emerson, "She is strong and brave as a desert cat, Father of Curses; if she had not fought back, Solimen would not have . . . I give him to you. Do with him as you like, he deserves punishment for his stupidity."

"A noble gesture," Emerson said dryly. "He is probably halfway to the Sudan by now. He would be wise to remain there. Whatever his reasons, he dared lay hands on my daughter. If I find him I will kill him."

The flat finality of the statement was far more terrifying than a shout of rage. A shudder ran through Hamed.

"As for you," Emerson went on, "I cannot murder in cold blood a wretched bag of bones like you, nor allow Abdullah to do so. I will break my own rule and give you a second—and final—warning. If you, or anyone sent by you, bothers me again I will give Abdullah permission to proceed with the activities from which I am presently restraining him. His large circle of friends and relations may wish to participate. You understand me."

"Yes, yes!" The old man scrambled down from his rocky seat

and dropped to his knees. "You are merciful, Father of Curses; the blessings of Allah be on you."

One twisted hand reached for the hand of Emerson, who pulled it away with a look of disgust. Then his expression changed. Taking the hand in a hard grip, he examined it closely.

"Look at this, Peabody."

I would rather not have had that repellent member so close to me, but as I inspected it I saw what had aroused Emerson's curiosity. Under the ingrained dirt a network of pale scars could be seen, covering the back of the hand and extending down the warped fingers.

"It was not rheumatism or arthritis that crippled him," I exclaimed. "His hands were broken—crushed—by a rockfall or . . ."

"A booted foot." Coolly Emerson pushed the sleeve of Hamed's robe up to the elbow. The exposed forearm was ropy and wrinkled, but unscarred. He dropped Hamed's hand and absently wiped his own hand on his trousers. "The injuries must have been deliberately inflicted. They are on both hands, and only on his hands. He feigns lameness, but as you must have observed he can move as quickly as a snake when he likes. Who did this to you, Hamed? And when, and why?"

The thin lips twisted in a silent snarl.

"I believe I can hazard a guess, Emerson," I said. "They are old injuries—ten years old or more. Hamed has been in the antiquities trade longer than that. We know who controlled the trade in Luxor at that time, and we know how he controlled it."

"Well done, Peabody. The only remaining question is Why?"

"He tried to swindle Riccetti, obviously," I said. "It is what he would do, and that is how Riccetti would react. Do the details matter now? For heaven's sake let us go, Emerson."

"Hmmm, yes, we may as well. I can't stand the creature's stench much longer myself. Come along, Abdullah."

I looked back at the house. The woman Layla stood in the open doorway, one hand on her hip. She gave me a broad smile and lifted the other hand in farewell.

"A wealthy widow, I think," said Emerson, who had observed

this exchange. "The house must be her own, and she has character enough to bully Hamed. How much, I wonder, does she know about his activities?"

I took a firm grip on his arm. "Not enough to warrant a visit from you."

"How do you know how much . . . Oh," said Emerson. "I grasp the subtle implication, Peabody. Or was it a threat? Unnecessary, I assure you. Where is the confounded cat?"

"Hunting," I said, as Anubis came trotting along with a fat rat in his mouth. He dropped it at the feet of Emerson.

"Most considerate of you," said the latter, picking the rat up by its tail and handing it to Abdullah. "Wait till we have gone a way before you discard it, Abdullah, it would be ungracious to appear unappreciative."

"Ugh," said Abdullah, lips pursed.

Emerson lifted the cat to his shoulder and I said, "That fellow—one of the thugs, I believe I may term him—certainly behaved very strangely. How did you manage to reduce him to a state of gibbering terror?"

"It was not I," Emerson replied. "It was you. Or, to be more precise, that absurd umbrella of yours. Are you unaware of the fact that it is considered to be a weapon of great magical power?"

"Surely you jest."

"You are become a legend in your own time, Peabody," Emerson said solemnly. "The tales are told and retold around the village fires, gaining in impressiveness with each repetition. Tales of the great and terrible Sitt Hakim, whose potent parasol can bring strong men to their knees, begging for mercy. You have our loyal men to thank for it," he added with a laugh. "Especially Daoud; he is the best raconteur of the family."

"How ridiculous," I exclaimed.

"But useful." Emerson sobered. "Don't rely on your legend, though, my dear. Only the most superstitious and least sophisticated of the locals believe it."

I turned to look at Abdullah, who was stamping along behind us, muttering to himself. I suppose he was still annoyed because he had not been allowed to mutilate Hamed. Catching my eye, he said, with a self-conscious air, "That is true, Sitt. Daoud does not believe the stories, he only tells them because he is a great liar and likes attention."

Once we were mounted, Emerson sat without moving for a few moments, his eyes fixed on the hills to the north. The longing on his face was as poignant as that of a lover watching an unattainable mistress, but, noble creature that he is, he put aside desire for duty.

"Go back to the tomb, Abdullah, and get the men started. I will join you as soon as I can."

Abdullah began, "The boy—"

"I'll see to him." Emerson did not have to ask which boy he meant. "Give me the statue, Abdullah, then go."

Only his concern for the horse he bestrode, which was not in good condition, prevented Emerson from urging it to a gallop. He was in a perfect quiver of frustration, for he had had hardly a glimpse of the long-desired object of his quest and he ached to start work on it. I shared his yearning, but archaeological fever, with me as with my husband, gave way to more sacred ties; and as we rode side by side, at a fairly sedate pace, we discussed our immediate plans and settled on a course of action.

Our first visit, of course, was to Ramses, whom we found sitting up in bed giving David a lesson in ancient Egyptian.

"Good Gad, Ramses, you are supposed to be resting," I exclaimed, as the other boy retreated to a corner, clutching the notebook and pencil. "Where is Nefret?"

"Making chicken soup," said Ramses. "I don't want any cursed chicken soup, Mother, I want eggs and bacon. She would not let me have breakfast, only—"

"Quite right," I interrupted. "As you can see, Emerson, your son is in fine fettle. Run along, my dear; I know how you ache to investigate your precious tomb."

"As do you." Emerson drew me to the door. "Thank you, my dear. I won't forget your noble sacrifice, and I will tell you all about it this evening."

The urgings of duty (and, of course, maternal affection) did not prevent my thoughts from wandering during the course of that busy day. How alluring were the images that filled my brain—the intriguing rubble littering the chamber, the painted image under its frieze of bats—and that dark, unexplored opening in the wall.

If Emerson goes through that hole without me, I will murder him, I thought.

I had the doctor over from Luxor—I remember with amusement the look of surprise on Emerson's face when I expressed my intention of doing so—and modestly received his congratulations on my professional procedures. Little else required to be done, he declared. At my request, strongly opposed by Ramses, he put a few stitches into the incision. Leaving Ramses mutinously contemplating a large bowl of chicken soup, I went looking for Gertrude. She was not on the upper deck or in the saloon, so I knocked on her door.

A long pause and a period of rustling, scuttling sounds followed the announcement of my identity. Finally she opened the door.

"I am so sorry to keep you waiting, Mrs. Emerson. I was—I was not properly attired."

I could only suppose she had been altogether unclothed, since the garment she wore was a loose wrapper. Wrinkling my nose against an overpowering smell of incense, I said, "Why are you hiding in your room on such a fine day?"

"I was studying—trying to study." She pushed a wisp of mouse-brown hair back from her cheek. "I cannot stop thinking about last night. I bitterly regret—"

"All the more reason to get out into the sunshine and fresh air," I said briskly, for I did not want to hear a repetition of her excuses and apologies. "Brooding in your room is not sensible. Take your book out onto the deck and ask Mahmud to bring you a pot of tea."

"Yes, that is . . . that is a good idea." She glanced helplessly over her shoulder. So did I. She had not been studying; the books on the table were closed and stacked in a neat pile and the topmost book was covered with a light layer of the fine, sandy dust that quickly collects on all flat surfaces in that region. Nor had she been resting on the bed. The coverlet was unwrinkled, the pillows plumped.

Gertrude said, "I hope you don't think, Mrs. Emerson, that I am neglecting my duties. I went to see what I could do for Ramses, but Nefret would not let me into his room, and when I asked if she would not like a lesson she said she was busy."

"Quite all right, Gertrude." I wondered what else Nefret had said. "Your duties do not include that of a nurse, and this is not the time to worry about lessons."

All the same, I decided I had better get Nefret out of Ramses's room, for he would never rest if she ordered him to. My premonitions were accurate and my advent fortuitous; Ramses, lips set and eyes furious, was resisting Nefret's efforts to "tuck him in." *I* tucked him in and removed Nefret. Seeing that Gertrude had obeyed my orders and was on the upper deck, a book in her hand and her eyes fixed unseeingly on the horizon, we retreated to the saloon.

I had expected Nefret would complain of Ramses's stubbornness and lack of appreciation, but she had something more serious on her mind. "I did not want to ask in front of Ramses, Aunt Amelia, it might upset him; but will you tell me what occurred this morning at the house of David's cruel employer?"

"How do you know that was where we went?"

A disturbing little smile played round her lips. "I know the Professor well, Aunt Amelia, and I have seen that same look in the eyes of other men. As you said, I have had more experience in such matters than English girls of my age."

"Oh," I said. "Well, Nefret, the Professor is not like other men, he is far superior to them, and he would not . . . He did not . . . Oh dear. Suppose I tell you exactly what happened. There is no reason why Ramses should not know of it; he is not easily upset."

When I had finished, she nodded thoughtfully. "It may be so. The man was standing by the bed when I first saw him, and it may have been some slight sound—a stumble or misstep—that woke me. He did not touch me until I called out. May I see the statuette of Tetisheri you found?"

The abrupt change of subject left me wordless for a moment.

"Yes, certainly. But don't you want to talk about the—the other business any longer?"

"What would be the point? The facts we know are few and they can be interpreted in several different ways. If you and the Professor believe the old man was telling the truth . . ."

"About that, at any rate," I murmured. "His terror appeared to be genuine—and, I assure you, well founded. I am not sure about the rest of it."

So I went off to fetch Tetisheri, whom Emerson had left in our room. The conversation had convinced me that Nefret was not hiding fears of which she was reluctant to speak. I am a keen observer, and I had watched her closely as she spoke of that unpleasant adventure; there had not been a tremor, a change in color or in the tone of her voice. I believe in the subconscious, but only up to a point.

Since I had not had an opportunity to look closely at the statue, we examined it together and compared it with the photographs of the one in the British Museum. They appeared to be identical. It was Nefret who pointed out that even the break in the hieroglyphic inscription on the base had been copied exactly.

I left her studying—with my permission—my translation of "The Hippopotamus Pool," and went about my duties. Domestic arrangements—ordering meals, checking supplies, washing the horses—filled several hours; it was almost teatime when I returned to Ramses's room, to find, as I had expected, that Nefret had returned to what she considered her duty. The atmosphere was surprisingly cordial, however. Selim was curled up on the mat, sound asleep. The cat Bastet lay across the foot of the bed, and Ramses, propped up with pillows like a young sultan, held the Tetisheri statue. The photographs of the original lay beside him; he and the other two had obviously been comparing them.

"I have told Ramses and David," Nefret was quick to remark. "You said I might."

I had not said she could tell David. However, there was no sensible reason why I should object. At a gesture from Ramses the lad fetched a chair for me and I seated myself.

"Did you make this, David?" I asked.

"No, ma'am."

Ramses and/or Nefret must have been teaching him manners as well as English—and heaven knows what else. On this occasion his English vocabulary was inadequate for the purpose; after a few attempts he gave it up and burst into excited Arabic. "I cannot do such fine work, Sitt—not yet. This was made by Hamed, long ago, before his hands were hurt. He was the master, no one was as skilled. He could not show me, but he could tell me what to do and correct me when I was wrong."

"With a stick, I suppose," I said dryly.

"It is how one learns." After a moment he added in quite a different voice, "I had thought it was how."

"And yet," said Ramses, who had been silent for longer than I had expected, "you found this, if Nefret's account of the event is accurate—"

"I am sure it was," I said quickly.

"Certainly," said Ramses, almost as quickly. "I did not mean to suggest anything beyond the inevitable and unconscious inaccuracies that creep in when a story passes from one narrator to another. As I was saying, you found this hidden away with other antiquities that were genuine. Why do you believe this one is not?"

He was looking at David, not at me. I was about to translate, or at least provide a more intelligible version of Ramses's comment, when Nefret said impatiently, "Ramses, don't be silly. The original is in the British Museum, so this must be a copy."

"Then Hamed made it more than ten years ago," said Ramses. "Mr. Budge bought the other in 1890, if I remember correctly."

David understood the first sentence at least. He nodded eagerly. "Many years, yes. He cannot work for many years. When I came to him his hands were hurt. But he was the master, he taught me."

Hamed's tutelage could not have been so successful, though, if the boy had not had exceptional talent to begin with. The manufacture and sale of forgeries is the most common occupation of the residents of Luxor and the nearby villages; Hamed must have come upon the boy one day when he was trying his hand at producing a fake, and recognized his undeveloped abilities.

And who better than Hamed to see it? He *had* been a master, untrained and unscrupulous though he was; to deprive him of the ability to practice his craft was a punishment as cruel as any sadist could have contrived. Only his hands had been injured.

Emerson was back before I expected him. I knew what had prompted this departure from his usual habits, and when he burst into Ramses's room, still in his wrinkled work clothing and dusty boots, he was quick to express his sentiments in characteristic fashion.

"What the devil are you all doing here? Ramses should be resting. This looks like a—an orgy!"

David was the only one to retreat before Emerson's blazing blue glare and lowering brows. Selim gazed at him admiringly and I said, "Come and change, my dear, and then we will all go up for tea. The doctor said Ramses could get out of bed for a while this evening if he is careful."

Somewhat sheepishly Emerson accepted a biscuit from the plate Nefret offered him and allowed me to lead him from the room.

"Well?" I demanded.

"Well what?" Emerson closed our door and advanced upon me.

"You smell terribly of bat, my dear," I said, evading his grasp.

"Do I? Yes, I suppose I do. My apologies, Peabody; one becomes accustomed to the odor, you know." Standing before the basin he began to remedy this difficulty, and as he proceeded with his ablutions I answered his questions about the doctor's visit and told him what David had said about the Tetisheri statue.

"Doesn't add much to what we already know," Emerson grunted. "I would like to ask that young man a few questions. You recall the statue we found yesterday in the antechamber—the hippopotamus goddess?"

"I could hardly forget it. Have you found out how it got there?"

"I have a theory or two, but I have not had the chance to investigate any of them. It has been a deuced unproductive . . . Where the devil are my clean shirts?"

They were where they always were, in the top drawer of the bureau. I got one out and as he turned to take it I let out a gasp. "Unproductive, you say? What happened?"

"Very little. As I said . . . Oh, that." He glanced down at the darkening bruise on his chest. "I am sorry to disappoint you, my dear Peabody, but nobody tried to kill me; it was a simple accident, due in large part to my own clumsiness. You see, I was on the rope ladder, pounding at that ledge of rock just below the entrance—"

"Emerson, for pity's sake! Why must you take such unnecessary chances?"

"It was not unnecessary." He pushed my hand away and finished buttoning his shirt. "It's a narrow squeeze just there, as you know; aside from the inconvenience to ourselves, we cannot lower any large-sized object, not even a basket, through that crack. It had to be widened and I was the obvious person to do it. The cursed sledgehammer bounced back at an unexpected angle, that is all."

He was out the door before I could reply. I followed him into Ramses's room.

"Why don't we have tea brought here?" he inquired. "Ramses seems comfortably settled."

"Too comfortably," I replied, studying the scene with dismay. It looked more than ever like an orgy. Nefret was sitting on the side of the bed, Selim had waked up and was looking hungrily at the biscuits, which the laws of Ramadan prevented him from eating, and Bastet's head was in the bowl of chicken soup. Anubis sat in the window watching Bastet and licking his whiskers.

"He will have to get out of that bed for a while," I continued. "It must be remade and various bits of food removed from it. Besides, it would be discourteous to ignore Gertrude."

"Hmph," said Emerson. "If you say so, Peabody. But first . . ." He turned to David, squatting at the foot of the bed, and addressed him in Arabic. "Hamed told me that the man who came here last night meant no harm to the maiden. He came for you, because Hamed had bought you."

"He lied." But the boy would not meet Emerson's eyes.

"There is no buying and selling of human beings under English law," Emerson agreed. "But there are older laws that some hold higher. Hamed has no claim on you unless you believe he does. Do you?"

The last two words cracked like a slap. The boy flinched—and so did I. Why had I not seen the implications earlier? There is a loyalty based on servitude—resented, hated, but admitted by those who believe in that code. For them it might supersede all other obligations.

"Father," Ramses began.

"Be still, Ramses. David?"

The boy shook his head. "No. No, Father of Curses. I swear by Sitt Miriam, by her Son, by the Saints—"

"It is good," Emerson said. "I accept your word. Did you ever make for Hamed a statue of the hippopotamus goddess?"

He did not know he was being unkind. Emerson is incapable of deliberate cruelty to a child. But the brusque questions fell hard on a boy who was accustomed to blows and curses, and who had yet to learn trust. David's eyes fell, and his mumbled answer was barely audible.

"Aywa. I did not know . . ."

"Stop bullying the child, Emerson," I interrupted.

"Bullying?" Emerson swung round to face me, blue eyes bright with indignation. "The devil, Peabody, how can you suppose I would do such a thing?"

David was no more appreciative of my intervention. With a resentful look at me, he straightened his shoulders and spoke up like a man.

"I made it. I made two. Taueret, the lady of childbirth. They were good work."

"Excellent work," I exclaimed. "So that statue we found in the tomb is also a fake?"

"Quite," said Emerson, reaching for his pipe. "I had a close look at it this afternoon. Do you know how it got there, David?"

The boy shook his head, and I said, "How could he? He was here, too ill to move, when the cursed thing was placed there. Emerson, don't smoke that pipe. Take it and Ramses up to the deck. Tea will be ready."

Ramses insisted he could walk—which was true—but since Emerson was determined, he submitted with ill grace to being carried. He had to endure further fussing from Nefret, who would have bundled him in afghans from feet to chin if I had allowed her, and from Gertrude.

However, after the appropriate expressions of interest, Gertrude turned her attention to Nefret. That her concern was genuine I could not doubt; it was also exasperating and unnecessary, and finally I was forced to cut her short before Nefret exploded into rudeness.

"Have another sandwich, Gertrude, while Professor Emerson tells us about the tomb. We have not yet had an opportunity to discuss the day's work."

As Emerson was the first to admit, there was not much progress to report. "I have decided to take Ramses's advice and widen the lower passage," he explained. "The danger of falling rock is too great. We can't use explosives, so it will take some little time."

Ramses expressed his pleasure at hearing this and his intention of being "back on the job," as he put it, by the time work on the tomb actually began. "But," he continued, without giving anyone else time to comment, "it is the statue you mentioned that interests me, Father. Did you mean to imply by your recent questions that it was not in the tomb when you and Mother first—er—dropped in on the thieves? It may be that you failed to observe it, being preoccupied at the time with one another's safety. The alternative, as I hardly need point out—"

"You are talking too much, Ramses," Nefret interrupted. "I am sure it is not good for you in your condition."

"Quite right," I said, while Ramses was trying to think how to respond to this disingenuous remark. "The statue was not there at first. I assure you I could not have missed seeing it. And you hardly need point out the alternative. Though how it could have been brought there, with our men on guard, I do not know. Unless . . ."

"I beg," said Emerson, teeth clenched on the stem of his pipe, "that you will refrain from saying it, Amelia."

". . . unless there is another way into the tomb. A secret passage."

"Nonsense, Amelia."

"How can you be sure? We have not cleared the antechamber. The entrance could be hidden under the debris."

"Because . . . Oh, but why try to introduce reason into a conversation like this one? The cursed thing came from Hamed's shop, but why it was put there and how it was put there is beyond definition at this time. I refuse to discuss it any further. What's this, the latest post?" Emerson flung the pipe into the receptacle, scattering ashes over the remaining sandwiches, and reached for the papers and envelopes on a nearby bench. "Anything of interest?"

"Not in my messages, no. Further than that I cannot say, since I do not open letters addressed to other people."

A somewhat uncomfortable silence followed this gentle reproof. Miss Marmaduke began talking about the fine weather and the beauty of the sunset. I responded automatically—the subject was not one that required the full concentration of my intelligence—and watched Emerson as he ripped open the envelope that had caught my attention earlier. It was the only one that promised the possibility of some interesting development, for it had been delivered by hand and the writing was unfamiliar. Would he share it with me? Would he admit me into his confidence?

He had no intention of doing so. His only visible reaction was a quiver of that handsomely indented chin and a movement of the hand holding the paper. He was about to put it into his pocket. I therefore reached out and took it from him.

After reading the message I said to the steward, "Tell the cook the Professor and I will not be here for dinner."

Emerson said, to no one in particular, "Hell and damnation!"

As Daoud pushed off from the shore, Emerson said grumpily, "At least the daily interruption begins earlier than usual. I may be able to get a full night's sleep for once."

"What do you suppose he wants?" I asked, adjusting a lacy scarf over my hair.

"Amelia, we have been over this at least a dozen times since you read that note. What is the sense of speculating? We will learn the answer from Riccetti himself soon enough."

"Now, Emerson, you know that is not true. He will tell us a pack of lies in order to mislead us. Misdirection is the reason for his invitation to us."

I had been included in that invitation. The realization of that quite removed any guilt I may have felt about reading someone else's letter—for if I had not done so, Emerson would not have told me what it said.

Emerson was still sulking and did not reply, so I continued. "It is a curious coincidence, don't you think, that Riccetti should come to Luxor immediately after we found the hippopotamus statue? Perhaps it was his quaint way of announcing his arrival."

As I had expected, this speech roused Emerson to fury, which, in my experience, is easier to deal with than sulking. "You are entirely too damned fond of curious coincidences, Amelia! He may have been here for weeks. As for the mystic import of hippopotami, I can only suppose that translating fairy tales has gone to your head. Why the devil . . ."

And so on. The discussion kept him quite animated and happy for the duration of the voyage. I leaned against his shoulder and enjoyed the view.

Riccetti had asked us to dine with him at the Luxor. He was already there when we arrived, the focus of all eyes. Except for the waiters in their tarbooshes and red slippers, the dining salon of the Luxor might have been located in any English hotel, with its damask tablecloths and serviettes, crystal glasses and fine china, and patrons wearing conventional European evening dress. Riccetti stood out in that setting like a buzzard in a cage of sparrows. The presence of the two guards, motionless as statues behind him, lent a particularly exotic touch. He had been given one of the best tables, in a corner near the windows, and when he saw us he raised an arm in greeting. The staring eyes swung toward us as if moved by a single spring.

Lecturing me had put Emerson into a (relatively) amiable mood. He allowed Riccetti to complete his apology to me for his failure to rise ("The infirmities of age, Mrs. Emerson") before planting his elbows on the table and remarking, "Let us get to the point, Riccetti. I have no intention of breaking bread with you or allowing my wife to remain in your presence for any longer than I must. Amelia, don't touch that wine!"

"But my friends," Riccetti exclaimed. "How can I drink a toast to your success if you will not join me in a glass?"

"So you know we have located the tomb," I said.

"All Luxor knows. It came as no surprise to me, of course. I had the greatest confidence in your abilities."

"You did not ask us here to congratulate us," Emerson snapped. "What are you after?"

"Now, Emerson," I said, "I am in complete agreement with you about prolonging this interview unnecessarily, but you are not asking the right questions. Signor Riccetti will only ramble on about renewing old acquaintances and the pleasure of our company. Let me handle this. Signor, how long have you been in Luxor?"

Riccetti had listened with interest. Now he displayed all his saurian teeth in a wide satirical grin. "I would not be lying, Mrs. Emerson, if I claimed that I greatly enjoy the pleasure of *your* company. How can I refuse to play a little game of question and answer with so charming a lady? I arrived here eight days ago, on the Cook's steamer the *Ramses*. I found the name particularly symbolic."

"And what have you . . . No, that is not specific enough. Have you spoken with Ali Murad?"

"I visited his shop on Tuesday last. I always visit the antiquities dealers, in the hope of augmenting my little collection."

"You have a collection of antiquities?"

"A few modest odds and ends. Someday, if you will do me the honor, I would like to show it to you."

Emerson began, "I will be damned—"

"Hush, Emerson. I admit I wandered from the subject. I will return to it. Do you know, signor, that Mr. Shelmadine is dead?

Riccetti bared a few more teeth. "My dear Mrs. Emerson, it was I who took the liberty of informing you of that fact—or rather, of sending you the clipping from the Cairo newspaper. I was certain your quick wits would arrive at the inevitable conclusion."

"Did you murder him?"

Riccetti appeared to be enjoying himself immensely. His jaws gaped wider, displaying an astonishing collection of dentures. "No, Mrs. Emerson, I did not."

I tried another tack. "Since you have been in Luxor have you visited Abd el Hamed?"

"Alas," said Riccetti with a hypocritical sigh. "I have been unable to visit my old friend Hamed. My increasing infirmities, Mrs. Emerson."

"Was it your men who left the statue of the hippopotamus goddess in the tomb?"

Riccetti's eyes widened and I thought for a moment that I had caught him off guard. Then he broke into a bellow of laughter. Every glass on the table quivered, and every head in the dining salon turned.

Riccetti laughed till tears filled his eyes. Wiping them on a napkin, he gasped, "Ah, bravissima! Che donna prodigiosa! Emerson, old friend, she is superb. I congratulate you."

"Another such reference to my wife," said Emerson between his teeth, "and I will knock you out of your chair."

"Mille pardone! I misunderstood. The British sense of humor has always been a mystery to me." He was not laughing now.

"Let me understand your question, Mrs. Emerson. You seem to be suggesting that someone has—shall we say, inserted?—an object into the tomb in recent days. I assure you it was not I. The farthest thing from my mind is to interfere with your work."

"Oh, balderdash!" Emerson burst out. "I know your real reason for coming to Luxor, Riccetti. You intend to reestablish your control over the antiquities market here. You lost it ten years ago to another, more skillful player. He is gone now, and the position is again open. I am uncertain as to whether you have competitors, or who they may be; frankly, I don't give a damn. I will crush anyone, including you, who attempts to harm my family and friends, or who interferes with my work."

Riccetti's teeth had vanished behind tightened lips. They parted only enough to articulate the words. "How many friends do you have, Father of Curses?"

"Oh, good Gad," said Emerson. "I haven't the time to exchange enigmatic innuendoes with you. If you have anything sensible to say . . . I thought not. Come along, Amelia."

When we reached the street Emerson shook himself vigorously. "Being in that villain's presence always makes me feel as if I were covered with crawling insects," he remarked. "What do you say we drop by Rohrmoser's for a glass of beer and some supper? I am feeling a trifle peckish."

CHAPTER EIGHT

No Innocent Person Can Lead a Life So Free of Harmless Vice

A week later we were all on the platform when the night train from Cairo drew into the station. Even Emerson had taken time from his work.

Evelyn was one of the first off the train. She was pale and thin, with dark stains of weariness under her eyes, but there was an indefinable change in her manner that made me hope the longed-for recovery had begun. I realized she had not received any of the encouraging messages I had sent, for after a quick glance at me she ran to Ramses and embraced him.

"Thank God! You are better, Ramses? You are recovered?"

"Yes, Aunt Evelyn," said Ramses. "Fortunately the knife missed all the vital organs and the doctor Mother consulted, contrary to her usual custom, proved to be competent. I lost a considerable quantity of blood, but thanks in part to the consumption of several gallons of chicken soup—"

"Knife?" Evelyn adjusted her hat, which had been knocked

askew by the impetuosity of her embrace. "Good heavens! Were you wounded, then? I was under the impression that you had been taken ill."

"Er, hmph," said Emerson. "Never mind Ramses, he is back to normal, as you can see. You look done in, my dear Evelyn; let us go straight to the hotel. Where is the rest of your luggage?"

There was no more, only their hand luggage. They had not taken the time to pack a trunk or to rest along the way, pausing only long enough to await the next method of transportation available. With Evelyn's arm around me—supporting me, as she believed—I felt a pang of guilt, but only a little one. Emerson's methods were unorthodox, but they appeared to have been efficacious.

By the time we reached the hotel, Walter was questioning Emerson about the tomb. I tried to persuade Evelyn to lie down but she would not, claiming the pleasure of the reunion with those she loved and the relief of finding her worst fears groundless had restored her; so we settled down in the sitting room of their suite and ordered tea while Emerson lectured.

"We have made less progress than I had hoped," he admitted. "I have had to spend time fending off cursed newspaper reporters and curious tourists, and we have been bedeviled by accidents. Two rockfalls—"

"Two?" Walter exclaimed, with an involuntary glance at his wife. "Are you certain they were accidents?"

"What else could they have been?" It was an evasive answer, but we had been unable to discover how the collapse of the rock could have been engineered; the tomb had been guarded night and day.

The smile that illumined Walter's thin face was the first genuine expression of amusement I had seen on his countenance for months. "My dear Radcliffe, I have never known you and Amelia to suffer from ordinary accidents. I took it for granted that as usual you had a gang of criminals after you."

"Yet you came," I exclaimed, much moved.

"All the more reason to come," said Evelyn firmly.

"In point of fact—" Ramses began.

Emerson and I said in unison, "Be quiet, Ramses."

"I intend to confide fully in you both," Emerson went on, taking a pencil from his pocket. "But first let me finish my description of the tomb. The access to it is difficult . . ."

Since there was not a sheet of paper handy, I let him draw on the tablecloth. He sketched a rough plan of the fissure and the tomb entrance, and finished, "After the second rockfall I decided to follow Ramses's suggestion that we clear the lower part of the fissure entirely. I don't want to risk rumors that there is a curse on the tomb."

"Not to mention the risk of one of the men or one of us being crippled or killed by falling rock," I interrupted. "There is no danger of that now, Walter, I assure you. The lower section of the crevice is open and the men are constructing stairs."

"But the tomb," Walter persisted. "Are there inscriptions? Has the burial been disturbed?"

"Now, Walter, don't get ahead of me," Emerson replied, infuriatingly cool. "Thus far we have not penetrated beyond the first chamber. Here is the entrance passage . . ."

His pencil dashed across the white cloth, and with a smile at me Evelyn moved a teacup out of his way. "The passage and at least part of the chamber beyond had been filled with rock chips," Emerson continued.

"Deliberately filled? How do you know the debris was not washed into the tomb by floodwater?"

"Curse it, Walter, are you questioning my expertise?" Emerson demanded.

Walter returned his scowl with an amiable smile, and Emerson said grudgingly, "It is a reasonable question. Though rain is infrequent here, severe storms are not unknown, and many tombs have been damaged by flash floods or seepage. For some reason, possibly because rainwater was funneled straight down the crevice, this tomb appears to have suffered very little. It was deliberately filled in order to protect it.

"The thieves dug a tunnel through the passage and removed some, at least, of the fill in the first chamber—I don't know how much, since I don't know how much there was to begin with, but there was a considerable accumulation of chips of that sort at the bottom of the crevice.

"At the far end of this room is a doorway"—he sketched it in—"blocked with slabs of stone. Our friends managed to remove one of the stones and began a tunnel through the filling of the passage beyond—for it too was closed by rocks and chips. I don't know what lies beyond that opening."

The abrupt conclusion left Walter gaping. "But my dear fellow, what inhuman lack of curiosity! Why haven't you investigated?"

"Because the tunnel is so narrow only a child could pass through, and of unknown length. Even if I were willing to allow Ramses to attempt something so perilous, he has not been in fit shape for such an exercise these past days."

"And you wouldn't trust one of the local lads to explore the place," Walter said thoughtfully.

"Not unless I searched him to the skin after he had come out," Emerson replied with a snap of his teeth. "And there are other hiding places . . . No, I won't chance it, or take the risk of an untrained boy destroying a fragile object."

He avoided Ramses's accusing eyes as he spoke. He had refused to allow David to enter the second tunnel, claiming he was, first, untrained, and, second, not yet fully recovered from his injuries. But I knew, as did Ramses, that Emerson was still suspicious of the boy. He appeared to accept Ramses's insistence that David could not have been the one who attacked Nefret, but the question of why someone should go to such lengths to incriminate the boy still remained unanswered. It was possible that the incident had been arranged for that purpose, and some people would have been too blinded by prejudice against a stranger and a native to weigh the evidence properly.

"Well, my curiosity is at fever pitch," Walter said. "I am ready to proceed whenever you are."

He had risen to his feet. Emerson studied him with affectionate amusement. "Dressed like that?"

Younger and more slightly built than his brother, Walter had led a much more sedentary life since he settled down to raise a family and concentrate on the study of the Egyptian language.

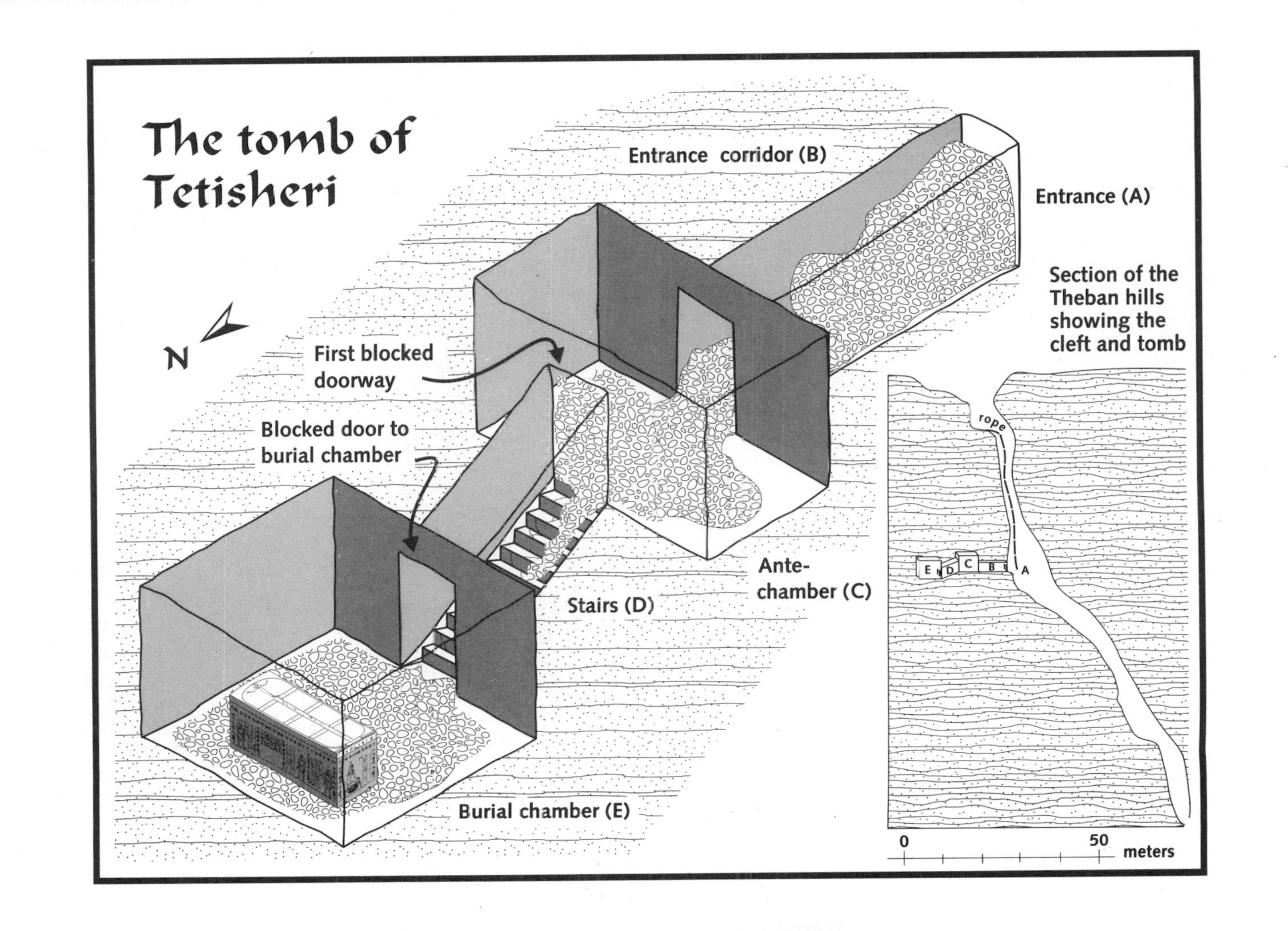
The tomb of Tetisheri
N
Entrance corridor (B)
Entrance (A)
First blocked doorway
Blocked door to burial chamber
Stairs (D)
Ante-chamber (C)
Burial chamber (E)
Section of the Theban hills showing the cleft and tomb
rope
E
D
C
B
A
0
50
meters

The stoop of his shoulders and the relative pallor of his complexion made him appear older than his real age, and his Norfolk jacket, wrinkled though it was by days of travel, would have been more appropriate for a stroll through English meadows than an archaeological dig.

"Yes, you must certainly change," Evelyn said. "I instructed George to pack your riding boots, but I am afraid there was nothing in your wardrobe suitable for strenuous activity."

She did not mean to sound critical, I believe, but her cool voice and the fading of Walter's smile assured me that relations between them had not measurably improved. I would have to attend to that matter, and I felt sure the arrangements I had made would facilitate the rapprochement I hoped for.

Evelyn was determined to accompany us and declared she would not delay us by changing; her traveling costume was a modish but practical tweed suit with ankle-length skirts, and stout walking shoes. She also refused a carriage. "We have got sadly out of condition since those days at Amarna; we must begin our program of exercise at once or we will never be able to hold up our end."

"Then you mean to stay on?" Emerson, whose arm she had accepted, looked at her questioningly.

She smiled at him, in almost her old way. "You have said nothing about the decoration of the tomb, but I know you well, Radcliffe; you are trying to whet my curiosity. Are the paintings as fine as you hoped?"

"They are unique, my dear Evelyn; they will revolutionize the history of Egyptian art. No decorated royal tomb as early as this has ever been found; if you had asked me, I would have said . . ."

Smiling with satisfaction, I fell back and joined Ramses, who was walking by himself, Nefret and Walter having preceded us.

"Are you feeling well, Ramses?"

Ramses started out of some dark—to judge by his expression—private thoughts. "It is good of you to inquire, Mother. I take the question as an expression of amiable affection rather than a request for information, for you must be aware of the answer, since you have insisted on inspecting the injury daily, though for at least the past two days there has been no need of that particular invasion of my—"

"For heaven's sake, Ramses, I was under the impression that you were attempting to correct the unnecessary prolixity and formality of your speech patterns."

"I am," said Ramses. "And I appreciate the reminder. I say, Aunt Evelyn looks better, doesn't she?"

Physically she was not visibly improved; the change was more subtle. Evidently Ramses's affection for his aunt had given him unexpected insight. I agreed, and he went on to suggest that since he was fully recovered I should persuade his father to let him investigate the second tunnel and the mysteries that lay beyond. (I quote.)

Our arrival at the ferry put an end to the argument. I settled myself next to Evelyn, since I had not yet had an opportunity to enjoy a comfortable chat with her.

"Words fail me," I said sincerely, "when I attempt to express my pleasure in seeing you—particularly in seeing you here, my dearest Evelyn. Dare I hope that you will remain for the rest of the season, and that you are indeed enjoying a new peace of mind?"

The wind brought a touch of color to her face and blew her curls around her face. There were threads of silver among the gold now, but it shone as bright as ever.

"We will stay as long as you and Radcliffe need us, Amelia. Not until his message came did I fully realize that I am not the only one to suffer a loss, and that others have borne it with greater courage and faith. Can you forgive me for behaving so badly?"

"My dearest girl!" We embraced. When I released her I saw that there were tears in her eyes, but her smile was her old sweet smile.

"I had ample time during our long journey," she resumed, "to consider my weakness and compare it with the fortitude of others. I remembered the innumerable times you had faced danger to those you love—those long days last winter, when you believed

Radcliffe was dead—or worse—the occasions, including the present one, when you feared for Ramses's life—"

"Ah well, where Ramses is concerned, one becomes used to it," I replied, feeling it was time to lighten the mood. "I claim no credit for fortitude with regard to Ramses. Paralyzed numbness would be a more accurate description."

"I know you too well to be misled by your modesty, dear Amelia."

"Hmmm. That word, I believe, is not one that has often been applied to me. But let us forget the sorrows of the past in the joys of the present. Look, Evelyn. Your artist's eye must appreciate the beauty of the view—the gold of the cliffs, the emerald green of the cultivation. And there, just ahead and to the right—do you recognize a familiar shape?"

"The dear old *Philae*!" Evelyn clasped her hands. "But I must call her the *Amelia* now. Radcliffe told us he intended to purchase her for you; in my selfish grief I failed to respond as he no doubt hoped I would, but what happy memories the sight of her recalls! She was not a large craft—only four staterooms, as I recall. You said you had employed a governess for the children . . ."

I burst out laughing. "My dear Evelyn, don't be so devious. I thought you would be happier at the hotel than in those cramped quarters on board, but I would evict ten governesses for you and Walter if you would prefer that arrangement. We will send Miss Marmaduke to the hotel."

I accepted her thanks and protestations with a modest smile. In fact, I had already booked a room for Gertrude at the Luxor, and told her to begin packing.

When we disembarked, Selim was waiting with the horses, and I realized that Emerson had intended all along to return at once to the excavation. By the time we arrived, the temperature had begun to rise, and I studied Walter's flushed face and the stiffness with which he dismounted with some concern. I must make certain he did not overdo or he would be sore and sunburned for days.

Tactfully I urged him and Evelyn toward the folding chairs and tables I had caused to be set up under an awning of sailcloth.

Emerson had fussed at me for "wasting time" with this, but unnecessary discomfort is a form of martyrdom with which I have no sympathy. Efficiency was also a consideration. There was no other shade when the sun was at the zenith, and it was very difficult to read Emerson's notes when he used a rock or the back of one of the men as a desk.

Gertrude was seated at the table, puzzling over the most recent notes. (Emerson's handwriting, even when he is not using a rock as a desk, is difficult to decipher.) Both of the cats were stretched out in the sun nearby, ostentatiously ignoring Gertrude. There is no creature better at delicate rudeness than a cat, and Bastet especially had gone out of her way to be rude to Gertrude, despite the lady's efforts to woo her with scraps of food and inappropriate compliments. I had warned Gertrude not to address Bastet as "pretty puss," and "sweet darling," but she went on doing it, to Bastet's deep disgust. No one, not even Gertrude, would have been moved to call Anubis "pretty puss."

I introduced Gertude, and the cats proceeded to underline the insult by sauntering up to greet Walter and Evelyn.

"They seem to be getting on better," Evelyn said, stroking Bastet as the cat rubbed against her ankles and Anubis favored Walter by clawing at his shoes.

"She allows Anubis to come within five feet of her without spitting," I replied. "That is progress of a sort, I suppose."

Hard workers though they were, our men were not averse to a little break in their labor. They gathered round; I introduced each by name and Evelyn smiled on them with her usual graciousness. Some of the older men were known to Walter, though he had not seen them for years. He was particularly friendly to Abdullah, wringing his hand and addressing him in stumbling Arabic.

"It will take me a while to regain my former fluency," he added with a laugh. "I have been studying dead languages too long, Abdullah."

"It is good to have you back," Abdullah said gravely. "And the Sitt your wife."

He withdrew when Ramses approached, tugging at a reluctant

David. It could not be said that David and his grandfather were on friendly terms; the boy got on much better with the others, especially his amiable, easygoing cousin Daoud. But I knew he would come to no harm with Abdullah's eagle eye upon him.

His appearance had improved since he came to us. Most of the sores and cuts had healed; I had trimmed his hair and prevailed upon him to wash rather more often than he considered necessary. The change was comparative, however, and I suppose he still looked rather pathetic, for Evelyn's face softened with maternal pity. She was wise enough to refrain from expressing that pity, however. Instead she said, "I am very pleased to meet you, David. If you are a friend of Ramses's, you must be a friend of mine."

"We are blood brothers," Ramses explained.

"Are you indeed?" I exclaimed. "Curse it, Ramses—"

"A small amount only of the vital fluid was required," Ramses said. He jogged David with his elbow, reminding him, I supposed, that he was expected to respond.

The boy jumped. He had been staring at Evelyn.

"How do you do?" He pronounced each word slowly and carefully. Ramses nodded approvingly, and David went on, "You have the face of Sitt Miriam in the book. She is beautiful. She hold . . . holds?" He glanced at Ramses, who was too thunderstruck to respond. "Hold," David repeated, "the Child. She look so to him. How do you do?"

Sitt Miriam is the name given by Egyptian Christians to the Virgin. The little speech astonished me as much as it had Ramses. I could not be sure how much of it Evelyn understood, but she was visibly moved. Impulsively she held out her hand. David took it and, after a moment of hesitation, shook it gravely. "How do you do? I am very pleased to meet you."

Ramses drew him away.

"Good Gad," said Emerson, staring after them. "We appear to have a courtier in our midst. I wonder how much of that pretty speech was drilled into him by Ramses."

"Very little, I should think," I replied. "Ramses does not excel at pretty speeches."

"Hmph," said Emerson. "Well, Amelia, if you have finished with the civilities, I would like to resume work."

The rest of us followed him to the bottom of the slope in time to see a basket being lowered into the hands of Selim, who carried it off a little distance and dumped it onto the growing pile of rock chips.

"Part of the fill?" Walter asked. "It appears to be devoid of artifacts; why don't you just shove it over the edge?"

"You seem to have forgotten my rules," Emerson replied with some acerbity. "We have found little as yet, but that is no excuse for slovenly excavation technique. If you will all excuse me, I am going up."

Walter was accustomed to his brother's manners. "I will go with you. I am anxious to see the tomb."

"I believe the stairs are not yet finished, Walter," Evelyn said.

It was obvious that they were not, for Mohammed was squatting on the ground nearby working on them—simple structures of wooden steps and supports, with stakes for a rope railing.

Walter stiffened. "The rope ladder is adequate."

"At least wait until you have proper boots, and perhaps gloves to protect your hands."

It was the wrong approach entirely, as I could have told her. Men behave like little boys when someone, especially a woman, questions their fortitude. Walter might have yielded—as men go, he is relatively sensible—had not another man appeared, descending the ladder with the speed and agility of an athlete. Dropping lightly to the ground, he removed his hat and bowed to the ladies.

His easy grace made poor Walter appear even frailer and more ineffectual. I have never encountered a man whose physique matched that of my husband, but Sir Edward's working costume—especially the shirt, damp with perspiration—displayed his athletic form to best advantage.

Emerson greeted him in typical fashion. "I told you you would not be needed today."

"I had nothing better to do," was the cheerful reply. "As I said, sir, when my photographic services are not required, I will turn my hand to any other task. I have been helping Daoud label the baskets."

I deemed it wiser to allow Emerson to make the introductions, which he did, albeit grudgingly. Sir Edward had taken Emerson's warning to heart; he had hardly ventured to speak to me since he joined the staff and he had kept well away from Nefret. He bowed deferentially over Evelyn's hand and exclaimed, as he shook that of Walter, that it was an honor to meet the man whose scholarship was revered by all who were acquainted with the field of Egyptology.

Emerson studied him suspiciously, but decided there was safety in numbers and that I would be adequately chaperoned. "Come along, Walter, if you are coming. You had better precede me; I will steady the ladder from below."

"Allow me to steady it for you, Professor." Sir Edward followed them, and I heard him add, "Mr. Emerson, sir, take my pith helmet, if it fits your head; there is some danger of falling rocks."

"Oh, dear," Evelyn exclaimed. "Amelia, do try to dissuade Walter, he is not in condition for this."

"It would be a waste of time, my dear. We may as well sit down in the shade, don't you think?"

We returned to the shelter, where Evelyn entered into conversation with Gertrude, apologizing for putting her out of her room. This display of consideration appeared to surprise Gertrude very much. I suppose she was not accustomed to it; courtesy to those they consider their inferiors is rare among the upper classes.

"Mrs. Emerson's wishes are, of course, my commands." After a brief pause she added, softly but with feeling, "I only wish you could persuade her and Nefret to join me at the hotel. It would be much safer."

"Safer?" Evelyn inquired.

"Oh, it is just the usual sort of thing, Evelyn," I replied, shooting Gertrude a look of reproof. "I had intended to tell you all about it at a later time; but since the subject has been introduced, I may as well begin now."

The narrative served at least to distract Evelyn from her expectation of seeing her husband come crashing to the ground. I did not go into detail since I expected I would have to repeat the story later to Walter, and since Ramses would undoubtedly want to give his own, embellished version.

"Quite the usual sort of thing," Evelyn said with a smile, when I had finished. "Poor Miss Marmaduke! I hope you don't blame her for being nervous, Amelia; it takes a while to become accustomed to your way of life."

"I certainly didn't mean to frighten *you*," Gertrude said earnestly. "You and your husband can be in no danger. It is Nefret I am concerned about. Won't you let her come with me, Mrs. Emerson? She could share my room and I promise I would watch over her every moment."

The very idea that Gertrude could guard the girl more effectively than we could was preposterous. She must think me a fool to propose such a scheme, and I hated to think of the language Nefret would use should I propose it to *her*.

"You alarm me, Miss Marmaduke," Evelyn exclaimed. "Why do you believe Nefret is in greater danger than the others? Ramses—"

"He is not a girl," said Gertrude, looking so prim and pious that I could not help laughing.

"That is undeniable. What are you trying to say, Gertrude?"

Her eyes fell and a deep blush suffused her face; but she spoke out stoutly. "My first impression, that terrible night, was that the man had entered her room in order to . . . to . . ."

"Ravish her?" I inquired. "I hardly think so. That particular crime is almost unknown in Egypt, and only a madman would attack a foreign female—much less a female under the protection of the Father of Curses."

"Perhaps you are right," Gertrude murmured. "But you cannot blame me for fearing the worst. The sight of the poor child, her garment torn, her terror so great that she flew at me when I attempted to reassure her . . ."

A shudder ran through her. I said impatiently, "Yes, Gertrude, I have heard your explanation. Enough; I don't want to spoil this joyful reunion with depressing conversation. Suppose we . . . Ah, but there are the men, returning. Walter is safe and sound, you see."

Safe he was, but not entirely sound; his hands were scraped, his face brightly flushed, his garments ripped and soaked with perspiration. However, when I proposed that we return at once to the dahabeeyah he looked at me in astonishment.

"Now? Out of the question. The men have found decorated fragments! They are lowering the basket now. Inscriptions, my dear Amelia, inscriptions! I distinctly saw hieroglyphic writing!"

He pulled away from Evelyn and went limping off toward Emerson, who was supervising the descent of the precious basket. I looked at Sir Edward, who had followed Walter at a discreet distance. Smoothing his damp hair, he said with his engaging smile, "I have been privileged to witness a professional discussion between two of the greatest experts in the field. There is certainly writing on one of the pieces. The Professor will want photographs, I expect; please excuse me."

"There is no use trying to get Walter away now," I said to Evelyn, who was murmuring distressfully. "Let us go to the dahabeeyah, you and I. The others can follow." Lowering my voice, I added, "I must talk to you in private."

I announced our departure to Emerson, who replied with an abstracted grunt. Ramses was in the thick of the crowd as usual, trying to get a look at the fragments before his uncle could do so. Drawing him aside I told him to find Nefret and stay with her.

"She is with David," Ramses said. "I trust you are not implying he—"

"I am not implying anything, I am giving you an order. Don't let her out of your sight. And don't ask me why. And try not to annoy her any more than you can help."

Ramses folded his arms and raised his eyebrows. "Is there anything else, Mother?"

"Probably. But I can't think what at this moment."

He escorted us to the donkeys. Nefret and David were sitting on the ground a short distance away. Her bright head and David's black were close together, bent over something David was holding. It appeared to be a notebook resembling the ones Ramses used.

"What are they doing?" I asked, as Ramses helped his aunt to mount.

"We are teaching him to read," Ramses said.

"English? He can't even speak the language!"

"He is learning it," said Ramses. "Do you object, Mother?"

"No, I suppose not. Tell Nefret . . . I had better tell her myself. Put on your hat, Nefret!"

"She does not like taking orders from Ramses," Evelyn said with a smile, as the donkeys trotted off.

"You noticed that, did you?"

"I was glad to see it, Amelia. When she first came to us she was so meek and obedient I feared she would allow Ramses to bully her—with the best of intentions, naturally. She has gained more confidence now and her natural strength of character has emerged."

"I hadn't thought of it quite that way," I admitted. "You reassure me, Evelyn, as you always do. Their constant quarreling tries my nerves, but that state of affairs is certainly preferable to Ramses's initial infatuation. He was so bedazzled he could hardly pronounce her name."

"He was only a little boy," Evelyn replied tolerantly. "I felt certain your worries on that score were unnecessary. After all, there is nothing like continued proximity to strip away the veils of romance."

It was a surprisingly cynical statement from that source. I decided not to pursue it.

"But what was it you wanted to tell me, Amelia?" Evelyn asked. "Are we private enough now?"

I slowed my mount to a walk, allowing Selim, who had escorted us, to draw ahead. "Yes, and we may not have another such opportunity in the immediate future. This is between ourselves, Evelyn. I don't want Emerson or Walter—and certainly not Ramses—to know what I am planning."

By the time we reached the *Amelia* I had explained my intention and the reasons for it. Evelyn's gentle countenance reflected a variety of emotions, but her only comment, as I had anticipated, was an assurance that she would do precisely as I asked.

We hastened, therefore, directly to the chamber Gertrude occupied. The door was not locked; there were bars on the insides of the doors but no way of securing them from the outside, and, under ordinary circumstances, no need to do so.

It was the first time since her illness that I had entered Gertrude's room. It was certainly a good deal neater than it had been. She had packed her belongings except for toilet articles and a change of clothing; two cases stood at the foot of the bed.

"What a nuisance!" I exclaimed. "I suppose she has locked them; look through the dresser drawers for her keys, Evelyn. I don't suppose she left them here, but I would rather not pick the locks unless I must."

Evelyn complied, though with visible reluctance. The task violated all her principles—and, I hardly need say, my own. However, I never allow my principles to interfere with common sense.

"Nothing," she reported, closing the drawer with her fingertips.

Expecting this, I had already extracted two hairpins from the knot at the nape of my neck. Ever since a certain memorable occasion when I had found myself with no more formidable weapon than those hairpins, I had made a point of selecting the longest and stiffest available. One had to take care when jabbing them into a chignon or braided coronet, since they did not bend at all, but the other advantages far outweighed that little difficulty.

Evelyn stood by, glancing from me to the door. "How long—"

"I have no idea, my dear," I replied. "Curse it! This is proving more difficult than I had expected. I ought to have asked Ramses to give me a lesson."

"Perhaps," Evelyn said timidly, "you might allow me to try."

I sat back on my heels and stared at her in surprise. Blushing, she continued, "Ramses always enjoys showing me his new skills. No, dear Amelia, I do not know how he acquired this one and I thought it wiser not to ask."

I handed her the hairpins, and watched interestedly as she deftly opened the locks.

She left the task of searching the cases to me. I carefully inspected each garment in turn. Searching a case or drawer without leaving evidence of that activity takes a certain knack—and a good deal of time.

"What are you looking for?" Evelyn asked.

"I have not the least idea. But I am sure I will recognize it when I see it."

I emptied and repacked one case without finding anything out of the way except a remarkable and voluminous garment of thin crimson silk embroidered with ancient Egyptian symbols. My understanding of human psychology reminded me that people who are shy and modest in public often indulge in romantic fantasies when alone. The robe was not evidence of guilt, nor were the books on Eastern religion. I had already deduced from her conversation that she had a leaning toward esoteric philosophies.

"Hurry," Evelyn begged.

"I am making as much haste as I dare, Evelyn. Lock the first case again, will you please, while I examine the second?"

The second case contained a number of interesting items, including the source of the strange scent—sticks of incense and a bronze holder for them. Most informative of all was a slim volume wrapped reverently in a square of gold velvet.

"Well!" I exclaimed. "This explains a number of things, including those questions on Egyptian religion Emerson enjoyed answering so much. The confounded woman is a Theosophist, Evelyn! This is a copy of *Isis Unveiled*, by Madame Blavatsky, the founder of the Theosophical Society."

"Is it a secret society, Amelia?" Evelyn inquired hopefully.

"I am afraid not, my dear. It is a perfectly harmless if fuzzy-minded blend of Indian philosophy and occultism. Dear me, what a disappointment. Perhaps Miss Marmaduke is innocent after all—of everything except gullibility."

"Are you satisfied, Amelia?" Evelyn asked uneasily. "They will be returning shortly, and it would be very embarrassing to be caught."

"My dear, we will have ample warning. Emerson's ordinary speaking voice is audible at a considerable distance, not to mention the shouts that will probably herald his arrival."

Knowing this to be true I was not at all worried about being caught red-handed, and I completed the search without haste and without result.

"Curse it," I exclaimed. "She must be guilty; no innocent person can lead a life so free of harmless vice! No love letters, no bottles of liquor, not even a hidden box of chocolates. But I suppose some would consider a belief in the occult to be a vice, of an intellectual nature at least."

I subjected the room to an intense visual survey. I had overlooked nothing; every inch had been inspected. Except . . .

I snatched up the pair of boots that stood at the foot of the bed, turned them upside down and shook them vigorously. Had it not been for the shaking, the little cardboard box would have gone undiscovered. It had been wedged into the narrowest part of the toe.

I untied the string and removed the top. Cotton wool filled the box and told me I must proceed gently; a gleam of gold gave me a premonition of what I would find. It was the ring I had first seen on the finger of Mr. Shelmadine—the jewel bearing the cartouche of Queen Tetisheri, which had disappeared from our sitting room on the night he vanished from mortal ken.

After luncheon, which was served on the upper deck, we dispersed. Emerson, of course, went back to the tomb, taking Sir Edward and the children with him. Since Gertrude had finished her packing, I accompanied her and the younger Emersons across to Luxor so that the exchange of accommodations could be made and some necessary shopping completed.

There had been no opportunity for Evelyn and me to discuss the astonishing discovery of the ring. Warned by Emerson's hail, we had barely time to conceal the evidences of our visit and beat a hasty retreat. When Gertrude joined us on the deck she had changed her clothing and was wearing the boots. If she had noticed anything amiss she showed no signs of it. I wondered what she had done with the ring. She could not be wearing it on a chain around her neck; I would have observed the bulge.

When we reached the hotel I went with her to her room to study the arrangements, in case I wanted, on some future occasion, to drop in uninvited. It was quite satisfactory—on the second floor, with a small balcony and a most convenient vine not far from it.

Gertrude was kind enough to approve of the accommodations, but seemed reluctant to let me go.

"Don't you want me to return with you and resume the children's lessons? It has been almost a week since—"

"They will not be in a fit state of mind to concentrate on English literature this evening," I said impatiently. "Discipline is one thing, Gertrude, unreasonable expectation is quite another. I will send someone to fetch you tomorrow morning, or perhaps you could accompany Sir Edward. That would probably be best. He will notify you of the time and place when he returns this evening."

She looked as if she would have objected, though I could not imagine to what—being forced to share a boat, unchaperoned, with a personable young man? Bidding her good afternoon, I left.

Shopping took hardly any time, since the shops of Luxor offer little to the traveler except antiquities, spurious and genuine. The most sensible course of action would have been for Walter to return to Cairo, where European goods are readily available, but this he stubbornly refused to do, so in the end I was forced to telegraph and hope that my friend Mrs. Wilson would be able to approximate Walter's sizes in trousers and boots.

When we returned to the dinghy with our few purchases, the sun hung low over the western cliffs and sunset colors spread across the rippling water. I looked forward to the moment when I could dismiss Walter—for a bath, a rest, anything—and converse privately with Evelyn, but it was not to be. The others arrived from the dig at the same time we reached the *Amelia*.

Hat in hand, Sir Edward drew me aside. He had got in the habit of dining with us; now he announced his intention of returning at once to the hotel. "You will want to be en famille this evening, Mrs. Emerson. Don't go to the trouble of sending the dinghy for me tomorrow, I will just take the ferry and go straight to the excavation."

It was a graceful, gentlemanly gesture, and I said as much. "Perhaps you would not mind bringing Miss Marmaduke with you tomorrow, Sir Edward."

"Not at all. I might—with your permission, of course—ask her to have dinner with me this evening. She seems very shy and timid; perhaps I can reassure her."

I was about to reply when Emerson emerged from the corridor leading to the cabins. "Amelia! What the devil are you doing? I am waiting for you."

Sir Edward removed himself and I attempted to calm Emerson by reporting the conversation.

"Hmph," said Emerson, leading me to our room. "So he has turned his attentions to Miss Marmaduke, has he?"

"Would that were the case, Emerson."

"Why, Peabody, you shock me!" His good humor restored, Emerson knelt and began to unlace my boots. (He is given to such boyishly sentimental gestures in private.) "Surely you wouldn't turn a worldly libertine like Sir Edward loose on a timid spinster."

"If she were a timid spinster, such an experience would do her a world of good." Emerson chuckled, and I went on, "But Miss Marmaduke is not what she seems, Emerson. I am not certain whether that dinner will be a conference between co-conspirators or a fencing match between rivals, but it was clever of him to make the suggestion openly, for most people would take it as you just did."

"He is a clever fellow," Emerson agreed. "But not, perhaps, as diabolically clever as you believe. We may be imagining enemies where none exist, Peabody. And now that we have found the tomb, even Riccetti may have given up."

"Are you suggesting that we refrain from telling Evelyn and Walter about the earlier attacks, the mysterious circumstances, the—"

"Yes, curse it, I am. Why alarm them unnecessarily?"

He took my bare feet into his big brown hands and looked up at me with a smile.

"Had I believed concern was unnecessary I would not have told Evelyn," I said.

Emerson unceremoniously let go my feet and rose. "I might have known. All right, Peabody, you got in ahead of me, as usual, and I suppose Ramses has been talking too. I sometimes wonder what it would be like to be the respected patriarch of an ordinary English family."

"Very boring, Emerson."

Emerson's scowl turned to a reluctant grin. "Right again, Peabody. Come up to the saloon when you have changed, I will have the whiskey ready."

We had our whiskey, Walter and Emerson and I; Ramses demanded his share—"By the laws of Islam, Judaism and several Nubian tribes, I will soon be a man, Father"—but it was a rather mechanical performance, since he did not expect the speech would have any more effect on this occasion than it had had previously. Night had fallen; stars glimmered in the dark depths of heaven, the breeze carried the soft sounds of lapping water and the mystical aroma of Egypt.

I was beginning to regret having been so quick to take Evelyn into my confidence. She looked very frail and ridiculously youthful that evening, her fair hair falling loose over her shoulders, held only by a scarf. Walter was in worse case, his face scorched by the sun and his movements as stiff as those of a rheumaticky old gentleman. A few weeks of ordinary archaeological activity would toughen him and do him good, but our archaeological activities were seldom ordinary, and this year's dig promised to be even more perilous. I could only pray that our well-meant attempt to assist our dear ones had not endangered their lives.

Not while we are on the job, I told myself, with an affectionate glance at Emerson's resolute profile and stalwart frame. I dismissed my forebodings and addressed Walter.

"Loath though I am to cast a shadow over this joyful meeting,

Walter, I must warn you and Evelyn of what has happened. It is a rather long story—"

Smiling, Walter interrupted me. "I daresay yours would not be as lengthy as was Ramses's version. No doubt, dear sister, your interpretation of those events differs from his, but you need not repeat the facts themselves."

"Amelia's interpretations generally differ from everybody's else's," Emerson said. "In the beginning, I admit, we were the subject of certain—er—attentions. All of them were designed to prevent us from locating the tomb. Now that we have found it there is no reason for those attentions to continue."

He took out his pipe, with the air of a man who has said the last word and does not intend to permit discussion.

Ramses cleared his throat. "With respect, Father, that hypothesis fails to explain certain of the—er—attentions. The most curious of them was the visit of Mr. Shelmadine and his subsequent disappearance. He must have known his hints of ancient cults and reincarnation would enrage rather than persuade you, and if the ring was not genuine, he went to a great deal of expense and trouble to have it made."

Evelyn gave me a questioning glance. I shook my head. This was not the moment to mention our recent discovery. I intended to save it for the final stroke that would demolish Emerson's skepticism and force him to admit I had been right all along.

"He was a madman," Emerson said shortly. "Egyptology inspires lunatic theories."

"True," Walter agreed. "But it is something of a coincidence, isn't it, that the fellow should turn up with that particular lunatic theory shortly after you had decided to search for that particular tomb?"

Emerson was beginning to lose his temper. Quickened breathing prevented him from speaking in time to prevent me from anticipating him.

"It is the other way round, Walter," I explained. "Emerson did intend to work at the Seventeenth Dynasty cemetery, but it was not until after Mr. Shelmadine's visit that he began to fit the other clues into place. Now, Emerson, don't deny it; you said it yourself. 'Someone has found Tetisheri's tomb. It is the only hypothesis that accounts for all this agitated activity.'"

"No sensible hypothesis accounts for Shelmadine," Emerson said furiously. "His visit was a coincidence."

"And his death was another coincidence?" I said. "The body has been identified, Emerson."

Emerson drew a long, shaken breath. "And how do you know that, Amelia? Confound it, have you been in communication with the Cairo police? How did you—"

"As you know, my dear, Sir Eldon Gorst is an old friend. He responded to my telegram a few days ago. Shelmadine was identified by . . ."

I paused. I do not often tease my dear Emerson, but this time the temptation was irresistible.

"Well?" he demanded. "Don't be so cursed theatrical, Amelia. I suppose it was the ring."

"No, my dear. I was about to say, by a female individual who recognized certain—er—physical characteristics. The ring was not on Mr. Shelmadine's person. It is now in the possession of Miss Marmaduke."

The theatrical profession has always interested me. I had employed certain theatrical techniques in building up to my announcement—delay, misdirection and finally the use of what is, I believe, termed a "throw-it-away" line—and the effect was all I could have desired. The entire company was struck dumb and motionless with astonishment. Even Evelyn looked surprised, not at the news, but at my method of delivering it, and, perhaps, at its effect on Emerson. The blood rushed into his face, and from his parted lips came a series of gasping wheezes.

"It is true," Evelyn exclaimed. "We found it in Miss Marmaduke's room, in a boot. Oh, dear. Take a glass of water, Radcliffe, please."

Emerson waved it away. "You—you two—you searched . . . Good Gad!"

"It was necessary, Emerson," I assured him. "Do you suppose I would have committed such a flagrant breach of good manners unless I had felt I must?"

The flush of fury faded from Emerson's cheeks. His lips

twitched. "A hit, Peabody, a palpable hit," he said. "And very neatly done, too."

"Then you concede, Emerson?"

"I owe you one for that," Emerson muttered. "I will be damned if I will concede anything, Peabody, until I know precisely what I am conceding."

"You are only making one of your little jokes, Professor," said Nefret. "You know as well as I do what the ring means. Miss Marmaduke is a spy and a member of the gang who murdered Mr. Shelmadine! He may have been a lunatic, but he was not harmless. He was killed in order to prevent him from giving you information his rivals did not want you to have."

Ramses cleared his throat. "There is another explanation which—"

"Ramses," I began ominously.

". . . which I am sure must have occurred to Mother and which she refrained from mentioning only because she was teasing you a little, Father, and was waiting for you to propose it yourself."

"Propose it," said Emerson, glancing at me.

"Yes, sir. I am sure you suspected from Miss Marmaduke's remarks one evening at dinner that she might be a follower of Madame Blavatsky and the Theosophists. Her reactions to the subjects I proceeded to introduce confirmed that impression. The mystical Hebrew book called *The Kabbalah* and the beliefs of certain Hindu sects are part of the philosophical foundations of Theosophy."

"We have already established that she is a believer, Ramses," I said impatiently.

"Ah," said Ramses, "but—as you are of course aware—another essential tenet of that dogma is the belief in reincarnation. 'This life' is only one of many, and an individual's behavior in this incarnation affects future lives. It is surely more than a coincidence that the man who visited you in Cairo claimed to be the reincarnation of an ancient Egyptian priest. We cannot be certain that the ring Mother found was the same one Mr. Shelmadine showed her. There may be two or more of them, insignia worn by members of a secret Theosophical society. If that is the case, Marmaduke and Shelmadine would have been acquainted, but not necessarily for criminal purposes. As yet," Ramses finished, "there is not enough evidence to substantiate this hypothesis, but it is as reasonable as any other, as I am sure you would all agree."

Emerson returned his gaze to me. We looked into one another's eyes. Our lips parted. We spoke as one.

"I was about to propose that hypothesis myself."

"It was on the tip of my tongue."

"It wasn't on mine," Nefret admitted. "But it is plausible, and it is substantiated by Signor Riccetti's statement that there are those who would aid us if they could. If the Theosophists are as harmless and high-minded as Ramses says they are—"

"High-minded individuals are much more dangerous than criminals," Emerson growled. "They can always find hypocritical excuses for committing acts of violence."

He had the last word. The servants began serving dinner; some of them understood English and it seemed advisable to drop the subject.

Except for confirming my story, Evelyn had said very little. I was anxious to hear her theories, for I had come to have considerable respect for her ability at ratiocination. However, it had been a long hard day for her and Walter, and I decided they had better go directly to bed after we finished our coffee. As Evelyn followed her limping spouse toward their room I presented her with a bottle of liniment.

"It is obvious from the way he moves that Walter has not been on horseback for months, Evelyn. He will be stiff as a mummy tomorrow morning if you don't use this. Rub it in well, especially on the—er—lower limbs."

She thanked me and bade me good night.

The room was rather small and the bed was narrow. But I pinned my hopes on the liniment.

CHAPTER NINE

Buried Alive!

The sun had just lifted over the horizon when I departed from our room, leaving Emerson attempting to conquer his habitual early-morning confusion by dashing cold water onto himself and the floor. As I strode briskly toward the upper deck I passed the saloon and saw, to my surprise, that Walter was there before me.

A smile warmed his face as he rose. "I hope you don't mind my looking at your work, Amelia. It was an impertinence, I know, but I could not resist when I saw you were translating Apophis and Sekenenre."

"Of course I don't mind." What I did mind was that he was up so early. That augured poorly for the reconciliation I had hoped for, and his expression, though affable as always, lacked the indefinable but (to my trained eye) unmistakable signs that (in my experience) follow such an activity.

"I have been forced to neglect my translation these past days,"

I continued, concealing my disappointment. "It is a curious text, isn't it?"

"You mean to supply an ending, as you have done with your other Egyptian fairy tales?"

"I had hoped to, yes, but I confess I cannot think of a logical ending. The text is far from complete and the implication of the Hyksos king's message eludes me. It is obviously a deadly insult—but why? Oh, of course the arrogant demand is that of a monarch to an inferior, but there is more to it than that, surely. And why are Sekenenre and his courtiers at a loss as to how to reply?"

"There may well be some obscure religious meaning," Walter agreed. "As you know, my dear sister, Egyptian religion is wonderfully inconsistent, and an animal like the hippopotamus could be good or evil—the benevolent goddess of childbirth in one aspect, the deadly enemy of the sun-god Re in another. Set, the murderer of Osiris, took the form of that animal when he fought Osiris's son Horus in the famous tale of 'The Hunt for the Red Hippopotamus.' The Hyksos were considered to be worshipers of Set—but that," Walter said, shaking his head, "only makes the situation more mysterious. Why should the Hyksos king demand the slaughter of the animal that represented his god?"

"Walter, I believe you have given me a clue," I exclaimed. "You are attempting to employ modern Western logic. It is necessary to put oneself into the illogical minds of the ancient Egyptians."

"No one can do that better than you, my dear sister."

Before I could reply to this graceful compliment, Emerson came bursting into the saloon. "We are late," he declared accusingly. "Where is everyone?"

"On the upper deck, I expect," I replied, rising. "We always breakfast there, as you know perfectly well."

Nefret and Ramses were already eating, for we never stood on ceremony at that first meal of the day. I was pouring when Evelyn joined us. I managed to catch the pot before much tea had spilled.

"Good gracious," Walter exclaimed, staring at his wife. "When did you acquire that—er—ensemble, my dear? I have never seen you wear it."

"Men never remember women's clothing," Evelyn said, taking the chair Ramses held for her.

"I don't believe I could have forgotten that!"

I did not believe he could have either. It was a copy of the working costume I had worn before I took the daring leap to breeches and coat like those of a man. Evelyn's Turkish trousers were even more voluminous than mine had been, and a brilliant blue in color. Her boots, reaching to the knee, had obviously never been worn.

"I don't know why you are wasting time talking about my wardrobe, Walter," Evelyn said coolly. "We should return to the topic we were discussing last night."

Emerson—who had, of course, observed nothing unusual in Evelyn's appearance—banged his cup into the saucer. "I have no intention of returning to it. Must I remind you that this is an archaeological expedition? The task before us is a formidable one, and we are still short-handed."

"Radcliffe, you know we are at your disposal," Walter said. "Tell us what needs to be done."

Emerson pushed his cup away and put his elbows on the table. "The tomb is unquestionably that of Tetisheri. But the paintings are . . . in short, they are not what I had expected. The answers to the questions that have arisen in my mind may come to light when we finish clearing the entrance corridor."

He paused to fill his pipe, and Ramses took advantage of his temporary silence to remark, "So little remains of the decoration of that corridor that I suspect it was deliberately destroyed."

"What?" Walter exclaimed. "How did you arrive at that conclusion?"

"A futile question, my dear Walter," I said, with a sigh. "Or rather, please don't ask him, because he will tell you, at considerable length. I suppose the paintings were on plaster, which has become detached from the rock to which it was applied, and fallen to the floor of the corridor. The inscribed fragments the men found yesterday were part of the decoration. Confound it, Emerson, I ought to be accustomed to your infuriating reticence, but why have you been so closemouthed about this? You must have come across other fragments earlier, or you would not have been sifting that rubble so carefully."

"Habit, I suppose," Emerson replied, looking a trifle shamefaced. "The truth is, I found only a few scraps, none larger than ten centimeters across. Most of it has probably been ground to powder, but I am hoping to find more pieces at floor level."

"So that is why you have been working so slowly." Admiration overcame Walter's annoyance. "Any other excavator would have missed that evidence, Radcliffe."

"It may not be important evidence," Emerson admitted. "But one never knows." Taking out his watch he glanced at it and sprang to his feet with a grunt of annoyance. "If you have all finished interrogating me, perhaps you will allow me to get to it."

Moving at a brisk trot, I was able to catch him up before he reached the gangplank. "Are there any other little secrets you have kept from me?" I inquired.

He glanced at me from under lowering brows. "Oh, you have become interested in the tomb, have you? I beg you won't give over playing detective on my account; far be it from me to distract you from the pleasure of searching people's rooms and engaging in pointless speculation about spies and criminal gangs."

I said, "It is odd, isn't it, that we have seen nothing more of Signor Riccetti? No doubt he is lurking in concealment, directing his—"

My breath went out in an explosive gasp as Emerson threw his arms around me and squeezed. "You are hopeless, Peabody! Speculate all you like, search every room in Luxor—only promise your long-suffering spouse that you will refrain from taking foolish chances. No following suspects into dark alleyways, no breaking into Riccetti's secret headquarters—"

"Oh, has he a secret headquarters? In Luxor?"

Trying to frown and trying not to laugh, Emerson silenced me with an emphatic kiss. "Promise, Peabody."

"Emerson, the others are watching. The children—"

"Promise!"

"Certainly, Emerson."

Calmly and decisively Emerson kissed me again. "Nothing wrong with setting a good example," he remarked, glancing at our audience, which included not only our family but Selim and Yussuf. He then lifted me onto my horse and mounted his.

If he had bothered to look at Nefret he might have had second thoughts about setting examples. It was not so much the curve of her lips as a certain dreamy expression in her eyes.

It took us three more days to finish clearing the entrance corridor. Emerson's extraordinary patience was rewarded; on the floor next to the walls, lying where they had fallen over three millennia ago, were approximately fifty fragments of painted relief. It was necessary to plot their location precisely, since that might give a clue as to their original positions on the wall. One by one the fragments, some as small as a fingernail, were lifted and placed into padded, labeled trays. Accustomed as I was to the delicacy of Emerson's touch, I marveled at how deftly those big brown hands of his handled the fragile scraps.

What blissful days they were! Squatting in the dust, backs bent over our labors—enjoying occasional encounters with fretful bats—rubbing eyes reddened with dust . . . I enjoyed every moment of it and Emerson was happy as only a man can be when engaged in the labor at which he excels. We were all kept busy; each fragment had to be photographed (Sir Edward) and copied (Evelyn and Nefret) and recorded (Miss Marmaduke). Walter, assisted by Ramses (at the latter's insistence), began fitting the fragments together. It was a frustrating task—like, as Walter remarked, trying to put together a jigsaw puzzle when most of the pieces are missing.

In the pleasure of professional activity, the companionship of those dearest to us, and the complete absence of attack, assault, or violence, I almost forgot my forebodings; when they recurred to me I began to wonder whether Emerson might not have been right after all. (It had never happened before, but there is always a first time.)

The first "distraction," as he bitingly termed it, occurred when we returned to the dahabeeyah on the evening of the third day. Mahmud our steward was waiting for us. "The parcels from Cairo have come, Sitt."

"Excellent," I said. "It must be the boots and clothing you ordered, Walter. Just in time, too, your shoes would not have lasted another day."

"The gentleman is in the saloon, Sitt," said Mahmud.

"What gentleman?"

"The gentleman who brought the parcels." Mahmud's smile faded. "He said he was a friend, Sitt. I hope I did not do wrong."

"Petrie or Quibell, I expect," Emerson grumbled. "Or Sayce or Vandergelt or some other inquisitive Egyptologist. Curse it, I knew they would turn up sooner or later, spouting questions and trying to worm their way into MY excavation."

He started for the saloon, and of course we all followed, curious to know who the visitor might be. I had my own ideas on that subject, and hurried to catch Emerson up. I did not quite succeed, but I was close on his heels when he entered the room. Too close. His roar almost deafened me.

"O'Connell! Damnation! What the devil are you doing here?"

Seeing me, Kevin, who had retreated behind the table, felt it safe to come forward. His nationality was writ plain upon his face: eyes blue as the lakes of Ireland, face as freckled as a plover's egg, hair bright as the rim of the setting sun. "Why, Professor, you don't suppose *The Daily Yell* would overlook a story like this? And whom should they send but their star reporter, eh? Good day to you, Mrs. Emerson, me dear. Blooming as ever, I see."

I squeezed past Emerson, who stood rigid with indignation in the doorway. If Kevin O'Connell was not the "star" reporter of London's most sensational newspaper, he certainly could be considered an authority on archaeological subjects and on the activities of the Emerson family. Our past encounters had not all been pleasant, but the brash young journalist had come to my aid often enough to leave me with relatively kindly feelings toward him. Emerson's feelings were not at all kindly. He had good cause to detest Kevin in particular and journalists in general. Their reports of his activities had made him, if not precisely notorious, only too well known to the reading public. (And it must be admitted that Emerson's hasty temper and rash pronouncements made for very entertaining copy.)

"Good evening, Kevin," I said. "What took you so long? I expected you yesterday."

"Bedad, but I'm twenty-four hours ahead of the *Mirror*," Kevin protested. "And a good two days in advance of the *Times*. Ah, but is it more friends I see? Mr. and Mrs. Walter Emerson! I had hoped to catch you up, but you were too quick for me. Master Ramses—what a fine, great lad you've become! And Miss Nefret—sure and it's a pleasure to the eyes you are."

Evelyn advanced toward him. "Mr. O'Connell, isn't it? I am glad to be able to thank you for the beautiful letter you wrote after—after the loss of our child. Your expressions of sympathy were so gracefully and touchingly expressed."

Kevin's face turned a shade of pink that clashed dreadfully with his red hair. Avoiding my astonished gaze, he shuffled his feet and mumbled something unintelligible.

"Hmph," said Emerson, in a milder tone. "Well, well, I suppose you may as well sit down, O'Connell. But don't think—"

"Oh, no, sir, I never think." Recovering from his embarrassment at being discovered to have the instincts of a gentleman, Kevin gave Emerson a cheeky grin. "I would not have intruded on you, only I happened to run into Mrs. Wilson in Cairo, and when she told me she had some parcels for you I offered to bring them, since I was leaving that evening; and once here, it was impossible for me to tear myself away without—"

"Yes, quite," I said. "Thank you, Kevin. We must excuse ourselves for a while, but stay and dine, unless you have another engagement. No? I rather thought you would not. Take a chair. I will send Mahmud with refreshments."

I wanted to get back to Kevin as quickly as possible, so instead of bathing I contented myself with a quick splash in the basin and a change of clothing. Following me at the washstand, Emerson grumbled, "You needn't have invited him to dinner, Amelia. We cannot talk freely with a cursed journalist present."

"Sir Edward and Miss Marmaduke are joining us, and we dare not speak freely while they are present anyhow. It is time we decided how to deal with the press, Emerson. You must have known that your public references to a royal tomb would attract considerable interest."

Stripped to the waist and dripping, Emerson reached for a towel. "I have already dealt with members of the press. I mean to go on in the same way."

"You cannot intimidate the English and European newspapers as you did that poor young man from Cairo."

"I never laid a finger on the fellow, Peabody."

"You *roared* at him, Emerson."

"I have never heard that there is any law against—er—talking in a loud voice." Emerson dropped the towel onto the floor and gave me a critical examination. "Are you proposing to appear in public in a negligee, Peabody? That garment—"

"Is my new tea gown, Emerson. Aren't you going to dress for dinner? Sir Edward will be in evening kit."

"No, he won't. I told him I never wanted to see him in that suit again." Emerson reached for a clean shirt. "I must warn him and Miss Marmaduke not to volunteer any information about our work. That applies to you as well, Amelia. I will do the talking. Now get to the saloon and watch O'Connell. He is probably searching my desk."

Emerson was clearly in one of his masterful moods. I always allow him to enjoy them unless I feel it is necessary to set him straight, which, on this occasion, it was not. So I said submissively, "Yes, my dear," and was rewarded by a pleased smile.

Kevin did not even have the decency to pretend he had not been snooping. Rising from my desk as I entered the saloon, he said garrulously, "What a fetching frock, Mrs. E. As always, you are a vision of loveliness. Is this your latest exercise in translating Egyptian? If you will permit me to say so, it lacks the charm of some of your earlier efforts. What is the point of the hippopotamus pool?"

"You will have to wait for the story to be published," I said.

Kevin cocked his head and gave me his leprechaun grin and an even more exaggerated brogue. "Och, must I? As one who has known and admired you for many years, I have not failed to note that several of your earlier translations had a peculiar relevance to the activities you were pursuing at the time. Your highly developed instincts for crime seem well-nigh supernatural. What are you up to this time, Mrs. E.? And what do hippos have to do with it?"

"Really, Kevin, you cannot suppose I am going to succumb to your flagrant flattery and unsubtle questions. I am not up to anything, and there are no longer any hippopotami in Egypt."

Expert at dissimulation that I am, my response gave no hint of the disquiet his seemingly casual question had aroused. What he had said was true. On at least two earlier occasions, the fairy tale I had been translating at the time had proved uncannily relevant to the events that transpired. Was this another such case? And, if so, what the devil *was* the point of the hippopotami?

I led him to the upper deck. The others soon joined us, except for Emerson, who was lurking below with the intention of intercepting Sir Edward and Miss Marmaduke. Darkness had fallen by the time they appeared. As he had been ordered, Sir Edward wore well-cut tweeds and a regimental tie. Gertrude's hair was coming down—obviously she had neglected to cover it with a scarf while on the river, as I had suggested—and she kept poking at it. She looked even more apprehensive than usual. I wondered what Emerson had said to her.

The sight of a female brought O'Connell to his feet, Hibernian flattery bubbling from his lips. Watching him escort Gertrude to a chair, I hoped he was not going to fancy himself attracted to her. She lacked the personal charms that fascinate a man, but Kevin always likes to be in love with someone. I suppose it is because he is Irish.

Conscious of Emerson's warning, we tried to avoid the subject of the tomb. However, there was no keeping away from it, since it was the major interest of all present. Sir Edward was the first to refer to it—or perhaps the culprit was Nefret. She had not had much opportunity to practice her wiles on him, since he had taken pains to avoid her; that evening, with O'Connell cooing compliments at Miss Marmaduke, and Emerson arguing with Walter about the Berlin Dictionary, and Evelyn occupied with Ramses, he had apparently felt it was safe to join her on the settee. In a lull in the general conversation I heard her say, "Then you believe your new camera can do the job?"

Kevin's head turned like that of a dog snapping at a bone. Sir Edward raised an inquiring eyebrow and looked at Emerson. A shrug and a nod gave him permission to reply, and, returning his attention to Nefret, he said, "It will require a long exposure, but I have had good results from the new film Kodak developed last year."

"Then you'll be photographing the interior of the tomb tomorrow?" Kevin inquired guilelessly.

Emerson glowered at him. "Yes. I'll give you that much, O'Connell, since you will probably find out anyhow, but don't ask to have a look for yourself. No amateur is entering that tomb until it has been cleared."

"So long as you don't let the *Mirror* in ahead of me," Kevin murmured. "Would you care to speculate, Professor, as to what you will find? Is the royal lady resting quiet in her coffin, bedecked with jewels and magical amulets?"

Mahmud's arrival, to announce that dinner was ready in the saloon, saved Emerson for the moment, but Kevin was not to be so easily distracted. Throughout the meal he peppered Emerson with questions. I believe it had not occurred to Emerson until then that his impulsive reference to an "undisturbed royal tomb" would arouse such intense interest. The London newspapers reporting the discovery had not yet reached us, and Emerson's eyebrows wriggled alarmingly as Kevin summarized the stories that had appeared in print.

"Headlines in the *Times*?" Emerson repeated in a faltering voice.

"You ought to have expected it," I remarked. "And you owe it to yourself to correct the—er—misapprehensions of the press. In justice to yourself, my dear."

"Hmph," said Emerson, giving me a very thoughtful look. There was no need for me to elaborate; Emerson is sometimes hasty, but he is not stupid. Exaggerated claims that proved to be unfounded would damage his scholarly reputation, and we now had reason to suspect the tomb had been disturbed. What an anticlimax it would be if the mummy were found stripped of its jewels!

So Kevin got more information than he had expected, though less than he had hoped. Emerson firmly refused to speculate and refused to go into detail. Still, it was enough to give Kevin a "scoop," as I believe it is called, and he made no objection when Emerson announced that it was time for our guests to leave. (I have often pointed out the rudeness of this, without the slightest effect.)

"May I beg a ride back to Luxor with me new friends?" Kevin inquired, beaming at Miss Marmaduke, who simpered, and at Sir Edward, who responded with a stony stare.

So it was arranged, and as Kevin tenderly escorted Gertrude down the gangplank, Emerson caught Sir Edward by the arm. "I need not remind you," he said, "that the photographs you take while in my employ are not to be sold or shown to anyone without my permission."

The moonlight glimmered in the young man's fair hair and made it possible for me to observe the stiffening of his frame. "No, sir, you need not," he snapped. "Good night, Professor, Mrs. Emerson."

"You have offended him, Emerson," I remarked, watching Sir Edward stalk angrily away.

"Better safe than sorry, Peabody. O'Connell will have made him an offer before they push off."

"I expect you are right, my dear. It was clever of you to think of it."

Pleased by this little compliment, of the sort husbands much appreciate and which I am careful to apply as often as I can, Emerson drew my arm through his and led me to our room. Conversation of a general nature was not resumed until a later hour, at which time I returned to an idea O'Connell's questions had recalled to my mind.

"I know your methods, Emerson, and I am in complete agreement with them, of course; but would it really constitute a violation of those methods to have a look—just a private little peek—into the burial chamber? I am dying of curiosity."

I had chosen my moment well. Emerson was in an extremely affable mood. "I sympathize, my dear, and I am as curious as you are; but it won't be as easy as you think. The debris beyond that door is not fill, like the rock chips in the antechamber; it resulted from a partial collapse of the roof of what appears to be a flight of stairs—leading down, as is commonly the case in such tombs. The modern thieves dug part of it out and shored up their tunnel with sticks and planks—"

"And how do you know that? Oh, Emerson, how could you? You have already investigated that tunnel. And you didn't confide in me!"

Emerson looked a little uncomfortable. "I only had a look, Peabody. Only a few feet, as far as I could reach, holding a candle. I couldn't get into the damned place, it is too narrow for me."

"But not for me. Let me have a go at it."

Embracing me, Emerson expressed his disinclination to permit this, adding, "Your dimensions and those of the tunnel, both familiar to me, are not compatible. You would stick, Peabody, I assure you you would."

"You could pull me out by my feet."

"And risk damage to your—er—your person? Not under any circumstances, my dear Peabody. Ramses might manage it."

"David is thinner than Ramses."

When Emerson failed to respond, I said, "You still harbor reservations about him. That is unjust, Emerson."

"Perhaps. But what has he done to prove his loyalty to us? Twice now Ramses has risked himself to save the boy, from death and from suspicion of a vile crime. Yet David continues to insist he can tell us nothing that would assist us or explain why he is allegedly in danger."

Owing to the press of work, I had not seen much of David for the past few days. He always went with us to the tomb, since I felt he was safer there than alone on the boat, but he kept to himself, avoiding all society except that of Nefret and Ramses. Emerson's remarks had made me more uncomfortable than I liked to admit and I determined to speak with the boy at the earliest opportunity.

I was able to do so on the morning following Mr. O'Connell's arrival. Mohammed had finished building the staircase the previous afternoon, and under Emerson's direction the men set to work putting the structure in place. There was nothing for me to do until they finished, and O'Connell—who had turned up bright and early, notebook poised—was absorbed in watching the procedure, so I sought David out.

There are many unfinished and unexcavated private tomb shafts along the base of the hill. Like an early Christian anchorite, David had chosen one of these as his retreat. He—or Ramses and Nefret—had made it as comfortable as possible, with a piece of matting on the ground, a water jar, and several baskets. David was squatting on the mat, busy at work with hammer and chisel at something he held between his knees. When he saw me approaching he made a sudden movement as if to conceal the object. There was no way of concealing it on his person, however, for it was as large as my joined fists—a sculptured head, in ancient Egyptian style. I could see only the back of it, which appeared to be wearing a headdress of some sort.

"Good morning," I said pleasantly. "I am glad to see you keeping busy, David. Practicing your craft, are you?"

"Good morning, Sitt Hakim," was the unsmiling response. "I hope you are well today? I trust you slept soundly."

The words were pronounced with meticulous care, and the formality of them would have made me smile if I had not feared that would offend the boy. "Thank you, I slept very soundly and I am very well. I hope you are the same. May I see what you are doing?"

He put his tools carefully into a basket and without comment handed the sculpture to me.

The piece was unfinished; the headdress was only roughed in. He had concentrated on the face. It was obviously a portrait of Nefret, for the likeness was unmistakable, but it was also, just as unmistakably, a portrait of someone else. An almost indefinable alteration of certain features strengthened the resemblance I had observed on one other occasion, and the headdress was a crown—the vulture crown worn by Egyptian queens.

David's eye was that of an artist. Was this only an innocent form of flattery, giving his new friend the attributes of the young queen—or had he seen even more clearly than I the coincidental and fleeting resemblance between Nefret and Tetisheri? Harmless, in either case, but it made me uneasy. Shelmadine had rambled on about reincarnation, and it seemed probable that Gertrude was also a believer in that abstruse doctrine. I certainly did not want notions like that entering Nefret's head.

The resemblance and the disquieting thoughts it aroused made my response slow in coming. "It is wonderful, David. Remarkable."

The boy's thin shoulders relaxed. "You are not angry that I do this?"

"On the contrary." I sat down on the ground next to him. "The exercise of a talent such as yours is a duty and a God-given right; only a vandal would attempt to restrain . . ." I broke off, seeing his puzzled expression. "I am not angry. I am very pleased. Only—why did you give her the vulture crown?"

He understood that, but he continued to look puzzled. Finally he said, "I do not know. It was . . ." He waved one thin, expressive hand. "It was the right way."

An artist with a better command of English and a better opinion of himself would have put it more elegantly. I knew what he meant, however.

"I do not waste the time." From another basket he removed a notebook and pencil. "I learn. Do you want I read to you?"

He proceeded to do so, opening the notebook to a page on which I recognized Nefret's neat printing. There were only a few sentences, employing the simplest words, but she had woven them into a little story about a boy who lived in Egypt where the sun was bright and the river was wide.

"Very good," I said. I was beginning to sympathize with the poor mother hen whose one ungainly offspring showed signs of turning into something she had not expected and did not know how to deal with. What would the boy do next—logarithms?

I got to my feet. "I must go back to work, David. I am pleased with you. But don't neglect—do you know that word?—the portrait of Nefret for your studies. It is quite . . . remarkable."

"I will make it well, Sitt Hakim. It is for you."

As I walked away I heard him repeating "re-mark-able," over and over, trying to imitate my inflection.

I decided to wait until the portrait head was finished before I showed it to Emerson. Surely he would be as touched as I had been, and as impressed by the lad's talent. However, Emerson's prejudices were deep-seated. It would require a great deal to convince him David was loyal.

How great we were soon to find out.

It was almost noon before the steps were finally in place. Men always make an unnecessary fuss about carpentry and other simple jobs—in the hope, I suppose, of making women believe those "masculine" chores are more difficult than they really are—but this particular job did present some problems. Affixing the structure firmly to the rock face required heavy steel bolts and a series of supports, and Mohammed had to make a number of final adjustments. After Emerson had stamped up and down the stairs several times to make certain of their solidity, I was given the honor of being the first to make the ascent.

The entrance passageway having been cleared down to floor level, we set to work on the antechamber. The photography took quite a long time, since Emerson wanted views from every conceivable angle and various distances. For light he had been using reflectors—large sheets of tin, angled to catch the rays of the sun and direct them onto the area to be photographed. They had proved to be remarkably effective. Sir Edward had developed his plates each evening, and the results were even better than we had hoped.

As the afternoon wore on, my impatience with these necessary but tedious tasks increased. I itched to begin the actual excavation—to expose fully the fascinating depictions of Tetisheri paying homage to the gods of the Underworld, partaking of offerings, seated in royal state with her deceased husband and dutiful grandson—to learn whether the animal under her chair, partially concealed by the rubble, was a cat or a dog or some other pet—to sift through the interesting debris, which contained broken pieces of coffins and bits of their former occupants. Ramses was equally affected; finally, unable to resist, he reached for a brown brittle object protruding from the mass. A peremptory comment from his watchful father made him jump and pull his hand back.

More and more frequently my eyes were drawn to the rectangular opening in the far wall. Interesting as the clutter in the anteroom appeared to be, it paled before the prospect of what might lie beyond that black hole. When Emerson called a halt to our labors, announcing that we would lay out a grid and begin clearing the room the following day, I could bear it no longer. He was, as always, the last to leave. I lingered.

"Emerson," I whispered. "Do you think—tonight?"

He understood. I had known he would. That ardent spirit was as open as mine to the lure of adventure and discovery. He too had shot increasingly frequent glances toward that mysterious opening.

Yet he hesitated, and when he spoke his voice held a note of unusual indecision. "I don't know, Peabody."

"Are you suffering from premonitions, my dear?"

"I never suffer from premonitions!" One of the bats, hanging from the ceiling like a living frieze, stirred, and Emerson continued in a more moderate tone but with equal heat. "Forebodings, premonitions, idle fancies! Keep your premonitions to yourself, Peabody, curse it!"

"I have none at the moment, Emerson. Only ungovernable curiosity."

"I am relieved to hear it." Still he hesitated to commit himself. I prepared to deliver the conclusive argument—or rather to voice it aloud, for Emerson was as familiar as I with his son's annoying habit of trying to steal a march on his parents.

"If we don't explore the tunnel, Ramses will—alone and without the proper safety precautions. I am only surprised he hasn't tried it already."

"Curse it," said Emerson.

Evelyn was waiting for me at the foot of the stairs, with a cup of water and a wet cloth. "You look exhausted, Amelia," she said anxiously. "Quench your thirst and wipe your face."

I thanked her and availed myself of the water, which was certainly welcome. "You must be tired of sitting alone down here," I said. "It won't be long, Evelyn, before your talents are required."

"Oh, I don't mind. I enjoy talking with David. He was a little shy at first, but he seems easier with me now. And," she added with a smile, "the cats have been excellent company. I thought they would be unable to resist the lure of a tomb filled with bats, but they have stayed with me."

"It must be your irresistible charm," I said. "Bastet is fond of tombs and she is seldom far distant from Ramses; but she has not come closer than the mouth of the entrance passage."

We did not inform the others of our scheme until after Gertrude and Sir Edward—and Kevin, whose hints that he might be induced to stay for tea I had ignored—were on their way to Luxor. It was Emerson who made the announcement, adding, with a stern look at me, "We will not attempt it until I have examined the place thoroughly and made certain there is no danger of further collapse. This will be a preliminary reconnaissance, and unless I am completely satisfied, we will not proceed. Is that understood?"

All insisted on accompanying us. I did not attempt, as I once would have done, to dissuade Evelyn. Those Turkish trousers, to which neither of us had referred directly, affected me to the point of tears (or would have done had I been given to tears). She must have had that ensemble made in secret, tried it on during the rare moments of privacy afforded a wife and mother, and hidden it away again. It was a poignant fantasy, a substitute for the active life she had been denied. Well, she had it now, and who was I to prevent her from taking the risks that gave such a life its piquant pleasure?

Ramses's reaction was the most interesting. He did not say anything at all. That was suspicious in itself. I said, "Well, Ramses?"

Ramses returned my steady stare for several seconds, and then admitted defeat. "It is safe enough, Mother, for a person of small girth. The debris slopes down and thins out as one proceeds."

"How far did you go?" I inquired, with the control I had gained from years of painful experience.

"Only a few yards. Father came back up the stairs and I—"

"Curse it!" Emerson exclaimed.

After some discussion it was agreed that Ramses would be the one to enter the tunnel. Nefret's objections were the most vehement. "I am no fatter than Ramses! Just because I am a girl—"

"Now you know I allow no such discriminatory practices, Nefret," I interrupted. "Ramses has had more experience than you."

"Er, hmmm, yes," Emerson agreed. In his case, Nefret's accusation had been only too accurate, though he would never admit it. "Ramses is skilled at squirming through narrow spaces. Are you sure you are fit, my boy?"

"Yes, Father, quite fit."

"He is not!" Nefret never argued with Emerson's decisions. She had other, more effective methods of persuading him to change his mind. I could judge the degree of her indignation on this occasion by her abandonment of those methods in favor of direct confrontation. "He will have to crawl on his stomach, and a sharp edge of stone may tear the wound open again and I—"

"That will do," Emerson said.

Nefret knew that tone, though Emerson had never used it to her. Her lips trembled and her eyes filled with tears. It was an extremely affecting expression. I wondered if she had practiced in front of the mirror.

Emerson looked so guilty one would have thought he had slapped her, but he stuck to his guns. "Your concern for your brother does you credit, Nefret, but it is unnecessary."

Her concern (if that was what had prompted her objections) might have been unnecessary, but I thought I had better make certain. After dinner, before changing into my work clothes, I went to Ramses's room.

The wound had healed nicely. However, I took the precaution of adding several additional layers of bandages and strapping them firmly in place.

We made no attempt to steal away unseen; our destination would soon be known to the men on guard. It was only our purpose we hoped to conceal, for the present at least. Our men were still gathered round the campfire when we arrived. Emerson's stentorian shout brought them to their feet, and Abdullah hastened to meet us.

"Is it you, Father of Curses?"

"If you thought it was someone else, why the devil didn't you challenge them?" Emerson demanded.

"Be reasonable, Emerson," I said, as Abdullah shuffled his feet and looked away. "They have just finished their first meal of the day and had their first drink of water since sunrise. We should have told you we were coming, Abdullah."

"Confounded religion," Emerson grumbled.

Candles in our hands, we mounted the steps. It must have been a pretty sight from below—the line of flickering flames rising slowly into the darkness. At the last moment Emerson relented and allowed Abdullah to come with us.

He had done it, I think, as a tacit apology for his rude remarks about religion, but the dear old fellow proved useful. Abdullah's strength and keenness of eye had diminished over the years, but he was the most skilled reis in Egypt. Together he and Emerson quickly constructed from the boards they had carried with them a ramp over the heaped-up debris to the opening. After Abdullah had had a look inside, he and Emerson engaged in a muttered colloquy, and then Emerson turned to Ramses. "He feels it is safe. Go ahead."

Ramses scampered up the ramp and inserted his head and shoulders into the opening.

"Curse it, Ramses," said his affectionate father, "don't you know better than to plunge headfirst into a dark hole? Light your candle and for God's sake try not to set yourself or any flammable objects you may encounter ablaze."

"I am chagrined to have neglected the candle, sir. Excitement overcame my customary caution."

"Ha," I said. "Proceed slowly, Ramses, and keep talking."

"I beg your pardon, Mother. Did I hear you correctly?"

It was certainly not an order I had ever expected to give, but I was in no mood for a display of Ramses's peculiar variety of humor. "You heard me, young man. You have not been farther than six or eight feet into that hole. Describe exactly what you are seeing and how you are feeling as you go on."

Candle in his outstretched hand, Ramses had already eased most of his body into the tunnel. His "Yes, Mother" echoed weirdly.

"Hold on a minute," Emerson ordered. The visible part of Ramses, his lower limbs from the knees down, obediently stopped moving. Emerson looped a rope around the boy's left ankle and drew it tight. There was no comment from Ramses. "Go ahead," Emerson said. "And keep talking, or at least making noises. If your voice stops for more than thirty seconds, I will pull you out of there."

We gathered together round the foot of the little ramp and the light of the candles showed faces as grave and anxious as mine must have been. Walter put a comforting arm around Evelyn, whose wide eyes were fixed on the opening into which Ramses's feet had now vanished.

Emerson's last gesture had brought home to those who had not already known it how perilous was the undertaking. The crudely dug tunnel might collapse. The air in the depths—their extent as yet unknown—might be poisonous. The list of possible dangers was too long to be comfortable, and the rope round Ramses's ankle could be his only hope if he encountered one of them.

It must have been difficult even for Ramses to continue speaking in that confined space and with dust choking him, but he complied. As he went farther in, it became more and more difficult to understand his words. "Opens out" was one phrase, and "mummy cloth" and, loud and clear, the word "femur."

"We might have expected he would notice bones," I said softly to Evelyn, in an attempt to lighten her obvious anxiety.

"I don't care what he says so long as he keeps talking," Evelyn whispered. "How far has he gone, Radcliffe?"

Emerson had been paying out the rope. "Less than three meters. It is slow going with—"

The shriek, hideously amplified by echoes, that burst out of the opening made him stagger back with an answering cry of poignant terror. Only for an instant did he give way; grasping the rope, he gave it an emphatic tug. Ramses continued to howl and Emerson continued to haul on the rope with all his might until Ramses's feet came into view. Dropping the rope, Emerson grasped the feet and pulled the boy out into his arms.

Ramses's eyes were tightly closed, which was not surprising, since dust covered his lids and blood from numerous cuts and abrasions streaked his nose and forehead. I got the top off my canteen and dashed the contents into Ramses's face.

"Thank you," said Ramses.

Evelyn, pale as a ghost, took out her handkerchief and wiped his face. "What was it? Where are you hurt?"

"I am not hurt," said Ramses. "Except for cuts and bruises which resulted from father's precipitate removal of my person from the tunnel. Please, Mother! There are ladies present."

I had ripped open his torn shirt, sending buttons flying with as much precipitation as Emerson was wont to do. The bandage was still in place and unstained. By blood, at any rate.

"He appears to be relatively undamaged," I said.

"Snakebite," Emerson said hoarsely.

"Don't be absurd, Emerson. What would a cobra be doing in the depths of a tomb?"

"Then what did he scream for?" The color returned to Emerson's face. "I never heard him make sounds like that."

"The initial outcry," said Ramses, with obvious chagrin, "was prompted by shock and surprise. I went on shouting because I was trying to get you to stop dragging me along with such painful precipitation. You can put me down, Father, I assure you I am quite capable of standing unsupported, and it is very humiliating to be held like—"

"Why did you scream?" Emerson's teeth were clenched and so were the arms that held Ramses.

"Not from fear, I assure you." Ramses glanced at Nefret. "I encountered nothing to provoke alarm. In fact, it is fairly easy going after the first few feet. The steps are steep and broken, but the lower portion is clear of debris—and of cobras. It must have been the modern thieves who removed the lid of the mummy case in order to look for amulets and jewelry . . . Mother! Stop her, Father, there is no physical danger, but the sight is . . . Oh, curse it!"

I got to the ramp a split second before Nefret, and was in the tunnel before Emerson could prevent me. I knew my son's expository style well enough to be sure that he would go rambling on, deliberately prolonging the suspense, until he drove me to undignified verbal or physical remonstrations. I had to see for myself.

A hand caught hold of my foot, but I pulled away. (I am just as skilled as Ramses in wriggling through narrow spaces, though I get less credit for it.)

The air deep in the depths of Egyptian tombs does not strike pleasantly upon the nostrils, but as I proceeded I began to be aware of a sickly odor quite unlike any I had encountered before. As Ramses had indicated, the debris covered only the topmost steps, and my heart quickened when the small flame of my candle showed the unmistakable shape of a mummiform coffin below. The air was close, the candle burned low. I was quite close to the object before I realized it was not the sort of coffin I had hoped to see. There was no glitter of gold or glow of inset stones, nor any sign of an inscription. Dust dulled only a plain white surface of painted wood.

Not a royal coffin, then. Disappointed but still curious, I rose to my knees. The lid had been removed and flung aside. The occupant of the coffin lay exposed.

Exposed indeed. The body was unclothed, without so much as a scrap of bandage covering it. It was—unfortunately—in an excellent state of preservation. The head was flung back, the mouth hideously distorted in a petrified scream of agony and despair. I turned away, clapping my hands over my mouth to hold back the nausea rising in my throat. The foul, sickening stench that rose from the coffin was bad enough. Even worse was the realization that had struck me when I saw the ropes that bound the clawed hands and rigid feet. The man had been buried alive.

CHAPTER TEN

Men May Be Violently Attracted by Attributes That Are Not Immediately Apparent

Though I have never been particularly fond of mummies, I have in the course of my professional career learned to deal with the nasty things efficiently and unemotionally. I retreated from that one in considerable haste. The hour was late when we returned to the *Amelia*, but I admitted the need for discussion and restorative libations. It was impossible to go tamely to bed after such an experience.

We had all shared it, except for Evelyn, who claimed our descriptions were quite enough for her. Emerson, who *is* attracted to mummies, would have crawled over burning coals to reach this one. With the help of Abdullah he managed to widen the space enough for him to squeeze through, and he was there so long, I regretted not having attached a rope to *him*. Not until I crawled partway into the tunnel and threatened to remove him bodily did he consent to return. Emerson is not especially sensitive to atmosphere, and it was that as much as the hideous aspect of the mummy that had affected me—the dim light and shifting shadows, the foul stench—and the fact that the plain white coffin with its dreadful inhabitant had guarded the burial chamber of a queen. Hasty as had been my retreat, I had observed the doorway behind the coffin—a doorway blocked with massive stones.

Contemplating contemptuously the glass of warm milk I had caused to be served to him, Ramses remarked, "The reason for the refusal of the cats to enter the tomb is now explained. Their sense of smell, so much keener than ours, must have caught a whiff of that vile odor."

"You are being unduly fanciful, Ramses," I said. "A cat's notion of what constitutes a vile odor is certainly not the same as ours. But we have the mummy to thank, I suspect, for the fact that the thieves did not enter the burial chamber."

"I wonder," Walter exclaimed. "Radcliffe, do you remember the story we heard some years ago in Gurneh? About the lost tomb into which three men had vanished and never come out?"

"Folktales," Emerson said impatiently.

"This had occurred within recent memory," Walter insisted. "The fellow who told us of it claimed to be the brother of one of the men who had disappeared."

"A typical folktale, no doubt," Ramses said thoughtfully. "But it would be interesting, would it not, if some of the bones crushed underfoot in the antechamber turned out to be of modern date?"

"Balderdash," Emerson said. "The first sight of the atrocious thing might have sent them into screaming retreat, but tomb robbers are accustomed to grisly sights."

"I have never seen one as grisly as that," I murmured.

Emerson considerately splashed more whiskey into my glass. "I have, though. It came from the royal cache at Deir el Bahri."

"Emerson, this poor fellow was buried alive!"

"For once, Peabody, your melodramatic interpretation is probably correct. This mummy shows the same characteristics as the other, which I was allowed to examine some years ago. In fact, the visible parallels are so exact that I can guess what we will find when I finish the examination I was not allowed to make this evening."

I ignored this provocative remark, and the glance that accompanied it. He was only teasing.

"Yes, I remember the Deir el Bahri specimen," Walter exclaimed. "Its hands and feet had also been bound."

"Instead of being wrapped with bandages, it had been sewn into a sheepskin," Emerson said. "The internal organs were still in place and there was no evidence that the process of mummification had occurred. The same seems to be true of our mummy. I found the sheepskin, pushed back from the exposed body, and I could see no signs of the incision through which the viscera were usually removed. The expression of intense agony is like that of the other example, and it certainly suggests that both individuals died . . . unpleasantly."

"His crime must have been heinous, to warrant such a fate," Nefret said.

I wondered if I would ever become accustomed to it—the contrast between her delicate English fairness and the placidity on that fair face when she spoke of matters the mere thought of which would have made an English maiden shudder or swoon.

"A good point," said Emerson. "Not only was the method of execution—for such it must have been—particularly cruel, but the man was stripped of his name and identity and wrapped in the skin of an animal which was considered ritually impure. Yet the body was not destroyed; it was entombed with the royal dead—as, apparently, was this individual. I confess an explanation eludes me."

"There's a mystery for you, Amelia," said Walter. "I don't believe you've had a murder this season; why not employ those detectival talents of yours on this poor chap?"

"I doubt that even the talents of Ramses's favorite fictional detectives could solve a case such as this," I replied in the same jesting tone. "So long ago as that—"

"Ha," said Emerson. "I believe I once heard you say that no mystery is insoluble. It is simply a question of how much time and energy one is willing to expend, you said."

"I was engaging in a little braggadocio," I admitted. "However . . ."

"Oh, you have a theory, have you?"

"Not yet. How could I, when the evidence is incomplete?" Emerson's smile broadened. The challenge in those mocking blue eyes was impossible to resist; I went on, "What I intended to say, before you interrupted me, was that at this stage one cannot state that a solution may not be arrived at. One or two ideas have occurred to me."

Observing that Ramses, who was never at a loss for ideas, was about to launch into a speech, Emerson said quickly, "The hour is late. Off to bed, eh? Not a word of this to anyone, mind you. If O'Connell gets wind of it he will drag out the old nonsense about curses, and I don't trust Miss Marmaduke to resist his confounded charm."

"So you find Mr. O'Connell charming, do you?" I inquired, as we left the saloon.

"Not at all," said Emerson coldly. "I was referring to his effect on susceptible females, which I have had occasion to observe."

Emerson's temper was sorely tried over the following days, for the *Mirror* arrived on schedule and the *Times* soon followed, and Cook's added us to their itinerary ("steamers twice weekly during the height of the season"). Emerson's face when he first beheld the troop of donkey-mounted tourists thundering down on us was a remarkable sight. The timider souls retreated at his first bellow, but some were remarkably persistent and did not go away until he charged them brandishing a plank.

Not only were we besieged by journalists and tourists, but the archaeological onslaught Emerson had predicted also occurred. The first to arrive was Cyrus Vandergelt, our wealthy American friend. Quibell and Newberry "dropped in," Howard Carter spent as much time with us as he could spare from his other duties, and we were even honored by a brief visit from M. Maspero, despite Emerson's efforts to head him off.

The only ones of our friends who did not turn up were the Reverend Sayce, who, I was sorry to hear, was suffering from an attack of rheumatics (Emerson was not sorry to hear it), and Mr. Petrie. The Petries were at Abydos that year, which made their failure to come even more surprising. Howard attributed it to Petrie's compulsive work habits. Emerson attributed it to spite and jealousy.

"At least," he remarked sourly, "we need not fear interruption by the local thieves. They couldn't get near the place without tripping over a journalist or an archaeologist."

There had indeed been a singular lack of interest on the part of our known and unknown enemies. We had heard nothing more from Riccetti; night succeeded peaceful night at the tomb and on the dahabeeyah. This was, in my opinion, an ominous sign, but Emerson absolutely refused to agree with me (or to discuss the matter at all). How true it is that there are none so blind as those who will not see! I must share some small part of the blame. Our work absorbed me. I became complacent and careless. And in due course of time I paid a terrible price for that complacency.

Yet what Egyptologist could resist the allure of that tomb! The painted reliefs were remarkable, the colors scarcely faded, the outlines sure and crisp. Emerson and Walter spent a good deal of time arguing about the historical implications of these scenes and the translations of the hieroglyphic inscriptions, but I will spare the uninformed Reader further details. (The Reader who wishes to be informed will find those details in our forthcoming publication, *The Tomb of Tetisheri at Thebes*; four volumes, and a fifth, folio-size, of color plates.)

Clearing the antechamber took less time than I had expected. The modern thieves had been busy there, shoveling the debris aside in their search for marketable objects, and disturbing the stratigraphy to such an extent that even Emerson admitted there was no hope of reconstructing the original arrangement. Most of the remaining objects were much later in date than the time of Tetisheri, and of poor quality. The tomb robbers had left very little of them, dismembering the mummies in search of amulets and smashing the flimsy wooden coffins. They had come from the burials of a priestly family of the Twenty-First Dynasty, who had used Tetisheri's antechamber as their family tomb before an avalanche or earthquake concealed the entrance.

We found the work fascinating, but the journalists did not. After an interval during which no mummies, jewels or golden vessels emerged from the tomb, they retired to the Luxor hotels, where they spent most of their time drinking and listening to the fabrications of the local inhabitants. Our archaeological friends also dispersed; they had responsibilities of their own, and as Mr. Quibell remarked, with a rueful smile, it took Emerson even longer than it did Petrie to clear a tomb.

Not even to our archaeological colleagues did Emerson admit we had gone beyond the antechamber. He had closed the opening in the doorway and refused to open it again even at the direct request of the Director of Antiquities.

It was amusing to see how M. Maspero's face brightened when he saw our nice wooden stairs. Like Hamlet, he was somewhat stout and scant of breath. After inspecting the reliefs, he interrupted Emerson's lecture on the artifacts we had found thus far.

"Mon cher colleague, I am confident that you are carrying out your excavations in a manner of the most irreproachable. But what of the queen's mummy?"

Emerson's face took on the expression that often preceded a tactless remark, and I said soothingly, "We have not yet investigated the burial chamber, monsieur. You know my husband's methods."

Maspero nodded and mopped his perspiring brow. With any other excavator he might have insisted on having the passage cleared, but he knew Emerson well. "You will notify me before you enter the burial chamber?" he said wistfully.

"Certainly, monsieur," Emerson replied in his fluent but vilely accented French. "How could you suppose I would do otherwise?"

"Hmmmm," said Maspero, and went puffing down the stairs.

The only visitor who persisted was Cyrus. His offer of assistance having been firmly rejected by Emerson, he began his own excavations in the Valley of the Kings; but since his Luxor home was located near the entrance to the Valley, he was able to "keep after us day and night," as Emerson sourly expressed it. The house, which the local residents referred to as the Castle, was a large, elegant residence equipped with every modern comfort. Cyrus invited us to tea, breakfast, luncheon and dinner, and offered to put any or all of us up.

"Mr. and Mrs. Walter Emerson, at least," he insisted. "They aren't used to roughing it like us old hands, Mrs. Amelia, and the dahabeeyah must be a mite crowded with six of you."

I refused the invitation, but kept it in mind. The Castle was fully staffed and stout-walled as a fortress. There might come a time . . .

We were dining with Cyrus at the Luxor hotel on the evening when the deceptive tranquillity of our existence was broken by the first ominous ripple that indicated the presence of inimical life below the surface. Emerson had grudgingly agreed to dine, moved more by the fact that the following day was Friday, and hence a holiday for the men, than by my insistence that we all needed a change of scene. I thought Evelyn was looking tired, and even Nefret seemed more silent and preoccupied than usual.

With his customary generosity Cyrus had invited our entire staff as well as the young Egyptologist he had hired to supervise his own work. We made quite a large party, and Cyrus's lined face broke into a smile as he surveyed the table from his position at its head.

"Now isn't this just fine?" he demanded of me—seated, of course, at his right. "The more the merrier, that's my motto. And a handsome lot too, if you except my weathered old self."

I was forced to agree. No one adorns a dinner table (or any other ambience) more than my dear Emerson, tanned and fit as always, his well-cut lips curving in a fond smile as he watched Nefret pretending to be polite to Ramses. She had developed quite a talent for sweet sarcasm, which of course passed right over Emerson's head. It did not pass over the head of Ramses, but he had not decided what to do about it.

Sir Edward, playing it safe, had rejected evening dress in favor of a suit in a heather blend that set off his blue eyes and fair hair. Kevin . . . Well, even his best friend could not have called him handsome, but his freckled face beamed with satisfaction at finding himself in such company. The annoyance of the *Times*, the *Mirror* and the *Daily Mail*, at a distant table, undoubtedly added to his enjoyment. Walter looked ten years younger than he had when he first arrived; his face was now healthily tanned and he had gained at least a stone.

Mr. Amherst, Cyrus's new assistant, was a fine-looking young fellow, with sandy hair and a neatly trimmed mustache. None of us had met him before, since he was fresh down from Oxford, where he had been studying classics. He was chatting with Evelyn, who had never looked lovelier.

The happiest face of all, however, belonged to Miss Marmaduke. As the only unmarried adult female present, she obviously considered herself the belle of the occasion and she blossomed under the attentions of the gentlemen. Her black frock had been altered to display her arms and throat and shoulders, and by some device not immediately apparent to me she had managed to put her hair up and keep it there. Her thin cheeks were becomingly flushed—or perhaps it was paint. The transformation was so great I wondered whether Sir Edward . . .

"A good many tourists in Luxor this year," said Cyrus, interrupting a train of thought which probably did me no credit. "I wonder how many have been drawn here by the news of the tomb."

"Some have tried to see it, at any rate," I replied, recognizing several familiar faces. "Lord Lowry-Corry and his lady actually threatened Emerson with dismissal when he refused to let them mount the stairs."

"Dismissal from what?" Cyrus inquired with a bemused smile.

"Heaven only knows. I suppose they believe archaeologists must be employed by the British government." I nodded distantly at Lady Lowry-Corry, who proceeded to cut me dead.

Cyrus, who had observed the exchange, laughed heartily. "I hope you will forgive me for saying so, Mrs. Amelia, but there are advantages to a democratic form of government. The aristocracy can be a nuisance."

"Emerson would agree with you. But if *you* will forgive *me* for saying so, Cyrus, some Americans toady to aristocrats too—not only ours, but the American aristocracy of wealth. I deduce, from the way the ladies are fawning on him, that the gentleman at that table is a member of that group, for his appearance is not so prepossessing as to inspire such a degree of admiration."

"Right again, Mrs. Amelia." Cyrus scowled at the little man with the enormous mustaches, who was holding forth in a loud American accent. "He is a New Yorker and an old business rival of mine. Apparently he has become quite fascinated with Egypt, for he had the almighty gall to visit me and pump me about my excavations. Watch out for him. He'll be trying to bully his way into your tomb next, and I wouldn't trust him any farther than I could throw him."

"You could probably throw him quite a distance, Cyrus."

"And Emerson could throw him even farther." Cyrus's face relaxed into an anticipatory grin. "I just hope I'm on the spot if he tries his tricks on your husband."

I caught the eye of another gentleman who immediately rose and came to our table.

"How is your son getting on, Mrs. Emerson? Since you did not call me back I assume there were no complications."

"As you see, he is the picture of health." Turning to Cyrus, I said, "You remember Dr. Willoughby, Cyrus. I am glad to be able to thank you again, Doctor, not only for your prompt attention to Ramses's little accident, but for your care of my husband last winter."

"He certainly seems to have made a complete recovery," said Willoughby, looking at Emerson, who was, to judge by his impassioned gestures, arguing about philology with Walter.

"It was just as you predicted," I said. "As his physical health improved the—er—nervous disorder disappeared."

"I am delighted to hear it. And so would my patients be," he added with a smile, "if I were so unprofessional as to discuss my other cases with any but the patient and his family. But I may tell you, Mrs. Emerson, that your husband's case aroused my interest in—er—nervous disorders, and I have been able to help several individuals who have consulted me with similar problems. My practice is constantly increasing."

"Luxor is becoming known as a health resort," I agreed, "and the presence of a physician of your reputation must attract many invalids to the city."

After a further exchange of compliments the doctor returned to his table, and Cyrus, who was studying me curiously, remarked, "So Ramses has had another little accident—and one serious enough to require the attention of a surgeon?"

"The maternal instinct quite frequently inspires an exaggerated reponse," I replied, and, in the hope of changing the subject, went on without pausing. "Are the other people at the doctor's table patients of his, I wonder? Some of them seem to be suffering from nothing more serious than overindulgence."

"That fellow in the red fez could certainly profit from a few weeks on bread and water," Cyrus agreed with a chuckle. "He is a Hollander, Mrs. Amelia, and quite a bon vivant. The lady in black next to him is a subject of the Emperor of Austria. She lost her husband not long ago in a tragic accident; he was an ardent sportsman who tripped over a root and shot himself instead of the stag he was after. The poor lady appears to be very frail; that forbidding female at her left is a hospital nurse, who accompanies her everywhere."

"What a mine of information you are, Cyrus. Do you know everyone in Luxor?"

"I am not acquainted with the other ladies at Willoughby's table. Wouldn't mind an introduction, though. Nothing wrong with any of them that I can see."

"Too much money and too few brains, no doubt. Which do you fancy, Cyrus, the dark lady or the one with the Titian hair? I doubt it is the original color."

"Why, either one. I make no bones about my admiration for the fair sex, Mrs. Amelia, and since you are unavailable I must seek consolation elsewhere."

I am sure I need not explain to the Reader that vulgar curiosity was not the cause of my inquiries. In recent days I had seen no signs of the vultures, but I did not doubt they were still hovering, intent on gaining control of the empire Sethos had left leaderless. The trouble with unknown enemies is that they are so hard to identify. Any or all of these seemingly innocent tourists could be such a foe.

After dinner we retired to the garden for coffee. Lanterns hanging in the trees cast their soft glow on luxuriant greenery and tender blossoms; the cool pure air was a welcome refreshment after the crowded atmosphere of the dining salon. Emerson promptly proceeded to pollute the air with his pipe and Cyrus, after politely requesting my permission, lit one of his cheroots.

"So," said the latter, getting down to business, "when do you expect to reach the burial chamber?"

With a glance at Kevin, seated at an adjoining table, Emerson said, "One can almost see his ears prick, can't one? Don't bother straining your neck, O'Connell. The answer to Mr. Vandergelt's question is an unequivocal 'How the devil should I know?' It will be several more days before I finish with the antechamber, and then there is a passage of unknown length to be cleared of rubble. We will be lucky to reach the burial chamber, wherever it is, before March."

"Another month?" Kevin exclaimed, pulling his chair closer.

"At least."

"But I can't be hanging around Luxor so long! My editor won't stand for it."

"Neither, I fancy, can the *Times* and the *Mirror*," said Emerson with a sinister smile. "You have my permission to pass the information on to them, O'Connell. Now, Vandergelt, you were asking about the next volume of my *History*. I mean to discuss at length the development of the temporal power of the priesthood of Amon and its effect . . ."

With a muttered "Begorrah!" Kevin got up and walked away. The ruse had been successful. He and his readers were not interested in Emerson's theories about the priesthood of Amon. I was, of course, so much so that it was not until after we had finished a refreshing little argument about Akhenaton that I realized several of our party had disappeared.

"Curse it!" I exclaimed. "Where is Nefret? If that girl has gone off with—"

"With Ramses, I expect," Emerson said ingenuously. "It is a fine moonlit night, Amelia, and young people are too restless to sit still for long."

"Have Evelyn and Walter gone for a moonlight stroll too?"

"It would appear so. Sit down, Peabody, what are you in such a state about?"

"It is her maternal instincts," Cyrus declared seriously. "I sympathize, Mrs. Amelia; the responsibility for two such young people must be stupendous. What with Ramses's propensity for accidents and Miss Nefret's pretty face . . . You'll be up to your—er—neck in lovesick swains before long, Emerson."

"Oh, good Gad," said Emerson, with a stricken look at me. "Peabody, perhaps you had better go look for her—them."

It was so like him to have ignored all the obvious signs, including my warnings, until a casual comment from another *man* caught his attention! I said coolly, "I intended to do just that, Emerson. Please do not disturb yourself."

Picking up my parasol (crimson, to match my frock) I followed the path leading into the shrubbery.

There were others enjoying the tropical beauty of the night—shadowy forms in the darkness, many of them arm in arm. As I went on, I began to regret I had allowed momentary pique to prevent me from urging that Emerson accompany me. Egyptian nights are made for romantic encounters—stars, soft breezes, the languorous scent of jasmine and roses heavy on the air. The moon, nearing the full, cast silvery rays across the path. How could I, who had been and still was susceptible to sentiments of that nature, entirely condemn a young person who yielded to its exquisite sensations?

Because she was fifteen years old, not . . . not as mature as I had been when I was swept off my feet by moonlight and Emerson.

It was the moonlight that betrayed them, glinting in his fair hair. Her form was in deeper shadow, half-concealed by a flowering vine. A breeze rustled the branches; the sound must have hidden the even softer brush of my skirts along the grass. I stopped; and then I heard a woman's voice.

"What is it they say here? Word of an Englishman?"

It was not Nefret's voice. In fact, it was hard to identify, for she spoke in a whisper and a hint of laughter colored the tones. I knew it must be Gertrude, though, even before the response came in the equally soft but unmistakable voice of Sir Edward Washington.

"You have it. Do you doubt me?"

"Give me your hand on it, then—as gentlemen do when they strike a bargain."

The only answer was an intake of breath. The gleam of fair hair vanished as he moved, and since I did not know whether he was moving forward or back toward me, I retreated at once.

Returning to the table, I was relieved to find the wanderers had come back.

"We went for a short stroll," Evelyn explained. "The view across the river is beautiful."

"Did you see the others?" I asked casually.

"We ran into Mr. O'Connell and Amherst," Walter replied. "They were looking for tobacco. The shops are open half the night during Ramadan, you know."

"Sir Edward and Miss Marmaduke were not with you?" Well, I knew they had not been, at least not all the time, but a proper investigator takes nothing for granted.

"What business is it of yours?" Emerson demanded. "You are not responsible for them, nor are they accountable to you for what they do in their free time." He pulled out his watch. "It is late. We must be getting back."

"What's your hurry?" Cyrus gestured at a passing waiter. "The ladies are just as entitled to a holiday as the workers. If you won't take a day off, I would be delighted to act as escort. Temples, tombs or shops, ladies—whatever your pleasure, Cyrus Vandergelt, U.S.A., is your man. What about the Valley of the Kings, eh? I believe I may claim that is my particular bailiwick, and Miss Nefret tells me she has not seen it."

We had not been debating the matter long when the others

returned. They were all three together. O'Connell was showering Gertrude with smiles and Irish compliments. Had she managed to work him in too? I decided I had better have a little chat with Gertrude.

In all fairness to myself, I must make it clear that my concern was dictated by simple duty. Emerson is always complaining about my weakness for young lovers, as he terms it, and I would be the last to deny that I take an interest in promoting alliances of a romantic nature. (Marital alliances, that is.) In this case there could be no question of marriage, but there might be a question of conspiracy. I owed it to my family to learn whether Sir Edward and Gertrude were in cahoots, as Cyrus might say, or whether the gentleman was only amusing himself. And in the latter instance my sense of moral responsibility demanded that I speak a word of kindly warning to a woman who had obviously not my experience with the masculine sex.

I explained this to Emerson later, after we had returned to the *Amelia*. I am sorry to say that he responded with remarks of the most frivolous nature, and proposed another theory which I prefer not to quote literally. To employ terms less vulgar than the ones he had used: Gertrude was not so inexperienced as she appeared. Sir Edward (ready as men always are to believe themselves irresistible) had been seduced by a cunning adventuress. Emerson added—let me think how to put it—that men may be violently attracted by attributes that are not immediately apparent.

It was difficult to deny the truth of this. I managed to counter it rather neatly, I believe. "I am in complete agreement, Emerson. In fact, it was I, if you recall, who first pointed out that Gertrude is not what she seems. She may be more than a simple adventuress. She may be a spy and a criminal! In fact—yes, the snatches of conversation I overheard strongly suggest that she is trying to enlist him in the conspiracy!"

"They strongly suggest to me the sort of idiotic verbal games males and females play when they are establishing a—er—romantic relationship."

"Possibly," I said magnanimously. "But it is our duty to ascertain the truth and warn poor Sir Edward if he has been taken in."

"He wouldn't thank you for it," muttered Emerson. "Oh, damnation. I don't know why I waste time arguing with you, Peabody, you will go your own way whatever I say. Ply Miss Marmaduke with tea and sympathy and pry into her innermost feelings. I would attempt to prevent you if I thought there were the slightest possibility that she is anything but a sentimental, rather stupid woman who would faint dead away if she ever encountered a criminal or a spy."

He was mistaken, of course. He had not heard the woman's voice—confident, amused, murmurously seductive—the voice of an experienced woman of the world.

We had settled on the Valley of the Kings for our excursion next day. Emerson had agreed to join us, though he complained about cursed tourists and missing a day of work.

"At least Ramadan is almost over," I said consolingly. "One cannot expect the men to work at their best when they fast all day."

"And gorge themselves all night," Emerson grumbled. "Then we must endure three days of overindulgence and distraction, while they celebrate the end of Ramadan. Religion is a confounded nuisance!"

Of course he insisted on stopping by the tomb first. The rest of us rode directly to the Castle, where we were to breakfast with Cyrus before beginning our excursion. The party was the same as that of the night before, since Cyrus had affably included everyone in his invitation. He took us on a tour of the establishment while we waited for Emerson to join us. The tour ended in the library; watching Mr. Amherst remove an enormous folio volume from its shelf so that Nefret could examine it, I drew Cyrus aside.

"Are you certain Mr. Amherst is who he says he is, Cyrus?"

"My dear Mrs. Amelia! You must get over this habit of thinking everyone you meet is in disguise."

"He seems very interested in Nefret."

"What young fellow would not be? He is just showing off, Mrs. Amelia, heaving that volume of Lepsius around the way another lad might lift weights, to impress a pretty young lady. Ah, but here is your husband. Let's go to breakfast."

The food was excellent, as Cyrus's cuisine always was. Basking in our commendations, he reiterated his invitation. "There's plenty of room here, folks. What about you, Miss Marmaduke? And Sir Edward?"

"Kindly allow me to make the arrangements for my staff, Vandergelt," Emerson growled.

"No need to put out good money for a hotel," Cyrus insisted. "And it would save them making that trip across the river twice a day. Willy and I rattle around in this big old place, and I'm not much company for an energetic young chap. Isn't that right, Willy?"

Amherst smiled politely. "Your company, Mr. Vandergelt, could never be dull. It is entirely up to you, sir, of course."

"Wrong," said Emerson. "It is also up to me. Oh, the devil. Do as you like. Everyone always does."

I expected Gertrude would jump at the offer. Not only would proximity make it easier for her to spy on us, but the accommodations, which she had seen earlier, were as elegant as any female could desire. She demurred, however, and when Sir Edward also expressed his reluctance to take advantage of Cyrus I thought I knew why. Both would accept, or neither would. They wanted to confer privately before deciding.

"Think it over, then," Cyrus said good-humoredly. "The offer stands; just let me know."

We were soon on our way, following a path through the wadi. I had of course visited the Valley innumerable times, but it never fails to cast its spell upon me. As we rode on, the gorge gradually narrowed between walls of bare rock, golden yellow in the sunlight and utterly devoid of life—only the vultures lazily gliding overhead and an occasional serpentine slither among the rocky slopes—and, of course, flies. They appeared to bother Gertrude most. She looked ridiculous, bouncing up and down in her saddle and flailing at the air with her whisk. Again I asked myself: Could this silly woman be an adventuress or a spy?

The answer, of course, was: Yes, she could. A talent for acting and for disguise is essential to both professions.

When the path forked we followed the left-hand branch through a natural gateway of rock and saw the Valley before us. As Emerson had predicted, the place swarmed with tourists.

Only a few of the royal tombs were considered by Baedeker to be worthy of starred entries, and it was around these that the tourists had gathered. Disdaining the vulgar mobs, we were led by Cyrus to the place he had selected for this season's work. None of the men was working that day, but the evidence of their labor was visible in holes and piles of sand.

"I figure there's got to be a tomb here someplace," Cyrus declared.

Miss Marmaduke studied the barren ground and piles of rubble with obvious bewilderment, and Emerson said with a snort, "You would be better employed, Vandergelt, in conducting a proper excavation of one of the tombs that has never been completely explored—number 5, for instance. Burton's incomplete plan has several interesting features."

"The doggone place is full of debris," Cyrus objected. "It would take months to dig it out. Anyhow, it's not a royal tomb."

"Typical," Emerson muttered. "That is all you care about, you and the others—royal tombs."

Whereupon he stalked off, leaving us to remain or follow as we chose. "Where are you going, Emerson?" I asked, trotting after him.

Courteous as always (when I reminded him), he slowed his pace. "I want to have a look at one of the tombs Loret found last year."

"Amenhotep II? It will be crowded with tourists, Emerson; you know how the vulgar are attracted by mummies."

"No," said Emerson.

The tomb he sought had been dug into the side of the Valley.

Like most of the others, it was open and unguarded, and I reflected, as we started down the stairs, that Howard had his work cut out for him if he hoped to protect the tombs.

We had of course brought our own candles. At that time none of the tombs were lighted by electricity, and the steps were steep and broken. Gertrude, gallantly assisted by Cyrus, let out little squeaks of alarm as she stumbled down them.

The stairs ended in a square, unadorned room. A second stone-cut staircase led down into the chamber that had been the king's final resting place. A red sandstone sarcophagus, adorned with images of protective gods and goddesses, gaped empty.

"Hmph," said Emerson uninformatively. He went to the right-hand wall and began examining it.

I did not need him to inform me why he had come there. The tomb had belonged to Thutmose I, the father of Queen Hatshepsut, but it was not that connection that interested Emerson. This was the earliest royal tomb in the Valley—later by several generations than our tomb, but closer in time to it than any other. It was much smaller than the long, elaborate sepulchers of later periods, and I saw what was in Emerson's mind. Since our tomb was earlier even than this one, it might be as simple. If so, the blocked doorway at the base of the stairs we had seen could lead directly into the burial chamber.

The others had gathered round the sarcophagus. Gertrude stood at the head, her head bowed and her hands clasped. I noted that the goddess portrayed on that part of the sarcophagus was Nephthys—no more veiled than Isis, since both ladies are usually depicted wearing an extremely skimpy, skintight garment.

After examining the sarcophagus and translating the inscriptions (though no one had asked him to), Ramses joined his father at the wall.

"It was decorated with painted stucco," he remarked dogmatically.

"Hmph," said Emerson, walking sideways and holding his candle close to the surface.

"Water-damaged," said Ramses to Nefret, who had come to see what they were doing. "The chamber has often been flooded.

That is the difficulty with these tombs located at the foot of the cliffs; one would have supposed—"

"Hmph," said Nefret, following Emerson.

"Haven't you seen enough?" Cyrus demanded impatiently. "There's nothing interesting here."

I had to tap Gertrude on the shoulder before she roused from her reverie—or meditation, or prayer, or whatever it was. She turned to me with a particularly foolish look. "It is wonderful," she breathed. "To see Her here, in this setting; the air is permeated with Her presence, with the intensity of belief."

"If by Her, you refer to Isis," I remarked, "you have picked the wrong goddess. That is Nephthys. Isis is on the foot of the sarcophagus."

Gertrude was not put out. "She manifests herself in many forms. All are She. She is all."

"Oh, really? Come, Gertrude, or we will be left behind."

"Not by me," Cyrus declared. "I have an arm for each of you, ladies."

"That would leave you no hand for your candle," I retorted. "Take care of Miss Marmaduke, Cyrus. I will follow behind with . . . Evelyn?"

She had already gone on—with whom I had not seen, but not with her husband. "With Walter," I finished. "May I have your arm, my dear?"

Not that I needed it. However, his hangdog look indicated that his fragile masculine ego required a little boost, and I was happy to supply it. We were the last to mount the stairs, leaving darkness to fill the desolate abandoned chamber once again.

At the suggestion of Ramses, who shares his father's interest in mummies (to an exaggerated degree, I might add), we went next to the tomb of Amenhotep II, which had been discovered only the previous year. Like the cache at Deir el Bahri, it had contained the remains of pharaohs and queens transferred from their own tombs for safekeeping. The royal remains had recently been removed to the Cairo Museum, except for the body of the tomb owner himself. It still lay in the open sarcophagus, and naturally it attracted the more ghoulish visitors. It was an unseemly sight—the still dignity of the shrouded form, a withered wreath still on its breast, surrounded by gabbling, sweating, gaping curiosity-seekers. Some humorists made rude jokes, and some dripped candle wax onto the mummy. I was obliged to take Emerson away.

We retreated into the next room, where was to be seen one of the most curious sights in the Valley. In addition to the shrouded and encoffined royal dead, the tomb had contained three other mummies. They lay where they had been found, naked and unnamed. Two had been sadly battered by the ancient tomb robbers and did not look very nice, though the effect was nothing near so ghastly as our unnamed mummy. One, that of a woman, retained even yet a remote beauty. Her long dark hair lay round her head.

Of course we found Ramses already there, bending over the mummies. Nefret was with him, and as we came in we heard Ramses remark, "The mummification technique is certainly that of the Eighteenth Dynasty. Observe the incision."

Which Nefret did, her face close to the unpleasant surface of the mummy. Emerson chuckled. (The most peculiar things put him in a pleasant temper.)

"I am glad to see you both working hard at your studies," he said. "Have you reached any conclusions, Ramses?"

"As to the possible identity of these individuals, you mean?" Ramses thoughtfully fingered his chin. "It has been suggested, I believe, that the older woman is the great Hatshepsut herself."

Nefret let out a little exclamation of interest and knelt to examine the body more closely. "Could the younger individuals be her children?"

"Impossible to determine," said Ramses. "And there is no more reason to suppose that this is Hatshepsut than any other royal woman of the period whose mummy is as yet unknown."

A loud "Pardon, madame!" behind me made me step aside. Two tourists entered, followed by Sir Edward, whose expressive eyebrow lifted at the sight of Ramses and Nefret crouching beside the mummies.

"Amazing young woman," he murmured. "Most gels would run shrieking from such a sight."

"Most gels have been trained to behave like idiots," I replied.

"I am entirely of your opinion, Mrs. Emerson. After the ladies whom I have had the good fortune to meet this season, the ordinary young Englishwoman will seem vapid and childish."

I acknowledged the implied compliment with a smile.

The tourists were, as the Reader has undoubtedly deduced, of the French nation. I deduced, farther, that they were on their bridal trip. (They were young, their clothing was new and of the latest fashion, and she clung to his arm in a manner typical of brides.) The young man's swagger and loud voice and the high-pitched giggles with which she responded to his feeble witticisms were also indicative.

Emerson was already simmering with rage; he had protested loudly to M. Maspero about leaving the mummies unprotected. The rude comments of the young male person did nothing to calm him. When the latter poked at one of the pitiful cadavers with his gold-headed stick, Emerson could contain himself no longer.

"Sacrebleu!" he shouted. "Que le diable vous emporte! Âne maudit!" and other, even more emphatic, expressions of disapproval.

The tourists went quickly away. I caught Emerson's arm and prevented him from pursuing them. Sir Edward began to laugh.

"Very eloquent, Professor."

Emerson's rigid arms relaxed. "Oh, curse it. I don't know why I bother. It is a wonder some collector hasn't walked off with these poor cadavers already. I must have a word with Carter about this."

Climbing back up the rough rubble-strewn stairs was even more difficult than the descent had been, with only a rope handrail to offer assistance. We stopped midway up to see the other peculiar mummy still remaining in the tomb—which Ramses of course insisted on inspecting. After stripping it of its wrappings and amulets, the ancient thieves had thrown it carelessly onto a wooden boat, where it had stuck fast (being still damp with the oils and unguents of anointing). At the sight of it Emerson exploded again.

"Chicken wire! Is that Maspero's notion of proper protection? Curse it . . ."

I will spare the Reader a repetition of his additional remarks.

Even the excellent picnic lunch Cyrus's servants produced did not relieve his feelings. He was still in a surly mood after we finished eating, and declined to join us in an inspection of Belzoni's tomb, as it is called after the name of its discoverer.

"I have seen it a dozen times. You don't need me; Walter and Ramses can tell you about the reliefs as well as I can. And Peabody, of course."

Since the tomb (that of King Sethos I, to be precise) is one of the most handsomely decorated of all, there were still a number of cursed tourists hanging about, but they did not mar the enjoyment of my companions. A thrill of affection ran through me as I beheld Evelyn, her face rapt, examining the beautifully painted scenes. Her first and only visit to Egypt had ended in marriage and persistent motherhood; it was all new to her and as fascinating as art can be to a true artist. Gertrude found enough goddesses to keep her happy, and Ramses lectured till he was hoarse.

When we came out into the sunlight again, everyone was ready for a rest and liquid refreshment. The air, particularly in deep tombs like Sethos's, is very dry. Comfortably seated in the shade, we finished the tea and lemon drink the servants had brought.

Most of the tourists had gone; purple shadows lengthened as the sun sank toward the cliffs. "Where's my old pal Emerson got to?" Cyrus asked.

"Deep down in a tomb, I expect," Walter replied with a smile. "He loses all track of time when he is absorbed in archaeology. We needn't wait for him if you are tired, Evelyn. He will find his way back when he is ready."

I rose and shook out my skirts. "The rest of you go on."

"If you wish to wait for the Professor, I will stay with you," said Sir Edward, gallant as always.

"I don't intend to wait. I know where he has gone, and I am

going the same way. I will meet you back at the dahabeeyah. Thank you, Cyrus, for a delightful day."

Cyrus slapped his knee. "Gee whillikers, but I am a stupid old goat! I should have known he couldn't stay away from that tomb of his. See here, Mrs. Amelia, it's a long, rough hike from here. You can't go on foot."

"Emerson is on foot," I replied.

"You are going over the mountain path?" Sir Edward shook his head and smiled. "One day, Mrs. Emerson, I will learn not to be surprised at anything you attempt. I will accompany you, of course, if I cannot dissuade you. And I feel fairly sure I cannot."

He really had a very charming smile. Before I could assure him he was welcome, Ramses, already on his feet, said stiffly, "That is not necessary, sir. I will escort my mother."

I was anxious to be off, so I cut short the agitated discussion that followed. Everyone offered to go; I selected the ones I knew could keep up with me. "Ramses, Nefret and Sir Edward. Good day to the rest of you."

The view from the top of the cliff was glorious at that time of day, but we did not linger to enjoy it. As the sun sank lower, my uneasiness increased. We ought to have met Emerson returning before this. He would not have remained away so long without warning me of his intentions.

Instead of following the well-marked path that led to Deir el Bahri, I struck out to the north, following what I deemed to be the quickest if not easiest route. The track was in some places almost too rough for human feet, and had probably been made by goats. Since I was in something of a hurry, I accepted Sir Edward's hand in the more difficult sections. Ramses and Nefret followed, and I am sorry to say that I heard a good deal of bad language from the latter as she fought off Ramses's attempt to assist her in the same way. Some of the words were Arabic (learned, I did not doubt, from Ramses), and Sir Edward had trouble controlling his mouth. He did me the courtesy of pretending he had not heard, however.

I was sadly short of breath, with agitation as well as exertion, when I saw before me, encrimsoned by the sunset light, an unmoving and monolithic form. It was Emerson, sitting on a rock.

"Ah," he said, as we came panting up to him. "There you are, Peabody. I rather expected you would turn up before long, though I clung to the forlorn hope that you would have sense enough to go back with Vandergelt."

The reproaches that hovered on my lips, awaiting breath enough to pronounce them, were never voiced. I had seldom seen even Emerson in such a state of disarray. His hands were bleeding and his shirt was ripped half off him.

"Curse it, Emerson, what the devil have you been doing?" I gasped.

"Language, Peabody. Sit down and catch your breath."

"Excuse me, sir, but is it wise to remain here?" Sir Edward inquired. "You appear to have had some trouble."

"Trouble? Not in the least. I banged myself up a bit descending that ladder in too great haste. Unfortunately I was not hasty enough. They got away."

"Ladder?" I started to rise.

Emerson put his hand on my shoulder and held me in place. "You will see it soon enough, my dear, unless you decide to go round the long way. So much for your mysterious secret passages, eh? It is quite a well-constructed rope ladder, and it has probably been used several times—for one thing, to put the hippopotamus statue in the tomb."

"But you said there was no need to guard the upper entrance."

"Hmm, yes, well, it appears I was wrong. What I failed to take into account was the confounded religious element. During Ramadan even our men are tired and less alert by the end of the day. As soon as the sun goes down they begin eating and drinking and relaxing. The small sounds made by someone descending would be unheard or taken for natural noises."

Ramses returned from the edge of the descent. "They arranged it rather ingeniously, don't you think, Father? The supports are inconspicuous but sturdy; the ladder could be put in place and removed quickly."

I was amused to observe that Sir Edward, normally so cool

and imperturbable, was beginning to show signs of perturbation. "Sir—with all respect—it is getting dark, and the return trip across the plateau will be difficult for the ladies—"

"What ladies?" Emerson grinned at me and put an affectionate arm around Nefret, who was sitting next him on the other side. "But perhaps you are right, we ought to be getting back. Will you go first, Peabody?"

"If you will permit me, Father . . ." Ramses was already on the ladder.

"Gallantry is not required, Ramses," said his father, with a laugh. "The thieves are long since departed, and there is no one below except our men. But go ahead. I left a candle burning at the entrance of the tomb, where the ladder ends. You might wait there for Nefret."

Again I demanded explanations, and while we waited for the children to make the descent, Emerson condescended to give me a brief account. "It had occurred to me that perhaps I ought to have a look round up here, so I came this way, meaning to descend, you know, by one of the paths a little farther along. They had posted a lookout. He saw me coming; the first I knew of his presence was when he called out a warning. He was on the ladder and halfway down before I got here, and although I went after him immediately, I was just too late. The others must have rushed out of the tomb and gone pelting down the stairs; there were enough of them to burst through our guards and bolt. They knocked poor old Abdullah flat and cut Daoud up a bit."

"Are you certain they are all right?" I asked anxiously.

"Oh, yes. Except for being extremely embarrassed. I have been up and down several times, which accounts for my improper appearance. Now then, Peabody, off you go."

He assisted me onto the ladder and addressed Sir Edward. "I don't want to leave the ladder here. Unhook it and bring it with you."

Sir Edward must have voiced a mild objection or question; Emerson's answer, couched in his normal voice, was audible even though I was some feet down the ladder.

"Of course you cannot descend a ladder while you are carrying it! Go back the way you came or follow the path farther to the north and east, where the slope is not so steep.

"Really," he added, after he had joined me on the platform outside the tomb entrance, "so-called higher education in England has deteriorated even further than I had believed. Can you imagine a graduate of Oxford University making such an idiotic remark?"

"It will be a difficult trip in the dark, whichever way he goes," I said.

"He ought to know the paths, he was here last season with Northampton, wasn't he? Anyhow," Emerson went on, "you do not suppose I would leave you and Nefret alone with him."

"Hardly alone, Emerson. Really, you . . . Oh, never mind. Did they do any damage? For I presume you have been in the tomb."

"Yes."

Night had fallen. There is almost no twilight in Egypt, only a sudden transformation from daylight to dark. Emerson removed the candle from its rocky setting. The flame illumined his grave, unsmiling countenance.

"They meant to break into the burial chamber tonight, Peabody. And they might have done it, too, if I had not startled them into flight."

"Yet they chose to face all our men instead of you." I squeezed his arm affectionately.

"They may have believed you were with me," Emerson said with a chuckle. "You and your parasol." But there was no humor in his voice when he continued. "The situation is more serious than I allowed myself to admit, Peabody. An attempt like this one, in broad daylight and in force, is uncharacteristic of the Gurnawis. Someone knows we are now within striking distance of the burial chamber, and he means to get there before we do. The next attempt may be more violent; one of the men, or one of us, could be seriously injured. It is against all my principles, but I see no help for it. We'll have to go straight for the sarcophagus and the queen's mummy."

CHAPTER ELEVEN

I have Known Several Villains Who Were Perfect Gentlemen

Emerson's announcement, made that evening to our assembled family, aroused universal approbation. His arguments were irrefutable. The contents of the burial chamber, whatever they might be, must be removed to safekeeping before they inspired another attack on us or our loyal men.

We resembled a little group of conspirators as we drew close together round the table on the upper deck, the light of the single lamp casting eerie shadows across our tense faces. Emerson's first statement, even before he announced his intention, had been a warning that our plans must be kept secret.

"As far as is possible, at any rate," he added grudgingly. "If I had my way I would allow no one but ourselves and the men in that tomb. I don't see how I can keep Sir Edward out, though."

"Do you suspect him?" Evelyn asked.

"No." Emerson's eyeballs gleamed as he rolled them in my direction. I contented myself with a sniff, and Emerson went on,

"I have no reason to suppose he is anything but what he claims to be, and if I let him go now, without a valid excuse, it would arouse suspicion and justifiable resentment. I shall caution him as I do you not to breathe a word of what we are doing to an outsider. That includes Vandergelt, Amelia. And your friend O'Connell."

"Fortunately Kevin is presently suffering from a touch of stomach trouble, so we won't have to worry about him for a while. But Cyrus—"

"No one!" Emerson's fist came down on the table. We all jumped and I caught the lamp as it tottered. "It may be that only the local talent is involved, but today's attempt was uncharacteristically bold. It suggests there is some unknown power directing operations."

"Riccetti," I said.

"Quite possibly. If he has informants and allies among the villagers, as he undoubtedly does, secrecy is essential."

"Am I to take it," said Ramses, "that David is one of those included in your prohibition?"

Emerson is not, by nature, an unjust man. He hesitated—but briefly—before he replied. "Particularly David."

To my surprise it was not Ramses who came to the boy's defense, nor even Nefret—though she bit her lip and directed a less than friendly look at her foster father. The quiet voice was that of Evelyn.

"I am sure he can be trusted completely, Radcliffe. I have had several long conversations with him. He is a dear lad, who deserves better of life than the misery he has experienced, and he is devoted to all of you."

Emerson's voice softened, as it always does when he speaks to his sister-in-law. "Evelyn, your good heart does you credit and I understand why at this particular time . . . er, hmph. Bear in mind that the boy has spent most of his life under the tutelage of a master thief and forger. Early impressions—"

"Don't patronize me, Radcliffe."

The reprimand was as startling as a slap in the face. Never had I heard Evelyn speak to anyone, much less Emerson, in that tone.

Emerson was the first to recover, and it is to his credit that he responded as he did. (Though I would have expected nothing less of him.) He laughed aloud and slapped his knee.

"Well done! I apologize, Evelyn, but I assure you I am not discriminating against David. Good Gad, Vandergelt is one of my oldest friends, and I trust him completely—but I don't mean to let him in on this either. I wish we could rid ourselves of that confounded Marmaduke woman."

"Ah," I exclaimed. "So you have come round to my belief that she is an adventuress and a spy!"

"No, Amelia, I have not. I believe she is a woolly-minded romantic from whom O'Connell could winkle the truth with a few florid compliments."

"You have the right of it," I admitted. "Do not concern yourself, my dear, I will think of a way to—"

"I shudder at the thought," said Emerson with considerable feeling. "Leave it to me, Peabody. Does she know how to operate one of those typewriting machines?"

"Yes, I believe she does."

"Then I will put her to work transcribing the manuscript of my *History*. That should keep her busy, and away from the tomb."

"It certainly should," I agreed. "How long is the manuscript—six-hundred-odd pages? And your handwriting, my dear . . . An excellent idea."

"So it is settled, then. We begin tomorrow."

"It will only take another day or two to finish with the scraps of painted plaster we retrieved from the entrance corridor," Walter said. "The majority of them are unfortunately too small to be of use, but I have found a portion of a cartouche that I believe will interest you a great deal, Radcliffe."

"It will have to wait, Walter. I need every pair of hands, especially yours." Walter looked pleased, and Emerson, in his bluff way, went on to spoil the compliment by adding, "You appear not to have forgotten *entirely* everything you knew about excavation techniques."

I yawned, and Emerson, always so considerate of me, said in

a friendly manner, "Tired, are you, Peabody? Yes, it is time we were all in bed."

"You will want to be up at dawn, I suppose," I said. "One thing, Emerson—what about storage? The saloon is already full of trays and baskets of scraps, and I absolutely refuse to share my quarters with that atrocious mummy."

"We'll have to have it out, I suppose," Emerson admitted. "I had thought of storing it temporarily in the antechamber, but the stench of the thing is so vile it would poison the air. There are dozens of abandoned tombs nearby; we'll use some of them. And a separate one for our odorous friend."

I was the last to leave the deck. It may have been my imagination, but I thought I saw movement—only the darkest shadow of a shape—at the far end of the rail. It was as if something had hung there, like a giant bat, and then had noiselessly descended.

As I believe I have said, the upper deck was formed by the ceilings of the cabins below. The room under that particular section of the railing was the one occupied by Ramses and David.

I was not the only one to be up before daybreak next morning. Walter was in the saloon, shuffling his plaster scraps around in the light of a lamp. He looked up with a guilty start when I opened the door.

"Oh, it is you, Amelia. I thought I would just get in a few more minutes' work before breakfast. The cartouche I spoke of last night is one I never expected to find in that context. I believe it to be the name of—"

"Breakfast is being served," said Emerson, behind me. "Lock that tray in the cupboard, Walter, and come upstairs."

Waiting for the others to join us, Emerson and I sat in silence for a while, watching the sky brighten and the light creep slowly down the slopes of the western cliffs. Emerson let out a sigh.

"I have been having second thoughts about this, Peabody. Has it occurred to you—but of course it has!—that I may be doing precisely what our unknown opponent wants me to do?"

"It had of course occurred to me, Emerson. Yesterday's attempt was a reckless and chancy business, if they really intended to enter the burial chamber. Perhaps our enemy is becoming impatient. If we clear those stairs we will save *him* the trouble of doing the work."

"I dislike being goaded and manipulated," Emerson muttered.

"Well, of course you do, my dear. But I don't see what choice you have now."

The advent of Mahmud with breakfast ended the discussion. Ramses was the next to appear. He was wise enough to allow Emerson one cup of coffee before raising a subject he knew would annoy, and we were still discussing it when the others came.

"Ramses is in the right, Emerson," I said. "David had better come with us."

"I will keep him with me," Evelyn said firmly. "He will not observe what you are doing."

"Can you keep the Marmaduke woman out of my way too?" Emerson inquired humbly. "There wasn't time to head her off this morning, and I need to locate one of those confounded writing machines."

"Certainly," Evelyn said. "Leave it to me, Radcliffe."

I know I was not the only one to feel a thrill of anticipation ripple through me when we set off that morning. Even Emerson's eyes shone with greater luster. We archaeologists are superior to the common herd in our appreciation of knowledge for its own sake, but we are human after all; the thought of what might await us behind that sealed door would stir the feeblest imagination.

No thrill of anticipation rippled through the frame of poor Abdullah, who was waiting for us. Chagrin and shame lengthened his countenance, and I deduced, from the crestfallen looks of his men, that they had been lectured at length on their failure to perform their duties.

Emerson wasted no time in additional recriminations. (There is seldom any need for him to repeat a reprimand, since he makes his feelings clear at the outset.) After Evelyn had gone off with

David, her hand on the boy's shoulder, Emerson drew his foreman aside and told him of our intentions.

Abdullah's face brightened at this evidence of confidence. He so forgot himself as to interrupt Emerson's admonitions about silence. "Our lips are sealed, Father of Curses. We will not fail you again."

"It was not your fault, Abdullah," I said, patting his arm.

"Yes, it was," said Emerson, dismissing the subject. He took out his watch. "Where are the others? I cannot wait for them. Send Sir Edward up as soon as he arrives, Evelyn, and keep that tedious woman out of the way. The rest of you come with me."

And off he went, up the stairs.

It was at my insistence that we stopped for luncheon. The air was thick with plaster dust and the bat guano stirred up by our movements; Walter's breathing had become uneven and even Sir Edward was showing signs of distress. I had, over her strenuous objections, sent Nefret down earlier.

She came running toward me when I descended the last steps. "Aunt Amelia, you look terrible."

"Do I? Then I had better tidy up a bit before we join the others."

We all made use of the buckets of water and towels, and then retired to the shelter. Knowing Emerson would refuse to return to the *Amelia* until nightfall, I had ordered picnic baskets, and we tucked into the food and especially the drink with gusto. It was interesting to see how the group divided. I joined Gertrude at the little table, the men distributed themselves on various rocks, and the children went to join David in his tomb. Evelyn had been with him; when she took her place at the table I saw she was holding a sketch pad. I asked to see what she had been doing, and she handed it to me with an odd little smile.

"Are you giving drawing lessons?" I asked, thumbing through the pages in growing amazement.

"Taking them, rather. What a talent the boy has, Amelia! He knows nothing of the conventions of Western art, of course, but he is quick to learn—and he is giving me a new understanding of Egyptian art. I believe he could help me with the copying."

"That will have to wait until we finish clearing the antechamber," I said, with a warning glance at Gertrude.

She looked not quite the thing that morning; her eyes were shadowed and she seemed abstracted. Catching my eye, she cleared her throat and said hesitantly, "I have been thinking, Mrs. Emerson, about the kind invitation of Mr. Vandergelt. I would like to accept it, but I don't feel it would be proper."

"Why not?" I inquired, selecting a second sandwich.

"To be the only woman in the house?"

"Such old-fashioned notions are passé, Gertrude. We are in the twentieth century now. Surely you don't suspect Mr. Vandergelt of improper intentions."

"Oh, no! Only . . . I would feel so much more comfortable if Mrs. Walter Emerson were there too. Or Nefret?"

Emerson had finished eating. He came up to us in time to hear the last exchange.

"*You* will be perfectly safe with Vandergelt, Miss Marmaduke," he said. "Do you happen to know where I can put my hands on a typewriting machine?"

"Now that I come to think of it," I said, "Cyrus probably has one. You know how these Americans are about machinery."

"Excellent!" Emerson gave me an approving smile. "That's settled, then. You can pack your traps this afternoon, Miss Marmaduke, and be in the Castle by evening. I will run by later with my manuscript and tell you what I want done. You may as well go now. I will have one of the men take you over to Luxor. Finished, Peabody? Come along, come along."

He trotted away, leaving Gertrude gaping. I provided the explanations Emerson had neglected to give—he assumes, incorrectly, that other people think as quickly as he and I do—and sent Gertrude off with Selim.

"It is a relief to have her out of the way," I said to Evelyn. "Now we can talk freely."

A reverberant bellow from Emerson reached our ears. Evelyn laughed. "We cannot talk at all, Amelia. I am dying of curiosity to know what you have found, but you had better go before Radcliffe begins swearing."

The others had already obeyed the summons. As I followed, I saw Evelyn return to the spot where David was sitting.

When Emerson was finally persuaded to stop, the barrier was gone and most of the fallen stone had been removed from the steps. The sight of what lay below—the rock-cut stairs, plunging down at a steep angle, the low, uneven roof—was not alarming or unusual, but I noticed that our workers departed with alacrity as soon as Emerson gave the word. Abdullah must have told them about the mummy. How could I blame the men for dreading such an omen, when it had affected even me?

"That will suffice," Emerson said, wiping his wet forehead with his filthy sleeve. "We will need more planks tomorrow, Abdullah, to finish shoring up the roof; I don't like the looks of it."

"It shall be as you say, Emerson. And then you will take . . ." His hand moved in an odd, shrinking gesture, as if he was reluctant even to indicate the mummy, much less name it.

"Yes." Emerson glanced at me. "Go on, Peabody, we will be along shortly."

Nefret and Ramses had already left the tomb with Walter. I allowed Sir Edward to offer me his hand.

"You must be very tired," he said sympathetically.

"No more than you, I think." He was a far cry from the elegant gentleman I had first met, his clothing sweat-stained and wrinkled, his hair white with dust. From the filth that smeared his face a pair of red-rimmed blue eyes met my eyes with visible amusement.

"I had believed myself to be an old hand at this," he admitted. "But compared to your husband, Newberry and Spiegelberg, with whom I worked last season, are effete dilettantes."

"He will maintain this pace until we have finished, you know. Can you keep up?"

"I will drop in my tracks before I admit defeat," was the laughing response. "I am concerned about Mr. Walter Emerson, though. If there is anything I can do—with the utmost tact, of course—to relieve him . . ."

"A considerable degree of tact would be required. But I thank you, and I will bear it in mind. Have you decided to accept Mr. Vandergelt's invitation to stay with him?"

My knees buckled as I stepped onto the ground. It was not fatigue; I had trod on a pebble. His hand was quick to steady me.

"I would prefer to remain at the hotel, if you and the Professor do not object."

"I do not object," said Emerson. "If you need a hand, Amelia, take mine."

Sir Edward hastened toward the water bucket and I said, "Emerson, you must stop creeping up on people like that. It is not only rude, it is unnerving."

"I wanted to hear what he was whispering so tenderly into your ear," said my husband.

"He was not whispering, and it was not tender. It was interesting, though. I had expected he and Gertrude would want to remain together."

"You were mistaken, Peabody. It does happen occasionally."

I had observed earlier that Walter did not look well, but I did not take it seriously until after Sir Edward's concerned comment. Even I had been affected adversely by the strenuous effort and bad air and the sickening stench from the bottom of the steps. He looked better—so did we all!—after a bathe and change of clothing, but when we met for an early supper I took a closer look at my brother-in-law and was not pleased at what I saw. I refrained from comment, however, until Emerson informed us that he meant from now on to spend the nights at the tomb, and Walter insisted on sharing the duty with him.

"You will not wish to be away from . . . away from the boat every night," he said, carefully not looking at me. "We will do it in turn, Radcliffe, as we used to do."

"I don't see why either of you has to be there," I said. "Abdullah will not be tricked a second time and it is sheer arrogance and prejudice to suppose the presence of a single Englishman will prevent what five loyal Egyptians cannot."

I had hoped this would be convincing and that I would not have to voice my belief that Walter was not up to the job, since that would only make him more determined to prove he was. Oblivious to my subtle intent, Emerson foiled my plan by announcing loudly that he was not talking about Englishmen in general but himself in particular, and that if anyone doubted his effectiveness he could produce affadavits from most of the residents of Egypt.

So I was forced in the end to tell Walter he was not fit, and Walter indignantly denied it, and I sent him straight to bed.

After Emerson had gone off, carrying the manuscript he meant to leave with Miss Marmaduke before going on to the tomb, I returned to the saloon. I was alone; Nefret and Ramses were in his room, with David—giving him a lesson in English or ancient Hebrew or astronomy, I supposed—and Evelyn had taken Walter a tray. I had thought to distract myself by working on my translation, but the words never penetrated my head and finally I gave up, watching the moon rise over the silhouetted cliffs and trying not to think about Emerson.

I had arranged with Ibrahim, one of Abdullah's nephews, or cousins—it was difficult to keep track of them all—to stand watch some little distance from the camp and to report instantly to me if anything untoward occurred. (I had not mentioned it to Emerson; he would have made indignant remarks about nursemaids.) I felt a little easier after doing this, but not much. Our foes were cunning and unprincipled.

The door opened and Evelyn slipped in. "If you are working I will not disturb you," she said softly.

"You are the person I want most to see," I said, realizing, with some surprise, that this was true. "Or at least—"

"I understand. There is no use telling you not to worry about him."

"No. I hope you are not worried about Walter. I think he is only suffering from exhaustion."

"He is asleep," Evelyn said dismissively. She sat down and arranged her skirts. The lamplight aureoled her golden hair. "I wish there were something I could do. If only I were a man!"

"Well, as to that, I would not say that men have all the advantages. Poor creatures, they are singularly lacking in certain intellectual qualities."

Evelyn's tight lips relaxed into a smile. "That is not the common view, Amelia. Are not men supposed to be ruled by reason, and women by irrational emotion?"

"Ah, but who defines those views? Men, my dear—men! Only consider the facts. I have been attempting for weeks to convince Emerson to take a rational view of the situation, but he won't even admit the facts, much less the logical conclusions to be drawn from them. They would be self-evident to any woman."

"Perhaps not to me," Evelyn said with a smile. She seemed easier now; her hands lay loose in her lap and her stiff shoulders had relaxed.

"You do yourself an injustice. In case I have not mentioned it, Evelyn, I have come to have great respect for your ratiocinative abilities. I feel certain that if we put our heads together we can solve the problem of who our enemies are and decide on the best method of defending ourselves."

"My abilities, such as they are (and I fear affection makes you rate them too highly), are at your disposal, Amelia dear. You have already given me a brief account of what has transpired. Perhaps you would be willing to go over it again in greater detail?"

She was not really interested in hearing my account; she was hoping to keep my mind occupied so that I would not fret about Emerson. Mine had not been an empty compliment, however. I launched immediately into my narrative, beginning with the visit of Mr. Shelmadine. Evelyn listened in silence, and I must say it was a pleasure to talk with someone who did not interrupt every thirty seconds.

When I had finished she drew a sheet of blank paper to her and selected a pen. "I find it easier to keep things straight in my mind when I write them down. Do you object?"

"Not at all. I do that myself occasionally, though I have found that my mental processes do not readily lend themselves to organization of that variety."

"Your mental processes are too complex," Evelyn agreed gravely. "Let me see if I can summarize them." She inscribed a list of names. "These, if I understand you, are the persons of whose integrity you are not certain."

"That is a genteel way of putting it. You must add another name, Evelyn. I am fond of the boy too, but we cannot clear him completely of suspicion."

"Yes, of course." With a steady hand she added David's name to the list, and took another sheet of paper. "Let us start with the assumption—which seems to me reasonable—that there are two different groups of thieves involved. Which is which?"

By the time we finished, the paper was all scribbled over and crossed out. "Well," I said doubtfully, "I cannot say my mind is any clearer on this."

"But we have made a beginning." She pointed with the pen as she spoke. "Riccetti is the head of one such group. Shelmadine was his man. The horrible old man at Gurneh—Abd el Hamed—is connected with the second group. Shall we call them A and B, for easier reference?"

"More distinctive names are easier to keep straight," I said. "Let me see. Nefret calls Riccetti 'the Hippopotamus Man,' and there is unquestionably a certain resemblance to that beast. Supposing we refer to his gang as the Hippopotami and to the other group as the Jackals."

Evelyn laughed. "Those are certainly distinctive names. Then we can assume Abd el Hamed is a Jackal. His hatred of the man who crippled his hands must be intense. And if that is so, then David . . . Oh, Amelia, I cannot believe the boy would betray you. Any of you!"

"It would be a serious error to believe we can understand his motives," I said soberly. "An old, long-established fear may be

stronger than a new loyalty. If David is guilty, he is working for Abd el Hamed. What of the others?"

Evelyn shook her head. "I don't see how we can possibly tell. The antiquities dealer in Luxor must be involved, but he could be in terror of either group; they appear to be equally unscrupulous. It is difficult for me to picture a gentleman like Sir Edward taking orders from a man like Riccetti—"

"I have known several villains who were perfect gentlemen. And there are Europeans, English and Americans up to their necks in the illegal-antiquities game. Leave him in the list of uncertains. What about Miss Marmaduke?"

"On the surface she is a perfect example of a certain type of English spinster," Evelyn said thoughtfully. "Too perfect, perhaps? I have had a number of conversations with her, and I cannot find a flaw in her performance. There is only one thing that gives me pause, and that is her—excessive, don't you think?—interest in Nefret."

"Almost as if she knew some particular danger threatens the child," I agreed uneasily. "Yes, I do think it is excessive. She suggested more than once that Nefret would be safer in her care."

"She may be only superstitious and fanciful. A childless woman sometimes develops strong attachments to pretty young creatures in her care. Especially girls."

"Gertrude certainly has not shown any strong affection for Ramses," I agreed, laughing and yawning at once. "Emerson would say we are the ones who are fanciful, Evelyn. Our brilliant deductions are based on very tenuous evidence."

"It is up to us to procure additional evidence," Evelyn said. "But you are tired, Amelia; can you sleep now?"

"Yes." It was not true, but she was also in need of rest and I knew she would sit with me all night if she felt I wanted her.

I left her at the door of her room, with a kiss and a fond good night; but after that door had closed I went to another chamber than my own. The sound of soft breathing and the sight of a slight form curled under the blankets should have been enough, but I did not leave the room until after I had bent over it and made certain the form was Nefret's.

The conversation with Evelyn had brought into sharp focus fears that up till then I had tried to deny. In addition to the point she had mentioned—Gertrude's unnatural concern—there was another, more alarming indication of danger to Nefret. Abd el Hamed's excuses had been glib and reasonable, but the unpleasant fact remained: it was Nefret's room the intruder had entered, and it was she whom his hands had seized.

I lay long awake, and it was not only fear for Emerson that kept Morpheus at bay.

We did not linger over breakfast next morning. Upon our arrival at the tomb I hastened at once to mount the stairs; when I entered the antechamber I saw Emerson sitting on the floor, his head bowed and Abdullah bending over him.

"Now what?" I inquired, with admirable calm.

Emerson raised his head, displaying a countenance sicklier in hue than was its wont. "Good morning, my dear. I trust you slept well."

"Are you ill? Are you hurt?"

He pushed away my hands and those of Abdullah, and rose with all his old energy. "A passing queasiness, nothing more. I have just finished fixing the lid back over that mummy, and the stench was unpleasant."

"Did you have to do that?" I demanded.

"I should have waited for you to do it, I suppose," Emerson said mildly. The others filed into the room and he gave them an absentminded wave of greeting as he continued, "All right, Abdullah, let's get the gruesome thing out of here. Send Daoud or Ali up to give me a hand. I could carry it myself, but I don't want to joggle it."

Abdullah folded his arms and did not budge. "I will be your hands, Emerson."

Emerson stroked his chin and studied his reis thoughtfully.

Then he smiled and gave the old man a clap on the shoulder. "Is it so? You and I then, Abdullah, as so often before. Peabody, just trot down, will you, and disperse the locals? One glimpse of a coffin being carried out of here and they will spread the word. The rest of you clear out, you will only be in the way."

"Just a moment," I said. "At least protect your breathing apparatus. You ought to have done it before. Where is your handkerchief, Emerson?"

It was a foolish question. He never has one. While he was fumbling in his pockets Walter produced his, and Emerson bound it over his mouth. Abdullah wound his scarf over the lower part of his face, and then they started down the steps. Both had to stoop; they were tall men and the roof was low.

With the assistance of my trusty and magical parasol I dispersed the locals as requested. I had to chase them some distance, and when I returned I saw Emerson on the stairs. He had the front end of the coffin on his shoulder; Abdullah kept it level, his hands supporting the other end.

Once they reached the ground they moved quickly and without hesitation to the place Emerson must have selected in advance. It was hardly more than a pit, the entrance to a tomb half-choked with rubble. There was just enough room for the coffin.

The watching men moved rather too alertly out of its path. Nefret, standing next to me, said softly, "Is that what the Professor meant, Aunt Amelia, when he said 'Is it so?' And why Abdullah insisted on helping him?"

"In part it was Abdullah's pride that was at stake, Nefret. He hates admitting he is getting old. But I fear you are right; some of the men might have objected, or even refused to touch the thing. Oh dear, I hope we are not going to have another problem with curses, it is such a nuisance."

"It would give Radcliffe a chance to perform one of his famous exorcisms," said Walter. A night's rest had done him good; reminiscent amusement warmed his face. "Excuse me, ladies, I will just go and help them cover the pit. Better to do the job oneself than risk a flat refusal from the men."

Ramses was already with his father, helping him and Abdullah pour sand over the coffin. After a while Selim joined them, swaggering and smiling contemptuously at the other men. They could not be outdone; when they were all at work, Emerson and Walter returned to us. Apparently they had been arguing, for Walter's face was flushed and I heard him say, "Under no circumstances will I allow it, Radcliffe."

"Allow?" Emerson repeated. "I don't know how you've kept her under control all these years, Walter—I have never been able to do it—but I fear your domestic tyranny is ended. We could put it to the test. I will tell her what I want done and you will forbid her to do it, and then we will see what happens, eh?"

"What is the disagreement, gentlemen?" I inquired.

"I need a detailed drawing of the area before we demolish the doorway," was the answer I had expected. "Even with reflectors there may not be sufficient light for a photograph and . . . where the devil is Sir Edward? He should have been here by now."

"See here, Radcliffe," Walter began.

"Curse it, Walter, will you leave off badgering me? After all," Emerson added in an injured voice, "I was considerate enough to refrain from asking her to do the sketch while the repulsive thing was still in situ, although that would have been the proper procedure."

He strode off without giving Walter time to reply. I patted him on the arm. "Your concern is unnecessary, Walter."

"Hmph," said Walter, sounding astonishingly like his brother.

Evelyn promptly agreed to Emerson's request, of course; in fact she appeared delighted to be asked. She had been sitting with David, watching him as he worked on the sculptured head. I lingered long enough to commend him, for it really was quite a lovely thing. He did not reply except with a long steady look, and I felt his eyes upon me as I walked away.

The others were already at work when I descended the steps. The removal of the coffin had exposed a number of objects scattered randomly on the floor behind it. Evelyn was making a quick sketch of their relative positions while Nefret wrote down the numbers and descriptions Emerson dictated.

"Food offerings," said Ramses, before I could ask. "Jars of oil and wine, most of them broken, a mummified haunch of meat."

"For our mummy?"

"They wouldn't have been much use to him," Emerson said, without looking up. "Four and a half centimeters, Nefret. A nameless spirit could not partake of offerings. And five centimeters across."

Hearing footsteps on the outer staircase, I returned to the antechamber. The newcomer was Sir Edward, camera in hand. "I overslept—mea culpa, Mrs. Emerson, I confess it. I was up rather late developing the plates. And then the ferry grounded on a sandbar."

"That is always the way when one is in a hurry," I said. "Never mind, Sir Edward, Emerson is making drawings."

"I really am very sorry," the young man began, and then broke off, looking past me down the steps. "Is the coffin out already? You have been hard at work."

I had thought Emerson would be too preoccupied to notice my absence, but I was in error. "Peabody!" he shouted. "Fetch some of those baskets, and be quick about it."

Sir Edward politely took them from me. "Charming," he said with a smile. "His use of your maiden name, I mean."

"It is employed as a term of approbation," I explained. "A sign of professional equality and respect."

"So I assumed. Please allow me to precede you; the steps are very uneven."

Emerson took the baskets from Sir Edward without looking up. "That will have to do, Evelyn," he grunted. "Curse it! I will never forgive myself for this! Ramses, have you finished numbering the objects?"

"It is the only thing to do, Emerson," I said consolingly.

"Hmph." Quickly, but with the delicacy of touch that marked all his actions, he began lifting the objects into the baskets.

Then came the moment for which we had all been waiting. In silence Abdullah handed the chisel and hammer to Emerson. In silence Emerson gestured us to move back.

The ancient mud plaster crumbled and fell trickling to the floor under his precise, steady blows. At last he gave the implements to Abdullah, who placed a lever in Emerson's outthrust hand. Emerson inserted it into the crack and bore down. Under his sweat-soaked shirt the muscles of his back bunched and tightened.

An eerie grating groan, like the protest of an animal in pain, was the first indication of success. Until I saw a shadow along the edge of the block, I could not tell it had moved. Slowly the shadow lengthened. Emerson shifted his grip and spoke for the first time. "Twelve inches. Be ready, Abdullah."

The reis's hands were already under the front edge of the block. Sir Edward put me gently out of his way. He did not speak as he slipped past me; his eyes had a wild glitter. Dropping to his knees, he put both hands under the stone.

"Damn fool," said Emerson distinctly. "Don't try to hold it, let the back slide down and then get your fingers out from underneath. When I give the word . . . Now!"

The stone fell. Abdullah was slower than the younger man, but he knew exactly what he was doing. It was his skill that allowed the back edge of the block to hit the floor first, so that there was time for Sir Edward to pull his hands back. The block settled onto the floor with a thud.

"Bloody stupid business," Emerson grumbled, adding fairly, "My fault as well. If I were not in such a bloody damned hurry . . . I beg your pardon, Peabody; just hand me that candle, will you?"

I had hardly taken notice of his bad language. This was the moment. For the first time in heaven knew how many centuries, light would enter the eternal darkness of the tomb and the eyes of the profane would violate the rest of the royal dead. Or would they? Would we see the glitter of golden ornaments, the massive shape of an untouched sarcophagus—or only scattered wrappings and broken bits of bone? The flame wavered as I handed him the candle, and a tear blurred my vision. He had summoned me, of all those who stood nearby, so that I might be the first to share that moment with him.

He thrust his arm within. The flame flickered and burned blue and then went out. But before it died I saw what I had never dared hope to see—a chaotic tumble of decayed wood and fallen stone, yes; but the brief light had set off a hundred golden sparks, and looming high above the litter was a solid rectangle of stone—a sarcophagus, with its massive lid still in place.

It was a sober group that gathered round the picnic baskets. One would have supposed, seeing our gloomy faces, that we had found a looted, empty chamber instead of a discovery that would reverberate down the corridors of Egyptological history. The magnitude of the find and the enormous responsibility of it weighed on us all—most of all on Emerson, who sat with his face in his hands and his head bowed. After I had dispensed tea and sandwiches to the others, I touched his shoulder.

"Cheese or cucumber, Emerson?"

He lowered his hands. His face was haggard. "I can't do it, Peabody."

"I know, my dear," I said sympathetically. "I did not suppose you could."

"It is taking a risk." He grasped my hands and squeezed them. Had the moment been less fraught with emotion I would have screamed. "The longer we delay in removing the objects, especially the mummy, the greater the chance of attack. If you came to harm through my fanatical attachment to professional standards . . ."

His voice broke and he gazed intently into my eyes.

We might have been alone, "no one hearing, no one seeing," to quote an ancient Egyptian source. My heart swelled. The danger to others was equally great, but it was *my* danger that made him hesitate, *I* who came foremost in his thoughts. There had been many touching moments in our marriage, but none as poignant as this. I chose my words with care.

"Good Gad, Emerson, what a fuss you are making about nothing! If you had violated *our* professional standards I would have been forced to speak severely to you. Now go and tell Abdullah of the change in plan."

Emerson threw back his shoulders and drew a long breath. His eyes blazed, his firm lips curved; his face was that of the ardent young scholar who had first won my heart, and my wholehearted allegiance, in the necropolis of Amarna. Giving my hands a final, excruciating squeeze, he released them and jumped to his feet.

"Right you are, Peabody. Save me a few sandwiches, will you?"

I rubbed my numbed fingers and looked at my companions. The interest with which they had followed the conversation was evident from their expressions. For the most part, approbation and understanding marked those faces, but a shadow darkened Walter's brow, and Sir Edward was frankly staring.

The latter was the first to speak. "I beg your pardon, Mrs. Emerson, but I fear I missed the point of that exchange. Unless it dealt with personal matters which you would rather not discuss . . ."

"My husband and I are not in the habit of discussing personal matters in public, Sir Edward." I softened the seeming reproof with a friendly smile and an explanation. "We had determined to clear the tomb as quickly as possible, before robbers could get at it. It would have been a relatively simple job if this tomb had been like most of the others, empty of all save miscellaneous small objects. But now . . . The rubble you saw, Sir Edward, is the remains of the queen's original grave goods. Some were of wood, which has rotted and fallen apart, spilling the contents into a tangle. Part of the ceiling appears to have collapsed, crushing other objects. If we shovel the lot into baskets, any hope of restoring the original designs will be lost. And this discovery is unique—the first, perhaps the only, royal tomb to contain at least some of its original equipment. It would be a crime against Egyptological scholarship to overlook the slightest clue. The proper procedures will require not days but months, perhaps years."

"Yes, I see. I have heard of the Professor's meticulous standards." But his brow was still furrowed.

"Be candid, Sir Edward," I urged. "If you do not fully comprehend, ask questions and I will elaborate."

"Well, then, ma'am, since you allow me, I will be candid. What is the Professor worried about? I know the local thieves will steal anything they can lay their hands on, but he is not afraid of a motley lot of barefoot Arabs, is he?"

A stir of shared indignation ran through the others. Eyes flashing, Walter rose impetuously to his feet, and Ramses began, "The word 'afraid,' sir, in connection with my father—"

"Now, now," I said, waving Walter back into his chair. "I believe the question was not meant as an insult but as an expression of incredulity. My husband, Sir Edward, is utterly fearless—for himself. We are dealing here, not with a motley lot of barefoot Arabs, but with at least two gangs of ruthless, well-organized criminals."

Sir Edward was staring again. I went on to explain (for as the Reader may have realized, I had determined on a new strategy, whose details will become evident as I proceed). The young man's stupefied expression betrayed some evidence of intelligence when I mentioned Riccetti.

"I have heard of the fellow," he admitted. "And some unpleasant stories about him. If he is one of the people involved—"

"He is. No more of this now," I added, as I saw Emerson returning.

Sir Edward nodded. There was only time for him to say, "Count on me, Mrs. Emerson. In all ways and at any time."

Emerson was his old self again—cheerful, enthusiastic and autocratic. He began rattling off instructions. "I want a hundred photographs of that room before we touch a single scrap. No, I have not removed my ban on artificial lighting, we will use reflectors. I have managed it before under circumstances almost as difficult. We'll have to get you and your gear up on top of the sarcophagus, Sir Edward. Go back to Luxor immediately and bring more plates, you haven't nearly enough. And more reflectors."

"Let him finish his luncheon, Emerson," I said. "There is no need for haste now."

"Thank you, Mrs. Emerson, but I have finished." Sir Edward rose. "Excuse me, sir, but if I may ask . . . I thought you didn't want anyone moving about in the room. I don't see how I can get to the sarcophagus without wading through the debris."

Emerson studied him thoughtfully. "How are you at trapeze work?"

"He is just making one of his little jokes," I explained to the astonished young man.

"I had considered the possibility," Emerson said calmly. "However, I believe we can run a ramp from the doorway to the top of the sarcophagus. You will have to be careful, Sir Edward: if you slip and fall off onto my antiquities, I will murder you."

"Yes, sir. I will return as quickly as possible, Professor."

Emerson, devouring cucumber sandwiches, waved him away. Evelyn, who had been looking at the solitary figure sitting cross-legged in the shade, said, "I will take David his lunch and sit with him awhile."

"Bring him here," Emerson said.

"But you said," Ramses began.

"There is no hope of keeping this secret now," Emerson said. "If we had proceeded according to the original plan, we might have been able to keep it under wraps for a day or so, but our forthcoming activities will unquestionably be noticed. I will tell the boy myself—as much as I must."

Ramses jumped up. "I will fetch him, Aunt Evelyn."

I must give Emerson credit for more craftiness than I had expected from him. He put the case to David in such a way as to imply that he was one of a chosen few to be honored with our confidence. His peroration, though somewhat florid, was a masterpiece of persuasive rhetoric.

"There is danger still, to you and to us. Have no fear; I will protect you as I would my son. And you will watch over him—your brother and your friend. Is it not so?"

David moved his hand in a curious gesture; I could not make out whether he was crossing himself in the Christian fashion or performing the classic Arabic salutation. He spoke in English. "It is so, Father of Curses."

"Good," said Emerson, in the same language. Rising to his feet, hands on his hips, he looked us over one by one and smiled. "Let's get at it, then."

CHAPTER TWELVE

It Is Better to Have a Demon As a Friend Than an Enemy

"Obviously," I said to Evelyn, "we must take steps at once to render our enemies impotent."

The shadows of evening stretched across the ground as we rode side by side toward the *Amelia*. Behind us lay the hills and the desert plain; ahead and on either side, fields of barley and sugarcane shone green as emeralds in the golden light.

"I don't know what you have in mind, Amelia," Evelyn said, giving me an apprehensive look. "But surely attack is not only dangerous but unnecessary. If our defenses are strong enough . . ."

"Impossible, my dear. An armed regiment at the tomb and another guarding the boat would not suffice."

"I wish we had them, though."

"So do I," I confessed. "An abundance of dependable defenders would certainly mitigate the danger. Our stout fellows are completely trustworthy and would defend us to the death, but there are barely enough of them to guard the tomb. The guards employed by the Antiquities Service are worse than useless; most of them are local fellows who would just as soon rob the tomb themselves. But you know as well as I that if the local talent, as Emerson calls them, were our only concern, I would sleep sound as a baby. I know most of the rascals personally; they are dishonest and greedy and untrustworthy, but I do not believe any of them is capable of cold-blooded murder. Riccetti *has* committed murder—and worse."

Evelyn shivered. "It is the children who must be protected."

"My dear girl, I have been trying for almost thirteen years to keep Ramses out of trouble; it isn't a question of protecting him, it is a question of preventing him from locating a lion so he can put his head in its mouth. Nefret is almost as bad," I added bitterly. "I anticipated difficulty with her but I never expected it would take this form; they are in constant competition, each trying to outdo the other. No, Evelyn, defense is all very well, but it won't work where those two are concerned. We must find our foes and render them harmless!"

I was somewhat taken aback to learn that Walter had come to the same conclusion. It was not like him to advise direct action—at least it was not like the gentle scholar he had become—and I had intended to keep him out of harm's way. I thought I understood why he had become so bellicose, and I directed a silent curse at Emerson for refusing to allow Walter to share his vigil at the tomb. Had Walter been allowed to participate in that dangerous duty, he would not have felt obliged to prove his manliness. (Most men seem to think this can best be demonstrated by hitting someone.)

Yet I could not think harshly of Emerson; there was no room in my heart for any emotion except tender concern for my absent spouse. He had refused even to return to the dahabeeyah with us. "Tonight is the time of greatest danger, Peabody."

"You have said that before, Emerson! And what of tomorrow night and all the nights that will follow?"

"I'll think of something," Emerson said vaguely. Then his lips curved in a smile and his blue eyes shone with a look I knew well. "You don't suppose I will do without your—er—company indefinitely, do you? I would ask you to stay with me tonight if your presence on board were not absolutely vital."

Staying with him—and Abdullah and Daoud and six other curious, sociably inclined individuals—was not a prospect that held much attraction, except for the chance that I could be of help in protecting Emerson. But that would mean abandoning others more in need of my care. He was right; duty drew me, with what reluctance I cannot express, from his side.

The responsibility was daunting. It may have been that realization that made my dear ones appear particularly vulnerable that evening: Ramses and Nefret, vibrant with the reckless courage of youth; Evelyn, dainty and fragile as a girl in her beruffled tea gown; Walter, slight of frame and softened by years of study, nervously adjusting his eyeglasses. And, of course, the cat Bastet, who had selected Ramses's lap this time. In fact I was less concerned about the cat than about the others. She had better sense than either of the children. So did Anubis, who had gone with Emerson.

David was part of our company, though not, I thought, by choice. He had withdrawn to a corner, where he sat cross-legged chipping away at a bit of stone. It was not the head of Nefret, but a smaller, flatter piece, which seemed to be taking on the outlines of an ushebti figure. I supposed he was doing it to keep his hands busy, as a woman might embroider or sew.

We had talked only of archaeological matters during the evening meal. Not until after the dinner things had been cleared away did Walter abruptly introduce another subject. "Why didn't you and Radcliffe tell me you had seen and spoken with Riccetti?" he demanded.

"You speak of him as if you knew him," I countered, hoping I would not have to invent an excuse.

"I met him once. It was a good many years ago, but the tales that were told about him made him a character one would not soon forget. Confound it, Amelia, you had no right to keep this from me. If I had known he was back in business—"

"You would have tried to send me home," Evelyn interrupted.

"I would not have allowed you to come in the first place."

"Allowed?" Her tone of voice should have warned him to desist. Since he was a man, he began to lose his temper.

"You don't know what a cad like Riccetti is capable of. You are unaccustomed to violence."

Her voice rose. "You seem to have forgotten the circumstances under which we first met."

The reproof was just. Naturally this infuriated Walter even more. "I suppose you think you can defend yourself—and me?—with that absurd umbrella you have kept hidden all these years. I knew you had it, you know. I saw no reason to object if it pleased you to play at being a heroine—"

"Oh, dear," I said. "Please, Walter—Evelyn—not in front of the children."

They were both too angry to heed me. Evelyn had risen. The ruffles at her breast trembled with the rapidity of her breathing. "You did not object? How kind and generous of you. To allow me my toys, as if I were a child—"

"You are behaving like a child!" Walter shouted. "Denying your responsibilities—"

"And what of your responsibilities?"

I decided the quarrel had gone far enough. It was probably an excellent exercise for people who were too accustomed to keeping their feelings closely controlled, but Nefret and Ramses needed no lessons in bad manners, and David had crept closer, his chisel-like knife in his hand. I did not like the way he was looking at Walter.

"Enough!" I said loudly. "That will do. Apologize to one another at once. And," I added, "you had better apologize to me as well, Walter, for your derogatory remark about umbrellas."

As I had planned, my little touch of humor broke the tension. The apologies I had demanded were rendered (though not, I must say, with a great deal of conviction). Evelyn resumed her chair and Walter turned to me with a rueful smile.

"I beg your pardon, Amelia dear."

"Granted. We are all suffering from excitement and nervous strain. Instead of indulging in recriminations and asking idle questions, would we not be better employed at discussing how to deal with our various opponents?"

Walter said hesitantly, "I would never question your detectival abilities, Amelia, but what makes you so certain Riccetti is not our only enemy? I cannot see any evidence of a second party of villains."

I gave Evelyn a little sidelong smile. Walter's statement was a perfect example of that male illogic we had discussed the previous night. I said slowly and patiently, "Mr. Shelmadine was murdered, Walter. I assure you I did not do it and I really don't suspect Emerson either."

"How do you know he was murdered?" Walter demanded. "Was an autopsy performed?"

Nefret proved herself an admirable pupil by remarking interestedly, "I don't suppose they could do an autopsy, Uncle Walter. After being in the water so long, the body was probably falling apart and gnawed by fishes and lobsters."

"There are no lobsters in the Nile," said Ramses, in a peculiar voice. He covered his mouth with his hand.

"Never mind that," I said, before Nefret could take exception to his laughter. "For heaven's sake, Walter, Mr. Shelmadine fell down in a fit, Emerson was struck unconscious, Shelmadine disappeared, and two weeks later his body turned up in the Nile. Unless you believe that Shelmadine feigned his fit in order to strike down a man with whom he had been amiably conversing half a minute earlier and then dashed out of the hotel, unseen by the suffragi, and jumped into the Nile, I do not see how you can avoid the inevitable conclusion that some second party was responsible for his collapse and disappearance. As for Shelmadine himself, I hope you are not so naïve as to suppose he approached us out of sheer altruism, in order to share a golden secret with us. No! He had an ulterior motive—everyone does—and it was not altruistic."

Walter's lips parted. "And furthermore," I went on, "there were two groups of men in the tomb that first night. Emerson himself said one group evicted the other at gunpoint. Now pay attention, Walter, I admit this next part is a bit complicated. The only member of the second group—the one not run by Riccetti—whom we can certainly identify is Abd el Hamed."

"Certainly?" Walter repeated. He sounded rather dazed.

"Surely I need not recapitulate the steps of deductive logic that led me to that conclusion?"

"No, I think I would prefer that you did not, Amelia. Er—you won't object if I ask David a few questions?"

I looked round for the boy. He had not returned to his former place, but sat cross-legged beside Evelyn's chair. Either he had known more English than he had admitted, or he had picked it up quickly, for he understood what Walter had said. He looked up at Evelyn. Her hand rested for a moment on his curly black head, and she said, "It is all right, David. Answer him, if you will, please."

"Hmph," said Walter. "Well, then, David. Who was the man who hurt your master's hands?"

David had not expected that question—to be honest, it was one I had not thought of asking—but he replied readily, "It was before I came to him, sir. But they say he steal—stealed—from the Mudir."

"Mudir?" Walter repeated. "The Governor of the Province?"

"No, sir. The Governor of Antikas."

"Do you know his name?"

"No, sir. He was a great man, the antika sellers of Luxor were in fear of him."

"Riccetti," I said firmly.

"So it would seem." Walter adjusted his eyeglasses. "Has this man, this Mudir, come back, David?"

"They say yes."

"Who is 'they'?"

"Don't confuse him, Walter," I interrupted. "He is learning proper grammar. Who *are* they, David?"

Rephrasing the question did not lessen the boy's confusion. He gestured. "Men. All men in the village. And Abd el Hamed says . . ." He looked up at Evelyn. "I do not say those words. It is not polite."

"Abd el Hamed cursed him?" Walter was unable to repress a smile.

"Cursed." David nodded vigorously.

"Good," said Walter. "You are a great help, David. Did you ever see this Mudir? Did he come to the village or to the house of Abd el Hamed?"

"No, sir."

"Did any strange man come to the house to talk in private with Abd el Hamed, or to buy antiquities? A foreign man?"

David hesitated. "Foreign men, yes. The reverend sir from Luxor, the fat Inglizi from the museum, the man from Cairo who took the royal mummies away."

Despite his limited English vocabulary, he had labeled the individuals in question accurately enough for identification. "Chauncey Murch, Budge and Emile Brugsch," I said. "They all deal—more or less openly—in antiquities. Hmmmm. You don't suppose Mr. Budge—"

"No," Walter said. His voice was a trifle uneven—with anger, I supposed. "Amelia, you and Radcliffe really must get over suspecting Mr. Budge of every crime in the calendar. He is entirely unscrupulous in his methods of acquiring antiquities, but even you cannot suppose an official of the British Museum would resort to murder and assault."

"I suppose not," I said regretfully. "He *is* English, after all."

"Quite," said Walter. "David, I do not ask about men who are known and who came openly to buy from your master. Was there a man who came in secret, his face hidden?"

After a moment, the boy shook his head.

"If he came in secret he would make certain no one saw him," I said impatiently. "Negative evidence is not conclusive, Walter."

"Certainly. I don't deny the—er—logic of your reasoning,

Amelia dear, but since we have not the faintest idea who this individual is, I think we should concentrate our efforts on Riccetti."

"Fair enough, Walter. What do you suggest?"

"There is only one way of dealing with a hound like Riccetti," Walter said, with a snap of his teeth.

"Well, I would not be averse to employing—er—morally dubious methods. The trouble is, Walter, I don't know how to find him."

"You met with him at the Luxor."

"He is not a guest."

"How do you know that?"

"I asked, two days ago, when we dined at the hotel with Cyrus," I said calmly. "It took only a moment."

"One of the other hotels, then."

"The Luxor is the best. I would not have supposed a man so fond of luxury as Riccetti would settle for less. We could inquire, though."

"I will do so tomorrow," Walter said.

The very idea made my blood run cold. Walter, poor innocent Walter, alone in Luxor, pursuing inquiries the success of which might lead to his being captured or killed?

"No," I said quickly. "Your expertise will be needed at the tomb, Walter. Emerson cannot spare you. I will—uh—I will send one of the men."

I hesitated because at that very moment a particularly clever idea had occurred to me. I wanted to think it over before I proposed it, since I have learned that particularly clever ideas do not always stand up under close scrutiny.

I found the opportunity later, while I gave my hair its hundred strokes, to scrutinize it. I had brought Nefret to sleep in my room that night; she had given no indication of being nervous, but I was nervous—just a little—about her. I had given her permission to read for a while, and I could see her reflection in the mirror, her face absorbed, as she turned the pages. (The book, I remember, was *Wuthering Heights*. Some might not have considered it soothing bedtime reading, but a girl who could coolly discuss the decomposition of a corpse was probably not, I thought, of a nervous nature.)

After due deliberation I decided my idea was a good one. The only problem would be persuading Emerson to accept it.

I was in error. There was another problem, which did not occur to me until it was too late. The sheer brilliance of the inspiration concentrated my attention so that I failed to anticipate what might ensue from one casual sentence. It was certainly an error; it came close to being a fatal error.

When we reached the tomb next morning, Emerson was building a fence and cursing a great deal, because he hates spending time that could be employed in excavation. The task was necessary. Early as was the hour, a crowd of onlookers had already assembled. The word had got out. We never discovered how; the speed by which gossip spreads in small close-knit societies seems at times to verge on magic. I had often observed it in my own household. The servants always knew everything, occasionally before I knew it myself.

When I say Emerson was building the fence I mean that, unlike other supervisors who claim the credit for the actions of others, he was actually driving in stakes. Handing the hammer to Ibrahim, he hastened to greet me.

"All's well, Peabody?"

"Yes, my dear. And here?"

"Not so much as a thrown stone. Very annoying," he added with a scowl.

The light of the rising sun reflected off his sable locks and outlined his splendid form. Though his ablutions had taken place in a bucket of Nile water and he had not had more than a few hours' sleep, he looked fresh as a youth half his age. I knew what was in his mind; he yearned to come to grips with our foes and hoped that the news of our discovery would draw them here, away from those he loved.

"Have you eaten, Emerson?" I asked.

"Eaten? What?"

"I thought not. I brought breakfast for you; come and partake of it. You cannot begin work until Sir Edward gets here. I have a little scheme I want to propose."

That captured his attention. "What scheme? Now, see here, Peabody—"

"We did not have time to discuss all the permutations last night." I slipped my arm through his and led him toward the shelter, where the others were waiting. "If secrecy is impossible, the widest sort of publicity is our next-best course."

"Another of your aphorisms, Peabody?" Amusement brightened the blue eyes under the lowering brows. After greeting the others he condescended to take a chair and a cup of tea.

"Very well, Peabody, I am braced and ready. Propose your scheme."

"The news is out," I said. "If it has not already spread to Luxor, it soon will, and then it will be on its way to Cairo. We must send official notification to M. Maspero."

"Cursed if I will," Emerson growled. "He will come haring down here and insist on opening the sarcophagus. I won't have him tramping through my debris."

"Would you rather he heard of it from someone else? For he surely will, and then he would have grounds for resentment."

"We were planning to build elevated ramps and platforms," Ramses said.

Emerson turned an awful frown on his son. "Sturdy enough to support Maspero's weight?"

"That is rude, Emerson," I said, as Walter stifled a laugh behind his hand. "And, if you will forgive me, irrelevant. If we cannot prevent the news from spreading, we can at least control it—and make good use of the loyal friends who can now be taken into our confidence."

"Whom did you have in mind?" Emerson inquired suspiciously.

"Cyrus, of course, and his new assistant, Howard Carter—"

"If you mention the name of a certain redheaded journalist, Amelia, I may lose my temper."

"I am only suggesting, Emerson, that you leave that side of the business to me. You will be fully occupied with the excavation. I will handle everything else."

"You will anyhow," Emerson muttered. "Oh, very well. Is that Sir Edward coming? High bloody time! Nefret, get your notebook."

I could not resist going up with them to have another look. On the previous afternoon the men had removed all but the lowest course of the remaining stones, and constructed a sloping ramp to the top of the sarcophagus. It was firmly anchored at the base and secured at its upper end by a complex arrangement of ropes, but the slope was steep, and I must admit it was rather amusing to watch Sir Edward creep up it on hands and knees, camera and tripod strapped to his back. He had obviously taken Emerson's threat to heart, for he moved very carefully.

There were wonderful things in that small room. To the left of the door a carved chair or throne lay on its side in what appeared to be a pool of gold. The wood had shrunk and split, and the gold leaf that had covered most of the surface had fallen off. Those paper-thin sections of gold defined the original dimensions of the chair. It could be rebuilt if the gold was handled carefully. The same was true of the other inlaid pieces of furniture—a low bedstead with lion's feet, long poles that might belong to a carrying chair or a canopy. Leaning against the wall stood two large circular objects that had wrung a reverent "By the Almighty!" from Emerson. They appeared to be wheels—but belonging to what sort of vehicle? My suggestion, that it had been the chariot of a warrior queen, made Emerson groan aloud. "Impossible," he muttered. "Not at this period. At least . . . Oh, good Gad!"

He would have to restrain his burning curiosity, for the wheels were at the far side of the room, separated from us by several feet of incredible litter—baskets, pots, stone vessels, objects of bronze and faience. My eye was drawn to a tumbled heap of beads—gold and carnelian, lapis and turquoise—mixed in with gold spacers and exquisitely inlaid clasps. The queen's jewelry box had collapsed and shattered and the strings had decayed; but if we could preserve the present arrangement, the jewelry could be restored to its original beauty. Paraffin wax, melted and dashed over the fragments, would hold those beads in place. . . .

My fingers itched, but I turned away from the enticing mess. Emerson had not thanked me for my sacrifice; I felt certain, however, that he would acknowledge it at a later time. He knew—who better?—that I would have preferred to remain. Archaeological fever burned within me, but it must yield to the sacred ties of familial affection.

When I reached the Castle I learned that Cyrus had already left for the Valley of the Kings. Cyrus's steward—or majordomo, as he preferred to be called—was a Belgian who had lived for many years in Egypt. I knew him well, as he knew me; at my request he showed me at once to the library.

The typewriting machine stood on the table, with a pile of manuscript next to it. Not much had been done; only a few pages of typewritten material were there. Well, I thought charitably, perhaps it takes a while to become accustomed to a new apparatus—and Emerson's handwriting was admittedly difficult to decipher. But why was Gertrude not presently at work?

The majordomo informed me the lady was in her room. He led me there, and I knocked on the door.

Not until I announced my identity did Gertrude open it. She was wearing a loose robe and appeared a trifle dazed.

"What is it?" she exclaimed. "What has happened?"

"Why, nothing. Why should you suppose that?"

She took hold of my sleeve. "I had a dream last night," she whispered. "I was in my room on the dahabeeyah, and I heard a cry—"

"Now, Gertrude, I have not time to listen to your dream. I came looking for Mr. Vandergelt. Yes, I know he has gone on, and I must go after him, but I thought I would drop in and make sure you are comfortable."

"Why do you want him?" She maintained her grip on my sleeve. "Are you telling me the truth? Nothing has happened to her?"

I began to feel a bit uneasy—not for my own safety, since that was absurd, but for her sanity. She looked absolutely wild-eyed. The room behind her was dim with shadow, for the shutters had been closed, and there was a scent of that strange incense.

"Nothing has happened to anyone, Gertrude. I wanted Mr. Vandergelt to tell him what I am going to tell you—that we have entered the burial chamber and found great things."

Her hand went to her breast. "The burial chamber? Oh, heavens, is it true? But the Professor said—"

"He changed his mind. What is wrong with you? Are you ill?"

"No! No, thank you. I am well, I am strong. Only tell me—is she there?"

"Your references are more than a little ambiguous, Gertrude," I said—for a firm, even censorious, tone is necessary when speaking to incipient hysterics. "If you mean Nefret, she is there, working with the Professor and the others. If you mean Queen Tetisheri, we don't know. The sarcophagus is closed and it will remain so until the Professor decides to open it."

"Today?"

"No, not today nor within the next few days. I must go, Gertrude. You had better lie down."

However, I did not go at once to the Valley. I took up a position in the mouth of one of the innumerable little ravines that cut into the cliffs, and waited. I could see the front of the house, but I did not think I could be seen, immobile in the shadows.

It was less than half an hour before Cyrus's carriage drew up at the front door. Gertrude, hat askew and hair disheveled, hurried out and got into the carriage. It moved away in a cloud of dust, and I watched until it was out of sight. It had not taken the southern road, to Drah Abu'l Naga and Deir el Bahri, but had gone directly toward the ferry.

What I would have given just then for the ability to be in two places at once! However, it would have been difficult for me to follow Gertrude unobserved, and if she observed *me* she would not go where she planned to go. I regretted now the impulse that had led me to speak to her. Not until after I had seen her strange reaction did it occur to me that she might hurry to report to her unknown leader.

Ah well, I thought philosophically, hindsight is of little practical use. Urging my steed into a trot, I proceeded to carry out my original plan.

I beheld Cyrus looking on while his workmen carried off basket after basket of sand without—as was evident from my friend's gloomy expression—any sign of a tomb. I guided my steed rapidly through the inconvenient tourists and came to a sudden stop in front of Cyrus.

My appearance had, perhaps, a trifle too much panache. Cyrus jumped back and exclaimed in agitation, "Consarn it, Mrs. Amelia, what's gone wrong?"

I reassured him and made my announcement. Relief and pleasure succeeded one another on his expressive countenance, to be replaced by a look of poignant envy. "Can I have a look?" he asked hopefully. "I'll go back with you this minute if you say it's all right. Just let me stop by the house for my horse; I walked over this morning."

"I have a little errand to do before I return," I replied. "But you are welcome to pay Emerson a visit as soon as you like. I am sure he will be delighted to see you."

"I'm not so sure," said Cyrus, grinning. "But you couldn't keep me away with a club." Turning to his assistant, he remarked, "Sorry, my boy, but you will have to wait. Professor Emerson is not keen on company, and I would rather not try his temper."

"I would rather not do that either," said Mr. Amherst, with considerable feeling. "But sir, you will ask him—"

"Why, sure. He may want our assistance. If so, we'll close this pitiful job down and join him. I will let you know this evening. Mrs. Amelia, will you walk back with me to the Castle, or are you in a hurry?"

"I will be glad to accompany you, Cyrus. There is something I would like to tell you."

Excitement had rendered Cyrus unsteady on his feet. As my tale unfolded, he kept stumbling over things. "Holy Jehoshaphat, Mrs. Amelia," he cried when I finished. "Is this true?"

"You don't suspect me of prevarication, I hope? Or of imagining things?"

"You, imagining things?" Smiling, Cyrus stroked his goatee. Then he sobered. "I can't rightly accuse you of making up stories when I've seen with my own eyes the kinds of peculiar adventures you get yourself into. I can't for the life of me figger out how you do it."

"There is, I believe, something called a nose for news, Cyrus. Perhaps I have a nose for crime! And Emerson has—"

"A way of getting folks riled up. All right, ma'am, you know you can count on Cyrus Vandergelt through thick and thin, with a shovel or a six-shooter. You just tell me what I can do to help."

"I am counting on you, Cyrus, and I do need your help. I want you to watch Miss Marmaduke. You can trust your servants? Excellent. Any messages she sends must be brought to you, any visitors noted, all her actions observed."

Cyrus stumbled again. "Are you serious? That silly young woman? She's the most harmless-looking creature I ever saw."

I described Gertrude's reaction to my announcement, and her hasty departure from the house. Cyrus tugged at his goatee and looked grave. "I told her the carriage was at her disposal. No reason why she shouldn't decide to go shopping or sightseeing, I guess, but . . . All right, I'll do as you say."

We parted at the Castle; Cyrus, eager as a boy, went running off to the stable while I remounted and rode to the ferry, where I left my horse. Once on the East Bank I kept a sharp eye out for Miss Marmaduke, but saw no sign of her; she had been a good hour ahead of me, and might by now have completed her errand—whatever it was. After telegraphing to M. Maspero, I proceeded, still on the qui vive, to the Luxor hotel.

I had to detach Kevin from the *Times* and the *Mirror*, who were helping him celebrate his recovery by consuming copious quantities of beer in the bar of the hotel. Regrettably, I was forced to resort to underhanded means in order to do this, for they paid no attention to my hints that they should go away. Looking around in hope of inspiration, I saw the widow lady in black enter the lobby, leaning on the arm of her nurse.

Indicating the two women, I inquired of the *Times* in a thrilling whisper, "Is it true that the Duchess is suspected of having murdered her husband?"

Kevin, who knew me well, did not follow his fellow journalists when they rushed after their new victim.

"What are you up to now, Mrs. E.?" he asked.

"I haven't time to explain, Kevin. Excuse yourself to your friends, retire to your room, creep away unobserved, and come across to the tomb. If both or either of them succeed in following you, you won't have an exclusive."

"Say no more, ma'am," Kevin cried, eyes alight with professional fervor.

I said no more.

There were several other inquiries I wanted badly to pursue, but I dared not linger in Luxor; if I did not prepare Emerson for Kevin's arrival, a certain degree of unpleasantness might ensue.

After climbing over a wall at the back of the hotel, I decided to take a circuitous route back to the riverbank in order to throw off possible pursuers—including the *Times* and the *Mirror*. Although the increase in the tourist trade has brought about considerable improvement, parts of the old village of Luxor are unchanged even today. The narrow winding alleys, half blocked with stones and littered with trash and animal refuse, made it a perfect place for hide-and-seek, and I doubted the *Times* would risk dirtying his polished boots.

After proceeding some distance without observing signs of pursuit, I was about to turn back when something caught my eye, through the ears of a donkey who had decided to stop still in the middle of the lane. The configuration of the stooped body was familiar—but surely Abd el Hamel's rheumatic-ridden frame was not capable of such lizardlike speed?

Becoming impatient, the donkey driver brought his stick down on the poor animal's flanks, and I was forced to speak firmly with him. By the time we had settled the matter and the donkey had moved on, Abd el Hamel—if it was he—had disappeared.

I decided to walk on a little farther. The narrow way appeared to end just ahead, but when I reached that point I saw that it turned, abruptly and without apparent reason, into a slightly wider thoroughfare lined with tall old houses. There was no sign of the figure I had seen, and when I had gone another fifty feet I found that this street did end, in a cul-de-sac closed by a high wall.

I decided I had wasted enough time on a pointless investigation, so I turned and retraced my steps. I had got about halfway to the turn in the path when the door of one of the houses opened, and a very large individual stepped out.

He made no threatening move. He simply stood there, staring at me; but he was large enough to bar my path.

The poor fellow must be deficient in intelligence, I thought sympathetically—a child in the body of a (very large) man—for his look held more of apprehension than menace. This proved to be the case. When I raised my parasol and walked toward him he let out a high-pitched cry and fled back into the house. I proceeded on my way and soon found myself at the riverbank and the ferry.

The sun had passed the zenith by the time I reached the tomb. I was relieved to see that despite the delay I was there before Kevin. The luncheon baskets I had ordered had come, but no one was at table except Evelyn and David, their heads together over a book. Evelyn was the only one to whom I had confided my plans. She had not been too pleased about them, and had even tried to dissuade me from "running all over the countryside alone," as she put it. When she saw me, she rose from her chair with an exclamation of relief. "Thank heaven you are safely returned, Amelia. You encountered no difficulty?"

"None at all, my dear. I told you there was no cause for concern. I suppose the others are still at work?"

"I tried to persuade Radcliffe to—"

"Evelyn."

"Yes, Amelia?"

"Emerson despises his given name. Passionately."

"I had no idea he felt so strongly about it," Evelyn exclaimed. "Walter calls him that, and since you use his surname as a term of affection, I thought it would be presumptuous of me to employ it. What shall I call him, then?"

"Emerson, of course. A number of other people call him that, including those who do not employ it as a term of affection. Just a little hint, my dear! I had better go up and insist they stop for a while, otherwise Emerson will drive them till they drop."

I have seldom seen such an unkempt group of individuals. All welcomed my interruption except Emerson, but he went when I told him to, moving like an automaton and mumbling to himself. I had to nudge him down the stairs. I believe it was not until after he had poured a pot of water over his head that he realized who I was. His eyes came back into focus and he exclaimed, "Where the devil have you been all this time?"

"Come and have luncheon and I will tell you everything."

I told him about Kevin first, since I anticipated that bit of news would be the most difficult for him to assimilate fully (and calmly). He received it better than I had expected.

"Offering him an exclusive is the best method of controlling him," he admitted. "And he will keep the other confounded journalists away. Where is he?"

"Eluding the other confounded journalists, I suppose," I replied. I had other reasons for wanting Kevin, but there was no point in mentioning them to Emerson. He would only have fussed.

We joined the others, who were sitting and lying about in various poses of exhaustion. Ramses was the only one who looked much as usual. He was filthy dirty, but that was normal, and his black curls only coiled tighter when they were wet. Nefret had unfastened the top two buttons of her blouse and pushed the sleeves up above the elbow. I could hardly scold her for wishing to be as comfortable as was possible under adverse conditions, but the effect was demoralizing; Cyrus kept glancing in her direction, and Sir Edward, gracefully reclining at her feet, could hardly keep his eyes off her.

Emerson reached for a sandwich. "Have you spoken with Carter?" he demanded of me.

"Confound it, I knew I had forgotten something. What with one thing and another—"

"What things?" Emerson demanded, his eyes narrowing.

I never allow Emerson to get me on the defensive. "Good heavens, my dear, I have already been to the Valley and to Luxor and back this morning. I will go looking for Howard as soon as we finish luncheon. It may take me a while to locate him."

"He is probably digging out that shaft near the causeway," Emerson grunted. "Waste of time. There is nothing of interest there. I need one of those gates of his. Tell him to fetch it here at once, I want it installed today, before I leave."

"Ah," I said, without commenting upon Emerson's autocratic demands and unreasonable expectations, "you are planning to return to the *Amelia* tonight?"

It really was pitiful to behold the struggle that raged in the heart and mind of my husband. Had there been no other distractions he would have camped on the spot until the tomb was cleared, no matter how long it took. But he was as aware as I of those distractions, and affection took precedence over even archaeological fever.

"I am," he said shortly. "So get at it, Peabody."

Walter cleared his throat. "Er—Radcliffe—you have already spoken with Mr. Carter. He came here earlier this morning, don't you remember?"

"What?" Emerson stared at him. "Oh. Oh, yes, so he did. I was trying to get that cursed grid laid out without damaging the . . . Never mind, Peabody. Sir Edward, what are you lounging around for? I want to finish the photography."

There was no holding him, and I did not try to do so. Walter and Nefret accompanied the pair. Ramses remained where he was, cross-legged on the rug next to David. I turned an inquiring eye upon him.

"There is no need for any of us to be there, really," he said. "Except for Nefret and"—a slight spasm that would have been imperceptible to any eyes but mine crossed his face—"and Sir Edward."

"You were only looking on this morning?" I asked. Looking on was not Ramses's forte.

"The fascination of the place and the procedures are difficult to . . ." Ramses glanced at David, caught himself and started again. "It is very interesting. I learn from watching Father. But just now I felt it would be more useful for me to talk with you, Mother, about how your detectival (oh, curse it!) about what you have found out about our enemies."

"I was not pursuing detectival . . ." I could have sworn my pause brought a gleam of amusement to David's black eyes. I resumed somewhat stiffly, "All I did this morning was call on Mr. Vandergelt and Mr. O'Connell and send a telegram to M. Maspero."

"Ah," said Ramses. "You did not inquire at the hotels about Signor Riccetti?"

"There was no time." I hesitated, for a well-honed instinct told me it might not be advisable to inform Ramses of certain of my intentions. The sight of an approaching form urging its donkey to a rapid pace convinced me that reticence on one of those intentions would be useless. I had to tell Kevin what I wanted him to do, and Ramses would find out, one way or another.

"I am going to assign that task to Mr. O'Connell," I explained.

"Hmmm." Ramses rubbed his prominent chin. "Do you think that wise, Mother? Mr. O'Connell is certainly adept at pursuing impertinent inquiries, but he has not, in my opinion, the necessary talent for dissimulation."

"I believe, Ramses, I have mentioned before that I would prefer you refrained from using the phrase 'in my opinion.'"

"I beg your pardon." O'Connell was almost upon us. Ramses lowered his voice. "It could be dangerous, Mother."

I had considered this, of course. I made Kevin sit down and listen to me instead of rushing straightaway to the tomb; and while he finished the rest of the sandwiches I emphasized most strongly the necessity of caution.

Kevin's eyes gradually widened and he swallowed the wrong way once or twice. However, he is a quick young fellow, and he had participated in other cases of mine. By the time I finished he was grinning broadly.

"Ah, Mrs. Emerson, me dear, you never cease to amaze me. I would say that you are the light of me life if I did not suppose the Professor would take exception to such a remark, though it is intended, I assure you, in the most respectful—"

"Spare me your Hibernian effusions, Kevin. This is a serious matter and you must take it seriously. Take no chances. Follow no leads that take you into solitary places. In fact, don't follow those leads at all! Just report to me."

Kevin cocked his head and looked at me askance, like a bright-eyed bird. "So that *you* can follow them into solitary places? Och, well, if the Professor can't stop you (and I know he cannot, for I have seen him try and fail) the admonitions of a friend will have no effect. Do take care, though, Mrs. E., will you?"

I was rather touched, for I thought he meant it. The softened look did not linger on his face, however; he gave himself a little shake, as if ashamed of his brief display of sentiment.

"So what do I get in return?" he asked, with his roguish journalist's grin.

At the risk of repeating myself I must say (as I will never tire of saying) that only Emerson could have accomplished what he had planned that day. Egyptian workmen are the merriest of fellows, but they are inclined to be nonchalant about doing things in a hurry. Our men, trained by and devoted to Emerson, had developed an esprit de corps and professional pride that would have driven them to extraordinary effort even without the passionate exhortations of their chief. They worked with grim efficiency to install the iron door Howard provided; it had been intended for one of the royal tombs in the Valley, and we were fortunate indeed to have it available. However, the job was not completed when Emerson came running down the stairs to tell me I must escort the others back to the dahabeeyah.

"Not without you, Emerson," I said. "You said you would not stay here tonight."

"So I did, my dear. But the sun will set shortly and I want you all safely home before dark. I will follow as soon as I have fastened that padlock with my own hands."

"You won't come alone? Promise me, Emerson." I caught hold of his shirt.

His firm lips curved in a smile and he took me in his arms. "You are particularly persuasive, Peabody, when you cling to me and plead like the timid little woman you are not. But then I suppose if you did it as often as I would like you to, it wouldn't have the same effect. I promise, my love. Run along now."

Sir Edward had already returned to Luxor with his precious load of photographic plates and Cyrus had reluctantly torn himself away, promising to return early the following morning. He had asked us to dine that evening, but I declined on the grounds that we were too tired to enjoy a social encounter. It was true; there was little conversation during the ride, and we went immediately to our rooms.

I waited there for Emerson. Darkness had fallen and it seemed to me that I had been at the window, watching, for hours before he came.

"So you missed me, did you?" he inquired, sometime later.

"I believe you have had sufficient evidence of that."

"Not sufficient, no. But it will have to do for the time being. Is dinner ready? I am famished."

"Oh, dear," I said, somewhat self-consciously. "I am afraid it is on the table and getting cold, Emerson. I told Mahmud to serve when you returned."

"You ought to have known better, Peabody."

"You are right, I ought. Hurry and dress, my dear."

As it turned out, Evelyn had sent the food back to be warmed, so that was all right. I waited until after Emerson had satisfied the first pangs of hunger before giving him the telegram from M. Maspero.

"On his way, is he?" was Emerson's response. "Curse it!"

"He is very polite," said Walter, who had retrieved the telegram from the floor where Emerson had thrown it. "Felicitations, hommages, chers colleagues, and all the rest!"

"Anything else in the post?" Emerson asked, dismissing M. Maspero and his courtesies.

"Evelyn's daily report from Mrs. Watson," I replied. "All well and happy, she says. Nothing else of interest."

I did not really expect anything from Kevin until later that night at the earliest. He had gone chortling off with a book full of notes and I assumed he would be busy writing up his dispatch. I only hoped he would remember to check round the hotels as I had asked him to do; when journalism took possession of him he was inclined to forget all else.

We took all our meals on the deck now, since Emerson had commandeered the saloon for a workroom and storage chamber. The sweet breeze and rising moon did not tempt him to linger; draining his cup of coffee he said, "Nefret, I have several more pages of notes that need to be copied."

"I will transcribe your notes, Emerson," Evelyn said. "Let the child go to bed, she is worn out."

She must have been practicing, for she got the name out without a hitch. Walter gave her a startled look. Emerson said, "Oh? Oh, well, er . . . Yes, quite. Off to bed with you, Nefret, my dear, you worked very diligently today. You too, Ramses."

Ramses had been feeding scraps to the cat Bastet. I expected him to protest. Instead he rose obediently. "Yes, Father. Good night, all. Come, David. Come, the cat Bastet."

They left in dignified procession, the cat bringing up the rear. "He really should not speak to David as he does to the cat," Evelyn said.

"It is the other way round, I fancy," I said. "He should not speak to the cat as he does to a human being. Where has Anubis got to? I haven't seen him this evening."

"I told him to stay with the men," Emerson said. He chuckled. "Or rather, I requested that he do so. He is as effective a guard as you and your parasol, Peabody. The locals are terrified of him."

"So is Abdullah. I am surprised he didn't object."

"Abdullah has had a change of heart." Emerson got out his pipe. "He still believes Anubis is an afreet in feline form, but he has very sensibly concluded that it is better to have a demon as a friend than an enemy. Nefret, my dear, why are you still here? Did you want to ask me something?"

"No, sir, only I am not at all tired and I don't want to go to bed."

A statement like that would have won Ramses a firm rebuke, but Emerson only smiled fondly. There is no question but that a pretty face and golden curls lend a person an unfair advantage.

"It will be another difficult day tomorrow, child. Give me a kiss and run along."

Pouting, but to no avail, Nefret bestowed kisses all round and went with dragging feet toward the stairs.

I don't know what impulse made me go after her. When I caught her up at the door of her room, her surprised look made me feel a little foolish. "I thought perhaps you had left your nightgown in my room this morning," was the only excuse I could think of at the moment.

"No, Aunt Amelia, I dressed in my own room. Don't you remember?"

"Yes, of course."

She set her candle on the table and I gave the room a quick but thorough inspection. There was nothing out of place and nowhere to hide—only the curtain hung across the corner where her washstand was placed. I drew it casually aside.

"Is something wrong?" She stood by the bed, watching me.

"No. You don't mind being alone, do you? If you would like me to sleep here . . ."

"That is a very generous offer, dear Aunt Amelia." She spoke sweetly and gravely. "No such sacrifice is necessary; I am perfectly comfortable in my mind. Good night. Sleep well."

I withdrew in some little confusion. Had I heard a hidden meaning in several of those phrases?

I feared I had.

After an hour or so I convinced Emerson to stop working. Naturally I did not mention the odd sense of foreboding that had prompted me to search Nefret's room, but I did ask whether one of the men would be on guard that night.

"Do you suppose I would neglect that precaution?" Emerson

asked. "Ibrahim will make a circuit of the cabins every ten minutes and be on the alert for the slightest sound. I believe it to be needless; the tomb is as secure as I can make it, and Riccetti is not so rash as to play his old games with me. Better safe than sorry, however, as you would say, Peabody."

"I would not say anything so trite, my dear. Thank you for putting my mind at ease."

"Have I done so? Then let us turn our attention to other matters."

I slept soundly that night. To have Emerson safe with me again, to know that the tomb had been secured and our loyal man was on guard outside—these considerations and others must have been responsible for the failure of the sixth sense that normally warns me of danger. The room was dim with dawn light when I was rudely aroused by the door bursting open. Even Emerson, who is usually slow to recover himself in the morning, sat bolt upright.

Nefret stood in the doorway.

"Ramses is gone!" she cried. "They are both gone—and so is the cat Bastet!"

CHAPTER THIRTEEN

Humor Is an Excellent Method of Keeping a Tight Rein on Unproductive Displays of Emotion

After Emerson had rained vehement reproaches on poor Ibrahim (and then apologized, since at that point in time it was premature to assume he had been at fault), I insisted that we calm down and apply intelligence to the matter. Emerson's curses had awakened Walter and Evelyn, and we gathered in Ramses's room.

"He must have gone of his own free will," I said. "There is no sign of a struggle."

"How can you tell?" Emerson demanded.

"It is a little difficult," I admitted. "His room generally does look as if a violent struggle had taken place there. However, nothing has been overturned or broken. Kidnappers could not carry both boys off without something being overturned."

Emerson's initial frenzy had been succeeded by the icy rage that rendered him so formidable. "They could carry one boy off, though," he said coolly. "With the aid of a little chloroform—and that of the other boy."

"No, Emerson!" Evelyn cried. "David would not betray his friends!"

"That has yet to be determined," Emerson said in the same quiet voice. "If Ramses had gone voluntarily, he should be back by now. He would have left a note if he expected to be delayed beyond the time when his absence would be discovered. You are certain you did not overlook such a message?"

I did nothing to stop him when he began looking, in the same places I had already searched. How well I understood the need for action of any kind, however futile! He even opened the box labeled with an emphatic "PRIVATE! PLEASE DO NOT INTRUDE!" I had never investigated the contents of that box, not only because I feel that even children are entitled to their little secrets, but because I assumed it contained disgusting treasures such as dried bones and bits of mummy.

When Emerson straightened, he was holding something. He stood quite still, turning it in his hands.

The little alabaster head was finished, or near enough. Emerson looked at Nefret and then back at the sculpture. "David's?" he asked.

"Yes. He said he was making it for me." I touched the rounded cheekbones of the face with a reverent finger. "It is lovely, isn't it?"

Emerson's eyes went again to Nefret. "Uncanny would be nearer the mark. It is Nefret, and it is also Tetisheri. What did he see or sense, that made him produce a thing like this?"

"Why does it disturb you?" I asked in surprise. "It is a beautiful piece of work and he is a talented artist."

"It does not disturb me," Emerson said shortly—but he was quick to return the head to the box and close it. "The boy has talent, I grant you. That does not prove his innocence."

"I told Mahmud to make coffee," I said. "I suggest we dress and—"

Nefret, who had been pacing restlessly around the room,

whirled to face me. "Coffee? Why are we wasting time? Let us go after him!"

"Where?" I asked. "Calm yourself, Nefret. There is nothing to be gained and a great deal to be lost by premature action."

"Quite right," Emerson agreed. "You can't go rushing off to Gurneh in your nightgown, Nefret; your aunt Amelia would never allow such a thing."

I never linger unnecessarily over my toilette, but I do not suppose I have ever dressed as quickly as I did that day. Emerson delayed only long enough to add a shirt and boots to the trousers he had assumed earlier. He and Nefret were on the deck when I got there.

Never (hardly ever) have I admired my dear Emerson so much as I did when I beheld the touching tableau. Nefret knelt at his feet, her face raised imploringly, her hands warmly clasped in his. Fear for his son raged within him; but he had put it aside in order to comfort his daughter. There was—to his infinite credit I proclaim it—there was even a note of amusement in his calm voice as he spoke, and a reassuring smile on his face.

"My dear, Ramses does this sort of thing all the time. No doubt he has got himself into another scrape. We will get him out, that's all."

"You won't try to prevent me from helping?"

"I depend on it."

So great was her agitation she had not been aware of my presence until Emerson glanced in my direction. Rising, she smiled self-consciously. "I apologize, Aunt Amelia, if I spoke rudely to you. I was not worried about Ramses, you know. I was only angry because he had been so inconsiderate."

"Yes, Nefret, I know. Try to eat something."

When the younger Emersons joined us I noticed Evelyn was carrying the black parasol and that Walter was rather red in the face. They had been arguing again, and it was not difficult to deduce what about. Walter's first remark made no reference to this, however.

"The evidence does seem to indicate that Ramses went off on one of his mysterious expeditions. I don't see how he could have been carried off, even with David's connivance, without the kidnappers' being seen or heard by Ibrahim."

"Not to mention by the cat Bastet," I said, pouring coffee with a steady hand. "She would not have stood by in silence while someone knocked Ramses on the head."

"She must have gone with him," Nefret said. "She usually comes to my room after Ramses has fallen asleep. She was not on my bed this morning."

"Was it in quest of her that you went to Ramses's room?" I asked. I had not thought of asking her how she had discovered Ramses's absence.

"No. Something woke me. A sound, a voice, a dream . . ." She hesitated, looking down at her clasped hands. "It must have been a dream. I thought I heard . . . someone . . . call my name."

"Who?" I asked.

Still she avoided my eyes. "Just someone. You know how vivid dreams can be. I went immediately to Ramses's room, and . . . Oh, but what does it matter?"

"Never mind that," Emerson said. "Walter is right, Ramses must have gone off on his own. He took the cat, or it followed him. As for David . . . I am sorry, Evelyn, but we must consider the possibility that it was David who lured Ramses away. If David suddenly 'remembered' something he had seen while he was with Abd el Hamed, he could easily persuade Ramses to investigate. You know Ramses's cursed reckless—er, adventurous—spirit."

"There is no proof of that," Evelyn said steadily.

"Well, where the devil else could they have gone but to Gurneh?" Emerson demanded.

My slight involuntary start would have passed unobserved by anyone else; but Emerson knows me well. His iron control was beginning to crack. Turning to—or rather, on—me, he growled, "Well, Peabody? If you have been concealing something from me . . ."

"I swear to you, Emerson, I just this instant thought of it. I confess it should have occurred to me earlier, but I have been somewhat distracted. . . . Now, my dear, don't shout. I think Ramses may have gone off looking for Riccetti."

That dreaded name produced the silence I required in order to complete my explanation. Horrified conviction whitened every face.

"My God," Walter whispered. "Not Riccetti!"

"I may be wrong," I said. "I hope I am wrong. But Ramses did express reservations about Kevin's ability to pursue the matter competently, and he has always been prone to take matters into his own hands."

"It's all right, Peabody." Emerson's affectionate heart saw the emotion I strove to conceal. His strong brown hand closed over mine. "Don't blame yourself. Wherever he went we must assume that he is being detained against his will, otherwise he would have returned by now or sent a message. I am off to Gurneh. That still seems to me the most likely possibility."

"I am going with you." Walter rose.

"If you like. The rest of you remain here. Abdullah has considerable influence with the Gurnawis; his assistance will be invaluable."

"What are you going to tell him?" I asked.

"What else but the truth? His grandson is missing too."

"You won't distress the poor man even more by mentioning your suspicions of the boy?"

"Unnecessary," Emerson said curtly. "Do you suppose he won't think of that himself?"

"I am going to Luxor," I said.

"No!" He grasped me by the shoulders. "Peabody, for the love of God, do as I ask for once. If there is no trace of Ramses in Gurneh, we—you and I—will go to Luxor later on and try to follow his trail. You must not venture there alone. If I lose you too . . ."

The prospect of waiting, helpless and inactive, for endless hours, literally sickened me, but Emerson was in the right. We could not scatter in all directions. I nodded dumbly.

"Thank you, Peabody," said Emerson.

"Be careful, Emerson."

"Certainly. I may be the one pursuing a wild goose," he added. "There is still a chance he will turn up, and if he is being held captive, we can expect to hear from the kidnappers before too long."

"You are right," I cried, hope rising. "I will send someone for you at once if either eventuality occurs."

"The kidnappers may wish to prolong our anxiety for hours or days," Walter said soberly.

"No, no," Emerson said. "They will want to get Ramses off their hands as quickly as possible. Wouldn't you?"

He ran down the stairs, followed by Walter.

"How can he joke about such a thing?" Evelyn demanded.

"Humor is an excellent method of keeping a tight rein on unproductive displays of emotion," I explained. "Evelyn, put that parasol down. Your hand will cramp if you hold it so tightly."

Evelyn relaxed her white-knuckled grip, but retained her hold on the implement. It seemed to comfort her. "As usual," she said bitterly, "we women are left here to wait while the men act. I did not think you would give in so meekly, Amelia."

"Do you suppose I would give in unless I knew it was the most sensible course of action? We would only be in Emerson's way. Walter won't be of much use either, but at least his Arabic is fairly fluent. Now for pity's sake sit down—both of you—and let us go over the evidence again. Ramses said nothing to you, Nefret, that might give us a clue as to his intentions?"

Nefret flung herself into a chair. "No, confound him. He is always trying to keep me out of things. I don't believe for a moment, though, that David is still loyal to that vile old man. The Professor won't find them in Gurneh. They must have gone to Luxor."

"How?" Evelyn asked.

"I have been wondering about that myself," I said. "Let us see if we can construct a possible scenario. You know Ramses's talents for disguise; it would take very little alteration for him to pass for an Egyptian lad. They could slip out and over the side unobserved while Ibrahim was out of the way. Both are at home in the water; they would stay in it, swimming or wading, until they were some distance from the dahabeeyah, and then steal a boat—or possibly beg a ride from someone."

"Then we should be able to trace them," Evelyn said eagerly.

"I don't doubt that Emerson has already begun those inquiries, my dear."

"Then what can we do?"

"Wait," I said. "Nefret, will you tell Mahmud to make more coffee? We will be having visitors soon, I expect."

Indeed it was not long before the visitors arrived. Emerson had not had to explain his plans to me; our minds work as one (except in extraordinary circumstances). He had gone to the tomb to get Abdullah, and I felt sure that owing to the delay he would find Sir Edward already there, and probably Cyrus as well. The gentlemen would insist on helping to search for Ramses, and Emerson, rather than have them getting in *his* way, would send them to me.

I was mistaken on only one count. There were four gentlemen, not two. Cyrus's assistant and an agitated Kevin O'Connell completed the party.

The others were concerned, of course, but guilt appeared to be one of the components of Kevin's explosive speech. "If my negligence is to blame for this, Mrs. E., I will never forgive myself! I meant to go round to the hotels last night, but it was late when I finished my story, and this morning I just plain forgot, and . . . I'll be off to Luxor straightaway."

"I don't blame you, Kevin, so stop babbling," I replied. "Ramses thinks he can do everything better than anyone else, and not even I can stop him when he is determined to act. But all this is surmise. We don't know that he has gone to Luxor."

"It will do no harm to ask," Kevin insisted. "I must do something, Mrs. E."

Sir Edward had not spoken except to greet us. Now he said quietly, "I agree with Mr. O'Connell. With his permission and yours, Mrs. Emerson, I will accompany him. My Arabic is perhaps more fluent than his."

"It would have to be, since mine is limited to half a dozen words," Kevin declared. The prospect of action (and my kindly reassurance) had cheered him. "I'll take you up on that offer, Sir Edward, and I don't mind admitting I'll feel safer with a friend to guard me back."

Nefret accompanied them to the gangplank. I did not forbid her since I knew there was not the ghost of a chance she could cajole them into taking her with them.

"No sense in me going along, I guess," Cyrus said. "I figger Willy and I can be more useful on this side of the river. Come on, Willy, we'll shake up a few of the local citizens."

"No, wait. Where is Miss Marmaduke?"

"Plugging away at Emerson's book, I expect. Said that's what she was going to do."

"I want you to send her here."

"Now, Mrs. Amelia, you can't suspect that poor feeble creature. She hasn't got the gumption to say boo to a goose."

"Cyrus, will you please do as I ask?" My voice was a trifle loud. I am not entirely impervious to nervous strain; the sun was high in the sky now, and still there had been no word. Nefret, returning with flushed cheeks and frowning brows, came to me and put her arm round my shoulders.

"Why, sure," Cyrus said soothingly. "I'll do anything you want."

"What I want is to interrogate that woman. It is time to take off the velvet gloves. I am in no mood to be trifled with, Cyrus."

"I can see that. All right, Mrs. Amelia, my dear. I'll have her here as soon as is humanly possible."

"What are you going to do to her, Aunt Amelia?" Nefret asked.

"You would like to assist, I suppose?" I had asserted my will; my voice was calm. "It won't be necessary to resort to physical violence, child, even if my moral code allowed such a thing. If she knows anything, I will get it out of her."

But I was not to have the opportunity. Cyrus had been gone less than a quarter of an hour when the message I had half hoped for and wholly dreaded was brought to me.

I was waiting on the bank when Emerson and Walter returned. Evelyn and Nefret were with me; they were still trying to persuade me to change my mind. "You cannot go," I said. "Riccetti's letter was most emphatic about that. Only Emerson and I."

Emerson flung himself out of the saddle and took the note from me. He scanned the message in a single comprehensive glance and allowed Walter to take it from him.

"Hmph," he said. "Are you ready, Peabody?"

"Good God, Radcliffe, you don't mean to take her with you?" Walter cried.

"It is her right," Emerson said quietly.

"This may be a trap! Even if Riccetti is holding Ramses—"

"I am in something of a hurry, Walter," Emerson said. "Please excuse me."

Daoud had the boat ready. As soon as we were on board he pushed off. Emerson took out his pipe.

"Obviously," I said, "you learned nothing in Gurneh."

"I would not say that." Emerson went about filling the pipe with precise, controlled movements. "Abd el Hamel has gone to earth again. This time no one seems to know where he has got to."

"Not even his wives?"

"None of them," said Emerson, with a faint smile and a glance at me.

This was not the time to pursue that particular matter. I tabled it for future discussion.

"His disappearance may have nothing to do with that of Ramses," Emerson continued. "But I would like to ask the bastard a few questions. Abdullah is still looking for him; he may have better luck than I, and he is as keen on the scent as either of us could be. What have you to report, my dear? For I do not suppose you have been idle all morning."

I told him of O'Connell and Sir Edward's plan to inquire in Luxor. "Have you removed Sir Edward from your list of suspects, then?" he inquired.

"No, but I can't see that he presents any threat to Kevin. If he is a member of the gang—either gang, any gang—he will make sure Kevin doesn't learn anything of importance. It did occur to me that that was why he offered to go along—to head Kevin off."

"Suppositions, guesses and theories." Emerson's fist clenched. "If we only had something solid to go on!"

"The message is solid enough," I said. "Riccetti is too canny to admit in writing that he holds Ramses prisoner, but his suggestion that we join him to discuss a certain missing object of great importance can have no other meaning."

My voice was not as steady as I would have liked. Emerson put his arm around me. "Peabody, my darling, you can be certain Ramses is safe and sound. Riccetti is too good a businessman to damage valuable merchandise."

"You know what he wants in exchange, don't you?"

"Yes."

Neither of us spoke again until we reached the East Bank. Riccetti had said there would be someone waiting to lead us to him. I think I would have identified the guide even if he had not, of course, immediately identified us. Though he wore a galabeeyah and turban, he was not Egyptian. His physiognomy and complexion were those of a Greek or Italian or Turk. He spoke only two words, in accented Arabic.

"Follow me."

I had assumed the rendezvous would not be at one of the hotels, for in that case there would have been no need for a guide; and I did not suppose Riccetti would take the risk of bringing us to the house where he was staying. Sure enough, our destination was a café, a coffeehouse less than a quarter mile from the river. Our guide opened the door and stood back, waving us in with a burlesqued bow and an anticipatory smile.

As soon as we were inside the room I moved slightly to the right, so that I would not impede any pugilistic gesture Emerson might make. (Though he is equally capable with either hand, he prefers the right.) My own right hand was in my pocket, fingering my little pistol; my parasol was in my left hand. I sincerely hoped that not all the patrons of the place were in Riccetti's employ. Every table was occupied. I calculated the odds at roughly twenty to one.

It was difficult to make out details, for the place was poorly lit and the air was thick with the smoke of tobacco and hashish. There appeared to be two other exits from the room, one at the back and one in the wall to the left. The windows were shuttered. Feeble rays of sunlight, penetrating the foul gloom through cracks in the shutters, reflected off the brass mouthpiece of a nargheelah, a copper bowl, and the knife in the hand of a man at a nearby table.

Conversation stopped abruptly upon our entrance. Eyes examined us as intently as we were studying them. I heard a few hisses of indrawn breath, and then, so silently and suddenly that a magician might have been at work, the place was almost empty. The lowering of the odds did not comfort me, however. Those who had wisely decided to leave must have been local residents; the faces of the remaining men were lighter in color, with the unmistakable stamp of city dwellers—men of Lower Egypt, Cairenes, the dregs of that teeming metropolis.

Emerson spoke in his normal tones and in Arabic. "The son of a dog is hiding in his kennel, I see. Tell him the Father of Curses and the Sitt Hakim honor his filthy den."

"Do you think it wise to irritate him, Emerson?" I whispered.

"Rudeness is the only way to deal with vermin, my dear," said Emerson, without lowering his voice. He added in Arabic, "Quickly! I will see him now."

He did not wait for a reply but strode toward the door at the back of the room, gesturing to me to follow. Before he reached it it was opened by an invisible hand and a familiar voice said, "Buon giorno, honored guests. Enter my . . . kennel."

The door closed after us with an unpleasantly solid sort of thud. A quick glance told me that the doorkeeper was one of Riccetti's bodyguards. The other stood behind the couch where Riccetti reclined on a damask counterpane woven with gold threads.

The furnishings were a distinct improvement over the ones in the outer room. This chamber must be one of those reserved for wealthier clients. I thought Riccetti had probably brought the counterpane and the cushions and the fine crystal goblets with him, however. They were of a quality finer than the wooden table and chairs, the verdigrised brass lamps and threadbare carpet. I knew why he had overcome his delicate tastes to meet us here. It had been meant as an insult to me, for no decent woman of any nationality would enter the place. More important, it meant Riccetti was not as sure of himself as he would like us to believe. A man who held all the winning cards would not take such precautions.

The forlorn hope that dawned in my heart was short-lived. Riccetti gestured toward an object on the table. "You recognize it, of course?"

It was Ramses's pocket notebook. He never went anywhere without it. Emerson picked it up, thumbed through it, and coolly put it in his shirt pocket. "Yes," he said curtly.

"Then we have established the first premise on which our conversation will be based? Good. You must forgive my bad manners, Mrs. Emerson. I would offer you a chair and a glass of wine if I thought there were the slightest possibility you would accept."

"I would not," I said.

"A pity." Riccetti sipped delicately at his wine. "It is an excellent vintage. You want the boy back, I suppose. I can't imagine why; he is a very irritating child."

"Tastes differ," said Emerson, as coolly as Riccetti. "And I would be averse to sharing any taste of yours. How did he find you?"

Riccetti chuckled. "It was I who found him. I have many—er—associates in Luxor; they were told to bring me word if anyone appeared to be interested in my whereabouts. I felt certain one of you would come looking for me sooner or later. The other day I came close to—" His jaws closed with a snap. "But I was about to boast about my cleverness. You English despise that sort of thing, don't you?"

"Let us get to terms," Emerson said. "I suppose that in exchange for Ramses you want me to remove myself and my guards from the tomb and leave it to you."

"Dio mio, no!" Riccetti's eyes widened. "You mistake me entirely, my friend. Would I interfere with the finest excavator in Egypt? I want you to go on with your work—to clear the tomb and preserve its contents with the utmost care."

Emerson was silent for a moment. "I see."

"I felt certain you would." Riccetti put his glass on the table and leaned forward. "Working in haste, as illicit diggers must, my people would damage some of the articles, thereby reducing my profits. I can't trust the swine, either," he added indignantly. "No matter how—er—forcefully I supervise them, there are always a few who will take the risk of robbing me."

Astonishment and—yes, I admit—admiration robbed me of breath for a few moments. The fellow's evil intelligence was brilliant. This scheme was worthy of Sethos himself—allowing us to carry out the work with the skill only we could demonstrate—then forcing us to hand the treasure over to him.

"I hope," Riccetti went on, "that you now have a reason to speed the work. The sooner you finish, the sooner you will have your son with you again."

"Aren't you afraid I will work too quickly?" Emerson asked ironically. "A devoted father might shovel up the lot without worrying about your profits."

"Not you, my friend. Your principles are too well known. Flagrant violation of them would arouse suspicion. A deliberate speed—a careful compromise—that is all I ask. Shall we say . . . two weeks?"

"Two weeks? Impossible!"

"Some of your colleagues would have it out in two days," Riccetti said with his saurian grin. "I don't care about the broken scraps of pottery and wood. Pick the plums out of the pudding, you know what they are as well as I. And make sure you open that sarcophagus. I want what is inside, all of it—coffins, mummy and any other objects."

"Wait," I said. "What about David? He must be returned to us too."

Riccetti appeared to be genuinely puzzled. "David? Oh—the native boy. Why should you ask about him?" And then a slow, sneering smile spread across his face. "That famous British sentimentality! Would it distress you to learn, Mrs. Emerson, that he does not feel the same loyalty toward you that you appear to feel for him?"

"He is not your prisoner?" Emerson demanded.

"I don't know where he is and I don't care. No doubt he will return to you if he chooses. No more questions. Are we agreed?"

"Yes," Emerson said.

"Excellent. One final word of warning. I know you too well to suppose you have given up hope of finding the brat and freeing him. I would be seriously annoyed if you tried to do so. Let me make it perfectly clear, so there will be no unfortunate misunderstandings. If you are not, both of you, at your excavation every day, I will assume you are doing something else—something I have warned you not to do. Your first duty, my friends, is to your child. Should you lose sight of that, I will send you a little reminder. A finger, perhaps, or an ear."

I cannot remember how I got out of the place. When I become aware of my surroundings I was sitting on the cracked rim of a fountain with water dripping off my chin and Emerson bending over me.

"Say something, my love. Anything!"

"Curse it," I muttered. "I didn't faint, did I? If I gave that son of a dog the satisfaction of fainting . . ."

"That's my Peabody," Emerson said, with a long breath of relief. "No, my dear, you walked out on your own two feet, steady as a rock. It wasn't until we got into the light and I saw your face that I realized you were not entirely yourself. Here, take my arm and let's get out of this."

He raised me to my feet. Though his voice was even, he was rather white around the mouth, and I said, "I am ashamed of myself, Emerson. Forgive me for behaving like a weak wom—— Like a weakling. That terrible threat must have shaken you as much as it did me."

"Not quite so much, for I was expecting something of the sort." He managed a fairly convincing smile. "You have encountered a good many criminals in your time, Peabody, but never one so totally without scruples as Riccetti. Do you know, I almost find myself regretting our old adversary. At least Sethos was, in his own fashion, a man of his word."

"He would never have harmed a child," I said. "And he would have made short shrift of a creature like Riccetti. Emerson, you don't mean to give up searching for Ramses, do you? We cannot trust Riccetti. We can't even be certain the boy is . . . is still living."

"I think we can be, though. Riccetti knows I won't turn over so much as a potsherd without proof of that rather important matter. Your assessment of his character is correct, however. He wouldn't hesitate to slaughter the lot of us, including Ramses, after we have done as he asks. We will pursue our inquiries, but we will have to proceed with great care. The bastard has us neatly boxed in."

"You needn't tell me that. Oh, Emerson, what are we going to do? I confess that for the first time in my life I feel just a little—well—out of my depth."

"That state of affairs won't last," Emerson said with conviction. "What you need, my dear, is a good stiff whiskey and soda. Shall we drop in at the Luxor bar?"

"No, we had better get back. The others will be on pins and needles. But," I added, smiling bravely at him, "I will take you up on that suggestion when we are at the *Amelia*."

I was surprised to see how late it was. The sun was low over the western cliffs when we set sail for the West Bank. Emerson smoked for a while in silence and then said, "For the time being we must do precisely as he ordered. The absence of either of us from the excavation would surely be noted and reported by one of his spies. Agreed?"

"We cannot do otherwise. What do we tell the others?"

"Everything. In a case such as this, even O'Connell can be trusted to keep the thing quiet. He may have a suggestion. We are in no position to overlook any possibility."

"True. And one never knows—something may yet turn up!"

The Reader may wonder why I had not seen fit to tell him about my summons to Miss Marmaduke. The omission was not because I had forgotten or because I anticipated a rebuke. I had realized I must change my strategy. If Gertrude was in Riccetti's pay, the direct, forceful interrogation I had intended might be viewed as a violation of his orders—and the consequences of that were too horrible to contemplate. I would have to proceed with the utmost subtlety, simulating absolute confidence in her, lowering her guard, remaining on the alert for the slightest slip.

Luckily I had cautioned Evelyn and Nefret to refrain from direct accusations and to behave normally. They did not have my skill at extracting information from a reluctant witness, and I had known, when Riccetti's message came, that I would have to reconsider the situation.

So there was no need to tell Emerson about it. Possibly she would have left by the time we got back.

She *had* left. And so had Nefret.

We did not discover this for almost an hour. I wondered why the girl was not waiting in anxious expectation, as were Evelyn and Walter, but when I asked about her, Evelyn explained she had gone to her room to rest after Gertrude's departure.

"I am afraid I was rather short with the poor woman," Evelyn admitted. "She kept weeping and wringing her hands and making futile suggestions. She tried Nefret's nerves even more than she did mine, I believe. We were so worried about you. It is a relief to have you safely back—but I can tell by your faces that the news is bad. What has happened?"

I allowed Emerson to tell them. Evelyn's distress was so great I had to administer a medicinal glass of whiskey. It did her good, but her agitated inquiries, and those of Walter, made me forget all else until I realized the sun was almost down.

"Where is Nefret?" I cried, rising impetuously to my feet. "She should have woken by now. There is something wrong."

She was not in her room, nor on the dahabeeyah. We searched it from stem to stern before one of the crewmen volunteered the information that the young Sitt had gone away in the carriage with the other lady.

"Did she go of her own accord?" Emerson asked.

"Would we allow one to take her away by force?" The poor fellow sensed something was wrong. His hands flew up in protestation. "She smiled at me, Father of Curses, and said she would soon return, and she ran to the carriage, which was on the road. No one was in it but the other lady, and only Vandergelt Effendi's man driving it . . . I thought no harm of it. What have I done?"

"Nothing," Emerson said. "You are not to blame. Peabody, what do you say we call on our friend Vandergelt?"

"I am going with you," Evelyn declared. "You cannot prevent me, Emerson, I insist."

"Certainly," Emerson said. "We will all go."

Cyrus had not dressed for dinner. He came hurrying to meet us, still in his dusty work clothes. "I was just about to ride on over to see you folks. Any news?"

"What sort of host are you, Vandergelt, to keep us standing in the hall?" Emerson inquired. "The library, I think; it is the pleasantest room in the house and I would like to see how Miss Marmaduke is getting on with my manuscript."

He led the way. Cyrus was so taken aback he forgot to offer me his arm. "I never heard my old pal sound like that," he exclaimed. "What's wrong, Mrs. Amelia? Good Lord Almighty, don't tell me the boy is—"

"It is not so bad as that," I replied. "But the situation could not be much worse. We have lost both of them, Cyrus. Nefret has gone too. I don't suppose Gertrude returned to the Castle this afternoon?"

"Why, I don't know. I just got back myself a while ago. Are you trying to tell me she's been abducted too?"

He ushered me into the library. Mr. Amherst rose politely from the chair where he had been sitting, a book in his hand. Emerson stood by the table at which Gertrude had ostensibly been working.

"Half a dozen pages copied," he remarked, indicating the manuscript of his book. "One is entitled to wonder how the woman spent her time. Where is her room?"

This time Cyrus led the way. Emerson did not speak at all; it was I who gave our friend—and his assistant, trailing timidly in our wake—a synopsis of what had occurred. Overcoming his alarm and distress with the sturdy American efficiency I would have expected from him, Cyrus snapped out orders.

"Willy, get the coachman in here. And the housemaid. Heck, may as well collect the whole staff. Vamoose."

With his own hands he assisted us in searching the room. Nothing was overlooked, not even the pockets of the garments hanging in the wardrobe.

"Her toilet articles are missing," Evelyn said quietly.

"And one of her traveling bags," I added.

"A good thing you ladies are here," Cyrus said. "I don't guess I'd have noticed that. She left most of her clothes."

"And her books." I tossed *Isis Unveiled* onto the table. "The incense and burner are gone, though. And the ring."

"The bare essentials," Emerson muttered. "And anything that might be of use to us in tracing her. Let us hear what the servants have to say."

The coachman, quivering with nerves under Emerson's searching questions, was the only one who could contribute anything useful. The Effendi had ordered him to drive the lady to visit her friends on the dahabeeyah. He had waited for her, as she directed, and waited again for the young Sitt.

"And then?" I broke in, unable to bear the suspense any longer. "Where did you take them?"

"To the ferry landing, Sitt Hakim. I asked if I should wait or come back for them, but the lady said no."

"Did they say where they were going?" I knew what the answer would be, but the question had to be asked.

"They spoke in English, Sitt Hakim." Observing our downcast faces, he added, with the obvious hope of being helpful, "The young Sitt gave me a paper for the Effendi."

"What!" Emerson shot out of his chair like an arrow from a bow. "God curse you for seven eternities in the deepest pit of Gehenna! Why did you not say so? Give it to me!"

With a faint shriek the man shrank back against the wall. "I do not have it, Father of Curses. I gave it to—"

He indicated the majordomo, who began gabbling. "I put it on the table, sir; it is with your other messages."

It was there, half buried in a pile of letters and newspapers, which must have arrived that day—a folded piece of paper which had obviously been torn from a small pocket diary. The flush of hope faded from Emerson's face, leaving it hard and drawn.

"No use," he said. "She must have written this with the woman looking on—dictating, even. It reads: 'I have gone to Luxor with Miss Marmaduke to meet someone who may know where Ramses is. We are only going to the Luxor hotel. I will come back as soon as I can.'"

"How could she be so gullible?" Walter demanded. "I had thought better of her."

"It is that infernal spirit of competition that has developed between her and Ramses," I said.

"And her affection for him," Evelyn said gently. "She has been desperately worried, Amelia."

"Wait a minute." Cyrus had been looking through the other papers. "What the dickens is this?"

The majordomo cleared his throat nervously. "You told me, sir, to copy any message that came for the lady."

For a moment no one moved. The disappointment had been so severe, we did not dare hope again.

"Read it aloud," Emerson said hoarsely.

Cyrus cleared his throat. "'Riccetti has the boy. Now is your chance; she will come with you if you promise to lead her to him. She must steal away unseen or they will try to stop you, for they do not walk in the light as you do. She who guards the gates of the Underworld has given us a sign. Do not fail Her.'"

"Oh, heavens," I said with a sigh. "Crushed again. That is the usual psychic mumbo-jumbo. It is of no more help than Nefret's note."

Emerson was poring over the message. "There is more in this than we thought," he said slowly. "You were right all along,

Peabody, and I hope you will be good enough to refrain from mentioning it more than a dozen times a day."

My heart swelled with affectionate admiration. No one, particularly myself, had ever doubted that Emerson was the bravest of men, but this quiet fortitude demanded more courage than the vigorous action to which he was usually prone. In an equally calm, cheerful voice I replied, "Yes, my dear. I congratulate you for grasping the implications so quickly."

"You might just explain them to me," Cyrus said, rubbing his forehead. "I guess I'm a mite dense this evening."

"I understand," Evelyn exclaimed. "There are two groups of criminals, just as you believed, Amelia—"

"The Jackals and the Hippopotami!" I cried. "And Gertrude is not a hippopotamus!"

"Yes!" We shook hands, and I clapped her on the shoulder.

Walter stared at his wife as if she had lost her mind. Cyrus gaped. Emerson studied me pensively.

"Peabody," he said, "in case I have not thought to mention it recently, you are the light of my life and the joy of my existence. Come, my dear, we must return to the dahabeeyah immediately."

There was no opportunity for conversation during the ride back; Emerson set a rapid pace and we were several minutes behind him by the time we arrived. I hurried at once to our room, where I found him wrapping a bundle of clothing in India-rubber sheeting.

"Remain in the saloon this evening," he said, tossing the bundle onto the bed and starting to unlace his boots. "If anyone is watching, it will be more difficult to ascertain how many of us are present."

"You need not spell it out. Emerson, must you go?"

"Now is the best chance, before the trail grows cold. It may be my only chance, Peabody; I must be seen to be at the tomb tomorrow, at the usual time. Curse it," he added, tugging at his shirt, "what did you use to sew these buttons, wire?"

"Take Abdullah. Or Daoud. Please, Emerson."

"I might as well wear a placard with my name in black letters," my husband replied acerbically. "Their faces are well known in Luxor."

"And yours is not?"

Emerson grinned at me. "I borrowed a beard from Ramses. A fine beard it is, too. I am leaving Daoud with you, you may need him, and I dare not risk having him take me across; we might be seen. Give me a kiss for luck, my dear."

Since I had intended to do so anyhow, I obliged. I sent him off with a word of cheer and a valiant smile, but after the door had closed behind him . . . But why describe my sensations or my actions? They did me no credit. Finally I stiffened my spine, fastened the smile back onto my face, and went to find Walter and Evelyn.

They had not anticipated Emerson's intentions as I had done, and were awaiting us on the upper deck. Walter raged at his brother for leaving him behind, and at me for allowing him to go. Evelyn's lips trembled as she contemplated the vacant chairs at the table. The steward had set six places, as usual. Six—and only three of us left. How many of the missing would ever return?

I instructed Mahmud to remove the dishes and bring the food to the saloon. Walter had calmed down a bit by then; he apologized to me and agreed we must carry on in the manner Emerson had suggested. No one had much of an appetite. We forced the food down, however, since it was necessary to keep up appearances.

It has often been said—and I firmly believe it—that Heaven does not try us beyond our strength. Scarcely an hour had passed (though I measured it, Reader, in units interminably long) since Emerson's departure and I was wondering how I could bear the endless hours that must yet pass, when Heaven came to my rescue. So tightly strung were my nerves that the voices outside the saloon made me drop my glass and leap to my feet. I knew those voices. One was Mahmud's, raised in shrill protest. The other . . .

I ran to the door and flung it open. Mahmud held the squirming, struggling boy by the arm. "You cannot enter, not like that. Go wash your filthy person and I will tell the Sitt—"

The boy raised a wild face toward mine. His black eyes were dilated, his black curls streaked with dust, his galabeeyah torn.

"Let him go," I said. "David—where is Ramses?"

Before Mahmud could obey or David could reply, the cat Bastet emerged from the shadows of the deck, considered the situation, and leaped onto Mahmud's back. Mahmud screamed and let go David's arm. Bastet jumped down and sauntered past me toward the dining table.

I drew the boy into the room and closed the door. At first I could not make him sit down or speak coherently. He kept pulling at me, demanding that I come with him.

It was Evelyn who intervened, gently detaching my hands from David and his from me. "Stop shaking him, Amelia. David, sit here by me. I am so glad you are safe."

"But he is not? He is not here?" His taut body relaxed as she put her arm around him, and he let out a long gasping breath.

"Tell us what happened," Evelyn said. "Tell us what you know. Speak Arabic, it will be quicker and easier."

Only she, I believe, could have got a sensible account out of the boy. He spoke in simple, declarative sentences, watching her anxiously as if it were vital that she understand. She appeared to follow him without difficulty. Perhaps those long conversations between them had improved her Arabic as well as his English. They had unquestionably established a bond of something warmer and more complex than friendship.

It was as I had thought: Ramses had decided to take it upon himself to track down Riccetti. David had not even tried to dissuade him; he had a wholly disproportionate respect for Ramses's abilities. "And is he not my brother? Where he goes, I go."

They had "borrowed" a boat and rowed across the river. "She," said David, indicating Bastet, "she came too."

"Has she been with you all this time?" Walter asked, eyeing without favor the cat, who was calmly browsing among the left-over food.

"Let him tell it in the proper order, Walter," said Evelyn. "Go on, David."

I had to admit Ramses had gone about the business more

intelligently than I would have expected. Knowing that an ordinary barefoot fellah would never be allowed in one of the large hotels, he had got himself up quite smartly in what might have been mistaken for a kind of livery—sandals, clean white robe and red fez. Purporting to have been given a parcel to be delivered to Signor Riccetti, he had gone the rounds of the hotels, without, I hardly need add, success. He had also taken the precaution of telling David to follow him at a discreet distance—with the cat.

"All in Luxor know her," David explained. "She cannot be seen with him. He ordered her to stay with me."

I looked at Bastet. She raised her head from my plate and gave me a cool, appraising stare. The creature really was rather uncanny, and Ramses's relationship with her was one I did not care to explore.

"Then what?" Walter demanded.

Then Ramses had called on the antika dealers.

"Oh, good Gad," I exclaimed. "That is how Riccetti found out! Half of them are in his pay and the other half are terrified of him."

"Hush," Evelyn said. "Let him go on."

The rest of the tale was soon told. Ramses had emerged from one of the shops with a particularly smug smile (David did not use that expression, but I knew Ramses well enough to picture it) and, after signaling David, had plunged straight into the back alleys. He had been given an address, or rather, since street names and numbers are unknown in Luxor, directions. Hanging back as he had been instructed, David was ten feet away when a man stepped out of a dark doorway and caught hold of Ramses, clapping a hand over his mouth.

He got a bit more than he had bargained for. Ramses was as slippery as an eel and unrestrained by gentlemanly scruples. He had managed to free his mouth long enough to call out.

"He said 'Run,' " David said. "I ran."

"And the cat?"

"He said to her, 'Stay with David.' I ran and she ran with me, to find you, to bring help. That is what he said to do." The boy was trembling again. "Another man ran after me. At the riverbank

I looked for the boat. It was not there. Then a man said, 'Do you want to go across the river? Get into my boat, you and the cat; I am going to my house.' The man who followed was close behind. I was afraid. So I got into the boat and called the cat Bastet to come. But when we reached the other side . . ."

He had woken up in a windowless, dirt-floored room, with no memory of how he had got there. His head hurt and his mouth was dry. Fumbling around in the dark, he had found a water bottle, and after assuaging his thirst he had explored the room by touch. The single door was of heavy wood; it must have been bolted on the outside, for there was no keyhole and it did not yield when he threw himself against it. There was no furniture in the room, not even a pile of rags on which to lie; but they had left him his knife. And so, after pounding on the door and shouting till he was hoarse, he began to dig at the mud-brick of one of the walls. He had not got far before dizziness overcame him and he fell asleep.

"There must have been some drug in the water," I said. "But then how did you get out?"

"When I woke up the door was open," David said. "And the cat Bastet was there, licking my face. So I came here. Now, please, will we go to find Ramses?"

CHAPTER FOURTEEN

Most People Obey the Orders of an Individual Who Is Pointing a Gun at Them

We could not have held him back, even if we had not been burning to pursue the same end. Every square inch of the boy's meager frame was quivering with frustration. I could only imagine how much it had cost him to run away instead of rushing to Ramses's aid. A rescue attempt would have been worse than futile, but most lads would not have exhibited that degree of self-discipline and common sense.

Our decision was unanimous and virtually instantaneous. Walter did not even protest when Evelyn declared she meant to go with us. Our forces were already dangerously divided; we must stay together from now on.

I persuaded David to take food and water while we made the necessary preparations. He had not eaten since the night before and had been afraid to risk another drink from the tainted bottle, but he was on his feet, ready and waiting, when I returned to the saloon and sat down to pen a brief note to Emerson, and another to Cyrus Vandergelt.

There were a number of questions I wanted to ask the boy, but they could wait. They would have to wait. It was obvious to all of us that we dared not delay. Once Riccetti learned of David's escape he might view it as a violation of his orders and if, as the boy claimed, he could lead us to the precise spot where Ramses had last been seen, the villain might decide to move his captive to a more secure location—before or after detaching the "reminder" he had promised us.

Walter had gone to tell Daoud we were crossing to Luxor. When he joined us to announce that all was ready, his resolute countenance assured me I could count on him not to fail me; but oh, how I wished it were Emerson at my side!

To conceal our departure would have been impossible. Speed was our best hope now. I could have wished for a few more weapons; I had my pistol and my knife, but owing to Emerson's prejudice against firearms, that was the extent of our arsenal. A paltry armament with which to face a man like Riccetti and his hired thugs! I reminded myself that fortune favors the brave, not the party with the most rifles. The adage would have cheered me more if I had not been able to think of so many examples that contradicted it.

It was not until Daoud ran to meet us and took his cousin in a warm embrace that I realized I should have sent word to Abdullah. His anxiety must of necessity be prolonged, however; there was not time to summon him and our men, nor even a messenger to send. We needed Daoud.

Once we had taken our places in the boat, I asked David to explain some of the details urgency had forced him to omit. My first question concerned the location of the place where he had been imprisoned. He informed me that it had not been in Gurneh, but farther south, near the small hamlet of Medinet Habu.

"Close enough," I muttered. "Evelyn, could we have been wrong about Abd el Hamel? His hatred of the man who maimed him might have been overcome by fear, or the desire for profit. It must have been one of Riccetti's people who caught David—but then who freed him?"

David was unable to satisfy my curiosity on that point. He had not lingered to examine the outside of the door; as soon as he made certain no one was lying in wait for him, he had run, straight to the dahabeeyah. However, he had no doubt as to the identity of his rescuer.

"She," he said, nodding at Bastet, lying along the bench beside him.

"Come now," Walter exclaimed. "The door must have been bolted or barred. Even granting the creature sufficient intelligence to comprehend the mechanism, it would not have had the strength."

"It would have been more sensible of her to come to us and guide us to your prison," I said, giving the cat a critical look. She yawned.

"He tells her to stay with me," David explained.

Walter shook his head so emphatically that his eyeglasses slipped down. He pushed them back into place. "David's pounding on the door must have loosened the bar; that is the only possible explanation. You are as superstitious as the boy, Amelia. It is only a cat, you know, not a supernatural being."

"She," I said, unconsciously emphasizing the pronoun as David had done, "has some qualities more like those of a dog than a cat. I am hoping she can pick up Ramses's trail."

"Ridiculous," Walter muttered.

I would not have had to convince Emerson, who knew, as I did, that Bastet could also be useful in a scrap. She had left poor Mahmud's back badly scratched—and she had only been mildly annoyed with him. I bit my lip to hold back an irritable response. Walter was doing his best; he could not help being what he had become, but I would have given a great deal to have him be the man he once was—the gallant youth who had risked his life for loyalty and love.

Evelyn was the first to break the ensuing silence. "We are halfway across. Shall we not assume our disguises now, and make our final plans?"

The disguises had been her idea. I doubted they would help us much, but she had been so keen on the plan I did not argue, nor did I ask where she had procured the black robe and face veil. I had my own, of course. I always have such an ensemble in my wardrobe. One never knows when an emergency may arise.

We put them on and Walter slipped a galabeeyah over his head. There was not much more we could do. Our plans, such as they were, had already been formulated. When we landed I gave Daoud his final instructions.

"Stay at a distance, Daoud, and in the shadows. Watch where we go. If we enter a house, wait for ten . . . Wait till you have counted to five hundred. If we have not come out by then, or if you hear sounds of gunfire within, go and tell Mr. Vandergelt what has happened."

Daoud was a big, easygoing man who held me in considerable awe. He had never opposed an order of mine. He opposed this one, heatedly. I was forced to brandish my parasol at him before he agreed.

Anonymous in our black garments, we women trailed humbly behind Walter and David. Walter's hand was on the boy's shoulder—an ostensibly friendly gesture, but I knew what Walter was thinking: that David might be leading us into an ambush. Evelyn would have indignantly denied the possibility; I did not believe it myself, but belief is not certainty. It was just another of the risks we had been forced to take.

Luxor has only twelve thousand inhabitants, but some of them live crowded together in areas as dark and cramped as the slums of a city. They were not so dark that night. The Lesser Festival of Bairam, which follows the fasting of Ramadan, was being celebrated with visits of ceremony and the giving of gifts. We passed doors that were hospitably open, and groups of people talking, but when David finally stopped, the voices had died away and the surrounding houses were dark.

"Here," he whispered. "It was here the man caught hold of him."

Instinctively we drew together, with a wall at our backs. It was up to the cat now, and when so much hung on her purported talents it was hard even for me to have much faith in them. I was about to speak to her when my eyes, searching my surroundings, fell on something I recognized.

"That is the house," I hissed, pointing.

"How do you know?" Walter demanded.

"It would take too long to explain." I studied the facade of the house.

Like the others that abutted it on either side, it was several stories high, its peeling stucco surface broken only by shuttered windows on either side of the doorway and a balcony over it.

Was this unpretentious dwelling Riccetti's Luxor headquarters? It was certainly the house from which the very large man had emerged and—I now realized—attempted to intercept me. As I continued to study it I observed several interesting features. For one thing, the shutters were solid, and so well secured to the frames that not a single ray of light escaped. The inhabitants must be unsociable individuals who did not encourage visitors, even during the days of the festival. The same was true of the houses on either side and those that faced them across the narrow way. The whole area was uncommonly dark and quiet; I wondered whether Riccetti owned or controlled every house on the street.

If he had stationed a guard outside we were done for, but I did not think he would bother. The solid walls and shuttered windows made the houses into virtual fortresses. I decided not to waste time looking for a back entrance. There probably was one, but we might not be able to distinguish it from others, and if it offered an easier means of entry, it would undoubtedly be guarded.

I removed the muffling black garments and kicked them away. "Lift me on your shoulders," I said to Walter, indicating the balcony.

It was the only possible way; he knew that too, but he felt obliged to assert his masculinity. "Not you. I will—"

"I cannot lift *you*, you idiot." I forced the words between clenched teeth. "If you argue with me, Walter, I will—I will—I may be forced to strike you."

"Do as she says," Evelyn said. She had her parasol in her hand now. It had been hidden under her robe.

It was rather a tricky business, since I was in a hurry, and even standing on Walter's shoulders I could not quite reach the balcony. Had Emerson been there . . . I forced that seductive image from my mind and found a crack large enough for the toe of my boot. From there—to be honest, I don't know how I managed it, but I did, because I had to.

The shutters here were not solid. I could see no light between the strips of wood and I hoped that meant the room beyond was uninhabited. I could not avoid making some small noises when I ran my knife blade along the crack between the shutters and forced the inner bolt. The cursed hinges creaked, too.

I had had to leave my parasol behind, but I had my usual tools, and as I hesitated in the dark opening, I knew I must risk striking a match.

The room was a sleeping chamber, skimpily furnished with cots and a few tables and an assortment of pottery vessels. It resembled a dormitory in one of the cheaper boarding schools. Quarters for the thugs, I decided, and served them right, too. It was lucky we had come when we did; a few hours from now the room might be filled with sleeping men.

It behooved me to make haste, in case one of them decided on an early night. I paused only long enough to light my dark lantern. Then I tiptoed to the door and eased it open.

The room was on a corridor that ran around four sides of an open stairwell. From below I heard voices and saw a glow of light. Indecision, which rarely afflicts me, struck me now. Should I attempt to open the front door, or should I immediately pursue my search for Ramses?

In fact, the decision was not difficult. There were people below; reaching the door unobserved and undoing bolts, bars and/or locks would be difficult if not impossible.

I had another reason for preferring the second alternative. I need not explain that reason to any parent.

I was nerving myself to leave the illusory safety of the room when something pushed against my ankle and a sound like the buzzing of a giant insect struck my ears. I whirled round, my knife raised, and saw a dark form silhouetted against the window opening.

"It is I, Sitt, and the cat Bastet. Do not strike!"

I swallowed my heart—at least that was how it felt—and managed to speak. "David! How did you get here?"

"I climb." He came to my side, silent as a shadow, on bare feet. "Mr. Walter Emerson says, open the door. If you do not he climb too."

I felt a little easier, coward that I was, at having him—both of them—with me. It is very lonely in a dark house filled with foes.

The cat was still purring. (It is a well-known fact that familiar sounds are not easy to identify in unfamiliar surroundings.) I bent over to stroke her head.

"I don't think we can get to the door," I whispered. "The most important thing is to find Ramses, if he is here."

"He is here. The cat Bastet know. She climb on my shoulder. Now you hear, she purr."

"Too loudly. Bastet, stop purring at once."

She obeyed. Walter would have said it was coincidence.

"We must not be discovered, David. If Ramses is not in the house, we dare not let Riccetti know we were here. And for heaven's sake, speak Arabic! Your English is coming along nicely, but this is no time to practice a new language."

I sensed rather than saw him nod. "Sitt, you hold the knife wrong. Strike up, not down."

It was good practical advice under the circumstances, though not what I had expected. "I know," I said meekly. "I forgot."

"Do not forget. Come now."

Confound the boy, he was beginning to sound just like Ramses, trying to order me around and take charge. So was the cat (but that is the habit of cats). She preceded us along the corridor, her tail switching, and led the way up the stairs.

The doors on this level were closer together and the floor was splintered and worn. Every step produced a squeak or a groan that seemed to echo like a pistol shot. I used my dark lantern as sparingly as possible; every time I opened the shutter, I felt as if the light must be visible throughout the entire house.

The cat Bastet moved on, past door after closed door. She appeared very confident—but that, again, is a characteristic of cats. My faith in her began to waver. How could she possibly know where she was going? This upper floor, bare and comfortless as it was, was not the most logical place for a prisoner to be confined. I would have expected Riccetti's tastes to run to something more unpleasant—a dank, dismal den far underground, with water dripping from the walls, and rats, and snakes . . .

So dreadful and pervasive was this mental image that David had to catch me by the sleeve before I saw it—a thin ray of light lying across the worn floorboards like a golden thread. The door from which it issued was closed, but the hinged side had warped a trifle.

The cat Bastet sat down in front of the door and looked at me expectantly. I closed the shutter on the dark lantern and leaned close to David. "I think there will be a guard."

"Aywa. If it is locked, let me speak. If it opens, I will go first."

Not likely, my lad, I thought, reaching for my pistol. I hoped I would not have to fire it and alarm the entire house, but if Ramses was there I would do anything I had to do in order to get him out. The sight of the pistol might be enough. Most people obey the orders of an individual who is pointing a gun at them.

David got to the door before I did. He pressed the latch and flung the door open in a single movement.

There was a guard. He was the very large man I had seen once before.

It is a mistake commonly made by criminals, I have observed, to hire a very large man instead of a smaller, quicker person. This fellow heaved himself up out of his chair with the ponderous deliberation of a moving mountain.

"Stop," I said softly but emphatically. "Do not make a sound or I will fire."

The large person stopped. David stopped too. He was holding

his knife in the manner he had suggested and I did not doubt he would have used it.

"Lie down on the floor," was my next order. "Quickly!"

Instead of complying, the fellow looked from me to the boy. His brow furrowed. He was thinking. It was obviously a painful process, but unfortunately he appeared to have sense enough to weigh his options accurately. His curious gaze moved to the cat, who was sitting to one side, watching as coolly as a spectator at a play; then it came back to me, and a slow unpleasant smile spread across his face.

I much regretted having had to abandon my parasol; it must have been the sight of that magical weapon that had frightened him off before. Now he had decided that a child and a woman deprived of her magic presented no real threat. Any sound, a pistol shot or the sound of a struggle, would bring the others running. We seemed to be at something of an impasse.

With a sound like a snort of disgust, the cat Bastet crouched and leaped, straight at the man's face. He staggered back, his scream muted, first by ten pounds of cat and then by the chair David smashed over his head. He fell sideways across the bed, and across the feet of Ramses, who was lying on the bed.

I had seen Ramses, of course, but I had been too intent on the guard to give him more than a fleeting glance. Nor was I able as yet to attend to him. I had to strike the man several times with the butt of my pistol before he stopped squirming. Since I did not want to kill him (not very much), he had to be bound and gagged. There was no sheet on the hard cot, not even a blanket. David had to give up his robe, which we tore into strips.

I suppose the whole business only took a few minutes, but it seemed to go on for hours. Expecting at any second to hear feet in the corridor—frantic to assure myself that my son yet lived—wondering how the devil we were going to get him out if we could not rouse him—well, it was not a pleasant interval. When I turned to the bed, Ramses had not moved. The cat sat beside him, licking his head. She was kind enough not to object when I pushed her away and gathered Ramses into my arms.

His head fell back against my shoulder. There was no doubt

as to what was wrong with him; his dirty, bruised face bore a look of utter bliss. Ramses had always wanted to experiment with opium—in a purely scientific fashion, he claimed. He had got his wish.

"Drugged," I gasped. "We will have to carry him. Take his feet."

I much regretted that Ramses had grown so much the past year. He was heavier than I had expected—not, heaven be thanked, a dead weight, but near enough. Getting him down the stairs was the most difficult part. My arms and shoulders were very tired by then, and his posterior kept bumping on the steps.

My goal was the room through which I had entered the house, and the image of that unprepossessing chamber hovered before my straining eyes with all the allurement of Paradise. If we could reach it before we were intercepted, we were safe. The sounds from the ground floor had increased in volume and in joviality; the thugs must be having their private celebration. I sincerely hoped they were enjoying themselves. If one of them tired of the party and decided to go to bed . . . I addressed a brief prayer to that Power that rules our destinies, but I am afraid it came out sounding more like an order: "Keep them downstairs!"

We were on the last stretch of corridor, with the desired door only ten feet distant, when it opened. I think I would have screamed if I had had breath enough. David, ahead of me, dropped Ramses's feet and reached for the knife he had stuck in the band of the loose drawers that were his sole remaining garment.

There was just enough light from the stairwell to save Walter's skin. David could not have recognized his face, but the European boots and trousers warned him in time. He returned the knife to his belt and Walter scooped Ramses up.

"They are coming," he said. "Hurry."

We never knew what aroused the suspicions of the men below—the thud of Ramses's heels on the floor, or some sound from without? It must have been just enough to alert but not alarm them, for they came slowly, and I heard one make a joking remark about hearing afreets.

Evelyn was waiting behind the door; she closed it as soon as we were all inside. "How—" I began.

"Secure the door," Walter cut in. "Bolt it and shove the furniture up against it." Carrying Ramses, he went out onto the balcony.

Evelyn slammed the bolt in place; it was a flimsy thing, only a hinged strip of wood, but it would hold for a while. I left her and David moving furniture, and followed Walter.

He was leaning over the edge of the balcony; I was in time to see him drop Ramses into the upraised arms of Daoud.

"Now you, Sitt," Daoud called.

I would have chanced it had I been alone, but there was not time for all of us to get out that way. Our adversaries had discovered us; they were shouting, and pounding on the door of the chamber. Sooner or later it would occur to one of them that the balcony was our only means of escape.

Walter ran back inside and I said to Daoud, "No, it is too late. Run—get Ramses to safety and bring help. Go now, before they come out of the house!"

Even as I spoke, I heard the rattle of chains and bolts inside the front door. Daoud stood gaping up at me.

I called him the worst Arabic name I knew. Between Ramses and Emerson, I knew quite a lot of them. He jumped as if I had struck him and then ran, with Ramses draped over one shoulder. They were still in sight when—as I had feared and anticipated—the front door opened. One of the thugs burst out, pistol in hand, and started in pursuit.

I shot him in the back. It was not a sporting thing to do, but the alternative would have been less acceptable. He fell, dropping the pistol, but I knew I had not killed him because he screamed a good deal. Finally someone dragged him back inside. I did not want to waste any more bullets, so I fetched a pot (smelling strongly of the remains of someone's dinner), and when the door opened again and another head appeared, I dropped the pot on it.

"That should hold them for a while," I said, returning to my companions. "But I fear that exit is now unusable. They can cover us from the doorway. How are things going?"

I could see the answer for myself, and a discouraging one it was. The door reverberated under the pound of hard blows; they must have been using a heavy article of furniture as a battering ram. Every cot and table had been piled against the portal, but they were flimsy things and could not hold long once the door yielded, as it soon must.

"Did they get away?" Evelyn gasped.

A truthful answer would have been "I hope so," but it was safe to assume that my companions' morale was in need of a little boost. "Yes," I said firmly. "Can we hold these fellows off until help arrives?"

"Oh, certainly, if it arrives within the next five minutes," Walter said with awful sarcasm. "I seem to remember your telling Daoud he must go to Vandergelt if we failed to return."

I had hoped he would not remember that, and I hoped even more that Daoud would not remember. There had not been time for me to give him precise instructions. "Nonsense," I said. "He has better sense than to delay so long. He will seek help closer at hand."

"Surely one of the neighbors will summon the police," Evelyn said.

Walter, who seemed to be in a state of some exasperation, would have made another sarcastic remark if I had not given him a little kick. "Yes, of course," I said. "But we ought to take stock of our weaponry, in case—er—in case."

One of the iron cots fell over with a crash. The door was vibrating violently. "David has his knife," I shouted. "I have a knife and a pistol. Walter, you had better take my pistol."

"I too have a knife," Walter said, taking it from his belt. "Daoud gave me one of his."

"Don't hold it that way!" I demonstrated with my own. "An underhand blow is more likely to strike a vital spot than . . ." One of the hinges gave way and the door buckled. A shout of triumph from without forced me to raise my voice even more. "Never mind, Walter, just do the best you can. Evelyn, would you prefer my knife or my pistol?"

"Whichever you like, Amelia," Evelyn said politely.

"Take the pistol, then," I screamed.

And suddenly the racket stopped. The door, hanging by one hinge, no longer shook. The voices outside dropped to a murmur. Heavy footsteps ran along the corridor.

The next sound to strike my ears came from outside the house. A high, undulating, inhuman shriek, it would have raised the hackles on the neck of a dog. Such a scream might have wavered through the night when Death rode the wind and a banshee on the battlements heralded the fall of an ancient house.

I knew that sound.

"Saved!" I cried, and ran to the balcony.

One of the men carried a torch. In its light Kevin's head looked as if it were on fire. He had stopped screaming and was calling my name. Daoud was there, and the *Mirror*; the *Times* was holding the torch. I did not recognize the others, but there were at least a dozen of them, some in evening dress, some in galabeeyahs and turbans.

"Saved!" I cried again. "Up the O'Connells!"

Kevin looked up. "And the Peabodys! Will you come down, Mrs. E., or shall we come in?" A bullet whistled past him and he added hastily, "The latter, I think. Hang on!"

Our rescuers took cover, and just in time; a fusillade of gunfire erupted from the doorway. I heard the *Times* swearing and deduced that a bullet had nicked him but not seriously enough to affect his vocabulary.

A hand caught hold of me and pulled me back into the room. "Damn it, Amelia," my mild-mannered brother-in-law roared. "Don't you know better than to stand chatting when people are shooting at you?"

"There is no need to use bad language, Walter," I replied. "Everything is under—"

The door fell with a crash, splintering tables and cots. A man plunged through the opening. Before any of us could move, he had seized the nearest person in a grip like iron. The person happened to be David.

After the first involuntary cry the boy remained silent and

motionless as a statue, as I believe anyone would have done when the blade of a knife rested against his throat.

From the open doorway a voice said, "Congratulations, Mrs. Emerson. It appears you have won this skirmish. The next victory will be mine."

For the first time since I had met him, Riccetti was standing unsupported. His great girth filled the doorway, but something about his stance gave me the feeling he was not so feeble as he had appeared.

For a moment I did not understand why he seemed to be conceding defeat. We were virtually weaponless. Like me, Walter stood frozen, unable to attack so long as the knife menaced the boy.

Then I saw that Evelyn was pointing my pistol at Riccetti. She held it with both hands, but the weapon did not waver.

"There will not be another skirmish," I said, letting out my breath. "You have lost the war, Riccetti. Tell your man to let the boy go or she will pull the trigger. You might just fire a warning shot, Evelyn—a few inches over his head, perhaps."

Evelyn gave me a quick, agonized glance, and Riccetti laughed. "I doubt she would do anything so unladylike. Rather than take the chance, however, I will run away and live to fight another day. My men will remain until I am out of the house, so don't follow me."

He turned away. The fellow holding David was the very large man we had left bound and unconscious upstairs. Apparently he was the sort who held a grudge. His eyes glittered as he asked, "What shall I do with this one?"

Riccetti did not even pause. "Cut his throat."

I don't believe Evelyn meant to fire. The movement of her trigger finger was involuntary, a reflexive start of pure horror. Though it came nowhere near its target, it had the effect of hurrying Riccetti and, more importantly, of distracting the very large man for a vital second.

In that second Walter sprang. Murderer, victim and rescuer tumbled to the ground in a tangle of limbs. I ran forward, knife at the ready; Evelyn was there before me, but we were both helpless to act. It was all we could do to avoid the thrashing bodies and flailing arms. First one man was on top, then the other; David lay curled in a ball, his arms over his head as feet and fists lashed out at him.

Walter's grip failed; his knife clattered to the floor and he caught his opponent's right wrist with both hands, exerting all his strength to loosen the fellow's hold on his own knife. For a moment it seemed as if he would prevail. Then the man shifted his weight and Walter was flung over onto his back. His head hit the floor hard enough to stun him momentarily. His opponent wrenched his arm free, rose to his knees, and struck.

With a scream almost as piercing as O'Connell's eldritch howl, Evelyn emptied the magazine of the repeater. Jumping over David, she pulled Walter out from under the fallen body of his foe and lifted his head into her arms.

I am seldom rendered incapable of action by sheer astonishment. I was on this occasion. However, it appeared action would not be necessary. The downstairs door had given way and our rescuers were in the house. David was sitting up, Walter's eyes were open, and the very large man was unquestionably dead. Evelyn—my gentle Evelyn!—had shot him four times full in the breast.

Feet pounded up the stairs and men crowded into the room. "God and all the saints be thanked," Kevin exclaimed. "We heard shooting and feared the worst."

I returned my knife to its sheath. "As you see, gentlemen, we have the situation under control. We are grateful for your assistance, all the same."

"My darling," Evelyn cried. "You saved him, he is unhurt. But oh, heaven, you are wounded!"

"It is nothing," muttered Walter. "But you, my dearest, are you injured?"

"No, sweetheart!"

"Darling!"

"Well, well," said a voice from the doorway. "I seem to have arrived just in time for one of those sickeningly maudlin conversations. What have you been up to, Peabody?"

"Emerson!" I threw myself into his arms. "Oh, Emerson, you are safe! My dearest—"

"Please, Peabody, spare me another exchange of public sentimentality. From the alacrity with which you moved, I believe I may assume you are undamaged." He put me gently aside and knelt by his brother.

"It is only a scratch," Walter assured him.

"Good Gad," said Emerson, "what an idiotic thing to say. You have been reading too many thrillers." He eased Walter's coat off. "Hmph. Not too bad. Don't sit there crooning over him, Evelyn, tear up some extraneous garment or other and bandage his arm." His hand closed over Walter's, and they exchanged a long look before Emerson rose to his feet.

"Ramses is safe, Emerson," I said.

"I know." He hesitated for a moment. "I am sorry, Peabody. Not a trace of her. Not to worry, I had barely begun my inquiries and I don't believe the situation is as desperate as this one was. Which reminds me: were you careless enough to allow that bastard Riccetti to get away?"

I knew Emerson's little jokes were only his way of concealing his own anxiety in order to lessen mine. I was about to respond in kind when one of the interested watchers cleared his throat.

"Excuse me, Professor. Would you care to give us a statement now?"

Kevin O'Connell ducked behind Daoud, and Emerson turned, snarling, on the *Times*.

"It was somewhat disconcerting," said Emerson, "to stroll into the bar at the Luxor hotel and behold my son being plied with brandy by a plump Dutchman in a red fez."

"I don't see what the fez has to do with it," I remarked. "I would not have recommended brandy to counteract the effects of opium, but it appears to have been effective."

My eyes kept returning to Ramses. I had put him to bed and washed some of the dirt off him and replaced his filthy robe with a clean one; except for his bruised face, he looked quite normal. All the same, I somehow felt the need to keep looking at him.

Emerson was looking at the bruises too. Most of them might have been made by a large hand clamped over Ramses's mouth. Most, but not all.

"Was it Riccetti who struck you, Ramses?" Emerson asked.

"No, sir. Signor Riccetti," said Ramses critically, "is not a well-bred person. He continually interrupted me. We had only been talking for a few minutes when he lost his temper and told the very large man to . . . if I recall correctly, his precise words were to 'teach the brat how to hold his tongue.'"

"So it was the very large man who hit you?" Emerson smiled at me. "You robbed me of the pleasure of returning the favor, Peabody. That was the man you killed, I suppose."

"It was Evelyn who killed him, not I."

Emerson looked askance at his sister-in-law. One hand in Walter's, the other resting on the head of David, who sat at her feet, she was the image of an English lady of impeccable lineage and good breeding. "So you told me," Emerson muttered. "I still cannot take it in. Well, well, life is full of surprises."

It had certainly surprised *me* to find Ramses drinking brandy with a Dutchman at the Luxor bar. He was still at it (and trying, rather incoherently, to persuade the kindly gentleman to let him follow the rescuers) when we stopped to collect him on our way to the dinghy. By the time we landed near the *Amelia*, the fresh air had restored him, but Emerson insisted on carrying him to his room. I sent Daoud at once to fetch Abdullah, and the rest of us gathered round Ramses's bed, where we were soon joined by Cyrus Vandergelt. I had left the door open, since Emerson was smoking his pipe and Cyrus had lit one of his favorite cheroots.

Silent and unheralded, robed in white and wreathed in smoke, Abdullah appeared in the doorway like a ghostly apparition. David got slowly to his feet. For a long moment neither moved. Then Abdullah held out his arms, and the boy ran into them.

After that was settled, Abdullah, and Daoud, who had followed him, found places to sit on the floor. The room was very crowded, but there was an empty place in our hearts, and no one wanted to be the first to speak of it.

Ramses cleared his throat. "I would like to say two things."

"Only two?" Kevin inquired sotto voce.

Ramses, who had ears like a cat's, fixed him with a cold stare. "First, I am deeply indebted to all of you. You risked your lives to save me."

"Och, 'twas nothing," Kevin said. "I rather enjoyed—"

"Second," said Ramses, "I apologize for my carelessness and lack of foresight. You would not have had to take those risks had I behaved more sensibly. It will never happen again."

"Ha," said his father. "Never mind, my boy, it was not your fault. Er—not entirely."

"It is my fault that Nefret is now in danger," Ramses said. "That is a fact, and nothing you can say will alter it. Nothing I can do will redeem my error, but . . ." He turned the catch in his voice into a cough and went on in the same cool voice, "But I would appreciate it if you would start planning how we are going to get her back."

"Well said, by Jupiter!" exclaimed Cyrus. He was sitting on the floor, since there were not enough chairs, and he looked rather ridiculous with his long legs doubled up and his knees on a level with his chin, but his eyes were cool and steady. "That's why I'm here. I sure appreciate you folks letting me know the good news about Ramses right away. Maybe I shouldn't have come barreling on over here at this hour of the night, but I couldn't sleep thinking about that purty li'l gal. If we put our heads together we should be able to figger out where they took her."

"That's the spirit, Vandergelt," Emerson exclaimed. "I will tell you what I learned this evening. It is not a great deal, but what the devil! It is a beginning.

"They were seen boarding the afternoon ferry and disembarking in Luxor. None of the crewmen could hazard a guess as to where they went after that, so I next inquired of the carriage drivers. I finally found one who remembered seeing Nefret and another Sitt get into a carriage. After some animated and maddeningly prolonged discussion they agreed it was the carriage of Ali Mohammed. He had gone off with a party of tourists, no one knew where, so I had to wait for him to return. I need not tell you," Emerson said quietly, "that it seemed an eternity. It was, in fact, over an hour, but I had no choice but to wait. He remembered them—Nefret is hard to forget—and offered to take me to the place where he had driven them."

"The Luxor?" I asked, as Emerson paused to light his pipe. "That was incredibly bold of the cursed woman. How could she hope to keep Nefret there?"

"I don't believe they remained at the hotel," Emerson said. "But before I could continue my inquiries I observed a group of men erupt out of the bar and onto the street. I recognized O'Connell; I caught only a glimpse of his companion, but that particular galabeeyah and turban were strangely familiar, so I looked into the bar to ask what had happened, and was thunderstruck—to say the least—when I saw Ramses. He was beginning to come round, but he was still uncertain as to where he was or how he had got there. Fortunately the Dutch gentleman speaks English quite well; he told me of the dramatic appearance of Daoud, a knife in one hand and the unconscious body of Ramses over his shoulder; he had forced his way past porters, clerks and doormen and was demanding assistance for Ramses and rescue for the Sitt Hakim at the top of his lungs."

"He was clever to think of going to the hotel," I said, with an approving nod at Daoud. "It was the nearest place in which he could count on finding help."

"I looked for him," said Daoud smugly, indicating Kevin. "He is always in the bar of the Luxor."

"A vile canard," said Kevin with a broad, unabashed smile. "It's thankful I am that I was there on this occasion, but once Daoud had told his story, he had every chap in the place ready to rush to the rescue."

"To resume," said Emerson loudly.

"I beg your pardon, Professor," said Kevin.

"Hmph," said Emerson. "To resume: I stayed with Ramses until I was certain he was all right. He had not the faintest recollection of how he had got there, but he was able to give me some indication of where he had been, and I began to put the pieces together. O'Connell on the rampage, Daoud in Luxor, Ramses delivered—who else could have instigated a melee like that but you, Peabody?"

"Thank you, my dear," I replied, much gratified.

"And I knew I was right," Emerson continued, "when I got near the place and heard shots, shouts, and people battering on doors. I apologize for being delayed, but luckily you didn't need me, did you?"

"No," Evelyn said. "Walter was there. But I think he should go to bed now."

Walter tried to look modest. His eyeglasses had been broken in the struggle but it was not their absence that made his face look so changed. A man does not have to be a hero to gain confidence in himself; he only needs a woman to think he is one. In this case, however, Walter had earned his laurels.

"I am perfectly fit, my dear," he said. "And I cannot rest until we have explored every possible clue. Radcliffe, has it occurred to you that the trip to Luxor may have been a blind? Suppose they returned to this side of the river?"

"In disguise," Ramses said. "Well done, Uncle Walter."

"Thank you, Ramses," said his uncle.

"However," Ramses continued, "it is my opinion that attempting to pick up the trail would be a waste of time. There is no one more anonymous in this land of black-veiled women than another black-veiled woman. We should rather try to determine the identity of the individual who has taken her. Miss Marmaduke is a dupe or a subordinate. She was given orders by someone else."

"The letter proves that," I said impatiently. "It also proves that Riccetti was not responsible for kidnapping Nefret."

Ramses coughed. (I was beginning to dislike that cough.)

"The phraseology of the letter leaves open the possibility that the writer was in league with Riccetti. However, other indications suggest that you are correct, Mother. If he were holding Nefret, he would have taunted you or threatened you during that dramatic confrontation you described so vividly."

"But he is not out of the picture," Emerson muttered, clenching his fists. "He will be back, more dangerous than ever."

"I'm not so sure about that," Cyrus drawled. "You folks haven't had time to sit still and think straight tonight, but consider what happened. Riccetti got away with his low stunts before because nobody in authority really cared what he did to a bunch of poor Egyptians. This time he kidnapped an English boy and tried to shoot up a whole crowd of foreigners. The British administration isn't going to put up with that sort of thing."

"And neither will British public opinion," Kevin said eagerly. "Don't underestimate the power of the press, Mrs. E. and gentlemen. My story and those of my colleagues will have every British citizen howling for justice."

"Hmph." Emerson stroked his chin. "Do you mean I may be forced to admit that the confounded press is of some use after all?"

"God forbid, sir," Kevin said piously.

"You may be right," Emerson admitted. "All the same, I hope we haven't seen the last of Riccetti. I would like to deal with him personally. See here, O'Connell, you do understand that no word of Nefret's disappearance must get out?"

"Yes, sir, I do." Kevin's face grew sober. "It's not a word I'll breathe till the little colleen is safe home again. You've no idea who could have engineered her disappearance?"

"We know how she was lured away," I said. "And by whom. That knowledge is of no use to us, since Miss Marmaduke has also vanished. At one time I believed that Abd el Hamel was a member of the same group, but of late I have begun to wonder about that. I saw him, or a man closely resembling him, near Riccetti's house a few days ago. Curse it, Abd el Hamel must be involved in some manner; on two occasions he sent would-be killers onto this boat. He wouldn't risk that unless he stood to lose something vital to his interests or those of the individual who employed him."

All eyes turned to David. He sat unmoving, his head bowed, and the silence lengthened.

"We are brothers," Ramses said finally. "He would tell me if he knew."

David raised his head. He looked, not at Ramses, nor at Evelyn, whose hand had stroked his hair, nor at Walter, who had saved his life that evening, nor at his grandfather—nor at me. His gaze locked with that of Emerson, blue eyes and black intent on one another.

"I have thought till my head was empty," he whispered. "I have told you all I know. I spied on Abd el Hamed, yes. I hated him! Often at night when I could not sleep for hunger or bruises, I would creep out and listen, hoping to learn something that would harm him. Many came to see him in secret—the thieves with their stolen goods from the tombs, the dealers from Luxor, the Inglîzi who bought the antikas. No strange man came in secret. No man who was—"

"Just a moment," Emerson said, his voice strained and harsh. "No man, you say? No strange human beings?" He used the plural word *nas*, which means "people."

A great light seemed to burst in my brain. "Good Gad!" I cried.

David's eyes grew round. "They said 'man.' " He used the English word. "I thought—"

"No blame to you," Emerson broke in. "There was a woman, then? A strange woman?"

"Women did not come to Abd el Hamel. He went to them. But . . . one night, not long ago . . ."

"What did she look like?" Emerson's voice was gentle and encouraging. He carefully refrained from looking at me. I appreciated that.

"She wore the black robe and veil, but she was not Egyptian. No! I cannot tell you how I knew, they spoke softly and apart, I heard no words; but it was not Arabic they spoke, there is a difference in the way the words rise and fall. And she walked like a man." He was panting with excitement now, his eyes shining. "Does it help? Do you know her? Is she the one?"

"It helps," Emerson said. "It may be the clue we needed. Thank you, my son."

"I might have known there would be a woman in this," I remarked sometime later, after exhaustion had finally forced us to disperse.

"That," said Emerson, dropping his shirt onto the floor, "was decidedly an uncalled-for remark, Peabody. After I politely avoided pointing out that you, of all people, ought to have realized—"

"Yes, my dear, and I appreciate your forbearance. All the same, you cannot deny that there is always some female in your vicinity. This is the third—or is it the fourth?—time in a row. I cannot seem to get rid of . . ."

Splashing at the washbasin, Emerson was unaware of my failure to complete the sentence. When he turned (after dropping the towel onto the floor), his face was grave.

"It helps, but not enough. We know the mysterious female was not Marmaduke; she was with us on the boat. Who the devil can it be? And don't suggest that Sir Edward is a woman in disguise."

"No, there can be no doubt of his masculinity." Emerson's eyes narrowed and I hurried on. "She must be a tourist—or pretending to be one. We will investigate them tomorrow."

"I wish to God it could be tonight." He sat down on the side of the bed and covered his face with his hands. "Forgive me, Peabody. I should try to put a brave face upon it—you are as worried as I, I know—but the thought of that child, imprisoned, threatened, afraid . . . I may as well go over to Luxor. I shan't be able to sleep."

I sat down beside him and put my arms around his shoulders. "You can do nothing tonight, Emerson; the managers of the hotels won't let you roust all the female guests out of bed so that you can roar at them. You must rest, my dearest, or you will be of no use to Nefret. Come, lie down."

"I shan't sleep," Emerson muttered.

I knew he would, though. I had slipped just a few drops of laudanum into his coffee.

I had not taken any myself. I lay down beside him, but long after his deep breathing assured me he was asleep I stared open-eyed into the darkness trying to think, not of Nefret—for I could not bear that—but of some way of finding her.

The pieces were falling into place. David's escape, the meaning of the hippopotamus goddess, the strange behavior of Gertrude Marmaduke . . . I had not told Emerson; it would have been cruel to raise hopes that might be dashed. And besides, he would have informed me that "this theory, Peabody, is even more fantastical than your usual theories, and that is saying a great deal!"

He would have been right. Moreover, there was no guarantee that my suspect would continue playing her role. She might have gone into hiding by now with her captive and her confederate.

I did not expect to sleep, but I did at last. When I woke, the cold light of dawn showed at the window; and the first object my drowsy eyes beheld was the form of a golden-haired girl sitting cross-legged on the floor next to the bed.

CHAPTER 15

No Mystery Is Insoluble—It Is Simply a Matter of How Much Time and Energy One Is Willing to Expend

"I hit her with the chamber pot," Nefret said.

It was not the first thing she said, but it was the first statement I clearly remember, out of the joyful confusion that followed. I believe I pinched myself; it was not until I had actually got hold of her that I could believe she was real and not a fantasy shaped by fear and hope. Then the others had to be aroused, and I had to remind Emerson to put on his trousers, and I had to tell Nefret of Ramses's safe return—which she already knew, since her first act upon returning had been to look into his room. At least I think she said that. She was certainly not surprised to see him, but Ramses's face, when he beheld her, was a sight I will long remember. Seldom if ever had I seen that phlegmatic countenance so unguarded.

A certain touch of chagrin mingled with his pleasure, however, after we had gathered on the upper deck and Nefret had begun her story.

"You escaped without assistance?" he asked. "You did not require to be rescued?"

"From Miss Marmaduke?" Nefret sniffed. "She took me for a silly, helpless, civilized girl, and I did all I could to confirm that opinion. You would have been ashamed of me, Aunt Amelia, if you had seen me pretending to believe all the lies she told me."

"No, my dear, I would have been, and am, immensely proud of you," I said warmly. "But did it not occur to you that Miss Marmaduke might be leading you into a trap?"

"Yes, of course," Nefret said, opening her eyes very wide. "Otherwise what would have been the sense of going with her?"

Yet Gertrude's initial actions had made her wonder if she had been mistaken. She had not objected to Nefret's leaving a message, and they had driven to the hotel without attempting to conceal their movements. She would not answer questions, however. She claimed she was only a humble servant of one greater than she, who would supply all the answers.

From Nefret's description I realized that the room to which Gertrude had led her was the same one I had booked for her. She must have kept it on after she moved to the Castle. Nefret noted and approved the balcony and the convenient vine. She still had her knife, and felt certain she could get away if the situation became dangerous.

"She was in quite a strange state," Nefret said. "She kept talking in that vague way of hers about the goddess and the Path; but the most peculiar thing was the way she behaved toward me—almost with reverence. I began to fear she was not a spy at all, but only a believer in some occult nonsense. She ordered tea to be brought to us . . ."

The first sip told Nefret that there was something wrong with the tea. She had to make a decision, and she did so without hesitation. She drank the tea.

Emerson could contain himself no longer. "Good God, child! How could you?"

"How could I not? I had learned nothing that would help me find Ramses or unmask Miss Marmaduke's mysterious superior. Unless they believed me to be helpless, they would make certain I did not learn anything. I threw up the tea, though, when Miss Marmaduke left the room for a moment. She was very nervous," Nefret said thoughtfully. "I have observed that when people are nervous they need to go—"

"Very true," I said. "How did you—"

"Over the balcony. When she came back, I complained of feeling dizzy. She helped me to lie down, and I pretended to fall asleep."

She must not have rid herself of all the drug, for her succeeding memories were hazy and confused. With the assistance of another woman, Miss Marmaduke removed her outer clothing—and her knife. She could not remember what the other woman looked like, except that she wore a severe, dark gown of European design, and that she was stout and strong. After wrapping her in a long hooded robe, the two women placed her in a large traveling trunk and packed pillows and blankets carefully around her before closing the lid. As she drifted in and out of consciousness she was aware of the trunk being lifted and carried and finally set down. The gentle motion that followed told her she was on a boat, and she deduced they were returning to the West Bank. At last it stopped; the lid of the trunk was opened and she saw stars shining in the dark sky. Someone bent over her. It was not Miss Marmaduke, for she heard the latter's voice, high-pitched with anxiety.

"Is she all right?"

"Yes." The other voice was a woman's, deeper and harder. "She will sleep for another hour."

Taking her cue from this, Nefret remained limp and unresponsive as she was lifted out of the trunk and onto a litter. To her annoyance the woman then covered her, even her face, with a cloak or coverlet. She could see nothing as she was carried rapidly along, but other senses told her when they left the cultivation: the scent of moist vegetation was replaced by the drier air of the desert, and then by the sounds and smells of habitation. Someone lifted her from the litter, carried her up a flight of stairs, and placed her on a hard surface. There was a murmured exchange in Arabic; a door closed; and then the cloak was removed. She dared not open her eyes, but she knew the hands that smoothed her hair and straightened her garment even before Miss Marmaduke spoke.

"She still sleeps."

"She will wake soon. Get her to take more tea."

"But you said—"

"This place is no longer safe. As soon as the lady comes, we will move on."

"She may not take it from me. She has no reason to trust me."

"There are other ways." Impatience and contempt hardened the woman's voice. "That is the easiest for her, but if you cannot manage it—"

"Oh, I don't like this," Miss Marmaduke moaned. "I was told it would be tonight. Surely, if I explain to her—"

"That she is Tetisheri reborn and that she must confront the remnants of the body she once inhabited in order to progress along the Way?" A contemptuous laugh. "Never mind the tea, I will deal with her."

The door closed and a key turned in the lock. Nefret ventured to open her eyes a slit. The first thing she saw was her erstwhile governess, pacing up and down and wringing her hands. The room was lit by a single lamp. The walls were of plastered mud-brick, the single window shuttered. The furnishings were meager—a few sticks of furniture, a few baskets, a few pottery vessels.

Her heart pounding, Nefret knew she must think as quickly as she had ever thought in her life. The outlines of the plot were clear now. Miss Marmaduke was just what she had appeared to be, a simpleminded believer in occult religion who had been duped by . . . By whom? The leader must be a woman, that mysterious "lady" to whom the other female had referred. And she, Nefret, was to be held hostage until Emerson gave up the mummy and the treasures of the tomb.

All this raced through her mind as she tried to decide what to do. She might learn more, including the identity of the unknown leader, if she remained; but the perils of that outweighed any possible advantages. There was no longer any reason for them to continue the pretense that had delivered her into their hands. She would be drugged or bound and carried off to another place from which escape might be impossible. And if she was to act, it must be instantly, before the other woman returned with the means to "deal" with her.

"So I hit Miss Marmaduke with the chamber pot," Nefret said. "She didn't even see me; she was standing at the window mumbling to herself."

As soon as Nefret looked out, she recognized the houses and walls of a village. Behind the dwellings, silvered by moonlight, rose the cliffs of the high desert. The room was on the upper floor; she was considering how she might best manage the descent when she heard heavy footsteps approaching. Climbing quickly out the window, she lowered herself by her hands and dropped onto a surface of hard-baked earth liberally sprinkled with animal droppings.

"Then you can lead us back to the house," I exclaimed. "Was it that of Abd el Hamel?"

"I don't know. The village was Gurneh, but I never saw the front of the house. The window was at the back, and after I got out the window I was too concerned with escaping to notice my surroundings. If I had not found the donkey, they might have caught me."

Ramses tried not to look pleased at this admission of fallibility. I thought he succeeded rather well, but Nefret saw the look.

"The place is a maze—no streets, hardly even alleyways! I had only been there once before, and . . . I suppose you think you could have done better!"

"No," said Ramses. "On the whole, I think I did much worse. I am . . ." He cleared his throat. "I am very glad to see you safely back."

Emerson went directly to Luxor next morning—accompanied, I hardly need say, by the rest of us. To his extreme annoyance, he discovered that the vulture had flown. The house was deserted, and further inquiries produced the information that a man of Riccetti's description had taken the train to Cairo early that morning. It was the quickest means of transportation available, and his willingness to sacrifice comfort for speed indicated that he had, somewhat belatedly, realized that his recent indiscretions might get him into serious trouble. We dispatched messages to the authorities in Cairo, telling them to intercept and arrest the villain, and then I persuaded Emerson to return to the West Bank.

"May as well," he agreed, brightening. "Riccetti got away from me, curse him, but if I can lay my hands on Abd el Hamel . . ."

My poor Emerson was due to be disappointed again. When we reached Gurneh the village was abuzz with the news. Abd el Hamel had been found in an irrigation ditch by two farmers setting out for their fields. He had not been identified immediately, since several parts of him were missing.

"Now, Emerson, calm yourself," I said. "You are always telling me you resent having your work interrupted by these little criminal encounters; this one is ended, so why don't you stop swearing and get back to the tomb?"

It was not ended, however. There was one more loose end to tie up, and I determined to deal with it later that day while Emerson was busy in the burial chamber. If he had known of my intentions he would have forbidden me to go or insisted on going with me—and in the (unlikely) event that my theory proved to be incorrect, he would never let me hear the end of it.

The only person who observed my departure was Sir Edward. In fact, he had the impertinence to ask where I was going. I informed him I had a little errand to do in Gurneh and that I would return shortly. When he persisted, declaring he would accompany me, I was forced to be blunt. "I am tying up a loose end, Sir Edward. It is a private matter, and I prefer to go alone."

I did not suppose I would be unobserved. When I opened the carved door, Layla was waiting for me, silver on her brow and slim brown wrists. The bracelets jingled softly as she raised her cigarette to her lips.

"Marhaba, Sitt Hakim," she said, blowing out a cloud of smoke. "It is kind of you to visit me. Have you come to offer sympathy on the death of my husband?"

"No; I thought congratulations might be more in order." She laughed, and I went on, "I wondered why you married him."

"And now you know?"

"I think so. I did not come to see you. Where is she?"

"She?" Her eyes widened in pretended surprise.

"You know whom I mean. Will you call her or shall I go looking for her?"

The curtains at the back of the room opened and a woman appeared. She was clad in the same severe, uniform-like dress she had worn at the hotel when attending upon the "widow"—and when she had helped Gertrude abduct Nefret. "What do you want of me, Mrs. Emerson?"

"Not you," I said.

She advanced toward me. She was indeed a large woman, several inches taller than I, broad-shouldered and stout as a man. "There is no one else here. Will you go, or must I—"

"No, Matilda." The voice was the one I had expected. It came from the room beyond the curtain. "Bring her here."

With a shrug that sent muscles rippling down her arms, the "nurse" held the curtain back for me.

The room was shadowy, the shutters tightly shut. She stood in a doorway opposite the one by which I had entered. She wore the long black garment of an Egyptian woman, uncannily similar in color and design to the widow's weeds she had worn in Cairo and in Luxor; but now the thin veil that had hidden her fair hair and blurred her features was gone. I knew those features well, though I had not seen them for almost a year—at Amarna, on the day Sethos met his end.

"Good afternoon, Berthe," I said.

The nurse had followed me in. Instead of returning my greeting,

Berthe said, "Search her. She is usually a walking arsenal, so don't miss anything."

I did not resist as the woman's hands moved over me, removing my pistol and knife. Resistance would have been futile and undignified. And those were not the weapons I meant to use.

"Now will you offer me a chair?" I inquired.

"Did you recognize me, then? I thought I had taken every possible precaution."

"No, I deduced your presence," I said. "Would you like me to explain?"

She studied me suspiciously. "I must admit you have aroused my curiosity, but if this is a ruse to detain me until your friends arrive—"

"Nothing of the sort. I came alone. Won't you sit down? In your condition you should not be standing."

"That too?" She laughed, briefly and harshly, but she followed my suggestion, smoothing the black fabric across her abdomen in a gesture that confirmed my diagnosis. "How?"

"Taueret. She was the patroness of childbirth. I didn't catch that at first," I admitted handsomely. "I believed the hippopotamus goddess had quite another significance. However, I had deduced that one of the tourists must be the unknown enemy we feared, and when I saw the poor widow lady in Luxor . . . There is a certain way of walking characteristic of a woman who is advanced in pregnancy. Six or seven months, isn't it? In heaven's name, Berthe, how could you risk your life and that of the child in this desperate enterprise?"

"It is kind of you to be concerned," she said with a sneer. "But I risked nothing. I expected to conclude the enterprise and return to Europe this month, and if I was delayed—well, Egypt is becoming known as a health resort and Dr. Willoughby has an excellent reputation. Aren't you going to ask the name of the father—or have you deduced that as well?"

"That is not my affair," I replied.

"So long as it is not your husband?" Another burst of harsh laughter. "I would like to make you believe that, but I could not, could I?"

"No."

The nurse had slipped out of the room. Now she returned and nodded at Berthe, who acknowledged the nod with one of her own.

"You did tell the truth; no one has followed you. Speak then, Mrs. Emerson. I presume you are anxious to prove how clever you are."

"Boasting is a habit in which I never indulge," I replied, settling myself more comfortably. "I sought you out because I too was curious about a few minor details. I knew that other criminals would attempt to take over Sethos's lucrative business as soon as the news of his death got out. Who would know of it sooner than you, who was with us last year when he met his end? You saw the opportunity, and, with a quickness and audacity I would admire had it been devoted to a nobler end, decided to take advantage of it. But no woman could assume that dominant role in this male-oriented society—or, if I must be honest, in our own—without male authority to reinforce hers. You have represented yourself as acting for Sethos, haven't you? The reference I overheard one night, to 'the Master,' ought to have made me suspicious. I ought to have expected as well that legends would form around that towering figure, as they formed around other great leaders, such as Charlemagne and Arthur. His superstitious followers considered him a mighty magician; it would not be difficult to convince them that he had survived and would return one day; and he had the ability, I believe, to command the loyalty—even the affection—of his lieutenants. By claiming to be his representative you could win that loyalty for yourself."

I waited for her to comment. She said nothing, only watched me with unblinking blue eyes and a most curious expression, so I continued.

"You needed all the help you could get against a man like Riccetti, but you had one advantage he lacked: you knew where the tomb was located. As I reconstruct the story, the tomb was found some ten years ago and certain objects, like the statuette of Tetisheri, were taken from it. After Sethos took over the antiquities trade, the looting of Tetisheri's tomb stopped. I am not entirely certain of the reasons, which are in any case irrelevant to this discussion. The discovery of the grisly mummy may have been a factor, or the mysterious disappearances of certain men of Gurneh, or fear of Sethos. After his death the Gurnawis decided it would be safe to renew their activities. You learned of this through your connections with the followers of Sethos, but you were not the only one who wanted to replace the Master Criminal. Riccetti, driven from his position by Sethos, determined to regain it. He knew there was such a tomb, but he did not know its location. He sent Shelmadine to us with a story he hoped would arouse the competitive instincts of my husband, and inspire us to find the tomb for him. He had already conceived the ingenious idea of allowing us to clear it and then steal the treasures.

"You had been watching Riccetti. You did not know how much he knew, and you were afraid Shelmadine would be able to direct us to the tomb. You were staying at Shepheard's; you sent one of your people—our friend Matilda here?—to kill Shelmadine. You dispatched the suffragi on an errand, and Matilda carried the body to your room."

She gave me neither yea nor nay; her unblinking blue eyes remained fixed on my face.

"You were less subtle than Riccetti," I went on. "At first you intended a straightforward robbery of the tomb. We fought off several such incursions, and then you had intelligence enough to revise your plans.

"You had a spy in Riccetti's camp—Abd el Hamed. His desire for revenge—and the persuasions of the female person in the next room—made him a ready ally. You knew where Riccetti was staying in Luxor and what he was doing; but you wisely refrained from challenging him directly. You waited, with that serpentine patience of yours, and finally Riccetti made the mistake you had prayed he would make, by kidnapping Ramses. It was your men, who had Riccetti's house under constant observation, who seized David. Riccetti (being a man) assumed we would not care about the boy's fate. You knew better. But then you had another idea. You made use of Ramses's disappearance to get your hands on Nefret, and once you had her, you no longer needed David. So you freed him, hoping he could lead us to Riccetti's headquarters, and that we would rid you of your most dangerous rival. It was a brilliant improvisation, worthy of a woman's superior intelligence. Riccetti learned of Abd el Hamed's treachery and—"

I broke off. It had only been a fleeting glance, at the curtained doorway behind me, and a faint smile; but something in that smile chilled my blood. Abd el Hamed had been horribly mutiliated. Surely no woman would . . .

Clearing my throat, I continued.

"The cleverest thing you did was to make use of poor stupid Miss Marmaduke. Hoping to enlist a spy in our camp, you had talked with her and about her while you stayed at Shepheard's; you knew of her belief in reincarnation. Lurking on the balcony, Matilda overheard the story Shelmadine told us. She took the ring—with no ulterior motive in mind at the time—it was gold and it was valuable. Later, when she repeated Shelmadine's story to you, you realized how it could be used to seduce Gertrude. You were not the only one to observe the coincidental resemblance of Nefret to Tetisheri; Gertrude was a willing believer when you made something more of it."

At last she broke her silence. "Is that all?"

"Yes, I think so. Oh—one more thing. It was you in the garden of the Luxor hotel that night with Sir Edward, was it not? I ought to have known it was not Miss Marmaduke, but you spoke so softly and so briefly, I did not recognize your voice."

"Is that all?" Berthe said again.

I nodded. She leaned forward, her eyes brightening.

"Very clever, Mrs. Emerson. So clever that I am amazed you would make the fatal error of coming here alone."

"What would it profit you to harm me?" I asked calmly. "The game is up, Berthe. You cannot hold me captive, not here in the heart of Gurneh."

"Is it a stalemate, then? You wouldn't send me to prison, would you? In my condition?" She spat the last word at me and then burst out laughing. "Careers for women! That is a favorite theme of yours, I believe? Why, then you should commend my efforts, for I have given gainful employment to women—downtrodden, oppressed females of this and other countries, who work not for men but for themselves—and for me. A criminal organization of women! Heading such an organization is a far more interesting and lucrative career than the one you once suggested. You thought I might train for a nurse—if I could overcome my squeamishness. I have overcome it, Mrs. Emerson—as you will soon see."

Before I could reply, her face underwent a dreadful change and her voice dropped to a whisper. "How can you be so blindly complacent? Don't you know how much I hate you—and why? Night after night I have lain awake picturing the ways in which I would kill you. Some of them were very ingenious, Mrs. Emerson—oh, very ingenious! Unfortunately there is no time for them now, I will have to do it quickly and more painlessly than I would like. Matilda—"

I had not underestimated the woman's strength; I had simply failed to anticipate this particular development. I was still pondering it, in some confusion of mind, when the nurse's muscular arm lifted me out of my chair and her fingers closed round my throat. The pressure was quick and cruel and skillful; my senses swam, and my efforts to free myself were as feeble as those of an infant.

"Don't let her lose consciousness," Berthe murmured, gliding toward me. "I want her to know what is going to happen."

From under her robe she took a jeweled dagger.

I tried to speak. Only a harsh gasp emerged from my lips, but the hard fingers tightened. Blackness covered my eyes and through the ringing in my ears I heard Berthe cursing. She was berating the other woman for squeezing too hard. I had planned to feign unconsciousness in the hope my captor would loosen her grip, but apparently I had waited a little too long.

My last thought, as I had always known it would be, was for Emerson. I imagined I could hear his agitated reproach: "Peabody, how could you be so bloody stupid!"

I did hear him! Or at least . . . My senses swam, but vision had returned to me, and sensation; I had fallen to the floor, and the voice was clearer now. Not Emerson's—but it was a man's voice, speaking English, and with considerable agitation.

"Are you mad? Give me the knife!"

The sentence ended in a grunt or gasp. I decided I had better find out what was going on, so I lifted myself onto my elbows. At first all I could see was his boots; then a hand caught me under the arm and raised me to my feet.

"Are you uninjured, Mrs. Emerson?"

"Yes, thank you, Sir Edward," I croaked, rubbing my throat. "But why the devil are you standing there? Go after them!"

The room was empty except for the two of us. He held a pistol—mine. His fair hair was unruffled, his face composed, his attire impeccable, except for the blood that saturated his left sleeve.

"I don't believe that is within my powers at this moment," he said politely, and slumped to the ground at my feet.

Well, of course, that was the end of that. By the time I had ascertained the extent of his injury and stopped the bleeding, there was no hope of catching them up. He came back to his senses while I was bandaging his arm and began apologizing.

"I was unarmed, you see; I found that pistol on a table in the outer room, but I simply could not bring myself to fire, even after she came at me with her knife. Not at a woman."

"Hmph," I said. "No doubt your sentiments do you credit, Sir Edward, but they can be cursed inconvenient. I presume that it was the lady who seduced you, instead of the other way round?"

"Seduced? Good heavens, Mrs. Emerson, what are you saying?"

"I saw you—heard you, rather—with her in the garden at the Luxor hotel the night we dined with Mr. Vandergelt."

"Heard," he repeated slowly.

"I thought it was Gertrude with you," I admitted. "But it was not she, was it?"

"No." The reply was prompt and emphatic. "I don't know what you heard, Mrs. Emerson, but your interpretation of my relationship with the lady—such as it was—is completely in error. I would never dream of—uh . . . Even if she had not been—er . . . I took her for what she appeared to be, a lonely, grieving woman in need of sympathy and friendly companionship. We talked, that was all. I assure you, that was all!"

"But you had some idea of its becoming something more."

His eyes shone with unconcealed amusement. "I have never taken you in, have I, Mrs. Emerson? You know how it is with us younger sons; an advantageous marriage is our only hope of getting on in the world. She represented herself as a wealthy widow; she was young, attractive, and—er—receptive to sympathy."

"And Nefret?"

He laughed aloud and shook his head. "You need have no fears for the virtue of your ward, Mrs. Emerson. I was unaware of her identity when I first met her. Once I learned that she was Lord Blacktower's heiress . . . Well, she is worth waiting for, don't you think? In a few more years she will be even more beautiful, and in control of her own fortune."

"I admire your candor if not your principles," I said. "It might be advisable for us to leave now, don't you think?"

Unaided, he got to his feet and preceded me into the next room. It was unoccupied; Layla had deemed it advisable to remove herself.

"Can you manage?" I asked. "Take my arm, if you are feeling faint."

"The injury is superficial. I feel very foolish for having behaved so feebly."

The injury *was* superficial. He had feigned faintness because he was reluctant to lay violent hands on a woman—not only a woman, but a lady, and a lady, moreover, for whom he had felt some tenderness. Some might call this chivalrous. I call it silly and impractical, but his action had relieved me of a painful decision. It would have been difficult to condemn a woman in her delicate condition to the rigors of prison, and in fact I had no proof of criminal behavior on her part except for her attack on me—and I understood the motive for that only too well. Had I not felt the same pangs of jealous rage when I feared I had lost Emerson's love to another? My jealousy had been transitory and without foundation; Berthe's was fixed and without hope, for Emerson would never be hers. No wonder she hated me!

Musing thus, I allowed Sir Edward to lead me to where the

horses were waiting. He tossed the urchin who had been holding them a coin, and helped me to mount. "Are you going to tell your husband about this little adventure?" he inquired.

"I see no other choice." Tenderly I touched my bruised throat. "Unless you would like to confess to throttling me."

He returned my quip with a jest of his own. "And you to stabbing me."

"He is going to roar," I said regretfully. "Ah well, venting his emotions will be good for him. Er—I will tell him the exact truth, of course: that I came to pay my respects to Abd el Hamed's widow and was astonished to discover she was harboring the mystery woman. She will claim, of course, that she was ignorant of her late husband's criminal activities, and that she had no idea the poor Inglîzi lady was involved in them. The lady came to her because . . . hmmm, let me think. Because she had wearied of the social life of the hotel and wanted solitude and peace, far from the madding crowd? Out of the kindness of her heart Layla took the lady in . . . Yes, something along those lines."

"Oh, well done!" Sir Edward exclaimed. "Have you ever thought of writing a novel, Mrs. Emerson? You have quite a gift for fiction."

"That is what *she* will say," I replied somewhat severely. "I never lie to my husband, Sir Edward. I will tell him the exact truth—that to my utter astonishment I was attacked by a female whose existence we had postulated, but of whose identity we were . . . Er, I presume, Sir Edward, that you arrived at the house only moments before you burst into the room? I am curious to discover how you knew I was in need of rescue, since I do not recall crying out."

"I do not suppose you could have cried out; you were being throttled very efficiently. No; what I heard was a woman's voice raised in anger, and employing language ordinarily considered very unwomanly. I took the liberty of investigating."

So he had not overheard any of the preceding discussion. That was a relief; I felt certain I could rely on his discretion but I was glad I did not have to. My—and Emerson's—previous acquaintance with the mystery woman was best kept secret.

I again assured him of my appreciation. "None of us can be

blamed for failing to realize that our unknown adversary was female," I explained. "Women, Sir Edward, are sadly discriminated against in this man's world, but their subordinate status does give them one advantage. They are always the last to be suspected!"

"I have learned my lesson," was the rueful reply. "Never again will I underestimate a lady's capabilities, for good or evil."

"You too must be entirely candid," I said. "You followed me because you feared Hamed's henchmen might still be in Gurneh. Emerson will be very grateful."

"Not so grateful that he will regret my departure," said the young man smoothly. "Yes; I must leave Luxor almost immediately. Urgent family matters have arisen that require my attention."

"I am sorry to hear it. Have you informed Emerson?"

"I intended to do so today. He will have no difficulty replacing me; every archaeologist in Egypt has offered the services of his staff."

"We will be sorry to lose you."

"It is kind of you to say so." He turned amused blue eyes in my direction. "You haven't seen the last of me, Mrs. Emerson."

"Give up all hope of Nefret, Sir Edward. Emerson would never stand for it."

"One never knows, Mrs. Emerson. I am reckoned a persuasive fellow." We were riding slowly side by side; smiling, as if to himself, he said musingly, "Miss Nefret is a beautiful girl and will be a wealthy heiress; but her greatest attraction to a man like myself is the possibility that she may one day become a woman of character—the sort of woman you are now. I hope you will take it in the spirit in which it is meant, Mrs. Emerson, when I say that were it not for the fact that you are esteemed by one whom I hold in the highest regard, I would venture to . . . But I believe you understand me."

It is difficult to be angry with a gentleman who pays you compliments, even impertinent compliments. Especially impertinent compliments.

On April 5, 1900, we opened the sarcophagus.

It had taken us almost two months, working day and night, to clear the way to that massive structure. Fortunately for Emerson's blood pressure, we were able to accomplish this without sacrificing his (our, I should say) professional principles. Starting from the doorway, we cleared a meter-wide path directly toward the sarcophagus, recording the contents of each section before proceeding to the next. Our labors were made easier by the fact that this passageway was relatively free of objects, as if someone had removed or pushed them aside. The tangle of jewelry was one of the prizes we preserved, but the tantalizing wheels had to wait; they were not in the direct path to the sarcophagus. Emerson calculated it would require at least two more seasons to clear the rest of the chamber, but it was imperative, in his opinion and mine, that the mummy be removed before we left Egypt. Though the tomb would be locked and guarded, we did not underestimate the industrious robbers of Luxor.

Curiosity and public interest had risen to fever pitch after Kevin published his first "scoop"—the fact that Walter's painstaking study of the scraps of plaster found in the debris of the entrance corridor revealed the name of Queen Hatshepsut. He and Emerson agreed that the fragmentary cartouche could only be hers. It appeared nowhere else; Emerson insisted that the remaining reliefs and the inscriptions on the sarcophagus made it certain that the tomb was that of Tetisheri, but that did not prevent the imagination of press and public from running wild. Tetisheri was virtually unknown, except to Egyptologists, but the great queen Hatshepsut was familiar to every tourist who had visited her temple. It was Kevin, I believe, who suggested the ladies might have shared the sarcophagus! This was nonsense, of course, but it delighted the readers of his newspaper—two queens for the price of one! I did not doubt that the fantasy would appeal as strongly to the Gurnawis. There is not a great deal of difference after all between so-called primitive and self-proclaimed civilized people.

Though we had tried to keep secret the precise day on which we would open the sarcophagus, a crowd of onlookers had assembled, and our men had their hands full restraining importunate journalists and curiosity-seekers.

As it was, the party admitted into the tomb was larger than Emerson would have liked. He had erected temporary walls along the pathway in the burial chamber, but he kept up a muttered undercurrent of expletives as our distinguished visitors—M. Maspero, the British Consul General (our old friend Lord Cromer, formerly Sir Evelyn Baring), Howard Carter in his capacity of Inspector, and a representative of the Khedive proceeded along the narrow passage. Cyrus was there, and—to the visible surprise of Maspero and the indignation of the Pasha—so were Abdullah and his grandson. I had agreed with Emerson that they had a right to be present.

The previous day Emerson and Abdullah had set up the necessary block-and-tackle arrangement, with heavy wooden tripods at either end of the sarcophagus, and had used levers and wedges to raise the top just far enough to allow the ropes to pass under it. As the great quartzite lid slowly rose, every eye was fixed upon it and every breath came quick and shallow. At last the gap was wide enough, and Emerson looked inside.

He stepped down from the stone on which he had stood. "Ladies and gentlemen," he said, "I regret to say that Queen Tetisheri is not receiving today."

The sarcophagus was empty. Not a scrap of wood, not a broken bone remained.

Because of the crowds we had to retreat to the *Amelia* in order to entertain our visitors. Toasts were proposed and drunk, but

Maspero's congratulations were mingled with polite commiseration. Emerson only shrugged. "A minor disappointment, monsieur," he said equably. "The paintings are masterpieces, the contents of the tomb remarkable. One could not reasonably hope for as much."

After the distinguished visitors had taken their departure I turned to Emerson. "You knew she wasn't there! You would not have taken it so coolly if you had not anticipated this."

"I was prepared for her absence, yes," Emerson said calmly. "You see, my dear, I have always believed that the bald little old lady from the Deir el Bahri cache is Tetisheri. She bears a striking resemblance to other members of the family who were also in the cache—those protruding front teeth are quite distinctive. Don't ask me to account for how she got there, though, or why her empty sarcophagus was so carefully closed. It is and will probably always remain a mystery."

"Oh, come," Walter exclaimed. "You must have a theory or two."

Emerson had already removed his coat and cravat. Leaning back in his chair, he took out his pipe. "What about a whiskey all round?" he inquired genially. "We have a great deal to celebrate, my dears. A mummy more or less does not detract.

"In fact, my brilliant deductions as to the location of the tomb were wide of the mark. This was not Tetisheri's original tomb; it was a reburial, made by Hatshepsut for her revered ancestress after the original tomb had been robbed or threatened—the latter, I think, since much of the funerary equipment survived.

"By that time the kings of the new Theban Empire had realized that conspicuous monuments like pyramids invited the attention of tomb robbers. Hatshepsut's father was the first to build his tomb in the Valley of the Kings—no one knowing, no one seeing, as the king's architect boasted. Hatshepsut concealed her own tomb so successfully that it has not been found. The location she selected for Tetisheri was equally obscure. She had the tomb decorated in the conventional style, and, with a modesty unusual in an Egyptian ruler, she had herself depicted only in the entrance corridor. Those reliefs and inscriptions probably described her pious restoration of her ancestress's burial.

"After her death her nephew, whom she had kept under her thumb for years, began attacking her monuments. As I reconstruct the case, it was his men who entered Tetisheri's tomb. Thutmose, whose mother was of humble birth, was probably collecting ancestors; he removed Tetisheri and some of her grave goods. And don't ask me me to speculate about why some things were taken away and others were left! Unlike some of my colleagues, I am an excavator, not a writer of historical romances. The last act of Thutmose's servants was to destroy the decoration of the entrance corridor, which mentioned Hatshepsut.

"The tomb was entered again in the Twenty-First Dynasty and used for burials of a priestly family—those whose coffins we found trampled and broken by the modern thieves. It may have been they who deposited the Nameless Mummy, but I am inclined to believe he was already there, and that it was his presence that deterred the priests from entering the burial chamber."

"Well done, Emerson," I said. "I agree in general with your reconstruction; but you have not offered a theory as to the identity of the Nameless Mummy."

"Come now," Walter exclaimed. "Not even you, Amelia, would have the . . . That is, would dare . . . What I mean to say—"

"What he means," said Emerson, "is that only you possess the imaginative force to invent—pardon me—deduce the solution to this ancient mystery. Proceed, my dear Peabody. I await your remarks with interest."

"It is only a theory, of course," I said modestly. "But as you said, we can be fairly certain that the tomb was entered by agents of Thutmose III. The king destroyed the reliefs that showed his powerful, autocratic aunt Hatshepsut, but he had no reason to resent Tetisheri. It must have been he who left the Nameless Mummy. So who was this unfortunate, horribly murdered, ritually destroyed? Obviously—What did you say, Emerson?"

"Obviously," Emerson muttered. "I said 'Obviously,' repeating your own word. Do go on, my dear."

"Obviously he was an individual of some importance, a priest or prince or noble. The body of a common criminal would not have been preserved at all. Obviously he had committed some act that won him the hatred of the pharaoh, for this was an official murder—an execution, in short. Now I ask you—what high official would have been hated by Thutmose? What low-born upstart had dared to—er—"

Emerson took his pipe from his mouth. The stem was quite badly chewed. "Defile?" he suggested, with deceptive mildness. "Just the other day, Peabody, you denied that the queen would have taken a commoner as her lover."

"You misunderstood me, my dear," I replied.

"Oh, good Gad!" Emerson exclaimed.

"Think it through," I insisted. "The king of Egypt—whether male or female—was divine, engendered by a god, but I don't doubt that the ancient Egyptians followed the same unfair double standard that prevails today. It was perfectly acceptable for a king to have as many concubines as he could manage, but a commoner who—er—had intimate relations with the queen would not enjoy a long life—unless the queen was also a king, who could protect her favorite! Once that protection was removed, the sinner met the fate prescribed for those who had violated religious and state law. But—and this, I think, is the conclusive argument . . . if I can think how to put it . . ."

"Of course!" Nefret exclaimed. "He had partaken of her divinity!"

"That," said Ramses in a peculiar voice, "is certainly one way of putting it."

"A very proper way of putting it," I said, nodding gratefully at Nefret. "That relationship imbued his physical remains with a certain sanctity; they could not be utterly destroyed. Yet they were also accursed, and that is why Thutmose removed Tetisheri from her resting place, lest she be contaminated by contact with them."

"You have it," Nefret cried. "Brilliant, Aunt Amelia! Who else could it have been but Senmut?"

"Who else?" Emerson repeated musingly. "Any one of—let me hazard a guess—five hundred princes, priests and high officials who were living at that time. Confound it, Peabody, you don't even know for certain when the fellow died! Mummification techniques are of no use in dating him, since he was not mummified! Five hundred be damned! Five thousand is more like it!"

"I am in complete agreement with Amelia," Evelyn said firmly. "Senmut is the most logical candidate."

Walter, who had opened his mouth, closed it again. Finding no support in that quarter, Emerson looked hopefully at his son. "You follow my reasoning, Ramses?"

Ramses's expressionless black eyes moved from Evelyn to Nefret to me. "Yes, Father, I do. However, I believe Mother has made a strong case. Hmmm. Yes. On the whole, I agree with her."

We sailed from Alexandria on the thirtieth, and I must say it was pleasant to feel the sea breezes after the extreme heat of April in Upper Egypt. It was also pleasant to have several able-bodied adults (not to mention David and Nefret) looking after Ramses, instead of being solely responsible for him. Terrible things happened when Ramses was on board a ship. Evelyn and Walter had agreed to come out with us again next year; they would collaborate on reproducing the decorations of the tomb, Evelyn doing the artwork and Walter copying the inscriptions.

Emerson and I were strolling the deck one afternoon shortly after our departure when I observed that a frown darkened the smooth surface of his noble brow.

"Unburden yourself," I urged. "You are not worried about the tomb, I hope? Riccetti is safely tucked away in a prison cell and his henchmen are incarcerated or have fled; Miss Marmaduke will remain in Dr. Willoughby's care until she is recovered from her nervous collapse; and after the lecture you gave her, Layla will not dare interfere with us again. You let her off too easily, Emerson. Women always know how to get round you."

"And what would you have done with her?" Emerson demanded. "We had not a shred of proof that she was criminally involved. If you had not let Berthe get away—"

"You would have done the same."

"Hmph," said Emerson.

"Proving her complicity would have been difficult. Her sisters in crime were, and if Layla is any example, still are, loyal to her. Perhaps," I said musingly, "the tender influences of motherhood will soften her and turn her from evil to good."

"Hmph," said Emerson, even more emphatically.

"At any rate we needn't worry about her for the immediate future, and the tomb is as secure as we could make it. Abdullah and the others will guard it well."

"It is Abdullah I was thinking about," Emerson admitted. "I don't doubt he and the men will keep careful guard. But he is getting old, Peabody. One of these days I will have to bully him into retiring before he injures himself. I can't think how to do it without hurting his feelings."

"If you replaced him with one of his sons—"

"They are all good men, but none has the necessary quality of leadership. I had thought of training David to take his place."

"Why not?"

Emerson stopped and turned, leaning against the rail. "Because the boy is too good for the job. There are others like him in Egypt, but there is no chance for them, not so long as our ignorant English prejudices keep them from being properly educated. We can give David that chance."

"And we will!" I cried. "Emerson, I am with you heart and soul. Evelyn and Walter will feel the same."

"I have already mentioned the possibility to Walter." Emerson added with a laugh, "He proposed starting to teach the boy hieroglyphs this summer while David is staying with them. I imagine Evelyn has other schemes in mind."

"It would be better for him to learn to read and write English first," I agreed. "Ramses will see to that; he has set aside four hours a day for lessons."

Emerson offered me his arm and we walked on. "Peabody, I have a bone to pick with you."

Oh dear, I thought. Now what? There were a few minor matters I had kept from Emerson, for his own good. Which of them had he discovered?

"It hurt me deeply," Emerson declared, "when you reproached me for not purchasing the little statue of Tetisheri for you."

"Oh, that," I said, trying not to sound too relieved. "I was only joking, my dear."

"Hmph," said Emerson. "My dear Peabody, have I ever thwarted a desire of yours? Have I ever failed to anticipate and satisfy your slightest wish?"

"Well, Emerson, since you ask—"

"I had a damned good reason for not buying that statue, and it had nothing to do with my principles. I have sacrificed them often enough for you, my dear."

"What reason, Emerson?"

"It was a forgery, Peabody."

It was I who stopped this time, catching hold of his shirt and forcing him to face me. "One of Hamed's copies, do you mean? The one you saw at the antika shop ten years ago? The one Mr. Budge bought for . . . Emerson! Are you telling me that the statue in the British Museum is a fake, and that you have always known it? Why haven't you informed them?"

"Why should I? They are enamored of Budge and his brilliant coups. One day someone—myself, if I so decide—will enlighten them, and Budge will look almost as foolish as he really is." Emerson's eyes glowed sapphire with anticipatory pleasure. "Who knows, we may be able to unearth the original. Wouldn't that do Budge one in the eye?"

It was impossible not to share his boyish amusement. We enjoyed a hearty laugh together, and then I glanced at my lapel watch.

"Goodness gracious, it is almost teatime. Let us collect the children. I promised I would read them my little fairy tale."

"Oh, so you have finished the hippopotamus story?" Emerson

took my arm and we strolled toward the stairs. "How, if I may ask? There is only a small part of the original remaining."

"It is only conjecture," I said modestly. "However, I believe it is psychologically sound. I refer to ancient Egyptian psychology, of course."

"Of course," said Emerson, smiling.

"You remember where the original leaves off—with the king and his courtiers at a loss as to how to reply to the insulting demand that they slaughter the bellowing hippopotami? Yes. Well, as they sit in baffled silence, up from her throne rises the king's mother, the dowager queen Tetisheri, the wise, the revered one, and addresses the arrogant messenger in ringing tones. I have composed rather a nice little speech for her; I modeled it on one of Queen Elizabeth's addresses to her troops before the arrival of the Armada."

"An excellent model," said Emerson.

"I had to change some of the wording, naturally. 'Servant of the Evil One, be gone,' Tetisheri cries. 'Our hippopotami will eat up the crocodiles of Set!' Inspired by her courage, her son also defies the messenger. The tale ends with the Egyptian armies setting forth, trumpets blaring and pennants flying, to drive the invaders from the sacred soil of Egypt."

"That would be a good place to end it," Emerson agreed gravely. "In view of the fact that her son lost his life in the ensuing battle, and most probably lost the battle as well."

"I thought that would be too depressing—and not at all in keeping with ancient Egyptian psychology."

"Have I mentioned recently that I adore you, Peabody?"

"I never tire of hearing it, my dear. Now, Emerson, don't do that; not just now. There is Ramses's room, and . . . and someone in the room is screaming! Good heavens, what an unearthly sound!"

I hastened toward the door, but before I reached it I beheld Ramses coming toward me from the far end of the corridor. His shadow—I refer to David—was close on his heels.

"Ramses!" I cried, tugging at the handle. "Unlock this door at once. What on earth is going on in there?"

Ramses, visibly perturbed, began rummaging in his pockets. "Anubis must have crept in while I was not looking. That is Bastet's voice. She is very angry."

"Er—Peabody," said Emerson, behind me.

"How could you have been so careless!" I cried, snatching the key from Ramses. "They despise one another! They are fighting. They—"

I flung the door open and stood transfixed.

"They are not," said Emerson, "fighting. Close the door, Peabody. Even a cat is deserving of privacy at a time like this."

So I did.